"YOU TAUNT ME, WITCH-WOMAN!"

She saw the fire in Tabor's blue eyes and knew that she was playing a very dangerous game. She knew, too, that if she should displease her Danish captor and he should complain to Ingmar that she was an unacceptable gift, she would live to regret it.

I must please him, Tanaka thought, her eyes burning with defiance and another emotion that even she was not entirely aware of. *Pleasing my captor, however distasteful that may be, is the lesser of evils!*

When Tabor had kissed her before, his strength was suppressed and his kiss was soft and sweet against her mouth. This time, when he took Tanaka into his arms, all his desire seemed to bubble toward the surface, driving him on. He crushed Tanaka's curvaceous body against his own, pulling her in tightly, forcing her plump breasts to compress against the powerful muscles of his bare chest.

Tanaka had not intended to touch Tabor. To *be* touched was perhaps necessary; to touch would be unacceptable. She would give to him whatever he wanted, but she would volunteer nothing.

Yet his warmth seared her senses, and her hands simply could not remain passive at her sides. Tanaka flattened her palms against Tabor's mighty shoulders, trembling as she did so, feeling the steely strength of him.

"No woman has ever made my blood burn so," Tabor murmured when the burning kiss ended. "You'll destroy me in the end. Of this I am sure . . ."

ROBIN GIDEON

VIKING ECSTASY

ZEBRA BOOKS
KENSINGTON PUBLISHING CORP.

*For Mom and Mural, and for
Lila, Phyllis, Don, Clayton, and Ken
—rg*

ZEBRA BOOKS

are published by

Kensington Publishing Corp.
475 Park Avenue South
New York, NY 10016

First Printing: February, 1993

Printed in the United States of America

Chapter One

It all felt wrong to Tabor. Wrong for a dozen very good reasons. He could smell danger in the air, death. Even though his instincts warned him to leave now, before blood had been spilled, before he actually committed himself and his men to anything, he stayed.

He looked over at Sven, standing to his left. He, too, had a concerned look on his face, the chiseled Scandinavian features seemed sharpened by his tautly stretched skin, defining his Viking heritage as surely as the battle-axe at his hip.

"I don't like it," Sven said when his gaze met his leader's. "It smells of a trap."

Tabor nodded. "I know, my friend. But we have a chance for peace. We've risked our skins for profit; shouldn't we risk as much for peace?"

"Aye," Sven agreed. "I just don't trust that Northman. He earned the title of Ingmar the Savage, he did. What makes him want to propose peace now? His fighting force numbers more than ours—"

"Aye, that's true," Tabor cut in. "But the advantage

5

he has in numbers does not equal the edge we have in fighting skill. I'll put any two of Ingmar's men against any one of us, and we'll win most every time."

Tabor grinned, and the brief conversation between them died away. He looked over the crowd of people at the trading village, pleased that he and Sven stood a head taller than the rest of them. The hawker was taking bids on yet another slave, and Tabor made no effort to hide his distaste for the business. Of all the villages he and his Viking warriors had raided, he could safely say that only one woman had been raped by his men (and that man paid the ultimate price for violating Tabor's orders) and not one house had been burned afterward. True, Tabor had allowed the villagers to build themselves back to prosperity only to be descended upon by himself and his men again, but the senseless slaughter, the savage rape and pillage of defenseless communities, the inhumane carnage that marked the behavior of so many other Viking warriors was never a hallmark of Tabor and his men.

Seventy feet to his left he saw the crowd part, and a moment later spied the coppery red hair of the man he despised most and respected least: Ingmar the Savage. Men and women scurried clear of Ingmar, clearing a wide berth for him. Everyone had heard the stories of this man or that woman being cut—literally—for not moving aside or showing sufficiently deferential behavior when Ingmar was near.

Tabor passed his left hand through his long blond hair. He did not have to look to know that thirty-five of the finest fighting men in the world—exactly one-half of the troops under Tabor's command—were now on battle alert and were ready to fight at the slightest provocation, though they remained hidden, interspersed in the crowd.

When Ingmar approached, Tabor could see that his adversary had arrived with very few men — certainly much fewer than the thirty to forty Tabor had anticipated. With his right hand, Tabor again ran his fingers through his hair; and thirty-five men slipped deeper into the Hedeby crowds, disappearing like smoke from a hidden fire.

"Hail, Tabor!" Ingmar the Savage said in his bellowing, too-friendly voice, striding forward as though he didn't have a care in the world.

"Ingmar," Tabor replied simply, nodding slightly. The unadorned simplicity of his greeting was an insult, and he made no effort to hide it. When Ingmar did not react either positively or negatively to the slight, Tabor privately wondered whether his formidable adversary had suffered some great war loss recently. Accepting insults without returning insults was not at all in keeping with the Ingmar the Savage that Tabor knew.

Ingmar stepped close to Tabor, and for a moment there was silence between them. Would Ingmar extend his hand in friendship? If he did, would Tabor accept it? And if he did not, would Ingmar challenge him, as was custom among Vikings for such a display of disrespect? Their gazes met and locked, two strong men long accustomed by might and self-won authority to having their own way and having strong men bow to their greater will.

Men and women near Tabor and Ingmar sensed the tension between the tall, dangerous-looking men and moved aside, giving them plenty of room should the thinly disguised contempt between them explode into action — violent action.

"Why have you called this gathering?" Tabor asked at last, breaking the explosive silence.

Ingmar hesitated, as though weighing how honest he should be, how much he should tell his nemesis. "We have been enemies for a long time, Tabor. And even though we have hated each other and fought each other many times, we have managed to amass fortunes for ourselves, haven't we?"

"Yes. And so?"

"And so I propose that we stop wasting our energies fighting each other. There's simply no money to be made in it." Ingmar passed a broad palm in the direction of the crowd of people who surrounded them. "I have come with the fewest amount of men, and you have brought how many warriors with you? Forty? Fifty? Does that show trust, Tabor? And the fact that your men are lurking in the crowd and that three of your best men, with throwing-daggers in their hands, stand ready to toss their deadly blades into my body, does that show trust?"

"Four," Tabor corrected, mildly impressed, despite his contempt for Ingmar, for his grasp of the situation.

"See? All this work, and for what? Neither of us are collecting a grain of gold for this. But if we work together, we could make much gold."

"I don't think so."

"Women, Tabor!" Ingmar whispered, leaning close, his green eyes fiery, glinting with avarice. "Why search for gold, gems, grains, or wines when women can be captured easily and sold for a profit that impresses even Odin?"

8

"I don't believe the gods are impressed with money made by kidnapping women and selling them into slavery," Tabor replied drily. Though not a squeamish man, he had always found the slave trade irredeemably appalling. "Is that why you brought me here?"

Tabor's contempt for the business was well known by all. Why would Ingmar even propose such a deal?

The hawker's voice rose dramatically, drawing Tabor's attention to the auction. Tabor watched as a dark-haired young woman, dressed in a torn and soiled gown that at one time must assuredly have been a fine and expensive garment, stepped onto the raised platform. Unlike the other young women who had stepped forward, she held her head high, her shoulders square. One need only glance into her angry, defiant brown eyes to know that she had been hardened and strengthened—but not defeated—by the cruel treatment she had received since her capture.

Though she was barefooted and her clothes were in rags, there was an unbending defiance in her eyes that gripped Tabor with a strange force deep within. It curled to life in a place inside him that he had not consciously known existed.

The instant the dark-eyed woman stepped onto the platform, a clamor of bids shouted by the men in the audience arose. The woman, clearly aware of what was happening and why, looked with unconcealed contempt at the men who bid to buy her as one might buy a prize mare.

"She is magnificent," Ingmar said softly, mentally calculating his profit. His ship had captured the fiery-eyed beauty off the coast of Egypt, near Opar, and Ingmar was entitled to eighty percent of whatever gold was paid for the woman. At present, she was his prized possession. "So angry! Look at those eyes! You can tell just by looking in her Egyptian eyes that she will be a thunderstorm in a warrior's bed. Don't you agree?"

The bidding for the silent, angry Egyptian woman was escalating quickly, moving far beyond the price paid for any other slave. Callously, Tabor thought that if Ingmar would take the time and spend the money to clean his captured slaves and dress them in fine clothes, he could command a much greater price for them. Hardly had the mercenary thought entered Tabor's head than he felt guilty for it, thinking of the heinous profit made from the purchase and sale of a woman's body.

"If it is the slave trade that you have come to discuss, then we have nothing to say to one another. You have wasted my time," Tabor said through clenched teeth, furious with himself for the unexpected sexual thoughts that had sprung into his head since the Egyptian woman had stepped on to the stage, even angrier since he was certain that Ingmar would profit greatly by the vast sum of gold that was now being offered for her.

Not far from where he stood, Tabor watched a man, a Moor, raise the bid on the woman. Tabor had seen the man in Hedeby before, and knew of his reputation as a man more inclined toward torture than sensuality. The slaves the Arab bought in Hedeby never lived long, it was said. In a blinding flash, Tabor saw in his mind's eye the stunning creature on the stage having her flawless flesh torn asunder by the Arab's destructive whip.

"Fifty kronor!" Tabor heard himself shout.

It took a moment before he realized he had actually tendered a bid on the woman. He felt the curious stares of people nearby surveying him and heard the stunned whispers. "He's got so many women who would gladly bed with him! What's Tabor want to buy a woman for?" And "She must be truly gifted in the sensual world to catch Tabor's eyes. Everyone knows he's got his choice of women!"

Even Ingmar, who was not a man easily shocked, looked at Tabor as though seeing him for the first time — or, at least, seeing him in an entirely new light.

"She meets with your fancy, eh?" Ingmar asked, his tone much too friendly and confidential for Tabor's liking. "I didn't know you have a taste for purchased flesh."

Tabor was furious with himself and livid with Ingmar. Worse, there was a grain of truth in what the vicious Northman was saying.

"I just didn't want the Arab to get her. She's got a warrior's spirit in her blood, and you know as well as I do what that man does to his slaves."

Tabor glanced up at the woman again, and he felt the strangest tightening in his chest — as though he had never before been held fast, enthralled by a woman's beauty. But this one — dark-skinned, voluptuous, spirited — not merely looked different from the assortment of women that Tabor usually warmed his bed with, she was different inside, in her heart, in a place deep within her soul. As he searched the depths of her eyes and realized that she was different from other women, he also realized that he wanted her, that he had tendered a bid for her, and that by doing so he had violated his own code of proper conduct. He would not

11

profit by the slave trade, and he would not help others — particularly not Ingmar the Savage — profit by it, either.

"If you brought me here to convince me to join you in the swinish business of buying and selling human souls, you have failed again," Tabor said, biting the words off caustically. "Stand aside. You have taken up more of my time than you are worth."

Ingmar stepped aside, nodding nonchalantly in the direction of the portly moor who had once again raised the bid on the Egyptian captive. "You want her, Tabor? Let me give her to you. Call it a peace offering. Something to make our time together profitable for you."

Tabor scowled, fighting the urge to draw the huge, heavy sword at his hip. Though Ingmar was a capable fighter and a powerfully-built man, Tabor was taller, stronger, and — he was certain — a better swordsman.

"If you don't accept her as a gift, then the Spaniard will get her. Is that what you want?"

Tabor's mind reeled. He did not want a slave, yet if he refused Ingmar's "gift," then the woman would surely live out her few remaining days in hideous agony. If even half of the stories that Tabor had heard about the Spaniard were true, he could not risk allowing such a fate to befall the proud, defiant Egyptian woman.

"I'll take her," Tabor said, his blue eyes burning bright with contempt for Ingmar.

Ingmar smiled pleasantly, but the triumph he felt showed in his eyes. He raised a broad hand to the hawker. "The auction for this one is off," Ingmar said, his voice just barely above a conversational level, not needing to speak loudly because whenever he spoke, everyone else nearby went silent. "I have decided to make her a gift to my friend, Tabor—" he hesitated a moment, then added the nickname "—Son of Thor."

A hush went over the crowd, followed immediately by the low murmur of voices as those nearest to Ingmar explained to those farther away exactly what had just transpired. The Spaniard who had been bidding on the Egyptian woman reddened with anger, his fleshy hands balled into impotent fists. He dared not challenge an edict from either Ingmar or Tabor—not here in Denmark, anyway—but his fury was consuming him inside, and everyone in the crowd knew that one day the Spaniard would want his revenge.

"I'm not your friend," Tabor said under his breath.

He felt like he had been outmaneuvered by Ingmar, perhaps even outwitted, and he did not like the sensation at all. And by referring to the nickname "Son of Thor," a ridiculous title pinned on him by a lover who thought such sensual skill must come directly from the gods, Ingmar implied an unearned, intimate knowledge of Tabor, as though they drank together and talked of their conquests of women.

Raising his hand again, Ingmar motioned for the woman to be taken from the stage and brought closer. Two thickly-muscled men took the woman by the arms and pulled her roughly from the stage, pushing through the crowd, nearly dragging the young Egyptian. Tabor scowled again, hating to see the rough treatment the woman was needlessly receiving, privately pleased to see that she was fighting against the men even though it was clear that she had no chance of winning even the slightest victory.

Tabor felt himself stir, part of him responding to the woman's beauty and allure, even if he did pity the cruel treatment she was receiving. Now that she was directly in front of him, he saw that she was very short—perhaps barely five feet tall—and rather slender though curvaceously built. Her ebony hair fell in curly waves well over her shoulders, and the wide, full-lipped mouth looked perfectly designed to give a man pleasure. Across the surface of his mind flashed images, suggesting the sensations he would know holding her slender body close, feeling the firmness of her supple breasts against him, her full, sensuous lips pressing tightly against his, her mouth opening to receive his questing tongue. For only a second, Tabor closed his eyes and fought against the almost tactile response to the mental images.

"What is your name?" he asked, his tone gruff. Now that he had been saddled with the responsibility of taking care of this poor, unfortunate—if exotically-alluring—soul, he wanted to take her some place safe, then be rid of her.

"Tanaka," the woman replied after some hesitation, her eyes dark and unflinching as she glared up at Tabor.

Ingmar grabbed her by the upper arm, his large hand almost completely surrounding her biceps. "Tanaka, if you give Tabor any trouble, if you deny him any pleasure, I will teach you why I am called Ingmar the Savage. Do you understand?"

Tanaka looked at Ingmar and replied, "The most that you can steal from me is my body, and that is only the outward appearance of who I really am. But I do not expect a barbarian like you to understand such a

14

truth." She spoke with a thick accent, though her intelligence and grasp of Tabor's language was readily apparent.

Ingmar swung his open hand toward Tanaka's face. No one had ever insulted him without paying a terrible price for their temerity, and the Egyptian slave would be no different. But before his palm could punish the smooth, flawless, dark-hued flesh of Tanaka's cheek, Tabor's reflexes proved to be superior. His right hand shot upward to catch Ingmar's wrist, preventing the arcing blow.

"You bastard!" Ingmar hissed, now even angrier with Tabor than with Tanaka.

"She is mine now," Tabor replied, still holding tightly onto his enemy's wrist. "I don't want you bruising what I own. Unless you want her back?" he asked, his voice rich with open challenge.

To a Viking, the only thing worse than being a coward was being falsely generous, giving something only to later demand its return.

"She's yours, Tabor, and good riddance." Ingmar pulled his wrist free of Tabor's grasp. The flesh was white and bloodless where Tabor had squeezed, the marks of his fingers still plainly visible on the pale flesh. "Have your pleasure with her, Tabor, if you can find any pleasure in her at all. Her skin is dark, and she lies there like a corpse."

Tabor tightened inside at Ingmar's words. What difference did it make if Tanaka had been raped by Ingmar? Tabor himself had no intention of sleeping with her. Still, it bothered him that such a small and delicate woman should have to suffer through the undoubtedly vile experience of being the

15

recipient of Ingmar the Savage's lust.

Suddenly Ingmar's expression changed, and though the smile did not reach his eyes, it did curl up the corners of his mouth. "We have managed to make each other angry again, haven't we, Tabor? Ha! Perhaps it will always be so, but I truly hope not. Take the woman. Enjoy yourself. Later, after I have taken beer and food, we can speak again."

"I told you, I'm not interested in the slave trade."

"So you have said. But there are many other ventures that I am involved in, ventures which could be even more profitable with a strong and capable partner like you." Ingmar held his hands wide apart, palms heavenward in the universal Viking sign of peace. "It is easy to keep fighting, Tabor, Son of Thor. It is difficult to find the path to peace. Wait a few hours until our passions have cooled, then let's see if we can find the difficult path together. Agreed?"

Tabor did not trust Ingmar, but the words he spoke carried much truth to them. If it was possible, the fighting and the destruction had to be stopped, and if that meant waiting at Hedeby for another couple hours and spending more time with Ingmar the Savage, then that was a small price to pay for the benefits everyone would reap from peace.

"Two hours. Then I meet you here."

"Make it three," Ingmar said, and his smile made Tabor agree. "I have a Viking's thirst and a hearty appetite."

Chapter Two

It had been four long months since Tanaka, Priestess of Opar, had been pulled off the small Egyptian sailing vessel by Ingmar. Four months of desolation and fear. She had at first dreaded the time when she would be put on the auction block and sold. Then, after weeks as Ingmar the Savage's personal captive, she figured that whoever purchased her could not be worse than the man who had captured her.

At least this one's handsome, in a light-skinned, harsh-featured sort of way, Tanaka thought as she allowed Tabor to lead her through the crowd.

To Tanaka, the Vikings seemed like a race of giants, the men all hovering close to six feet tall, at least six inches taller than the average Egyptian man. Yet even among these gigantic people, Tabor stood out a head taller than the others. His strength, too, was awesome. Tanaka had seen how he blocked Ingmar's attempt to slap her. It took incredible strength to stop the strike in mid-swing without appearing to even strain.

"Where are you taking me?" Tanaka asked at last.

Tabor did not answer, and a cold dread washed through Tanaka. She believed that, even though she needed to bathe and Tabor had not said a single word directly to her, there was only one thing he wanted and he intended to take it from Tanaka immediately. Though Tabor had treated her kindly so far, he was a man, and Tanaka had rid herself of any naive notions of the inherent goodness of men. Since her capture, the only kindness shown to her had come from another woman, also captured by Ingmar's Vikings during their vicious sweep along the coastal villages of northern Africa. She had suggested that when the "lustful madness" came over her captor, it would be best if Tanaka kept her eyes squeezed tightly shut and tried hard to think of other things while the foul deed was being done.

"I won't hurt you," Tabor said at last, speaking without looking down at Tanaka, whom he kept at his side, his broad palm resting lightly on her shoulder.

The statement was ambiguous and failed to put Tanaka's mind at ease. He might not *mean* to hurt her, but a man as tall and powerfully built as he could hardly *help* but hurt her. Tanaka knew that she would have to call upon all her inner strength if she were to survive an evening in the Viking's arms.

"Are you hungry?" Tabor asked when they had passed through the main crowd surrounding the slave auction and through the village square where tradesmen sold their wares of bronze spearheads, cooking pots and kettles, talismans, amulets, hogsheads of wine, and barrels of the beer that the Vikings were so fond of.

When he received no answer, a pained expression crossed Tabor's harsh features, as though the thought of having to put up with Tanaka was going to be a great strain for him. "Woman, I can't hear words that you do not speak. If you're hungry, tell me so and I will provide food for you. If you say nothing, then that is exactly what you will get from me—nothing!"

Tanaka did not trust this man that she had been given to. She had been fighting everyone who had power over her since her capture, and though she was afraid to admit it to herself, she was nearing the end of her stamina.

"Yes," she said suddenly. She could not escape if she were weak, and the only way she would recover her strength was with nourishing food. "I need food. It has been days since I have eaten well."

Tabor studied Tanaka for a moment and said, "And had a bath as well, I should think. Ingmar's never understood that people need to bathe and eat food."

"Ingmar's barely human," Tanaka said quietly. Though Ingmar had announced that he and Tabor were friends, she suspected their hatred outweighed whatever kindly feelings they had for each other. Her insult was a test of Tabor's loyalties.

"He is called 'The Savage' for good reason, and he likes the title. The day will come when he and I will square off with sword and axe, and then he won't be savage, he will be dead."

"You're that confident you will win? From what I have heard and seen, many men have challenged Ingmar. They have all died."

Tabor grinned crookedly and answered, "When a Viking ends his prayers, after thanking Odin for all he has and all he believes in, he says, 'I believe in my own strength.' It is the foundation upon which our lives and our faith are based."

It seemed a grim, aggressive approach to life; but Tanaka, not wanting to incur Tabor's wrath by questioning his beliefs, kept her opinions to herself.

They passed under an archway, stepping outside the walled city of Hedeby. The warmth of Tabor's hand upon her shoulder seemed to seep through her body to the marrow of her bones. Cautious of letting her guard down, she looked up at Tabor to remind herself that even though he was possibly the most handsome man she had ever seen, he was still a man—a Viking man at that—and though he spoke kindly to her now, there would come a time when he would drag her to his bed and force her to succumb to his greater strength.

"Where are you taking me?" Tanaka asked quietly. Now that they were no longer surrounded by a milling crowd, she felt more vulnerable to Tabor, as though the crowd and all the witnesses it represented protected her from Tabor's desires. When he took his hand away from her shoulder, she immediately wondered what her chances of escape were should she try to run. She looked at Tabor's thighs sheathed in the spun cotton, saw the outline of the powerful muscles beneath, and knew that she could never outrun him.

"I have a small home just beyond that rise." Tabor rested his right palm on the haft of his broadsword, and Tanaka wondered if he was making a subtle threat. "There is food—and privacy to bathe."

Privacy enough so my screams will not be heard, Tanaka thought angrily.

She looked right and left at the Danish countryside. The rolling hills and lush greenery was so different from her own homeland in Egypt. Even if it was possible for her to escape from Tabor, where would she go?

She was miles—thousands of miles!—from home. And here in Hedeby, she looked so different from the natives with her copper-hued flesh, high cheekbones, aristocratic nose, and flowing, wavy ebony hair that fell to a point between her shoulder blades. If Tabor sought her out, he could find her easily enough. With her coloring, she could no more hide in a crowd than could Tabor with his great size.

Glancing over her shoulder, she saw three men following at a discreet distance. Ingmar's men?

"We are being followed," she said in a frightened whisper.

"Of course we are. Never in a thousand years would Sven leave my back unprotected."

With a certain sense of fatalism, Tanaka decided she would try to consider herself lucky that she had been sold to just one man. She had heard what happened to some slaves who were purchased by groups of men, and the horrifying stories nauseated her.

Tanaka guessed that they walked two miles from Hedeby, following the shoreline for the most part. They rounded a curve and there, within a copse of trees, was a hut—perhaps twenty feet square—made of wood and thatch.

"You live here?" Tanaka asked. It seemed a very primitive living arrangement, particularly for a man of Tabor's apparent social influence and stature.

"Aye. For a month or two each year. Most of the time I am on my ship. But while I am in Hedeby to do my trading, buying, and selling, I live here."

"And no one steals your property while you are gone?" It seemed to Tanaka that all Vikings were nothing more than common thieves.

"No one who wants to continue living," Tabor replied.

Inside, it was nearly as Spartan as Tanaka had suspected. There were no inside walls to separate the structure into smaller, cozy, private rooms; and the only real furniture was several mats of straw and cloth that constituted beds. There was a single table, two three-legged stools, and an iron tripod holding an iron kettle over a cold fire. Along all the walls were various weapons, from bows and arrows to shields, swords, battle-axes, helmets, and spears. Tanaka didn't need to ask to know that the hut was occupied by Tabor and his men and that women did not stay long, if they were allowed in the hut at all. There was nothing feminine about the surroundings, and that seemed to fit Tabor perfectly.

"Sit," Tabor said, pointing to the mat at the far end of the hut.

For an instant, Tanaka felt her knees go weak. *This is it,* she thought, sure that her captor's patience had come to an end and that his passion would now rule his actions. On trembling legs, Tanaka went to the mat and knelt, keeping her back to Tabor. She squeezed her eyes tightly shut and thought, *I've lived through it before, I can live through it again.*

She heard Tabor picking things up and setting them back down and wondered what he was doing. When she heard him step up behind her, she stopped breathing.

"Here," he said in the deep, baritone voice that carried such natural authority in it. "This is all I can do for now. Later, we'll find something more suitable."

Tanaka opened her eyes, twisting just enough so

22

that she could look over her shoulder up at Tabor. He held a long garment in his right hand. Cradled in his left was a large section of cheese and a small loaf of bread. Dangling from his shoulder was a wineskin.

When Tanaka reached her hands out to take the food and coarse wool shirt from Tabor, he was able to see down the front of her soiled, much-torn gown. The fullness of her breasts, round and firm, brought a spontaneous warmth to his blood. Her flesh, golden by birth and darkened by the sun, appeared as smooth as velvet, and though Tabor had never forced himself upon a woman, he wondered if his willpower and his Viking code of honor were strong enough to prevent him from being overcome by the desires that this young woman from the strange, faraway land provoked.

He handed her the cheese and bread, then dropped his spare shirt on the mat beside her. Taking his dagger from its sheath at his hip, he dropped that on the mat, too, then turned away from Tanaka, not wanting to tempt his desires longer than necessary by examining her exotic, alluring charms.

She cut off a large slice of the cheese and bit into it, washing it down with a decidedly unladylike gulp of the wine, which—she realized after swallowing—was considerably more potent than wine from her homeland. Tabor had strode across the hut to where a battle-axe rested against the thick, grass-insulated wall. He kept his back to her; and, unconsciously, Tanaka's eyes drifted from the tall Viking down to the dagger on the mat beside her.

Could she do it—plunge the dagger into his back? And if she didn't, what fate would be hers? Surely the gods would understand the taking of a life under such a circumstance. Even she, Priestess Tanaka of Opar, personal high priestess to Pharaoh Abbakka, had the right to take a life to save her own.

She was deliberating her chances of success when Tabor half turned and froze her with his icy blue gaze. "Others have tried," he said quietly, without much malice, as though explaining something complex but important to a child. "Two men and one woman. Spies they were. Assassins." He wrinkled his face in disgust, not liking anyone who fought in a cowardly manner, not like a proud and brave Viking who faced his adversary head on, man to man.

"Others have tried to kill you, but you are still with the living," Tanaka said softly.

"Aye. I still sail the seas. The assassins have crossed to the other side."

"Even the woman?" Tanaka was afraid of the answer, but she had to know. Did this Viking warrior care whether his victim was a man or woman? Tanaka knew the answer shouldn't matter—the taking of life was the taking of life. Still, in her heart she felt there was a difference, and she had to know.

"When she was in my arms, she was a woman," Tabor explained. "When she tried to plant a dagger in my back, she was an assassin. I would never hurt a woman; I would never spare the life of an assassin."

He turned away from her, swinging the heavy battle-axe at his side. Tanaka suspected he held the weapon not as a threat to her but because it gave him some comfort against the memories of the men and women that he had killed. Apparently, the taking of

24

life did not rest easily upon his broad shoulders, and Tanaka found this curious.

Though quite aware that she could likely earn Tabor's anger by asking too many questions — she was, after all, his slave, and that hardly put her in any position to demand answers — her curiosity and inquisitive mind had always been too hungry to keep her ideas or her thirst for knowledge in check.

"That weapon you hold carries with it the weight of history. It is heavy, I feel, with memories."

Tabor turned fully this time to gaze down upon the kneeling woman on his mat. He stared at her critically, thinking that she must surely be a sorceress of some kind to see into his heart. Then, slowly, he smiled, for Tanaka had only deduced what was plainly there for anyone with open eyes to see. He twirled the smooth wooden handle in his hand, enjoying the feel of it. The wood gleamed from much use and great care, the kind of shine that comes to wood only after many years of handling.

"It was my grandfather's, then my father's, then mine. For nearly a hundred years this axe has slain the enemies of my family. When I hold it in my hands, I can see into my past and see the faces of my father and grandfather."

"And their faces comfort you?" It seemed an uncharacteristically tender notion that a Viking as tall and strong as Tabor should need comfort from anyone but a woman — and that to merely satisfy his sexual desires.

"Aye. They comfort me when I am troubled." Abruptly, Tabor set the axe down and motioned to the bread beside Tanaka. "For a hungry woman, you

25

ask many questions. Eat now. Then you can bathe."

Tanaka averted her eyes from Tabor, eating quickly, afraid that he might suddenly decide that she was not worthy of food and would take it from her before she had her fill. She drank freely of the wine, too, wanting to dull her senses for the terrible thing she knew that Tabor would do to her, but long before the wineskin was empty it was taken from her.

"Drink too much of this, and when you bathe, you'll drown," Tabor explained with apparent disgust in his tone.

Chapter Three

The place where Tabor chose to bathe was a short walk from his hut, off a small finger of rocks that trailed out into the sea. The area was moderately secluded. Nevertheless, Tanaka was mystified that the Vikings apparently bathed with extraordinary frequency — usually every other day — and they usually bathed in the sea, which to Tanaka's Egyptian blood was positively freezing.

"Go on now," Tabor said, squatting on his haunches. On the rocks beside him was a large square of cloth used to dry a person after bathing as well as the spare shirt he had selected for Tanaka. Tabor had a twinkle in his eye as he took a long swallow from the large drinking horn he carried, downing the beer with obvious relish.

Tanaka looked at Tabor, then to the sea. She could drown herself, and that would put an end to her troubles. But if she did, she would be giving up, and that was something she was not yet prepared to do. She had been beaten physically, emotionally, even spiritually, but not broken. Though she had been knocked down by Ingmar, she continued to get back up, and as long as she could continue to see within herself and find something worthy of saving, she would continue to struggle and fight however she could.

With an angry, defiant thrust to her chin, Tanaka asked in her most haughty tone, "I suppose you will be here to protect me?"

Tabor smiled. "Of course. I wouldn't want you to get hurt."

All that was left of the clothes that Tanaka had worn when she was kidnapped by Ingmar the Savage was the torn gown that now hung limply on her curvaceous body. Standing, looking down at Tabor, she thought, *At least he's handsome*, then immediately cursed herself: a handsome barbarian was *still* a barbarian.

"Where are your guards? Are they watching, too?"

Tabor grinned again. He looked over his shoulder into the trees. "They are out there somewhere, and I suppose they are watching. But they are discreet men, my lady. Their word is their honor, and they are honorable men."

"Where are they?" Tanaka asked, peering into the shadows of the trees.

"You may find the others, but you will not find Sven. If he doesn't want to be seen, then he isn't seen."

Tanaka hesitated a moment longer. Was Tabor's control over his men so great that they could see her naked and not rush forward to force themselves upon her? One savage barbarian was hideous; four would be hell on earth.

"He isn't smoke," Tanaka whispered. "He can't make himself appear and disappear at will."

"You, clearly, do not know Sven. Hurry, now, I have agreed to meet again with Ingmar, and I want him to see how you look when you have been treated properly." Tabor shook his head, sending his long blond hair swirling around his shoulders. "Such a brilliant warrior, but such a stupid man."

There seemed to be much more behind Tabor's conflict with Ingmar than just predatorial adversaries both hunting the same victims; but, at present, Tanaka forced those questions from her mind in favor of more pressing ones—like whether or not she was going to take her gown off, as Tabor had instructed.

"Hurry now!" Tabor said, then drank again from the horn. He leaned back, his massive upper body propped up with an elbow beneath him, his long, powerful legs lazily stretched out toward the sea. "You are making me impatient."

Tanaka turned her back on Tabor, then pulled her gown off and tossed it aside. After stooping to pick up the ham-sized soap made from, among other things, whale blubber, Tanaka dashed into the water.

She had hardly reached knee-deep when the icy water nearly paralyzed her. She inhaled in a great rush and tried to stop her forward movement in a single step. But the slippery rocks beneath the water provided poor traction; and, with arms and legs outstretched and the sound of Tabor's laughter echoing in her brain, Tanaka flipped through the air and crashed into the water. She came to the surface, sputtering and frozen, angry with herself for being foolish enough to run in waters she knew nothing about, mad as hell at Tabor for finding so much humor in her predicament. She stood in waist-deep water, her eyes shooting daggers at Tabor, arms crossed over her bosom to hide her nakedness.

Tabor's laughter subsided presently, and he called out, "Apparently this land you come from has warmer waters."

Tanaka bent her knees, sinking into the water until it was up to her shoulders. To her surprise, after a minute or two, the water didn't seem quite so frigid and in a strange way was rather invigorating.

"Much, much warmer," Tanaka replied. She was farther north than any of her peoples had ever been — farther north than she had thought existed. The winds were coming almost steadily from the north now, with autumn on its way and winter soon behind it. She could only imagine what winter was like in Viking country.

Tanaka was surprised when she rubbed the soap over her skin and it foamed nicely, having both a pleasant cleansing action as well as an appealing fragrance. She rubbed her arms and legs vigorously, getting the blood circulating in the frigid waters, then worked the lather into her long, thick, wavy hair. She rinsed the soap from her hair, then worked up the lather once more; and when she dipped beneath the water a second time, her hair felt as clean as it ever had in her life. The Vikings were barbarians, but at least they made good soap, she concluded.

Tanaka worked the soap over her legs again, displeased with the hair stubble she felt. In her culture, only the lowliest and most slovenly of women would allow hair to grow on their legs, under their arms, or on their pubes. Tanaka had not been allowed to have a razor since her capture; and, even if she had, she doubted she would have used it. What difference did it make if she felt filthy when she was forced to be with

30

barbarians? She had noticed that the custom of shaving was not something the Scandinavian women followed.

However invigorating the icy water was, it wasn't pleasant enough to make Tanaka linger in its cold clutch. Less than six minutes had passed before she was finished and wanted little more than to feel the relative warmth of clean, dry clothes upon her.

She looked over her shoulder at Tabor, who was on the rocky bank, leaning back on one elbow, surveying her with an unreadable look in his blue eyes. Was it lust? Yes, she suspected so. Lust. . . . and something more. But what? He was such a mystery to her. She did not understand his strange and unbending code of honor, nor the bizarre gods he prayed to. Her ability to learn languages quickly made it possible to understand his words; but, beyond that, she understood almost nothing about him at all except that he wanted her as a man wants a woman and yet he would not take her as a barbarian takes a woman.

Who was this Tabor, Son of Thor?

"Skinny creature, come and get warm," Tabor said. He raised the edge of the drying cloth invitingly. "You shiver like a frightened hare. Don't be afraid. I'm not the seawolf you think I am."

It was Tabor's good humor more than anything else that infuriated Tanaka. She squared her shoulders, forced herself to stop shivering, and walked toward land with the bearing and pride of what she was: a High Priestess.

As Tanaka emerged from the sea, Tabor caught his breath. When Ingmar the Savage had foisted the Egyptian captive upon him, Tabor had no intention of keeping her. His first thought was that he would feed and clothe her, then bundle her off to Rollo's, where she could work for her food and lodging and perhaps find herself a husband who would care for her. But now, as he watched her rise out of the fjord, with the grace of a copper-skinned sea-goddess, he thought only of what extraordinary ecstasy he would know by inviting her to his bed and warming her body with the heat of his own.

Tabor had been stunned by Tanaka's beauty even when she was dirty from the arduous trek to Hedeby. Her hair and body were clean now, revealing her comeliness and a regal bearing heightened her physical charms.

She was more slender than Tabor had thought; and, as he watched the clear, cold water streaming down her body and between her breasts as she walked toward shore, he saw she was also more buxom. Unlike those of the tall, blonde, ivory-skinned women Tabor was accustomed to, Tanaka's areolas were a deep brown. Glistening now with sea water, the nipples stood tight and erect from the cold. When the water level reached Tanaka's waist, her stride broke for only a fraction of a second, her gaze challenging Tabor. Another two steps, and the brine splashed the tops of her thighs, exposing her femininity to Tabor.

The visual charge from the sparse triangular thatch of hair and the soft pink flesh gripped Tabor savagely with greater magnitude than it should have for a Viking of his experience.

Inhaling deeply, Tanaka searched inside herself for strength. As she drew breath, her breasts swelled out, rising, drawing Tabor's hungry stare.

Let him look, Tanaka thought defiantly, her cheeks turning pink with a mixture of anger, helplessness, and embarrassment. *He looks at me without clothes and can't speak. My beauty makes him stupid. . . . and I can defeat a stupid man.*

She walked up to Tabor and looked down at him, still fighting against the shivers that tried to grip her body. She dropped the bar of strange soap that she had found so pleasant and extended a hand toward the drying cloth. "If you please?"

Tabor's too-confident grin quickly returned. He picked up the towel; but, instead of handing it to her, he set his empty drinking horn down and got to his feet.

"Your hair is so thick," Tabor said, his dry mouth at last able to form words as he stepped behind his newly acquired "slave." "I'll have to dry it last, or the cloth will be too wet to dry the rest of . . ." His words trailed off, but in his mind he concluded with *your magnificent body.*

Delicately, as though she were very fragile, Tabor eased Tanaka's thick, heavy, wet hair away from her shoulders, then he began patting her shoulders, arms, and back dry with the cloth. Even as he did this, touching Tanaka's flesh only with the cloth, Tabor was shockingly aware that he was using his power over her to touch her, and this was a direct violation of the code of conduct he had set and rigorously maintained for himself and his men. Could he expect his Viking warriors to follow rules that he could not adhere to himself? This violation made him feel weak, as though his will power—the single, driving force that controlled his life and his beliefs—were no longer strong, true, or unbending.

33

He dried her body slowly, allowing himself the hypocritical rationalization that if he touched her only with the towel and never with his bare hand, then he really wasn't using power over her for his own sexual pleasure.

He patted dry the small of her back, then knelt behind Tanaka to dry the taut, smooth curves of her buttocks. As he did this, his mouth felt dry; and in the core of his soul, Tabor realized with embarrassing certainty that he had never before been so powerfully affected by a woman's beauty, not even when he was a very young man and the pleasures of sexuality were new and mysterious to him.

He dried her thighs and calves, and Tanaka raised her feet one at a time to allow him to dry them as well.

"Turn around," Tabor said, still kneeling behind the standing woman. "I'll dry your front."

Tanaka half-turned. This, she sensed, was a moment where she might have the ability to recover some of the power over her own life and actions that she had lost in the months since her capture.

"No," she said quietly, with some authority in her tone without being commanding. "I'm quite capable of doing that myself." She extended her hand for the cloth, her brown gaze locked with Tabor's icy blue one as she looked over her shoulder.

For several heavy seconds, they just looked at each other in a silent duel of wills. Then, Tabor's gaze swept slowly down the length of Tanaka's naked body. He met Tanaka's gaze; his grin broadened, and he handed her the cloth.

"Aye, my lady," Tabor said, the mischievous expression on his ruggedly handsome face much too enticing for Tanaka's peace of mind. "Your wish is my pleasure to grant."

I wish you weren't the strongest, tallest, most blatantly virile man I've ever seen, Tanaka thought, holding the cloth in front of herself modestly.

She dried herself quickly; and, though her skin still tingled from the icy waters of the sea, Tanaka knew in her heart that she tingled from something else — Tabor's touch. It didn't matter to her that *he* actually hadn't touched her, only the towel he had held had. And, infuriatingly, it didn't matter to her body that she had been given as a gift to Tabor as though she were a commodity to be bought and sold without regard for her own wishes and desires. When he graced her with his rare smiles, Tanaka could understand, at least vaguely, why a woman would want to be with a man. Her entire experience in such matters began and ended with Ingmar the Savage, which had colored how she saw men in every aspect of life.

Lastly, as suggested, Tanaka rubbed her wavy, ebony black hair vigorously with the cloth to dry it. When she was at last satisfied, she held an open hand behind her. "Please?"

She felt the coarse linen shirt against her palm and clenched her fingers around it. But when she started pulling it toward herself, she heard the deep chuckle. Tabor held the opposite sleeve and was refusing to release it.

"Please?" Tanaka asked again, irritated that she should have to ask repeatedly for something that she should be given without hesitation. She tugged again on the shirt, and managed to pull it from Tabor's grasp. One look at his forearms, bulging with muscles,

35

crisscrossed with veins pumping his life's blood, and she knew that he had *allowed* her to take the shirt from him.

The shirt was heavy, made from the fine wool produced near Hedeby and Kaupang. The tight neckline was made to prevent drafts, and the bottom hem cut a horizontal line across the middle of Tanaka's shapely thighs.

Only when her nakedness was at last covered did she turn to face Tabor. "Thank you," she said quietly, averting her gaze. She was afraid of what she might see in his icy blue eyes. She was also a little surprised that Tabor had allowed her to put the shirt on and that he hadn't yet forced himself upon her. In fact, though he had teased her some, he had behaved astonishingly well.

Or was that *deceptively* well?

"Come," Tabor said with sudden and surprising brusqueness. "I have a brush at the shelter. You can use that on your hair."

He rose quickly; and, though he made no threatening move toward Tanaka, she took a step away from him. His size alone was threatening, and whenever he moved quickly, her heart seemed to skip a beat.

Tabor took a lock of wet, wavy hair and twisted it around one long finger. "Your hair is so thick, I doubt you will even be able to pull the brush through it."

Tanaka could not tell if that was meant to be a compliment or not. The only thing that she was absolutely certain of was that occasionally Tabor's tone became low, resonating with a confidence and warmth that touched Tanaka deep within her own being in a private and tender place. The tone seemed to imply that whomever Tabor chose to protect would be protected for life. No harm could ever come to anyone under Tabor's protection. It whispered this — and something more: that enemies of Tabor died harsh, violent deaths.

As they headed back to the shelter Tabor shared with his men, Tanaka wondered whether she could continue to receive protection from this great Viking leader without having to share her body with him in return.

Ingmar the Savage looked over the high wall surrounding Hedeby, standing atop the small, solid-roofed structure that was populated mostly by women who traded passion for financial survival. There were many ships at anchor near the sea entrance to the Danish trading port, but those boats didn't interest him. Ingmar was looking for the large square blue and white sails and the high wolf's head frontpiece that so clearly defined his raiding boats.

If his younger brother Hugh had followed the instructions and plans Ingmar had devised, within hours Tabor would be nothing more than a memory of troubles that once plagued him. *If* . . .

The trouble was that Hugh had a habit of creating his own battle plans, and thinking had never been one of his strengths. He lacked Ingmar's size, power, and cunning. But what he lacked he made up for with savagery, a lust for cruelty, and a willingness to commit any heinous crime against humanity he deemed necessary. As such, he had the skills to support Ingmar if he were to rule the Scandinavian seas, since every captain needs a mate to carry out his orders. But Hugh's inability to understand his limitations made it impossible for Ingmar to put complete faith in his brother.

"What is so interesting out there?" an intoxicated woman of questionable virtue asked from the top rung of the ladder that led to the roof. "There's more to look at down here."

Ingmar examined the woman. She needed a bath and smelled of soured wine. When she ran a hand suggestively up and down her side, he scowled. On principle, he never paid a woman to have sex with him. If a woman didn't want to sleep with him, he forced her; he *never* paid. That was for powerless men who were not in control of their own lives.

"Leave me, woman, or I'll make you suffer for disturbing my concentration."

The woman instantly disappeared from view. Ingmar turned his attention back to the water, looking for the approaching boats that signified the return of his fleet . . . and the first stage of the total destruction of Tabor.

Chapter Four

Tanaka could tell that Tabor was disturbed by the postponement of his meeting with Ingmar. He was not a talkative man even under the most favorable conditions; since receiving the request from Ingmar's servant that their meeting wait until dawn, Tabor had been stony in his silence.

"He drinks much," Tanaka said quietly, kneeling on a thick wool blanket near the fire in the center of the hut. "Perhaps he has had so much wine that he is afraid."

Tabor cast Tanaka a sideways glance. It surprised him that she could know him for such a short period of time and yet be able to read his thoughts and moods with startling accuracy. Her grasp of his language — though she spoke with an accent — shocked him, too; and he wondered whether she had really learned it during her captivity with Ingmar as she had claimed.

"Sometimes you speak like a witch-woman," Tabor said, slowly twisting the handle of the double-bladed dagger between his palms. "Perhaps you know more than you say?"

Tanaka shook her head, sending her damp, unbound hair back and forth over her shoulders. "No, I am no witch from the underworld. I do not pretend to see into your heart, but to look into your eyes is to see a man who is thinking many thoughts . . . troubling thoughts."

A grin pulled up the right side of Tabor's mouth. "If my eyes show you that much, then I must be careful not to let you see into them."

Tanaka almost replied that to not see into his eyes would deprive her of one of the few pleasures she had known since her capture, but she was able to stop the words before they escaped.

What was happening to her? she asked herself, more mystified than angry. *Why wasn't she more contemptuous with this huge Viking who held her captive?*

As though to confirm to herself that she was a captive, Tanaka boldly asked, "What do you intend to do with me. . . . When you are finished with me?"

For no more than a second, anger flashed bright and fierce in Tabor's eyes. Then his features softened almost imperceptibly. "I will take you to Kaupang by the first available boat. There you can find a husband to take care of you. With your beauty, you should have your pick of successful men who will want you as their bride. And I will give you something so that you have a dowry."

Demeaning insults that Ingmar had hurled at her over the past weeks still burned in Tanaka's consciousness, destructive words that forced her to ask, "My skin is not too dark to be beautiful?"

Tabor, sitting cross-legged beside Tanaka, set the dagger down on the blanket before the fire. He twisted to face her more directly, then cupped her chin gently in his large palm. "Your skin is the color of gold, the

40

most precious metal in all the world. Any man who cannot see that does not deserve you."

The words thrilled Tanaka, and the touch of his battle-calloused palm against her chin, his fingers lightly touching her cheek, sent a strange warmth rippling through her. "Why . . ." she began, then had to stop to moisten her dry lips with the tip of her pink tongue, unaware of the erotic vision she presented to Tabor. "Why would you give me a dowry? You do not have to do that."

Tabor looked at her strangely, at first not understanding why she would say such a thing. "You come from a land far from here, so perhaps you do not understand the ways of the Vikings. I did not ask for you; you were given to me. Though you are called a slave, I do not recognize any human as slave. But you are my responsibility, and I must do what I can to see that you have food to eat, clothes to wear, a home to live in. Without a husband, you will not have these things." He shrugged his broad shoulders in his characteristic way, as though there were many things in the world that he simply accepted as immutable laws sent down from the heavens. "Some men find women more attractive when they have a dowry. It is the least I can do."

For a while, neither spoke, contemplating the full impact of what Tabor had said.

"Put your feet in my hands and I will warm them," Tabor continued finally, breaking the silence. "After they are warm, I will give you thick woolens to keep you comfortable."

He wants me to trust him, but in the end, though he does not insult me like Ingmar the Savage, Tabor is still a man and only wants what it is men always want, she thought with grim

41

resolve, determined to keep her soul as isolated and protected as possible.

"You don't need to be frightened," Tabor whispered.

"No?" Tanaka asked.

Though she did not trust Tabor, though recent history with these barbaric Viking tribesmen had taught her that they took whatever they wanted and asked permission of no one, Tanaka twisted on the blanket until she was sitting with her feet extended toward Tabor. She did not trust him, but she dared not openly defy him. She grabbed the shirt and pulled it down as far as she could, to about mid-thigh level.

Smiling, Tabor took her feet in his hands and cradled them in his lap, his large hands engulfing and surrounding her.

"Your feet are so delicate," Tabor whispered, running his hands over the soles and toes of Tanaka's feet.

It was difficult for Tanaka to remain in that position while holding onto the bottom hem of the shirt with both hands. She felt disturbingly vulnerable and attracted to Tabor, and she welcomed neither emotion. At last, afraid that she would fall backward and completely lose whatever modesty she had been able to maintain, Tanaka cautiously placed her right hand behind her to keep herself propped up as Tabor slowly and sensually warmed her feet. With her other hand she stretched the shirt as far down her thighs as she could manage.

Tabor ran his fingers over Tanaka's feet slowly, warming them. But his hands strayed upward until he was massaging the gentle curve of her calf. Tabor watched his hand, his flesh pale against her golden-hued skin. Never had he felt skin so velvety smooth; and, though he prided himself on his control over self, desires, and instincts, he felt a stirring within—even though pleasuring himself with Tanaka was not proper Viking conduct.

"This Kaupang . . . it is far away?" Tanaka asked, but she was not entirely interested in receiving an answer. Her entire concentration was on the strong fingers that had worked up her calf and were now above her knee, kneading the muscles at the lower part of her thigh.

She should say something appropriately scathing to Tabor. She had never let Ingmar touch her without grimacing, without in some way letting him know that she loathed his touch and everything about him. Yet when Tabor touched her, she felt his fingers and did not feel violated. She was torn between what she *felt* she should *say*, and what she actually *felt*.

Tabor answered her, but Tanaka did not—*could not*—pay enough attention to hear the answer. The kneading fingers were now at her mid-thigh, just beneath the hem of the shirt which she still held tightly to; and the warm tingles that had started in her leg were now traveling slowly but steadily throughout her body. Most surprising of all for Tanaka was that she felt moist high up, at her private area, and this had never happened when Ingmar the Savage had pawed her.

She watched Tabor's hand moving over her thigh. His massive forearm was solidly hewn with thick muscles, crossed with blue veins.

How far will he want to go?

It was a tantalizing question to Tanaka. With a certain horrifying dread, she wanted Tabor to continue touching her, exploring her body with his calloused, powerful hands. She knew, too, that she would do

43

whatever it was he demanded of her. Denial, she had been taught, accomplished little with a Viking—he would simply take from her whatever he wanted and perhaps beat her for her defiance. That was the lesson she had been taught by Ingmar the Savage, and she would not forget it now that she was the captive of Tabor, Son of Thor.

If I have to take him inside myself, will I enjoy it?

The thought made Tanaka's heart leap in her chest and her eyes open wide. It was too easy for her to forget the horrors she had been taught now that she was influenced by the gentle ministrations of the Viking called Tabor. Tanaka turned angry eyes on her captor with renewed vigilance against the weakening of her defiant spirit.

Choosing her words very carefully, angry with herself and with Tabor for his seductive ways, she said, "If you're going to do it, have done with your foul deed. I'd like to get this over with as quickly as possible."

The words stabbed Tabor, piercing his contentment, insulting him, reminding him that he was going further with the Egyptian beauty than his personal code of honor allowed. He tossed her legs off his lap, twisting Tanaka sideways. For an instant he was given a glimpse of Tanaka's buttocks, and the reflexive hardening of his groin further irritated his increasingly savage mood.

"If I had wanted to rape you, I would have done it long ago," Tabor said. He bolted to his feet, glaring down at Tanaka. "If I had wanted to sell you for profit, I would have done that, too. You see, I have complete and total power over you. In Hedeby, you are my *property.*" He drew the last word out slowly, venomously, for maximum effect. "Do not try to vex me, woman, or

44

you may succeed; and if you do that, I promise you will harbor many regrets."

Tabor wheeled away from her, picking up the battle-axe. "You must come with me . . . now!" he said, barking out the words. He was a man long accustomed to giving orders.

Fear lanced through Tanaka like the razor-sharp iron tip of a fighting spear. She spun quickly on the blanket, pulling her knees beneath her, turning beseeching eyes that silently asked for sympathy from Tabor.

"I am sorry! Sorry for everything!" Tanaka said, her tone rising sharply with her fear. "Don't sell me back to Ingmar! Please don't!"

Tabor grabbed her by the upper arm, hauling her roughly to her feet. Tanaka, afraid that she would be sold yet again — either back to Ingmar or someone even more heinous — threw herself at Tabor, trying to get her slender arms around his neck to kiss him. When she collided with his body, it was like crashing into an oak tree, and Tanaka realized how truly small she was compared to the broad-shouldered Viking.

In vain she tried once more to kiss Tabor's mouth; since he was well over a foot taller than she, all he had to do to avoid her lips was keep his back straight. The horrible stories she'd heard of women who were sold to *several* Vikings drove her to behave shamefully . . . appallingly. However bad Tabor could be, however great her humiliation before him, one man was not as bad as a dozen.

"I will be good to you, Tabor!" Tanaka said, nearly crying now as his huge hand clamped around her wrist as he pulled her toward the door of his hut. "Do not

45

send me away! I can be the woman you want! The *slave —*"

"Silence!" Tabor bellowed. When Tanaka tried again to kiss him, he pushed her to arm's length, his gigantic hands now on her slender shoulders. "If you think I need to use force to get women to come to my hut, you are greatly mistaken. And if you believe that I would sell you back into slavery, you are doubly mistaken." Tabor's blue gaze spit flames of rage at the trembling, frightened woman. "If you do not want to stay here with me, then you can stay with Knut and his wives. He would not mind another mouth to feed."

"W-wives?" Tanaka stammered, thinking these Vikings were surely the most barbaric people ever to curse the face of the earth.

"Yes. The last time I talked with Knut, he had four. He's probably got more now." Tabor started to push Tanaka toward the door again. "You will be safe with Knut."

Tanaka doubted that she could ever feel safe with any man who had four wives. She pushed against Tabor's hands, resisting the powerful Viking's pull as much as she could.

"I do not want to go," she said, looking straight into Tabor's eyes, her will challenging his. "I tell you the truth. If I insulted you, I did not mean to."

Tabor laughed at that, shaking his head slowly. Eventually, even Tanaka smiled.

"Perhaps I *did* mean to insult you," she said, her back to the pinewood door. When Tabor was smiling, the full force of his masculine magnetism struck her. "I am scared. Many bad things have happened to me since I was taken by Ingmar the Savage. You can understand, can't you?"

Tabor nodded. "Yes . . . I can understand. You do not need to be frightened of me."

He pulled her close, wrapping his powerful arms around her in a loose embrace. Tanaka's arms were at her sides, her cheek against his chest, her plush breasts pressing firmly against him. He stroked her hair and whispered once again that she did not have to fear him, but Tanaka knew better. She *had* to be afraid of Tabor—to fear him more than she had feared anyone, even Ingmar—precisely because he made her aware that she was a woman and because he could make her wonder whether all men were inherently evil, a truth she had to hold onto.

"Let me stay," Tanaka whispered, her words muffled slightly against Tabor's rough wool tunic. "I promise I will not cause you any more trouble. Promise."

Tanaka was distinctly aware of several things. She could feel the powerful beating of Tabor's heart. She could feel, too, the fearful, frantic beating of her own heart and the scratchy texture of the thick shirt against the erect tips of her breasts. Inhaling, she caught the faint, distinct scent of Tabor and found it disturbingly pleasing. Only moments earlier she had been chilled, her feet actually cold, but now she felt almost overheated from head to toe. Never before had an embrace offered comfort. Tabor stroked his palm down her hair and over her shoulders, sending an unprecedented sensation shimmering through her.

"Tanaka . . ." Tabor whispered.

It was the first time he had spoken her name, and Tanaka thought the sound coming from Tabor was wildly arousing. She tilted her head back to look up into his face, and he cupped her chin in his palm.

47

Tabor bent low until his lips were just inches from hers, and he purred, "Do not fear me."

"I must," Tanaka replied a moment before Tabor's mouth dropped down to cover hers, claiming her lips in a possessive kiss that took her breath away.

After being captured by Ingmar, Tanaka had sworn to herself that she would never close her eyes, no matter how horrifying the world became. But now, with Tabor's warm lips pressing firmly against her own, his arms like bands of iron encircling her, closing her eyes was the most natural thing in the world to do. Sighing, aware simultaneously both of Tabor's great strength and great tenderness, Tanaka tried to pretend—at least to herself—that the kiss did not affect her. She had been kissed before, and the kisses had left her feeling defiled; Tabor's kisses were no different.

Liar! her body shouted, refusing her even the small comfort of self-delusion.

Each passing second heightened Tanaka's passion, weakening her resolve to feel nothing at all in Tabor's embrace. Her full breasts, held tautly against Tabor's body, felt painfully compressed, the nipples hard and aching, roughly tantalized by the coarse texture of the shirt she wore and by the heat of Tabor's powerful body.

Time lost meaning, and she did not know how long the kiss lasted. When she felt the tip of Tabor's tongue against her lips, she willingly opened her mouth to accept his deeper exploration. A deep, rumbling groan of pleasure rumbled from Tabor, the sound reverberating through Tanaka, almost drowning her own throaty moan of excitement.

His hands roamed from her shoulders down her back, forcing her to arch backward, demanding that her body mold to his. Everything that Tanaka thought she believed grew faint and indistinct as she feasted on Tabor's mouth, dancing her tongue against his. When she felt Tabor's hand sliding lower, rounding the curve of her buttocks then moving back upward only to slide beneath the shirttail to feel her silken nakedness, she knew that she should protest.

But to what good? She could no more stop Tabor than she could stop the sun from rising on the morrow.

Telling herself that she had no choice in the matter helped salve Tanaka's conscience when Tabor's hand cupped her more firmly against him, forcing the strangely moist petals of her femininity to press intimately — pleasantly — against the hard-muscled surface of his thigh.

When at last the kiss ended, Tanaka felt as though some unseen force had mysteriously stolen all the strength from her body. Her heart raced in her chest; and, though she still held her hands passively at her sides, she longed to have the courage to reach out and explore Tabor's body precisely as he now explored hers, running his powerful hands over the backs of her thighs and the smooth curve of her buttocks.

"Tanaka . . . Tanaka . . ." Tabor whispered, his lips caressing the velvety arch of her neck.

Tanaka tilted her head to the side, giving Tabor more room. It was surely madness, she told herself, that she assist him in his decidedly unwelcome — though erotic — quest. The tip of his tongue, moist and pink, traced the outline of her ear, sending hot waves and cold chills racing through her. His hands never left her, exploring the contours of her back, hips, thighs, and buttocks, never lingering long, igniting a flameless fire wherever he touched.

Raising up on her tiptoes, Tanaka slipped her arms around Tabor, touching him cautiously, mystified by her behavior, yet helpless to stop herself. This was folly, she knew. An insanity of sorts. She tried to tell herself that Tabor was forcing her to kiss him, but when she thrust her tongue deep into his mouth to kiss him with as much intensity and yearning as he had kissed her, she knew it for the lie it was. Her breasts throbbed with desire, aching to be touched by the demanding hands that were so capable of such exquisite tenderness.

It wasn't until Tanaka felt Tabor's hand, the fingertips trailing featherlight caresses, slip around her hip and move toward the front of her body that reality at last registered in her brain.

"Wait! Tabor, wait!" Tanaka said in a breathy whisper, twisting until she slid out of his embrace and away from his touch. She felt warm and wet, oddly sensitized by this man's embrace. Her heart hammered, and she knew that she would not think clearly as long as she allowed Tabor to touch her, as long as she could taste the sweet, intoxicating nectar of his kisses.

She took another step backward, colliding with a shield that leaned against the wall. Startled, she turned to Tabor, silently pleading that he understand actions she herself could neither explain nor comprehend.

Her palms pushed at Tabor. "Please," she implored, the single word a tremulous plea that pulled at Tabor's heartstrings. Only once or twice in his life had Tabor questioned whether or not his personal code of honorable conduct was correct. But as he looked at Tanaka, he wanted to ignore the fear he saw in her eyes. Her slender, naked legs drew his gaze, and she wrenched sideways as though to protect herself from him.

It would be so easy, he told himself. She was small and wore only the shirt he'd given her. And she was his slave, properly given to him by her previous master, Ingmar the Savage. If he raped her, no one in Hedeby would think the lesser of him for it.

No one, that is, except himself.

Tabor growled, "Stand aside. I need to walk."

Two long strides brought him out of his hut, and he inhaled the cool evening air and wondered why a copper-skinned beauty from a faraway land called Egypt should captivate him so thoroughly. He thought, too, of "visiting" one of the women he knew. There were several in Hedeby—women who would take him into their homes, their arms, their bodies, at a moment's notice, never complaining of how long he had been gone, only happy that he had returned to them. Though he always brought gifts, they were happy just to have Tabor to themselves for an hour or two—or perhaps an entire evening.

But, somehow, the thought of satisfying his lusts with one of them no longer appealed to Tabor. As he looked up at the moon glowing pale in the dark sky, he cursed Tanaka because she had bewitched him and no other women could spark the fire of want within him.

Chapter Five

Ingmar was restless, and not even the young woman slave beside him that he'd just purchased could take away his sense of foreboding. It wasn't so much concern for his brother's safety that stirred a sour brew in the pit of his belly but knowledge of what would happen if Hugh had failed in his attack on Tabor's men. Since nightfall made sailing or even rowing through the fjords to Hedeby virtually impossible, Ingmar knew that there was nothing to do but wait until morning to find out if his plan to divide and destroy Tabor and his Viking warriors had proven successful.

If Hugh had failed, if word of the unprovoked attack should reach Tabor's ears . . .

The thought sent a shudder through Ingmar. He well knew the tales of what happened to the enemies of Tabor, particularly to anyone foolish enough to hurt one of his Vikings. Tabor's wrath was legendary, and it was something that Ingmar had no desire to witness firsthand.

Pushing the disquieting thoughts from his head, Ingmar concentrated on what pleasures he would know when Hugh returned with his full fighting force intact and with fully half of Tabor's men killed. The remaining rival force would be outnumbered four or five to one, and Ingmar and his men would make short work of Tabor's warriors. Perhaps in the end, when Tabor was thoroughly vanquished, Ingmar would slaughter the tall, powerful Viking himself. He had always resented how the villagers in Hedeby, and even in Kaupang in Norway and Birka in Sweden, feared yet respected Tabor, but only feared and despised Ingmar the Savage.

A smile curling his mouth into a hateful sneer, Ingmar promised himself that he would personally execute Tabor. He would do it publicly, at the slave auction block where so many people had seen him give Tabor the Egyptian slave. That would prove to everyone that he—Ingmar the Savage—was the ultimate Viking who ruled the lands and the seas.

The woman beside him in the bed shifted slightly, and Ingmar glanced at her. She wasn't bad-looking, but she certainly wasn't as beautiful as Tanaka. Why *had* he given *her* to Tabor?

Ingmar knew why. It was because her skin was dark, not pale like Scandinavian women, and he was afraid that his men would talk behind his back about it. He had pretended that her dark skin made her ugly, but now that he had given her away, he was angry with himself. Something about the Egyptian fascinated and aroused him. In all the time that she had been his captive, her spirit had not broken. Tanaka had not been defeated by her master's open contempt of her. Nor by his physical and sexual demands. Nor the humiliation he had heaped upon her. Even when he sent her to the slave auction she had held her head high, unsubdued, dressed in regal pride no rags could obscure. Perhaps that was the reason she had caught Tabor's interest.

A new burst of anger fired to life within Ingmar's breast as he thought about Tabor and the Egyptian woman lying in bed together at that very moment. And, as it always did, anger fueled Ingmar's desire for women. He rolled over, cruelly entwining his fingers into the blonde hair of the heavyset woman at his side.

"Wake up, wench! Wake up and be of use to me!"

And Ingmar was upon her even before she stirred.

Tabor squinted to see better in the moonlight and recognized Sven's familiar stride. He saw a smaller shape to Sven's right and knew that his friend had found a woman to keep him company while he kept guard.

"Hail!" Sven called out quietly as he approached.

"Hail!" Tabor returned, letting his friend know in the age-old sailor's tradition that it was safe to advance.

When ten yards separated the two men Sven motioned for the woman beside him to stop. Then, coming forward, he spoke privately with his leader. The smile on Sven's face told Tabor he thought the Egyptian woman beautiful and he considered his leader lucky to be the one who shared her bed.

"You think too much," Tabor said, accurately guessing Sven's thoughts.

"Out here to catch your breath? I thought you couldn't get tired out until the dawn."

"I haven't touched her," Tabor replied, his anger aroused, though he couldn't exactly say why. He realized, too, that he had not spoken the truth, and this was particularly disturbing since Tabor never lied.

Eager to change the subject, he asked, "You've got men watching Ingmar? When did they last report?"

Sven would not be so easily diverted. "I'll find quarters for all the men. You'll have the hut to yourself all night long."

"That won't be necessary." Tabor looked away and a muscle flicked in his jaw. "You know my rules. No slaves. No rape. If I should lie with her, it would not be with her consent. I will not violate my law."

"Aye, your law . . ." Sven replied, letting the words trail off. He cocked an eyebrow to suggest that while laws should not be broken, perhaps the bending of them by the man who had made them might not be altogether unforgivable.

"Ingmar—I want to know what he's up to. I don't trust him."

Sven nodded at last, his smile disappearing. It was time to be serious. Ingmar's name caused trepidation in even the bravest man's heart. "I have two men watching him at all times, and they are relieved every two hours by two fresh men. There are also men moving throughout Hedeby looking for signs of whatever plot the Northman has concocted."

"Good man," Tabor replied. He could always count on Sven to follow his orders to the letter. "What is Ingmar doing?"

"He's with a slave—has been for several hours now. No sign of his brother Hugh. That worries me."

"Me, too. Ingmar never lets his brother far from his sight."

"Hugh would get lost if Ingmar weren't holding his hand." They laughed briefly, then Sven nodded toward trees to their left. "I've got men in those trees as well as two groups of two men in each roving patrol. If

Ingmar's planning to pounce, he's going to meet with great resistance."

Tabor was pleased with Sven's thoroughness. He never had to issue orders for his own safety—his personal security was something Sven had overseen for many years.

The leader said with a smile, "I see you found someone to keep you from getting too lonely."

"It is a cool night." Sven grinned rakishly and slapped Tabor lightly on the shoulder. "Go back inside. We'll be fine. As I said, you have the hut to yourself tonight."

"It isn't necessary," Tabor said, finding it strangely important he convince his friend that he had behaved honorably, that he really hadn't forced himself upon the Egyptian slave who had been foisted upon him.

"Wait here," Sven said. He walked back to the woman waiting in the shadows, took something she handed him, then returned to Tabor. "We thought she might like this."

Tabor accepted the white cotton underdress from Sven, silently cursing himself for not having thought of it himself.

Sven said nothing more as he turned from Tabor, slipping his arm around the comely young woman before disappearing back into the shadows of the cool Danish night.

Tanaka was sitting near the fire with her knees pulled up tight to her chest, her arms around her legs. It was difficult to tell how long Tabor had been gone, but each passing minute heightened her fear.

Had she made him so angry that he would sell her?

And what would happen to her if he gave her back to Ingmar and complained that she had not treated him properly? Ingmar was a cruel man even when no one had done anything to make him angry. What would he be like if Tabor complained of Tanaka's defiance?

Though she sat close to the fire, Tanaka shivered. She turned so that the flames could warm the rest of her body. A thousand unanswered questions danced maddeningly in her brain, preventing sleep despite her exhaustion.

The memories of Tabor's kisses came back in full force, haunting Tanaka, stripping away some once-comforting illusions that she had held about herself. No man's touch could ever please her, she had stubbornly maintained; no man's kisses would ever taste good upon her lips. While Ingmar's captive, Tanaka had found it easy—even essential—to hold onto those beliefs. His cruelty and unceasing need to dominate all those around him only reinforced her dark view of men. Now a different man—a man of gentle, fiery touches that awakened her, a man of velvet kisses, a man of warmth in a land of cold—had scaled the protective stone walls of her illusions, and she was left naked with her realization: A man's touch *could* please her; his kiss *could* taste as nectar on her lips.

She touched her lips softly with the pads of her fingers, as though to feel the kisses that had been there. She moistened her lips with the tip of her tongue, and the small, insignificant act conjured up memories of how she had parted her lips to accept Tabor's tongue and how she had explored his mouth with bold curiosity that now made her feel so shameless she blushed crimson.

And it was precisely at that moment, while Tanaka

relived her wanton behavior and her cheeks were pink with embarrassment, that Tabor chose to step back into the hut.

"Why aren't you asleep?" Tabor asked, his tone hard-edged. Tanaka's presence was a magnetic confrontation to his senses that he was not sure he could continue resisting.

Dominating her fear of Tabor's lust was her greater fear of Tabor's anger. She was determined to do something that she never had done for Ingmar: pretend that she welcomed his passion.

"I didn't want to be asleep when you returned," Tanaka said softly, her eyes uncharacteristically turned down demurely. "I thought you . . . you might . . . require me."

Tabor saw through her pretense, sickened that she believed he would so use her. She had been taught by Ingmar to expect no better.

"I don't *require* you for anything." Tabor bit the words out caustically, making Tanaka wonder again if it was the olive hue of her skin that made her unacceptable in Tabor's eyes. He stripped off his vest and tossed it toward his bed, then pulled loose the tie that held his shirt closed. "It's time for sleep. Sven brought you something to wear." He dropped the white underdress at the foot of his sleeping mat. "You'll be more comfortable sleeping in this than in that scratchy shirt."

Her palms sweaty, her heart agallop, she looked at the underdress and realized what had been requested of her. Tabor seemed to ignore her as he prepared himself for bed, and she wondered whether he was being courteous of her modesty or snubbing her.

"Thank you."

She rose to her feet, unsure of what was expected of

her. Then resolve and courage sprang to renewed life in her breast; and, without further hesitation, her lips tightened into a determined line, she pulled the shirt over her head and extended it toward her captor.

Tabor had removed his own shirt when he knelt to retrieve the underdress. He turned, about to hand it to Tanaka, and stopped, awed by her naked splendor. His mouth dry, he stood motionless for several seconds, transfixed by her beauty and unable to speak. This small woman had a greater impact upon his senses than any other he'd ever known.

Although totally exposed, she held her chin high. Her eyes, however, while retaining their vitality lacked the mocking insult they'd always turned upon Ingmar. To her surprise, Tanaka enjoyed the effect her nudity had on Tabor. She saw desire explode in his eyes, brightening them. His jaw clamped tight, as though he were undergoing a great physical strain.

Go ahead and look at me, you Viking bastard, Tanaka thought savagely, keeping her hands at her sides, allowing Tabor an unhindered view. *Someday I'm going to escape and make it back to my own land, where I am the powerful Tanaka, High Priestess of Opar! I will have my pharaoh send a thousand men — ten thousand men — to these infernal, frigid Scandinavian waters, and they will vanquish all of you! You will be as insignificant as a single grain of sand in the Egyptian desert!*

The hunger in Tabor's eyes made Tanaka feel strong, confident in herself in a way that she never had before. She looked straight at Tabor and asked, "Did you want me to put that on now . . . or afterwards?"

"You taunt me, witch-woman!"

She saw the fire in his blue eyes and knew that she was playing a very dangerous game. She knew, too, that if she should displease her Danish captor so thoroughly that he complained to Ingmar that she was an unacceptable gift, she would live to regret it.

I must please him, Tanaka thought, her eyes burning with defiance and another emotion that even she was not entirely aware of. *Pleasing my captor, however distasteful that may be, is the lesser of evils!*

When Tabor had kissed her before, his strength was suppressed and his kiss was soft and sweet against her mouth. This time, when he took Tanaka into his arms, all his desire seemed to bubble toward the surface, driving him on. He crushed Tanaka's curvaceous body against his own, pulling her in tightly, forcing her plump breasts to compress against the powerful muscles of his bare chest. He lifted her easily, his mouth never leaving hers, his fingers pressing deeply into the firm flesh at her hip.

Tanaka had not intended to touch Tabor. To *be* touched was perhaps necessary; to touch would be unacceptable. She would give to him whatever he wanted, but she would volunteer nothing, feel nothing, and certainly not permit herself any attraction to this virile Viking.

Her unaffected aloofness had been planned, and she might have been able to maintain it if Tabor had been shirted when he took her in his arms. Sensation shot through Tanaka when her breasts, nipples already taut, crushed against Tabor's chest. His warmth seared her senses, the blood raging—almost boiling—in her veins. She opened her mouth and, with a throaty moan, played her tongue against Tabor's.

Her hands simply could not remain passive at her sides. Tanaka flattened her palms against Tabor's mighty shoulders, trembling as she did so, feeling the steely strength of him. Her legs, responding to a will of their own, wrapped around Tabor's waist, and his arms held her easily.

"Witch-woman!" Tabor murmured when the burning kiss ended. "You'll destroy me in the end. Of this I am sure!"

No, I could never destroy you, Tanaka thought. But with another kiss, she amended the thought to *I would never destroy you!*

Never in her life had she felt so small as when she was held suspended in the air by Tabor. Her legs wrapped tightly around his waist, her ankles hooked together. She clutched his shoulders as she feasted on the openmouthed kisses that stripped away her inhibitions like candle wax melting beneath the flame.

In a corner of her mind still capable of coherent thought, Tanaka realized that she was moving, that Tabor was walking. Tabor knelt at the edge of his mat and pushed Tanaka backward until she was stretched out and he could recline beside her, half resting upon her, his lips nuzzling hers.

"No woman has ever made my blood burn so," Tabor whispered between kisses, shocked at the intensity of his own need. He cradled Tanaka's head in the crook of his left arm. When she began to roll toward him, he pushed her hips away so that she again lay flat on the mat. "I must explore you! I must know all your secrets!"

Tanaka was confused by Tabor's words, but asked no questions, not entirely certain she could make her mouth form the foreign words properly. Tabor's kisses had been harsh and demanding, and forcing her to respond. She could not remain cold and detached as she had with Ingmar.

Now, with Tabor, she found the act different. Erotic. When his tongue touched her lips, she opened her mouth willingly. The exquisite heat of his body ignited a flame within Tanaka that burned away hesitation and doubt. Now needy, she hungered for Tabor.

When she felt his hand at her hip, turning her and pushing her away, she was confused at first. Tabor's mouth had not left hers, but she felt his fingertips inching up from her hip, following the line of ribs upward to the steep valley of her breasts.

Tanaka trembled, anxious for Tabor's touch and shocked by her desire. With her savage captors to be touched had been to be defiled. And yet now, held by this giant of a man who "owned" her, Tanaka wanted that contact. She mewed when Tabor caught her lip between his teeth. She writhed when he pressed against her left nipple, forgetting for a moment that she was an Egyptian high priestess.

He kissed the corner of her mouth, her cheeks and ears, her chin and throat. He kissed her everywhere; and as he caressed her with his lips, his right hand played over her body with consummate skill, touching and caressing her breasts, stomach, thighs, even the backs of her knees. He touched her everywhere but at the place where she most craved him.

Tanaka could not find the courage to explore Tabor as he explored her. She kept her hands at his shoulders, going no further, despite a wanton curiosity about this singular man — and his body.

When he leaned away, Tanaka kept her eyes shut, though she could feel Tabor looking at her, perusing her nakedness with his eyes. His fingertips circled her navel, tickling her yet arousing passion.

Tense seconds passed, and the fear that was never

far from the surface of Tanaka's thoughts began to build. Had she displeased Tabor? Did he not like the way she looked? Kissed? Should she have been bolder with her hands or had she been too bold already?

She also questioned her response to Tabor. Who was this stranger, this Tanaka who had suddenly sprung to life, taking delight in what she had once reviled?

"Witch-woman!" Tabor whispered again, and Tanaka could hear in his voice both adoration and anger, for he clearly was not entirely pleased with the desire he felt for her.

Then he took her breast between his lips, and Tanaka's questions vanished. Astonished by the intensity of her reaction, she pushed her fingers into Tabor's long blond hair. But rather than pushing his mouth from her breast, as she had intended, she hugged his face closer to her bosom. His lips, his tongue, even his teeth aroused her, and Tanaka trembled uncontrollably upon Tabor's mat.

She had thought nothing could feel better than Tabor kissing her breast until his hand pressed at the juncture of her thighs. Lightning bolts jolted through Tanaka. Spontaneously, she arched her back as his fingers probed then found a point of raw pleasure that caused Tanaka's mouth to open wide.

She felt him moving beside her, but a new sensual appetite dulled Tanaka's awareness. Tabor's tongue—slippery on her navel—made Tanaka flinch. Though she kept her eyes shut, she reached down to entwine the fingers of both hands into his mane and pushed him down, farther than she had intended. Between her thighs, she felt the erotic play of his mouth against her, his tongue probing, flicking, and circling. With serpentine ease, he stripped away her doubt, shame, and inhibition, and she no longer felt fear.

The pleasure too great, Tanaka struggled against Tabor. She could not breathe and so she pushed at him. But he held her wrists against the mat and did not stop his kisses.

Tanaka stared, unseeing, at the ceiling of the Viking hut. *What is happening to me?* she asked herself as the pressure built. Tanaka's hands were balled into futile fists pinned to the mat. Her body tightened inside, coiling, knotting painfully, until suddenly, the pleasure bordering on the brink of pain, she tumbled headlong into an abyss of white hot waves.

She screamed, a wordless scream that existed only in her mind. Her hips churned, jerking up and down as Tabor rode her with his mouth. She twisted from head to foot as the burning passion flowed in her.

And then, the tumult was over. Spent, Tanaka gulped in air greedily. Tabor's grip loosened on her wrists, and she raised an arm to her forehead, blinking to focus her vision.

"What was that?" she asked, the startled words out before she thought the question through.

Tabor's throaty chuckle drew her attention outside herself and back to him. With the return of logic, the sight of him was once again disturbing. She knew what he would want, and perhaps, with him, with the man who had taken her to such exulted heights, she might even have wanted it, too. But Tanaka had never been taken so high before; and, consequently, reason decreed, the crash to earth would be harder as well.

"There are many things I can teach you," Tabor said, getting to his feet. He removed his knee-high soft leather boots and cloth trousers. "Let me teach you how beautiful it can be."

Fully naked and fully aroused, the Viking frightened her. She had never intended for this to happen. Tanaka had wanted to please Tabor so that he would not be angry with her, but that was all. She had never thought *he* would please *her;* she had never even thought it was possible for a woman to experience pleasure. And now he wanted more—more than she was willing to or could give him. Her body tingled with a strange, gripping madness.

"Wait," she whispered. He looked down upon her as a wolf would upon his prey. "Please. . . . wait."

"Don't be afraid," Tabor said in that throaty whisper that was warm and sensual and made Tanaka want to trust him. "I can take you back there. I can make it happen again very soon."

But Tanaka did not trust his words. He was too big in too many ways, and she was convinced that to take him into herself would tear her apart.

He can give you back to Ingmar the Savage if you don't please him, an insistent voice inside her head warned.

A shiver passed through Tanaka as she realized the truth of the warning. She closed her eyes, turned her face aside, and whispered, "Do whatever you will. I'll not try to stop you."

Tabor got down beside her again, hungry for the taste of her mouth, aching for the release of his own passion. But her eyes had turned cold and fearful. He had seen this before. Often, when he'd brought a woman to the summit of pleasure for the first time in her life, it frightened her. But he had always been able to allay the fears, and satisfy both himself and the woman.

When Tabor tried to kiss Tanaka, she turned her face away, but his desire was too intense for him to be easily dissuaded. He wedged against her, manhood meeting thigh, and the heat of her flesh urged him closer to her fire.

"Look at me," he coaxed. "I want to see your soul when I take you to that special place again."

Shamed by the pleasure she'd felt—pleasure at her own defilement, she spread her thighs apart with cold detachment. "Do what you must," she said. "I am your slave and can deny you nothing."

She could have cut him with a knife and not have injured him more deeply. Tabor was not a rapist. His jaws clenched tight in rage, and he bolted to his feet, pulling on his clothes with feverish haste.

"Cover yourself, wench!" he snapped at the woman in his bed. "My warriors will be coming in soon, and I don't want them driven mad by the sight of you."

Tanaka sat up, raising one knee to hide herself as she crossed her arms over her bosom. "Have I displeased you? I would have done whatever you commanded."

Tabor picked up the blanket by the corner and tossed it partially over Tanaka. "Displeased me?" he asked tersely. "I doubt you have the knowledge and skill to please me."

He left the hut abruptly, and Tanaka lay trembling, wondering what punishment would be hers when the Viking warrior returned.

Chapter Six

Tanaka awoke into the disquieting reality of nearly a dozen broad-shouldered, heavily-armed Viking warriors. Adding to this confusion was the unsettling fact that she was nude, with nothing but a heavy, coarse-textured blanket to cover herself.

Sven noticed first that she had woken. He smiled. "Morning, miss," he said respectfully. "We didn't wake you, I trust. If so, let me apologize for myself and the others."

Tanaka shook her head, realizing how extraordinarily quiet Tabor's men really were. She knew that this was testimony to their discipline and training.

As she tried to form a question about Tabor, the leader strode into the hut. It was the first time she had seen him fully armed, and the sight was as pleasing as it was disturbing. He wore woolen trousers with soft, knee-length boots with leather strappings from ankle to knee, a dark blue shirt beneath a leather jerkin, and a vest of leather-plating for protection against swords and arrows. At his left hip was a long scabbard for a sword, the haft of which glittered with an enormous ruby embedded in its crown. At his right hip was the fighting axe that Tanaka had become all too familiar with. He wore no helmet, and his blond hair fell across his broad shoulders. His arms, bulging with muscles, were adorned with leather gauntlets at each wrist.

"She is awake," Sven said, then moved away, allowing Tabor some privacy.

Tabor knelt beside Tanaka, and her heart quickened. She pulled the blanket more tightly around her, tucking it in securely beneath her arms. These signs of apprehension brought a scowl to Tabor's lips.

"I have found clothes for you," he said, nodding to a pile of the neatly folded garments at the foot of the mat. "You will not have cold feet again. Hurry now, for I must meet with Ingmar, and then we will be off to Kaupang. I want to set sail within the hour."

Tabor stood, and with a flick of his hand, indicated he wanted the hut emptied. In less than a minute Tanaka was alone in the hut.

Tanaka was aware that she had witnessed a small display of Tabor's power. He had ordered strong, fierce Vikings to vacate the hut, and he had done it without uttering a single word. The men responded to his command without question or hesitation.

Nevertheless, she tossed the blanket aside and reached for the clothes that Tabor had provided, convinced that the men were waiting just outside the door, ready to burst in upon her in her unclothed state.

But if they were going to do that, why wouldn't they have simply taken the blanket from her while she slept? And why had Sven smiled at her and treated her so courteously if he was a vile Viking warrior bent on rape, murder, and senseless destruction?

Tanaka pushed the thoughts away. She couldn't allow herself to be confused about these Vikings. She knew what kind of men they really were.

When she picked up the underdress to put it on, the sight of the garment brought on a rush of memories. What had happened to her? What had caused her body to writhe and convulse in sweet ecstasy? Tabor called her a witch-woman, but surely he was the one practicing sorcery if he could create such a madness and fire within her.

Stop thinking about last night! You didn't please him, and he'll probably give you back to Ingmar within the hour!

Tanaka slipped the underdress over her head and pulled on the wool dress of bright green. It had a high neckline and came down to her ankles. Thick woolen stockings that came to mid-thigh and soft leather slippers completed the attire.

She pushed all memories of the previous evening to the back of her mind. What was past was history that she could not change, and no amount of worrying could alter that. Besides, with the challenge of a new day, its new problems would require her undivided attention if she were to have even the slightest chance of regaining her freedom.

She stepped outside, where thirty men were packing weapons of war and stowing away items purchased in Hedeby. Tabor gave orders casually, stating them as requests rather than demands, but Tanaka wasn't fooled. She saw how the men immediately did whatever he asked, how their stride became just a little bit quicker and their movements crisper when they knew Tabor was watching. Whenever a Viking locked eyes with her, he would smile and go about his work.

Tanaka suspected the men assumed that she had slept with Tabor; she wanted to scream to them that she hadn't.

Or had she?

It was a puzzling question. The sweet things that Tabor had done with his mouth had taken her to incredible heights of ecstasy—but did that mean she'd made love with Tabor? She had done *something*, but she wasn't at all certain what that *something* was, except that it was different from the rape that Ingmar called lovemaking.

Tanaka was turning this over in her mind when Tabor stepped up to her. Her unpredictable heart skipped a beat.

"You look good dressed like a Viking maiden." Gently, he lifted a lock of her jet black hair and twisted it around his forefinger. It seemed not unlike a caress. "Of course, no Viking maiden has hair as black as midnight."

Tanaka could not tell if she'd been insulted or complimented, but she a felt warmth from Tabor's presence. With memory refreshened, she did not step away, and the hard light in Tabor's eyes let her know that he was still unhappy with what had happened—and what had not happened—the night before.

He released her hair and, turning to his men, announced, "Let's get this over with quickly. Keep your wits about you, your eyes and ears open. This seems harmless, but we've all heard the stories of Ingmar's murderous treachery."

"Aye, we've all heard," Sven agreed. He was the only one of Tabor's men who dared interrupt—or was allowed to. "But what can that bloody Northman do?

He's left all but a handful of men behind. There are thirty-five of us."

Several Vikings voiced their agreement.

"He has *seemed* to leave himself defenseless, and that's one of the reasons why I don't trust these talks. There are many men who would love to see Ingmar dead. Why would a man with so many enemies leave himself so vulnerable to attack?"

Sven withdrew a deadly-looking dagger from a sheath at his waist and twisted the handle so the early morning sunlight reflected off its flawless, silver blade. "If you give me the word, we could be rid of Ingmar."

"A tempting offer," Tabor said, "but murdering him here in Hedeby, when he has come ostensibly for peaceful purposes, would not be honorable. It wouldn't be the Viking way."

Tanaka shuddered as she watched Sven brandish his dagger. His offer to murder Ingmar, she knew, was genuine. Yet he had also been polite to her. Tanaka wondered if Sven would cut her throat if Tabor gave him the command and suspected that he would. It reaffirmed her belief that she had to convince Tabor that she could please and be of value to him. That insight was still with her when Tabor commanded everyone to lift their trunks and bags of goods and start for Hedeby.

Ingmar squinted, trying to see better through sheer force of will. He was standing atop the wench's hut, staring out to sea. Off in the distance, just specks upon the sea, were ships. He could not yet make out their design, and since they were being rowed against the wind from the north, he could not identify them from the size, shape, and color of their sails.

But it had to be Hugh, returning from Medworth. It had to be.

In his mind, Ingmar could envision what had happened in the small village of Medworth, the home of Tabor and his men. Three ships and nearly one hundred twenty men would have landed at dawn the previous day, descending upon thirty-five Vikings, their women, and their children. It would be bloody hand-to-hand combat. Axes, swords, daggers. The kind of fighting that Ingmar himself avoided. He preferred his powerful bow, a quiver full of iron-tipped arrows, and plenty of distance separating himself from his intended victim.

The fighting would be fierce, for Tabor's men were the best. Perhaps that is why Hugh was late returning to Hedeby, Ingmar thought. For only a second he wondered if it were possible that Hugh and all his men, despite their enormous advantage in numbers, had failed to destroy Tabor's Vikings. What if it were Tabor's men in the longboats making their way slowly against the wind to the port city? The moment Tabor learned of his treachery, Ingmar would be as good as dead.

"Hugh is a fool, but even a fool would taste victory with my plan," Ingmar said aloud. The sound of his own voice, especially when he spoke in a confident tone, always reassured him.

Turning, Ingmar looked inland. Just barely visible beyond the high protective wall that completely surrounded the city, a queue of men were making their way toward the village, led by a tall, broad-shouldered blond man. Ingmar cursed. He turned back toward the sea, and now he recognized his own ships. Hugh, and what was left of the fighting force he'd attacked Medworth with, would soon be in Hedeby, attacking

72

Tabor and his men. Judging the distance and speed, Ingmar guessed that Tabor would be inside the walls of Hedeby for an hour before Hugh would arrive. As long as Ingmar could keep Tabor occupied for an hour, victory would be his! Just one more hour, then Tabor, Son of Thor, thorn in Ingmar the Savage's side, would be dead!

Tabor sat on the long wooden bench, leaning back, his legs crossed ankle upon knee. A maiden approached with a drinking horn filled with hearty ale, but Tabor refused. He did not care for strong drink in the morning, nor would he allow it with his men, believing that it made one stupid and weak-willed.

"How many years have we . . . disagreed?" Ingmar asked. He tore a large chunk of bread from the loaf and popped it into his mouth, washing it down with ale. "Why must we be enemies, Tabor? You want riches, and I want riches. If we work together, we multiply our forces, increase our strength. No country would dare stand against us."

Coldly, Tabor replied, "Aye, I want riches, but not if it means my men and I burn villages to the ground. Not if it means I must sit by and watch men under my command rape and murder. I'd rather be a poor Viking warrior, living by a code of honor that assured me a place in Valhalla."

Ingmar laughed softly. They both knew that, while Tabor's wealth did not equal Ingmar's, he was still a man of considerable wherewithal. The lavish gifts he showered on his lovers was testimony to that.

"Perhaps. But we can all use a little more than what we have now," Ingmar said. He felt a dribble of sweat trickle down his spine. He resisted the urge to wipe his brow. It was not warm enough for him to be perspiring so, and he prayed that Tabor wouldn't notice. If the trap were detected by Tabor, he would seek revenge upon Ingmar in true Viking tradition. He would kill the man responsible for attacking him. Though Ingmar was certain he was a more deadly warrior with bow and arrow, he was also certain that with sword, broadsword, battle-axe, or dagger, Tabor's size, strength, and speed made him a lethal foe.

When Tabor did not respond, Ingmar continued, "My gift. . . . she was entertaining?"

Tabor scowled. He disliked the male habit of detailing sexual conquests as though they were war victories. Ingmar saw his scowl and assumed that the Egyptian slave had been as cold and unresponsive to Tabor as she had been when he'd tied her to his own bed.

"I'll give you another, if you'd like," Ingmar said. "I have many slaves, and my ships will soon sail to the west again. Would you like me to bring you back a dozen or so?" He chuckled as though he and Tabor were confidants. "A man as lusty as you can surely go through a dozen slaves without tiring!"

Tabor stood abruptly. "Enough," he said. "You said you wanted to see me in the free village of Hedeby, where we commit no violence, and I have seen you. You stated that you want peace, yet you offer nothing to make me want to grant you that peace. You do nothing but talk, Ingmar, and your talk has wasted my time."

Ingmar stood then, too, and Tabor saw an undercurrent of desperation behind his eyes that he did not understand. "Wait. . . . we must talk."

"I'm weary of conversation." Tabor turned his back

to Ingmar, heading for the door of the tavern. "In another place, we shall meet again, and then we will not have any need to words to end our differences."

Tabor had just passed through the tavern doors into the early morning hubbub of the Hedeby marketplace, when one of his men rushed forward, his face flushed. "Tabor, there are ships at port! Ingmar's ships! They bear their bows and swords at the battle ready!"

In that instant it all took shape in Tabor's mind. He wheeled upon Tanaka, sure that it had been her job to keep him occupied while the attack began. "You are deadlier than I thought!" he spat contemptuously. "But you will not live to brag of your treachery this time! Sven, see that the wench's fate is tied to our own!"

Sven grabbed Tanaka by the collar of her dress with his left hand as his right removed the dagger he had previously threatened to kill Ingmar with. "Fight me now, and you'll die quickly," he promised.

Tabor, drawing his battle-axe, rushed back into the tavern, but Ingmar had already departed. The tavern owner pointed to a window in the back. Tabor rushed to the opening in time to see Ingmar pushing his way through the sparse crowd at a dead run, moving toward the dock where his men waited.

The willful betrayal of Ingmar's plan stunned Tabor. Hedeby was a free village, a place for commerce and entertainment. It had been a tacit agreement by Vikings everywhere that the villages of Hedeby, Kaupang, and Birka were to be free zones where violence and raiding would not be tolerated. Ingmar had to know that to break that pact would make him an enemy to Viking leaders everywhere.

But then, who besides Tabor, Son of Thor, had the strength, the will, the resolve, the well-trained Vikings, and the courage necessary to confront Ingmar the Savage?

The battle began in an instant when the leading edge of Ingmar's troops clashed with Tabor's Vikings. Tabor met two men head on. Axe in one hand, sword in the other, he slew them both in short order and looked for more.

"Behind you!" Tanaka screamed.

Tabor did not trust the woman, believing that she had been used by Ingmar to distract him, but without hesitation he ducked, bending his knees and wheeling to his left. The sharp edge of a sword sliced through the air a fraction of an inch from his head. Still crouched low, Tabor lunged out with his sword, driving the deadly blade in deeply. As he pulled his weapon from the corpse, he was aware that he owed his life to Tanaka; and the question of why she would warn him of the blind-side attack, even when she herself had been sent by Ingmar to subvert his defenses, took root deep in his mind.

Three more of Ingmar's men were felled by Tabor's axe and sword, but though he was successful in his own skirmishes, he sensed around him that the battle could not be won. His own Vikings, though fighting bravely and skillfully, could not match the monumental advantage of sheer numbers that Ingmar's warriors possessed. Although retreat was something that Tabor and his Vikings had never before had to do, to continue fighting would only result in their death.

"Be gone with us all!" Tabor shouted. "We'll fight these swine another day!"

He looked to his right and was surprised to see Tanaka. Sven had released her to put both hands and all his attention to the fight, so she had had plenty of opportunities to escape. Why had she chosen not to?

"To the ship! To the ship, good men all!" Tabor shouted above the cries of the villagers, who had never before witnessed carnage within the walls of Hedeby.

Tabor confronted one last warrior, slaying him with his bloody axe, then looked about him again. Though the lives of all of his Vikings were precious to him, he valued Sven's most. Tabor would not retreat until he knew that his friend was alive and capable of retreating. Sven and Tabor had saved each other's life many times, and neither would abandon the other.

Tabor found Sven with his back to a wall, fighting off three of Ingmar's swordsmen. Though attack from behind was not an honorable method of attack, Tabor launched into the three with ferocious wrath, swinging battle-axe and stabbing with sword. He felled two of the men as Sven dropped the third.

"To the ship," Tabor said to Sven. "There are too many of them to fight now!"

"Aye! And I fear that our warriors in Medworth have already fallen!"

Tabor nodded, about to fight his way to the rear entrance of Hedeby, when an arrow pierced his left biceps. He growled more in rage than pain as the battle-axe that had been his father's, and his father's before that, dropped from his hand. Blood spurted from the wounds fore and aft, the arrow lodged through the muscle.

"I'll kill the dark wench for you, my friend!" Sven hissed as he snapped the shaft of the arrow very near the inside of Tabor's biceps. Before he could pull the arrow from Tabor's arm, another arrow cut through the air, narrowly missing them.

In unison, they looked in the direction of the attack

and saw Ingmar, standing atop a building, shooting down at them.

The ensuing chaos made it possible for Tabor and Sven to rush between buildings and briefly avoid further arrows. Sven pulled the remainder of the arrow from Tabor's arm, but blood spurted freely from the wounds, soaking into the heavy fabric of Tabor's clothing and staining it red down to his waist.

Tabor sheathed his sword and used his hand to clutch his wound closed. He had already lost a great deal of blood, enough to weaken him. When even the slightest diminution of his fighting skills could cause his death. Now, for the first time since he'd taken command, he felt defeat, as though he had let down the men who trusted in his leadership.

As they made their way toward the landward entrance to Hedeby, they gathered together those Vikings who had survived the assault. Of thirty-five men, just fifteen remained. Only the lack of discipline among Ingmar's warriors made escape possible, since many of the men were already searching out women to molest, goods to steal, and wine or ale to gulp.

Sven stayed by Tabor's side until they reached the gate. Then, looking back one last time, Sven saw the Egyptian slave. Rage boiled in his veins. "Continue on. I'll be with you shortly." Sven nodded in Tanaka's direction. "The wench tricked us, but she'll not live to boast of it."

Tanaka stood about fifty feet away, timorous and dwarfed by Viking clothes that were far too large. Tabor's company had been decimated and the remaining men were in full retreat, yet under continued attack. The possibility of being overrun in the Danish countryside was still great—more likely than not. His own life's blood was squeezing between his fingers and running down his side.

Why wasn't she overjoyed with all that she had accomplished?

"Bring her," Tabor said. "If she's guilty, we can exact justice later. If not . . ."

Sven cursed savagely. "She's the cause of this! Don't let your lust make you a fool!"

"Get her," Tabor said, his eyes locked with Sven's. Very seldom did he actually give a direct command to his friend.

Sven rushed to Tanaka, taking her by the wrist to drag her along with him, though she seemed to be willing to come of her own volition. They fought their way through the gates of Hedeby into the thick forest that surrounded the village. With each step he took, Tabor felt himself growing weaker. Though he tried to keep pressure on the arrow wounds on his arm, the ongoing battle forced him to react and the lacerations kept re-opening.

"To the boat," Tabor said to Sven during a lull in the fighting. "We must make it out to sea if we are to live."

Tabor's ship was the fastest in the Scandinavian waters, his crew the ablest sailors. Even with the shrunken ranks of fifteen men, he was certain that he could find safety and recover his strength once he was upon the waters, where he felt most at home.

The battle had begun shortly after sunrise. Eight hours later, Tabor, his bedraggled crew, and Tanaka reached the inlet where he had anchored his boat. The crew he'd left behind was dead, and the ship was still burning, resting low in the water, about to sink. Tabor cursed as he watched the yellow, orange, and blue flames eating away at what was left of his vessel.

"You'll have other boats," Tanaka said softly, sympathetically, standing just behind Tabor.

Throughout the pain and turmoil he'd endured since she'd been given to him, she'd not seen him look defeated . . . until now. She did not know that to a Viking, his boat is more than a means of transportation and a place to live, it is also a personal shrine that has mystic and religious importance. The expression of defeat lasted no more than a moment before Tabor closed his eyes and heart to the painful sight. When he reopened his eyes, there was an icy hardness in their blue depths that lacked any human warmth.

"If she says another word, tie her up and gag her."

"Aye, Tabor. As you command," Sven responded.

Tanaka shivered because she knew that Tabor meant the threat and Sven would carry it through without a moment's hesitation. When the weary band of warriors continued on their trek across the Danish countryside, Tanaka got in step with Tabor, casting occasional sideways glances at him, wondering constantly if he hated her as much as he seemed to, if he blamed her for Ingmar the Savage's treachery, and what her fate would be if she could not convince the tall Viking of her innocence.

Chapter Seven

With nightfall, the constant threat of exposure and renewed battle lessened. Although Ingmar's men could no longer spy Tabor from a great distance, it was equally true that travel had slowed to a crawl so they wouldn't inadvertently stumble into a search party. Thick, autumnal clouds blotted out the moon; and, though it did not rain, the threat was constantly there. No one spoke a word as they trudged through the night, staying near the shore line in hopes of finding a boat to use for their escape.

It was shortly after midnight when Carl, a short but powerfully built youth who'd been sent ahead to scout, rushed back to the main body of men. "There's a group of maybe twenty just over the next rise," he whispered to Tabor and Sven as they huddled together in the dark. "I recognize them. They're Hugh's men."

Sven and Tabor exchanged glances. In the hours since the attack at Hedeby, they had deduced that Hugh had led the attack force which had slaughtered Tabor's men left in Medworth.

"Have they a craft?" Tabor asked, and though he

had lost a great deal of blood from his wound, the will to win rang strong and clear in his voice.

"Nay. They were afoot, bragging of their bravery and of the men they'd killed."

Tabor thought about the good men who had fallen in battle, fighting valiantly despite the incredible odds. He touched his shoulder, which throbbed, then the biceps, which still jolted him with stabbing pain. At least his arm had finally stopped bleeding.

"Let's give them an hour or two to settle under their blankets and get comfortable," Tabor said with venom and resolve, "then we'll see how uncomfortable we can make their lives."

Tanaka approached Tabor later as he rested, his back against the trunk of a tree. She had not uttered a word since Tabor's threat to have her bound and gagged many hours earlier. She waited until Tabor noticed her and motioned for her to move closer.

"You are pale . . . so pale," she whispered, kneeling at Tabor's side. The bandage of white cotton Sven had wrapped tightly around his biceps was now solid red, caked with dried blood.

"I only appear so to you," Tabor replied with little conviction. He attempted a smile, but did not succeed. "You think that everyone should have skin like yours — the color of gold in the moonlight."

His gaze briefly met Tanaka's; and, though no words were exchanged, she thought there was some lessening of the distrust between them, though she did not dare mention this for fear of piquing his Viking anger once again.

"May I look at the wound?" she asked. "I can put a fresh bandage on for you."

Sven, who had stepped closer once Tanaka began speaking with Tabor, said in a low, ominous voice, "I'll be the one to change his bandage." It was all he said, but the threat of violence was unmistakable.

Tabor said, "Let her put on the bandage." Then, to diminish the sting, he added, "That is woman's work. They are good at it. We, Sven, are Vikings."

Sven smiled, nodded in agreement, and stepped away.

The insult did not offend Tanaka. She had seen past the words to their cause.

"Yes, you are a Viking. . . . and Vikings are only good at killing." She softened the effect of her words with a gentle touch and began unknotting the bandage.

Tabor was shocked that she would have the temerity to taunt him. She was the only woman who'd ever shown the courage to tease him, and that, among so many others things, made her completely different from all the other women he'd known. Though he was in no mood for a verbal duel with the sharp-tongued woman, the corners of his mouth curled up in appreciation and, for the first time in hours, his eyes strayed down from her face to the breasts which quivered beneath her woolen dress as she unwrapped the saturated cloth from his arm.

"We're good at more than just killing," he said, the husky timbre of his voice intentionally conjuring up the erotic memories she had tried to forget. "It's just that killing is what frightens the men in the lands we sail to. Did you know that Normans end their prayers with 'Oh, Lord, protect us from the Northmen'?"

Tanaka had removed the bandage from his arm.

83

Tabor grimaced, not because he was in pain, but because he had seen men with similar wounds get sickness in their blood and die. Bad wounds bred poison; it was a hideous way to die.

She felt her insides constrict at the sight of the wound. As a priestess, she had been protected from the unsightly, but on two occasions she had been summoned to tend injured high-ranking men under Pharaoh Abbakka's command. Though she had done everything she could to save the men, one had died within hours and the other lasted less than two days. But the memories had lasted much longer for Tanaka, and the frustration and sense of loss and failure had never left her.

Turning to Sven, she said, "Bring strong drink to me." The icy glare she received from the Viking warned Tanaka that she was no longer in Egypt and could not issue commands.

Tabor added, "Do as she says, Sven . . . for now."

"He doesn't like me," Tanaka said, when Sven stormed off.

"He doesn't trust you. That isn't the same as not liking you," Tabor replied. "He used to like you . . . before the attack."

Tanaka refused to take her eyes away from Tabor's wounded arm. She was afraid to look into his eyes, afraid of what she would see if she looked there. The attack. The damned attack. Sven blamed her. Tabor, too. The men, she knew, blamed her. As if she'd wanted to be kidnapped by Ingmar the Savage. As if she'd planned to be given, like a brood mare, to Tabor.

With some difficulty, Tanaka forced such thoughts

away. They were too infuriating, and they did her no good. It wasn't fair that she should be blamed, she wanted to shout. But nothing had been fair since she'd been snatched from the security of Ofar.

Sven returned with a skin full of potent liquor and a cloth that had been torn into strips.

"Thank you," she said.

Sven got down on one knee and whispered into Tanaka's ear, "If he dies, so do you."

Although he walked away, Tanaka felt as though he had already stabbed the dagger into her heart. She tried to pretend that he had said nothing, certain that if she mentioned the threat to Tabor, he would not believe her. She picked up the skin of liquid and removed the stopper to sniff it. It smelled vile — and very strong.

"What are you going to do with that?" Tabor asked, aware that the priestess tending to his wound would never drink the heady brew.

"It is said that potent drink can prevent the sickness from spreading," Tanaka explained, hoping that what she had heard was more than just a story.

Tabor reached for the skin, but Tanaka held it out of arm's reach. "No," she said sternly. "It is not to be drunk."

"What *else* would you do with it, woman?"

Tanaka knew that strong drink upon an open wound was painful. She knew, too, that Tabor did not trust her and would not be willing to allow her to cause him pain. So, without warning, she said, "You do this!" and poured a long stream of the liquid onto Tabor's wound.

He flinched but made no sound. His eyes blazed

85

brightly, the question implicit, demanding response.

"It is said that strong drink can prevent the sickness," Tanaka said, relieved that he had not struck her. "I do it only for your own good."

Beads of perspiration had formed on Tabor's forehead; and, though it was clear that he was still in considerable pain, he tried to jest. "It's a good thing you're not angry," he said, "or you might go out of your way to hurt me."

Tanaka raised the skin over Tabor's arm again, but this time there was a question in her expression. She waited for Tabor's nod before she squirted the amber liquid onto his arm again, much more liberally this time to make sure she saturated the wounds on both sides of his biceps. Then Tanaka took a rolled strip of cloth and quickly bound the arm again.

"You're so strong," she said, tying the bandage into place. "You're upper arm is as big as my thigh."

As Tanaka began wrapping a second layer of cloth around his arm, Tabor placed his hand on her thigh. Tanaka's hands hesitated for just a second before she continued her work, outwardly steady as though she could not feel the heat of his hand and gaze upon her.

"Your thigh really is no larger than my arm," he agreed, his voice gravelly, mixed with fatigue and desire.

As she ministered to him, he wondered if she were capable of deception, of being a "distraction" so that Hugh's attack would have maximum telling effect. He played his hand along her leg from knee to thigh, touching her through the dress and underdress. He glanced in Sven's direction, not wanting his advances to be observed. Though it hurt to move, he ran his palm down her leg to her ankle. When he reached upward again, he slid his hand beneath the wool dress until he felt the satiny texture of her flesh. He pushed the wool up until his hand rested above her knee, his fingertips tracing tiny circles on her inner thigh.

Tanaka's heart was racing. She, too, cast a cautious glance in Sven's direction. *Tabor wouldn't force himself upon me here, now, with everyone watching. . . . would he?*

She wanted to clamp her knees together to trap his hand between her thighs so that it could not stray higher; but, having already denied him the pleasures he sought, she was hesitant to refuse him anything now.

"Y-You should save your strength," Tanaka stammered, reaching for the courage to refuse. "Soon you will be fighting again, and you will need all your strength. Besides, you have already lost so much blood . . ."

Tabor chuckled, amusement fading into a groan of pain. With his uninjured right hand he caressed Tanaka's cheek, running his thumb lightly across her mouth.

"Yes, I must fight again, but I have enough strength to take you to Valhalla and carry you back." He grimaced, not liking his words. He'd always believed that men who boasted of their sexual prowess did so out of some deep-down belief that they were sexually inadequate. "But I am indeed tired. Tired of fighting, to be sure. Aye. . . . and we have even less privacy than I have strength." He looked away, saying nothing for several seconds. His hand remained on

Tanaka's thigh, but he no longer caressed her. "Another fight. . . . I've been in so many wars . . ."

Tanaka's heart went out to Tabor. This side of him — the battle-weary warrior — was something she hadn't seen before, had not even suspected existed.

She said quietly, "Maybe when you find a boat, we can sail away. Then you'll be able to stop fighting. We'll go where there are no wars, no battles to be fought."

"And where, this side of Valhalla, might that place be?"

Tanaka remembered that Valhalla was the Viking word for heaven. She smiled, almost forgetting about his hand on her thigh, and began to tell Tabor of a place where the fish were plentiful, the marshes thick with waterfowl, and the sun ever-warm. Tabor, though, did not hear her soothing words because he had drifted into a healing, exhausted sleep.

Since Tabor was sleeping, Sven postponed the attack upon Hugh's hunting party. Tanaka saw that the men maintained silence not from fear but because they respected Tabor and wanted him to get as much strength-giving sleep as possible. When, two hours later, Tabor awoke, he cursed Sven out resoundingly for allowing him to sleep. But there was no anger behind his words. If anything, Tabor was angry with himself for his fatigue.

As the men prepared for battle, Tanaka stayed close to Tabor. She saw through the courageous facade that he presented to his men. She knew that he was still in enormous pain and that the huge loss of blood, which very likely would have killed a lesser man, had dangerously sapped him of his strength.

How much fight was left in him? she wondered. They had joked of the size of his mighty arms, but how much energy could be left when so much of his blood had drained away.

Tanaka resolved to remain close to Tabor. Perhaps she could prove her value to him in some way other than as a sexual object, and if she did that, then he just might not believe that she was responsible for Ingmar's ambush.

Tabor hooked the thumb of his left hand into his wide leather belt. He gestured extravagantly with his right hand; and, though Tanaka had at first thought this was a sign of good health, she now realized it was an act to draw attention away from his wounded left arm. With his thumb hooked in his belt, he appeared confident and at ease but never had to move his arm. His face, too, was gray; and, no matter how rakish the grin, he could not hide that he was a strong man fighting bravely against serious injury. Nothing could help Tabor now except time, nourishing food, and—most importantly—rest.

"Remember, they slaughtered your brothers-in-arms," Tabor instructed his men as they prepared to begin their trek to the enemy camp. "Expect no mercy from them. Show no mercy to them."

"Aye, Tabor. . . . as you command," the men replied in unison.

The tallest of the Vikings looked from his men to Tanaka; and, though he said nothing aloud, his expression warned her that she was to remain absolutely silent. If their approach was discovered because of sounds she'd made, she would suffer the consequences.

In the time that she had been forced to spend with Ingmar, Tanaka had witnessed several battles. But nothing she had experienced could prepare her for what it was really like to be in the middle of a fight, close enough to the soldiers, to the killing, to the carnage, so that she could smell the fear and sweat and blood.

Tabor and his men fought for revenge as well as victory, and they found in Hugh's men able fighters. The initial seconds of the assault caught Hugh's forces by surprise, even though two men had been posted as sentries. Several in their ranks died swiftly, some without realizing that their attackers were the men they hunted. This attrition made it numerically an even fight between Hugh's men and Tabor and his Vikings; and the surprise assault soon progressed into a contest of swordplay, strength, and stamina.

"Tabor, behind you!" Tanaka shouted when one of Hugh's warriors attacked him from the rear.

Tabor swung his mighty sword in a blind arc, and its deadly edge struck the soldier in the head. Despite his formidable helmet, the man crumpled to the ground and did not move.

Tabor looked at Tanaka. Could she really be responsible for saving his life? This was the second time she had intervened, but the Egyptian priestess was ashen, shrinking from the fray.

"Have you been hurt?" Tabor asked, holding his bloody sword in his good right hand. His left hand was still tucked inside his belt to keep the nearly useless arm out of the way.

Tanaka nodded, looking into Tabor's determined face. Suddenly, he raised the blade over his head and cut the air in a decisive motion as he lunged at her!

His elbow struck her shoulder, knocking her onto a corpse. Stumbling forward, she understood that she would have been stabbed in the back if Tabor had not reacted so quickly.

"There!" he said, grinning. "Now I've repaid the debt!"

The battle blurred, and Tanaka struggled to stay near Tabor, yet out of his way. And though he fought valiantly, it was clear that having the use of only one arm hampered him greatly. And once, locked in combat with one of Hugh's men, Tabor was forced to use his left arm in battle, and Tanaka could see the bandages she'd placed upon his wounds turning from white to pink to bright red.

When the fight ended, all of Hugh's men were vanquished. The dead were carted away, and Tanaka was saved the horror of watching this grisly task because she was once again tending to Tabor's wounded arm.

"You warned me during the fight," Tabor said, holding a drinking horn of beer in his good right hand while Tanaka carefully unwrapped the blood-soaked bandages surrounding his left upper arm. "Very bold of you. You have the spirit to be a Viking woman after all."

Tanaka said nothing at first, concentrating only on the wounded arm. When she had removed all the bandages, she was shocked to see that the wounds both in the front and in the back of his arm had completely reopened. Now more than ever, with so much of his blood staining the field of battle, she was astonished that Tabor was still alive.

"And I suppose you'll be wanting to waste good drink to pour on my arm?"

"Yes, I will. I know it burns, but it's important to keep the creeping sickness away."

"I am a Viking. From the time a Viking child stops feeding from his mother's breast, he's raised to ignore physical pain. It is in our blood."

Tanaka bit her tongue to prevent the words from escaping her mouth. Though there was much about this strange Viking culture that she found laudable, the warrior mentality, the willful struggle to strip themselves of their humaneness, was mystifying to her. She could hardly help her disdain.

She looked at Sven, who was issuing orders for the preparation of food, the location of sentries, the collection and cleaning of weapons taken from the conquered foes. She *knew* that Sven was also — covertly — watching her, and Tanaka came to understand with certainty that her life was inextricably tied to Tabor's.

"Sometimes when he looks at me, I feel he hates me, that he would like to kill me," she said avoiding Tabor's eyes.

"Sven enjoys killing no one," Tabor corrected. He sounded tired, now that the battle was over, the adrenaline no longer charging his system. "He does not trust you to care for me. You are dark and mysterious, and with your arrival, bad things have happened to us."

"And that's my fault?" Tanaka asked with more forcefulness than she intended. Her questioning gaze went up to Tabor's, and he raised his eyebrows to indicate that he did not know. She took the drinking horn from him. "Are you ready?"

"A Viking is always ready for anything."

"Fine," Tanaka snapped caustically. "Then you won't mind this at all."

She poured the entire contents of the drinking horn onto Tabor's arm. The veins and tendons stuck out in his neck, and every muscle in his body tightened; but he made no sound, and, other than flexing his muscles, he did not move as the strong drink was poured into his open wounds.

"I'm astonished you didn't scream," she said, sympathy now in her tone. Tabor's body had remained flexed until the pain lessened. "If that had happened to me, I would have gone into the black sleep."

Beads of perspiration dotted Tabor's forehead and temples. The pain was excruciating, and he did not dare speak for fear that his voice would crack. He stared straight at Tanaka until he was sure of himself. Only then did he say, "A Viking warrior does not scream in pain, nor does he go into the black sleep. . . . whatever that is."

"The black sleep," Tanaka explained, "comes sometimes with intense pain. It's brief—perhaps a minute or two—but it is said that the soul leaves the body when this happens."

The loss of blood had turned Tabor's skin gray, disgusting him and worrying Tanaka. Though he could, when not injured, imbibe an extraordinary quantity of strong drink, the few sips he'd had had sapped his energy. Pride prevented him from admitting this to Tanaka.

"I must sleep now," Tabor said suddenly, feeling the fatigue slithering through him, settling into his bones. Tanaka stretched a thick blanket over him, but he was so tall that when she tucked it under his chin, his feet were left uncovered. "Sleep. . . . so that I can fight tomorrow."

Tanaka looked from Tabor to Sven. She understood that Sven loved his leader and only wanted to do what was right, but to blame her for Tabor's injury was wrong. So unfair! And yet to argue this point with Sven would do her absolutely no good at all. When she looked at Tabor again, his eyes were closed, though she could tell that he was not yet asleep.

"Can I get anything to make you more comfortable? Is your bandage too tight?"

Tabor shook his head. "No. . . . you have done well . . . all that you can."

"You should eat. The food will make you strong."

"Later . . . later. . . . now I must sleep." He moved slightly and placed his right hand beneath his head to cushion it.

"Let me help you," Tanaka said.

She felt something akin to tenderness take bloom inside her heart for this strong man laid low by the loss of blood. Easing Tabor's shoulders up, she cradled his head in her lap.

"Is that better?" she asked.

"Much . . . much . . . bet—" he began, then drifted into sleep.

Tanaka felt the salty sting of tears for the fallen warrior, and she wiped them away quickly, angrily. What was wrong with her? It meant nothing to her

94

that he was weak with injury and might very well die. Nothing to her at all!

But it did, and she knew it. She had spent very little time with Tabor, yet she knew much about him as a person. In all the time that she had been Ingmar's captive, she had learned nothing of him except his language and the extraordinary lengths to which his cruelty could go.

Tanaka stroked Tabor's hair, smoothing it away from his gaunt cheek. Even now, asleep and injured, he was the most ruggedly handsome man she'd ever seen and easily the most muscular. There was a virility about him that was undisguised, even weakened by pain as he was now.

She placed her palm on his chest, feeling the hard pectoral muscles beneath his shirt and vest, feeling his heart pumping.

"I'll make you well again," Tanaka whispered, her vision blurred with unshed tears.

At that moment, Sven approached. Tanaka, startled by his presence, recoiled at the sight of him, unable to forget the cold-blooded threat he'd issued. But instead of suspicion on his face, there was understanding. In his hands he held a brass plate filled with the hearty stew that the Vikings favored, and a warm blanket hung over his arm.

Hunkering on his knees beside Tanaka, Sven handed her the steaming plate. The aroma of cooked beef, potatoes, and carrots made her mouth water. He slipped an arm around her shoulders to help her lean forward away from the tree trunk, then carefully wrapped her in the blanket.

He was gone a moment later, and Tanaka could

only wonder how difficult it must have been for a Viking warrior like Sven to serve her food and arrange a blanket around her shoulders. She had no illusions as to why he'd been so kind—because she was holding Tabor's head in her lap and Sven did not want his wounded leader to be disturbed—but nevertheless, the courtesy surprised her with new insight about those strange men called Vikings.

Chapter Eight

When Tabor awoke at dawn, his head on Tanaka's lap, he instinctively reached for his sword. He squeezed the familiar handle tightly and surveyed his surroundings with no further movement, not wanting yet to draw attention to himself.

The encampment was at peace. Tanaka, sleeping, leaned against a tree. He noted the blanket but was struck again by her extraordinary beauty. When he'd first seen her, he'd thought her features were too exaggerated: high cheekbones and wide-spaced, almond-shaped eyes that reminded him of a cat at night; a slender chin and full-lipped mouth; round, heavy breasts that rested high on her rib cage; and jet black hair falling in loose springy ringlets. It astonished Tabor now that he had ever, for even a moment, found her beauty displeasing.

He might have kissed her awake, but pain ripped through him the moment he moved his shoulder. Tanaka's eyelashes fluttered upon her cheeks, and she looked down at Tabor's head, still cradled in her lap.

"Are you all right? What woke you?" she asked in

a whisper, respectful of the other men who were still sleeping. She pushed a long strand of blond hair from Tabor's face, and her fingertips lingered longer than necessary.

"I moved is all. I forgot about my arm." He found it easy to be honest with Tanaka, yet another way she differed from other women. "Did you sleep well?"

"Don't worry about me. I'm not the one who had an arrow shot through my arm."

Tanaka was pleased that he did not don a brave facade, and she was suddenly aware that this was as domestic and as tranquil as she'd ever been with a man. She raised Tabor's blanket and saw that he had not bled through his bandage.

"You must be hungry. You ate nothing last night."

"I'm ravenous!"

"I'll get you something."

"In a moment," Tabor replied.

He let his senses absorb Tanaka. He could smell her female scent. The thighs beneath his head warmed him, and looking up above her breasts he connected with clear brown eyes. To see Tanaka's face upon waking every morning, he mused, would not be a bad fate. He'd never before had such feelings; and, though he tried to dismiss them as side-effects of his injury, he knew they were more than that.

Tabor clenched his left hand into a fist to test the injured biceps. He felt the pain and eased off. The arrow wound frightened him, though he did not want to admit it. Last night, he had not merely slept, he had fallen into the black sleep. And today, even though he smiled, a terrible weakness tore into his soul.

Eyes closed, he recalled the fighting of the night before, the killing. It had been necessary, but it tired him. The victory had given him none of the pleasure of accomplishment, and he blamed his wound and weakness for that lack. And it bothered him that he had lost the cherished battle-axe of his father's fathers.

At the sound of approaching footsteps, Tabor opened his eyes. He felt as if there were weights on his eyelids, but Tabor would never show his frailty. He was the leader of a fearless band of Viking warriors; his strength was legendary.

Sven approached, carrying two plates heaped with steaming portions of stew.

"Thank you," Tanaka said as she accepted the plate. "But I'll never be able to eat all this."

"I know. Tabor will need more than a single plate if he is to get well again," Sven said, with neither respect nor antagonism in his voice.

Tabor pushed himself to a sitting position, regretting that he could no longer rest his head on Tanaka's slender thighs. He accepted the plate from Sven, wordlessly fighting the pain that exploded with movement, once again in his arm. Tabor rested the plate in his lap, leaning back against the tree beside Tanaka, and took the wooden spoon.

They ate in silence; and, true to Sven's predictions, Tabor ate heartily. And by the time he had finished, some of the color had returned to Tabor's face.

Their dawn meal concluded, his men gathered around Tabor, who stood propped casually against the tree. Some of the men regarded Tanaka with suspicion, but she remained at their leader's side. Since Tabor did not refer to her presence, no one else did, either.

"We've got to find a fully stocked boat," Tabor said. "As long as we stay on land, our strength will be sapped, our movements slow, our progress minimal." There was a low murmur of agreement from the men. Seafaring Vikings, they preferred a boat, especially in difficult times. "Ingmar. . . . Ingmar has outwitted me," Tabor said, and it was clear that the admission was difficult. When the men began to protest, he motioned them to silence. "Ignoring the truth helps no one now. What Ingmar did is behind us. We must concentrate on the future."

"Lead us, Tabor, and we will follow," shouted Carl, Tabor's third in command. "Let us defy the Fates. Ingmar has many warriors, but he does not have the support of the people. They despise him!"

This news did not surprise Tabor, but though his men were in better spirits, Tabor knew they must hide until everyone had recovered from the wounds of battle. Hide. . . . or be found and killed. Ingmar was an experienced tactician who understood that unless Tabor were killed, he would return and seek revenge.

"I don't doubt that they despise him," Tabor said. "And I also do not doubt that he will kill everyone who wags a tongue against him." As he spoke, Tabor looked at each of his men directly. He was not talking to them as a group, but as individuals, reinforcing their belief that each life was valued by their leader. "We have our bellies filled with food. Soon, Ingmar's men will comb the countryside looking for us. They will find this camp and know that we were here. We must keep moving. . . . we must find a boat large enough to take us far away. . . . far enough away so that we can recover our strength and numbers. . . . and then, we will return to these waters and this land. . . . and we will have our revenge!"

"Although we are forced to flee from Ingmar's men now," Tabor continued, "the time will come when we can challenge the Norwegian and his bloodthirsty Vikings head-on." But as he spoke, the tenuous reservoir of Tabor's strength slipped away, and Tanak saw the strain upon him.

They left camp, with Sven taking the first shift as advance scout, walking ahead of the main body of men by a mile or more. Twice they stopped at homes to ask questions and glean what they could of Ingmar's movements and attack plans. As they walked, Tabor and Tanaka said little to each other, though they never were far apart. And when the weary Vikings paused near a cool running stream to drink and rest, Tanaka sat so close to Tabor that her knee touched his.

They were still beside the stream when Tabor caught the smell of smoke. He searched the sky but found no signs of fire. Then, from the direction they'd just come, he saw the gray smoke staining the clear midday air. Tabor dispatched a man to investigate, and it wasn't long before the man returned.

"It was Ingmar's men," the scout reported. "They killed everyone—even the children." He didn't have to say it was the family that they'd spoken to earlier for Tabor and the others to know who the victims were. "They set the house and barn on fire. The cattle and sheep have been slaughtered."

A deep, low sigh escaped Tabor as he listened to the tale of pointless murder. What kind of warrior murdered children? It was horrifying for Tabor to ponder. Even worse was the knowledge that the family had quite likely been slaughtered because Tabor had stopped at their home. That offense alone, for which neither the man nor woman—and certainly not the children—were responsible, had been reason enough to justify Ingmar's slaughter.

"Are they following us?" Tabor asked.

"Nay. They are roasting a slaughtered cow. They are in no hurry."

Tabor shook his head sadly. "Then they killed just for the thrill of killing. The family told them nothing." Tabor looked from one man to the next, seeking answers that none of them possessed. "What kind of monsters are these who chase us?" He ran his hand through his hair, pushing damp strands off his forehead. "We can no longer stop at any houses. Everyone we come in contact with we put in danger," he declared, his heart heavy with self-inflicted guilt. He did not look at Tanaka, afraid she blamed him for the innocent deaths. The memory of the children, their faces bright and animated, excited because visitors were unusual in their sleepy, green valley, tore at Tabor. "We must press on until we find a ship. Then we must sail far away, refortify ourselves, and then return to expunge Ingmar and his men from this earth. To a man, they must all be held accountable!"

Ingmar backhanded the messenger so hard that the sound of knuckles striking cheek was sharp and ominous in the tense evening air. When the messenger did not fall, Ingmar struck him again, this time with a closed fist to the stomach, and the young man crumpled to his knees.

"That was *not* what I wanted to hear!" Ingmar shouted, bending low so that his face was close to the breathless youth's.

Finished, he turned to the other men. They were gathered where, earlier in the day, a wine merchant who had shown courage and foolishness by complaining to Ingmar that the warriors were taking wine they had not paid for. The merchant's corpse now lay in the swine trough and crowded into the house was a collection of women of purchasable virtue and Ingmar's most trusted men.

"Where is Tabor?" Ingmar asked. He picked up the battle-axe that had been Tabor's, turning the weapon over in his hands. The axe was Ingmar's greatest possession. He knew its value to Tabor, and stealing it was a magnificent coup. "Why hasn't Tabor been found? Why isn't Tabor dead?" Ingmar raged. His red-rimmed eyes bore into each of his men in turn. "I have more than a hundred men in my command, and he has less than twenty! Why hasn't he been found and killed?"

No one said a word. To speak now would almost surely mean death. Ingmar wanted to be told what he wanted to hear—not the facts.

Though Ingmar would never admit it to his men, he feared Tabor's retaliation. But he did not know— because none of his men would tell him—was that although when the fighting began, Ingmar had many more than a hundred men, now there were fewer than seventy.

Ingmar held out his drinking horn, and it was immediately refilled with beer. As he drank, he brooded. As long as Tabor lived, the Viking was a threat. Ingmar promised himself he would not rest until his enemy's corpse, like that of the insolent wine merchant, had been tossed into the swine trough for everyone to see. No man, no matter how powerful, no matter how admired, could challenge Ingmar the Savage.

"Within the hour, the sun will set once again," Ingmar reasoned. "We know that under cover of night, Tabor has already attacked and killed one hunting pack sent to find him. With darkness, he'll probably attack again, so that is when we've got to stop him."

"But," countered one of the younger warriors, "knowing what Tabor is going to do and knowing how to stop him aren't the same thing."

Ingmar's lips twitched before he replied, "How right you are." Then, to the other men, he said, "Remove this insufferable fool, cut his throat, and throw him to the swine."

Without hesitation, the warriors carried the thrashing young man outside, where his screams were abruptly silenced. His cogent comments would no longer interrupt Ingmar's peace of mind.

Tanaka watched as Tabor tilted his head back and sniffed the night air. It was the act of a predatory, hunting animal, not that of a man.

"It will be a harsh winter," Tabor said under his breath, kneeling beside Tanaka. Sven, at his other side, knelt too. "The autumn winds are severe—and early."

"Strong winds from the north . . ." Sven said, letting the words die away.

Disconcerted, Tanaka felt that she alone did not understand the significance of strong northern winds. It made her feel ignorant, despite the fact that in her homeland she was considered a woman of considerable intellect.

"The winds will carry us far," Tabor said. He tilted his head back, looking straight up into the night sky at the star. Would he be able to guide the boat through the rocky, treacherous fjords? "But only if I'm as capable a seafarer as I sometimes think I am."

"You'll get us through the fjords into the open waters. I know you will," Sven said with confidence.

"At night? It's a difficult task in the day; it is

105

tougher still when the mist and the fog hamper a man's vision; it's probably impossible at night."

"Aye, it probably is. But if ever there was a man who could sail us through the narrow fjords, it is you, Tabor, Son of Thor."

Tabor rolled his eyes expressively. He did not care for the title, and he did not like it when his own men used it—especially not when Sven used it. Any association to a deity was insufferable arrogance as far as Tabor was concerned; claiming to be the son of the god of thunder surely had to be hubris to the nth degree. Besides, whenever Sven used it, there was an undercurrent of sarcasm that simply could not be mistaken.

A smile pulled at Tanaka's mouth, and she turned her face away so that Tabor would not see it. Tabor, Son of Thor . . . a title given to him by a woman who considered his lovemaking superhumanly satisfying. When she'd first heard the story, Tanaka had grimaced. *A self-promulgating lie,* she'd thought. Then she found out that the story was true. The emotion she felt was akin to jealousy, and she pushed *that* away and denied its existence.

What difference does it make what other women think of Tabor's lovemaking? Tanaka asked herself. Whatever had happened between Tabor and her had been foisted upon her, physical acts that were against her will and for which she could not be held accountable. But though she tried hard to convince herself, she didn't believe it.

A hundred yards away, torches lit the night as men loaded the boat with stolen provisions. It

106

wasn't a large boat—it had a maximum capacity of sixty men—but Tabor had concluded that its size might be to their advantage since it would be easier for a small crew to sail.

"We wait," Tabor whispered, reading Sven's mind as they knelt in the shadows, watching Ingmar's men piling stolen stocks of food and goods onto the boat. "We'll let them finish, then we hit them hard."

"I'll tell the others," Sven said, disappearing into the shadows.

Tanaka took Sven's place at Tabor's side. Though he did not take his eyes from the boat moored to a newly-built dock, she knew that he was aware of her presence. She studied his profile at her leisure, remembering what he had looked like before Ingmar's arrow had cut through his arm, thinking how nice it would be if she could again see that healthy gleam in his sea blue eyes. She would like to see a vital glow to his flesh and boundless strength in his movements.

"Can you fight?" Tanaka asked softly, keeping her voice low enough so that only Tabor could hear.

"I am a Viking warrior." To him the statement answered every question. Tanaka felt it answered nothing at all.

"And I am an Egyptian priestess, but that is not in question here." Tabor gave her a quizzical look, and Tanaka merely smiled back, wondering why she had told him when she hadn't admitted that in all the time that she had spent with Ingmar. "You will soon be in another battle. Are you strong enough to fight?"

Tabor fixed his icy blue gaze upon her. "You are a most persistent woman." It was not a compliment.

"Yes, I am." Her eyebrows arched above challenging eyes. "I need to know if you can fight. Sven has promised that I will live only as long as you do."

Tabor's expression told her that he had not known of the threat and that he did not approve.

"You can fool the others that your arm is not bad by holding onto your belt and not using your hand," she continued. "But I've seen your wounds. I know how much blood you have lost."

He had spent many years telling glib lies to women who wanted to know more about him than he was inclined to reveal, so he had a battery of smooth retorts to deflect a woman's questions. But, for reasons he did not comprehend, he needed to tell Tanaka the truth.

"You are really a priestess?" he asked. She nodded, her eyes demanding an answer to her original question. "I can fight, but I do not know for how long," he murmured.

"Every time you fight, you reopen your wounds. The sickness has not come to your arm yet, but sooner or later it will. And each time you lose blood, you are weaker than the time before. Sleep allows you to recover, but only partially." She placed her palm against Tabor's cheek, looking deep into his eyes. "Unless you stop fighting, unless you bring peace into your life, I fear you will not live much longer."

"No one but you would dare say such a thing to me."

108

Tanaka smiled indulgently. With more confidence than she had felt in months, she replied, "But I am not just anyone." She passed her thumb lightly across his mouth, remembering the wild thrills she had known from those lips. "Promise me you will stop fighting."

"Soon. . . . I promise," Tabor said, conscious that he had never before promised a woman anything other than pleasure.

"It must be soon. . . . or it will be too late," Tanaka replied, moving away. Soon it would be time for the attack.

Chapter Nine

Tanaka added one more layer of cloth to Tabor's arm, binding the wound with an especially tight bandage. She was not unmindful of the groan of pain he emitted when she tied the bandage off; and when she looked into his eyes, she realized he'd made the sound for her amusement.

"Don't look so frightened," Tabor whispered. "I've been in a hundred battles."

With an edge to her voice, Tanaka replied, "And how long do you think you can challenge the Fates by staying alive?"

Keeping to the shadows, Tabor and Sven led the Vikings toward the freshly loaded boat. Toward the rear, Tanaka was surprised that she wasn't as nervous as she had been just prior to the previous battles.

Don't tell me I'm becoming hardened to violence and killing, Tanaka thought, afraid that the savage days and cruel nights had stripped away the humanity and goodness she'd believed innate.

The Norwegian Vikings, fresh from their victory

over Tabor's men at Medworth, never expected an attack from a force they considered annihilated. The sentries on land were dispatched quickly and silently. From there it was a mad rush down the narrow, swaying dock, Tabor and Sven shoulder-to-shoulder in the lead, screaming to further disorient the Norwegians.

Though the initial stages of the battle had gone precisely as Tabor had planned, Ingmar's men were seasoned warriors and they would not fall without a fight. Swords were crossed, battle-axes met with shields—sometimes with flesh and bone. Tanaka watched a man only a few feet in front of her get struck down by a Norwegian's deadly, iron-headed axe. As the corpse fell, the dagger the Dane carried rattled across the dock to rest at her feet. An omen? She picked up the dagger, holding it awkwardly in front of her. The Norwegian—a member of Hugh's band of cutthroats whose face she recognized though she didn't know his name—paused a moment to look at Tanaka. Judging that she could not possibly be a threat to him, he moved on to resume fighting.

To follow the man down the dock meant lunging deeper into the heart of battle, but Tanaka felt compelled to do exactly that. She was oblivious to everything but the axe-wielding Norwegian.

An instinct that she knew she must trust warned her to act immediately or it would be too late. She ran onto the boat, leaping over two figures wrestling in deadly combat. Before she reached the Norwegian, her conscious mind finally grasped what her subconscious had known all along—that the man was going to use his lethal axe against Tabor, striking him down from behind.

"No-o-o!" Tanaka shrieked, rushing forward, leading with the dagger as the Norwegian stepped behind Tabor, who was locked weapon-to-weapon with his adversary.

The Norwegian raised his axe, envisioning the honors and riches that Ingmar would bestow upon him for slaying Tabor.

Unmindful of the threat behind him, Tabor feinted a move to his left, then came in hard from the right, bringing the sharp edge of his sword across his foe's throat. A moment later, Tabor heard Tanaka's high-pitched warning cry, and he wheeled around. He saw the axe, but it did not come down in a deadly arc to render bone from flesh, though Tabor could not possibly have raised his blade in defense. He drew back, prepared to strike the Norwegian warrior in the midsection, but the man fell face down at Tabor's feet, a dagger protruding from his back. Tanaka stood motionless, unable to tear her eyes away from the man she had just killed.

Heedless of his own safety, Tabor sheathed his sword, rushed to Tanaka's side, and lifted her into his arms, ignoring the screaming pain in his injured biceps. He carried Tanaka away from the fighting, concerned only for her safety.

"We're ready to set sail," Sven said brightly, too brightly.

"Then set sail!" Tabor shouted with as much pride as he could muster, wanting to savor this victory over his nemesis. But hardly had the words escaped his mouth when he slumped in the captured boat. He pushed himself erect again and sat upon a barrel of salted meat. His face devoid of color, he struggled to appear hale and hearty, but there wasn't a member of his crew who didn't know that their leader was clinging to life through sheer force of will.

It was madness to be sailing the fjords at night. Even during the day the barely submerged rocks could rip out the hull of a ship. At night, only the ablest of navigators could guide the boat through the waters — and then only with the guidance and blessings of the gods.

The sail was green-and-white-striped, as was the custom for Norwegian sailing vessels. It was not a boat that pleased Tabor, but it had enough provisions for many months to come and he was determined to be happy with what he had. Besides, as a Viking, he was always happiest and felt safest when he was on the water.

They headed toward Kaupang, Norway, running silently in the night. Tabor instructed Sven, who manned the rudder, guiding the sturdy boat through the rocky waters.

It was on the first morning of their escape that they were seen. Though they were a hundred yards from shore, the sail was recognized, and the call went up among Ingmar's men on land. In short order, a boat, fully manned, chased after them, sailing a mile or more behind.

By midday, there were three ships following Tabor's stolen boat; and as the sun was setting, five swift boats joined the chase, each struggling to eke just a little more speed out of the wind in hopes of catching the "renegade Dane."

Through it all, Tanaka kept a close eye on Tabor. She was mindful that his cheeks appeared a bit more gaunt than before, his eyes a touch more sunken. Twice she approached him, suggesting that he eat and get some rest, and on both occasions she was rebuffed.

"I am in command," Tabor told her curtly, his haggard features making him look even more threatening. For the first time, Tanaka looked and saw a man capable of atrocity, a man carrying an enormous burden of responsibility—besieged by enemies and pushed into a corner. "In command is where I will remain until it is time for the Viking funeral."

Irked by Tabor's stubborn refusal to rest, Tanaka wanted to say that the traditional Viking funeral for a man of his stature required that he be burned at sea in his boat, which would make it difficult for the rest of the men aboard ship to continue sailing. But she kept her comments to herself, wrapping the blanket around her shoulders to ward off the early evening chill.

When the sun set, the first of Ingmar's chase boats ran aground on the fjords. At night, over water, the slightest noise can carry great distances, so Tanaka was able to hear the hideous sound of timber snapping like twigs, the high screams of strong men about to die, and the sudden silence as the struggle for life ended.

The smile Sven and Tabor exchanged when they realized a chase boat had been shattered by submerged rocks infuriated Tanaka. She wanted to scream that men had died and that no man should take pleasure in that, but she kept her thoughts to herself. At best, her opinions would fall upon deaf ears; and, at worst, they would give further credibility to the suspicions that she was in league with Ingmar.

During the dead of the night came the most dangerous moment for Tabor and his men. They made the hard southbound turn, at last catching the wind coming from the north to head toward the English channel. Though this was exactly what Tabor wanted, it also put him within visual range of the mainstay of Ingmar's forces and loyalist population.

A second following-ship sank on the treacherous seas and rocks, and a cheer went up from Tabor's men.

"Even in their own waters, you've bested them!" Carl shouted, raising his fist heavenward, proudly, defiantly. "Tabor, Son of Thor, shall never be vanquished!"

Tanaka's heart skipped a beat when Tabor raised his hand briefly to acknowledge the compliment. Then, pale and drawn, his head slumped back on his shoulders, and he entered into the black sleep that she had feared would claim him.

Tabor was carried to the bow of the open boat, a bed of blankets made for him. When a light sprinkling of rain began, Sven ordered the whalebone supports put in place and the tightly woven-wool coverings stretched over them to provide a tent-like protection from the elements and to preserve heat.

Tanaka stayed at Tabor's side, oblivious to the

cold and rain, holding his hand between her palms and feeling for his pulse. If she did not hold him, she thought, if she did not touch him, his mighty heart would at last give out. When she asked Sven if it were possible to erect a barricade to give her privacy while she tended to Tabor, he fixed her with a hard, suspicious gaze. Then, softening, he ordered a blanket placed between the bow and the main body of men, creating for Tabor and Tanaka a small bedroom about fifteen feet long.

At the bow she was able to look out to sea. Perhaps, if Tabor escaped from the black sleep, he would be revived further by seeing the waves.

It was a race now, and everyone knew it. The festive mood of the boat had vanished; and, throughout the day, as the ships followed—sometimes inching closer, sometimes falling back—no one spoke a word. Sven remained at the rudder until fatigue got the best of him, and Carl took over.

To their port side, the coast of France slipped by. The hours passed, and exhaustion mingled with fear for those things which never changed—like the ships that followed relentlessly. The northern wind pushed them southward constantly, but the boats were evenly matched in speed and the chase continued. The tension mounted with the passing hours, the participants in this struggle of life against death paralleling their relationships of the earlier battles.

The shores of England were to the west, France to the east. Sven and Carl talked briefly of seeking refuge in England but abandoned that line of thought. Better to be on the water like a Viking, they decided. Besides, neither Carl nor Sven knew much of the English, and they had raided France too many times to believe they would find friends there. So onward they sailed, always moving south, afraid to pause for a moment, afraid that the wind would stop. If the oars were needed, then Tabor's crew of twelve would not stand a chance against the crews of sixty or seventy that followed them.

It was brilliantly sunny, and Tanaka rolled back the tent over her living quarters to feel the warmth of the sun. She rolled up the sleeves of her dress and, using a hair brush that one of the men had found on board, she pulled the tangles from her long, wavy hair.

"Tanaka, I have food for you," Sven said, his voice muffled slightly, speaking through the blanket that served as a wall.

Tanaka set aside the brush and rolled back down the sleeves of her dress. The Vikings, she had noticed, were far more inclined to keep their bodies covered than the Egyptians were. Once, when she had her dress raised up enough to show her knees, virtually every man aboard the ship had turned his eyes modestly away. Tanaka accepted this as a sign of growing respect, and that Sven had announced his presence rather than simply pushing the blanket aside and stepping into the bow was proof that the men now considered her more than just the slave who had been given to Tabor.

"Enter."

Pulling the curtain aside, Sven stepped onto the bow, a plate laden with food in his hand, concern in his eyes. He hardly glanced at Tanaka before turning his attention to Tabor, who remained on the bed of blankets, body swathed except for his head.

"Has he said anything?" Sven asked, though he knew that the black sleep still claimed his leader.

"No. But I have hope. He is a strong man, and I have been able to get some food and drink into him." Tanaka took the plate of pickled fish and dried meat and began tearing the portions into even smaller pieces. She was always afraid that the food she forced down Tabor's throat would choke him, so she kept the morsels extremely small. This, however, made feeding him a task that took many hours, and she always made sure that he ate before she did.

The land off to the west was unfamiliar to her, and she asked, "Where are we?"

"That is Spain," Sven replied, though his eyes never left Tabor. "I think it is, anyway." There was a pause, and then he said, "Tabor would know. He'll tell us later, I suppose."

Sympathy warmed Tanaka's heart. Sven was a strong man, and yet he seemed lost without Tabor. "Yes, I suppose he will," Tanaka replied, hoping to give Sven confidence.

After Sven left, Tanaka patiently began feeding tiny pieces of fish into Tabor's mouth. He was so thin now. How much more weight could he lose before he could lose no more? What would happen to her if he died? It surprised Tanaka that she was more concerned about what would happen to her heart if Tabor died instead of what Sven or the others might do to her if their leader died.

"Come on, Tabor, return to us," Tanaka whispered, stroking his face with her fingertips. "Every-

118

one is counting on you. We all look to you for strength, for guidance. What would we do without you?"

Tanaka could tell they had travelled far to the south, not only because of the warmth, but because of the countryside. It was much greener, the vegetation more lush and lavish. She ached for the feel of solid ground beneath her feet. She hungered, too, for the taste of something other than the nourishing though utterly bland Scandinavian food that the boat was packed with. When Tanaka thought this, she cursed herself for being so churlish. Not long ago, when she had been Ingmar's slave, she had not been given enough to eat. If she didn't particularly like the taste or variety of the food she was given now, that seemed a petty and minor inconvenience.

The blankets were pulled tight and tied back to allow in the golden rays of the sun. Tanaka yanked the blankets off Tabor and wiped him with a damp cloth. She had stripped him of his shirt and trousers several days before. She ran the cloth over his chest, marveling once again at his breadth, noticing that even though the definition of his pectoral muscles wasn't what it had been, he was still astonishingly, awesomely masculine.

She wiped his chest and stomach, moving downward slowly, averting her eyes, even though she had thoroughly washed him previously. *There is no cause for embarrassment,* she admonished herself. Tabor still slept in the black sleep. He didn't know she was there. He probably didn't know he was alive. Still, when she touched him, careful to touch him with nothing but the damp cloth, she felt strange, as though she were violating him — committing an act she shouldn't and that she would be punished for.

She squeezed water from the cloth, brought it back to Tabor's body. . . . and jumped when Tabor groaned and grabbed her by the wrist. He held her hand where it shouldn't have been at all!

"You're alive!" Tanaka breathed, afraid that in wanting him to open his eyes she had constructed an all-too-real illusion.

Tabor's lips moved, but no sound came out. After a moment, he simply nodded his head. Then, despite his weakness, a sly smile curled his mouth, and a twinkle lit his eye. Still holding her by the wrist, he kept her hand against him until she jerked away. Although happy that he was alive, she was about equally angry.

"What . . ." he said at last, his voice faltering. He moistened his lips and started over. "What you were . . . doing . . . would bring any man back to life."

Tanaka gave him a cross look, though her anger quickly dissipated. Tabor wanted to talk, to question, but she wanted him to eat and drink. Since she was the more determined of the two, she won out. But almost as soon as Tabor managed to get several mouthfuls of fish and cold potatoes into his stomach, followed by several hearty swallows of wine, he fell asleep.

"It is just sleep this time," Tanaka whispered, stroking Tabor's blond hair as she knelt beside him. "Strength-giving sleep, not the black sleep." She said the words aloud to give herself strength and confidence. Then, with the blanket still in place so that she had privacy, Tanaka stripped off all her clothes and sat cross-legged facing the sun, concentrating on a mental image of the lotus blossom, the Egyptian symbol of regeneration, and seeking the strength of the heavens to bring all of life's glories back to the tall, powerful Viking who lay beside her.

The news that Tabor had spoken and eaten elated the crew. Huge quantities of food and wine were prepared for Tabor, even though Tanaka said it wasn't necessary yet. When Tanaka stepped out from the bow and presented herself to the crew, a cheer went up that had to be loud enough for the two ships that continued to follow to hear.

"I think the worst is behind him now," Tanaka told the men "Soon you will have your leader again."

Looking into the faces of the men, she could see the strain of the days at sea. Continually chased, they knew that when the wind from the north died, so, too, would they all. She felt proud, also, of the work she had done to save Tabor's life . . . and she felt relief that he would live.

Sven leaned close to Tanaka and whispered, "You have my eternal gratitude. You have done a great thing, and for that great thing I will always remember you."

"He's still in danger," Tanaka said, not wanting anyone to forget that Tabor's wounds were still with him.

"But he has your love to sustain him."

The words shocked Tanaka, and she could think

of nothing to say in reply. Sven saw her surprise and confusion and said, "You have saved his life, and now you will love him. It is destined. You cannot help it. We all love those we save."

Excusing herself, Tanaka closed the blanket curtain behind her to be alone with the sleeping Tabor. She needed to think, to sort out what she truly knew and what she just believed to be the truth. But the words that Sven had spoken kept coming back to her; and each time they echoed in her mind's ear, she heard the ring of truth. Sven and Tabor loved each other and felt a bond of loyalty because each had risked his own life for the other many times. Indeed they had saved each other's life many times. The men loved Tabor because they trusted him to keep them alive in troubling times. They believed that he, with his superior judgment and skills, could save them; and because he *had* saved their lives, Tabor loved his men.

He is a Viking . . . a barbarian Viking . . . I am an Egyptian high priestess. . . . a priestess would never allow herself to love a barbarian, she thought with straining conviction, hoping that Sven was wrong in his prediction.

Tabor's recovery was not as swift as Tanaka wished. That first day, when Tabor was awake, he ate, and then sleep would reclaim him. But the color in his face had returned, and his wounded biceps appeared to have avoided the sickness in the blood altogether.

Once, while Tabor slept, the wind died and the two trailing ships brought out their oars and closed the distance between them to less than fifty yards.

But then the wind picked up again; and while the Norwegian ships transfered back to running under sail, Sven put almost a mile of sea between himself and his pursuers.

It was during the second day after Tabor crept out from the black sleep that the chills struck him, making him shake no matter how many warm blankets were piled upon him. The crew fell silent, their thoughts with their leader, all of them knowing that there were limits to human endurance, even for Tabor, Son of Thor. He had battled constantly for their welfare, and they prayed to the gods that his life would be spared and that the copper-skinned slave with the strange name and odd accent had the healing magic in her fingertips.

Tanaka's emotions ran wild. One minute she was convinced that Tabor had finally shaken off the shackles of his sickness and that he would be fine in just a few hours. The next moment, watching him shake as though he were cold and, at the same time, perspire as though burning from excessive heat, she was convinced that he could not last much longer. He had suffered as much or more than any man could be expected to; and if he chose to die, no one would blame him.

When the sun went down, the tension and the fear rose. The wind generally dwindled, hinting at the possibility that the trailing ships would use their oars to close the protective gap. Also, the sea darkness was so complete that the possibility of becoming beached on a sand bar, or shattered on rocks, was dangerously heightened. And it was during the night, when the rays of the sun were no longer there to warm Tanaka and to give her comfort and confidence, that her fears took on the strength and force of physical beings. She had loved desert nights in Egypt but she was afraid of the night now that she spent them aboard a Viking ship.

Rising up on her knees, Tanaka pulled the dress and underdress over her head. Naked, she added one more blanket to those already over Tabor, then crawled in beside him, careful to be on his right side so that she would be away from his injured arm.

Very gently, she placed her cheek on his chest, where she was able to hear Tabor's heart beating. It was a reassuring sound for her, even though he still shook from the fever as he slept.

Tanaka raised her knee, sliding it over his legs as she rolled closer to him. She placed her hand lightly on his stomach and in the midnight darkness whispered, "Please don't die. I'm not as afraid when I'm near you, even if you can't hear what I say. You inspire me, Tabor. You inspire everyone who is close to you."

Closing her eyes, Tanaka snuggled a little closer, pressing her small, naked body against his large one, hoping that somehow the life energy within her could be transferred to him.

Chapter Ten

Tabor woke with a jerk of his body, his eyes bursting open to complete and utter darkness. Though he was a brave man, the apparent blindness frightened him until he saw the twinkling of a few stars that had managed to peek through the clouds. There was nothing wrong with Tabor's eyes or with his sense of touch, for Tanaka lay naked beside him and her breasts, pressed against his side, were as firm and warm and tempting as he remembered.

His first instinct was to roll toward Tanaka and pull her in tighter, but he took a moment to mentally readjust himself to his surroundings and get his bearings on who and what he was and all that he had been through.

It took a few seconds, but Tabor was able to recall the fierce fever that had gripped him. Vaguely, he recalled Tanaka trying to get him warm enough to stop the shakes; at other times she was taking the blankets off because he was burning up with the fever. He recalled, too, how she had slowly and cautiously fed him. This was not an easy revelation for a proud Viking warrior like Tabor.

He recalled, too, coming out of the black sleep and being able to eat hearty meals, and that was when the fever hit him. Though his powerful muscles felt stiff from disuse, as he cautiously moved his arms and legs, he understood that the ship of his body had weathered this particular storm in good fashion. With the exception of his left arm, which still throbbed and itched from Ingmar's arrow, his ship, as his Viking mind put it, felt seaworthy.

Once he had come to the conclusion that he was alive and, at least for a little while, likely to stay that way, there was the matter of the unclad woman beside him.

He inhaled and smelled the intoxicating aroma of Tanaka. The warmth of her next to him—her body curled up along his side, her thigh thrown over his with her right arm resting lightly across his stomach—was an aphrodisiac that Tabor, no matter how battered and beaten he'd been, responded to with a slow but insistent hardening.

He grinned as he sensed himself lengthening, thinking that this surely had to be a sign that he was regaining not only strength but appetite.

Her cheek was against his chest, and he felt the soft, brushing warmth of her breath against his nipple. Tanaka's hair—the color and texture of which had so fascinated him from the very beginning—was spread over his right arm and along the blanket near his head.

Curling his arm around Tanaka's shoulders, Tabor

126

moved cautiously, not wanting to waken her yet, and he was pleased when—with a sleep, mewl—she snuggled closer to him. The movement of her thigh against his own brought fresh waves of stimulation streaming through Tabor's body, jolting his manhood to its full potential.

Tabor dismissed the practical, pragmatic questions that nudged against desire. There would come a time when he could find out how long he had been recovering from his wounds and the sickness, a time when he could find out where they were and where they were sailing to, a time to discover if they were still being chased by Ingmar's boat. But the time for that was not now. Tanaka was at his side, and she had never seemed more alluring to him.

Perhaps it is just that I am happy to be alive, Tabor thought, looking for a rational reason for his passion. Then, from an inner recess, another voice whispered, *Or perhaps you are just happy to be with her.*

The amendment did not rest easily with Tabor, and he cast the secondary thought aside as quickly as he had the questions of health and battle.

He started to encircle Tanaka with his left arm, but the pain in his biceps stopped him instantly. This pain, however, was the hot burning of regenerating tissues coming back to life, not the rotting of damaged flesh. Consequently, even the pain felt good to Tabor, and he chuckled a bit, sure at last that he would not lose his life because of Ingmar's arrow.

It was the chuckle that triggered Tanaka's protective instincts. She had developed the skill of awaken-

127

ing at Tabor's slightest sound, afraid that he would succumb to his wounds. She twisted sharply, rolling around so that she could tuck her knees beneath her.

"Are you awake? Are you all right?" she asked in a breathy whisper. She placed her fingertips against Tabor's throat, feeling for his pulse. It was strong and steady, though beating considerably faster than it had before. In the darkness, it was difficult to see clearly, so Tanaka had to lean forward over Tabor, placing her face close to his, trying to see into his eyes. "Tell me where you hurt. Is it your arm?"

Tanaka was completely unmindful of the fact that, leaning over Tabor, her breasts brushed erotically against his chest. And even as she looked into the depths of his blue eyes, her breasts were pressing warm and soft against him. But though she was unmindful, her body was not. Her nipples became hard and erect, and a gentle fire flamed to life within her.

"I am quite well," Tabor said, speaking slowly as though to test his own voice. He kept his words soft, having no desire for anyone's attention but Tanaka's. "Better than you will probably believe."

Tanaka had been confused so often by Tabor and his Viking ways that she let the comment pass. But why, she asked herself, did he have that damnably devilish grin on his face? When she had crawled under the blankets with him, he was shaking with the fever; now the light in his eyes suggested an entirely different kind of fever.

Tanaka sat back on her heels, crossing her arms

128

over her breasts. Her eyes spit flames as she glared down at the infuriating Viking that she had been silly enough to worry about. In sitting up, she had drawn the blankets to her, leaving Tabor exposed.

Though she had avoided looking at him, her eyes instinctively sought his body, and not even the midnight darkness could hide the full glory of Tabor's arousal.

Embarrassed, Tanaka tried to cover him with a corner of the blanket, but Tabor laughed, amused.

"I can see you are feeling *much* better," Tanaka whispered. Though she was angry she was also relieved. Tabor would soon recover his strength and vigor.

His smile faded, but the warmth in his eyes did not. He placed his hand on her thigh. To feel her beside him, to see her cast in soft starlight and shadows, was the most perfect vision he'd ever known.

"Don't . . . don't hide yourself," he whispered. "You're so beautiful, you should never hide yourself . . . from me."

Those were not the words that she had wanted to hear him say. Or so she told herself.

"You scared me," she said at last, arms crossed over her bosom. She shook her head so that her ebony hair fell down the front of her body like a robe. "I thought you were going to die."

Tabor, his hand still on her thigh, replied glibly, "I am not so easily killed."

Tanaka's mind whirled. Before, it had seemed as though the Vikings were far more modest, more inclined to feel shame at displaying the human body, than the Egyptians. But here on the boat on this starry night, Tabor was perfectly at ease despite his flagrant excitement. It was Tanaka who felt jittery and unnerved.

"That is good for me," she said at last. "Sven would have killed me if you'd died."

"He can be protective," he said, as though that explained and excused the threat. "But let's not talk about Sven now." Even in the darkness, Tanaka could see the light that sprang into Tabor's eyes. "There is much that we have left unfinished, isn't there?"

Tanaka looked away. *Yes,* she thought, *there is much that we have left unfinished. You gave me pleasure, and I gave you nothing at all.*

She felt that she owed him something, but almost as soon as this emotion blossomed, she crushed it. She owed him nothing at all! Whatever magic he'd performed with her had been done for his own benefit. Besides, feeling that she *owed* Tabor took something away from the feelings of the moment; and, though it was an uncomfortable realization, Tanaka knew that she was more than just curious about sharing herself with this handsome Viking once again.

"There is anger in your heart," Tabor whispered.

"And how do you know what is in my heart?" she asked, letting an unmistakable edge tinge her voice.

"I can see into your heart through your eyes. What have I done to make you angry? Is it that I am alive and will stay that way?"

130

"No," Tanaka said quickly. "It's not that at all. I was just thinking that . . ." Her words trailed off.

She was thinking that Tabor was much more perceptive than she'd given him credit for. She was thinking, too, that the fever—the sickness—had stripped several pounds from his magnificent body, but that had only served to make him look more dangerous and predatorial, like a hungry lion on the prowl. And why, Tanaka wondered, would she want to be the prey that satisfied this lion's hunger?

As innocently as she could, Tanaka murmured, "You must be cold," and pulled the blanket—successfully this time—over Tabor.

"Actually, not in the least." He raised his hand from her thigh to boldly brush her hair over her shoulder. Tanaka closed her eyes, turning her face away, but in no other way made any move to block him. "I have a feeling that I owe you my life," Tabor continued, staring at Tanaka's crossed arms and envisioning what lay bared beneath them. "How can I repay you for your kindness and generosity of spirit?"

The teasing undercurrent in Tabor's tone was playing havoc with Tanaka's senses. He was much too weak for this kind of banter, she told herself. At least she *wanted* him to be too weak to follow through with any of his unspoken sexual promises. And he was promising to take her to that special mindless place he'd taken her to before, wasn't he? That place where nothing existed but feeling—pure, physical, feeling.

131

Memories, warm and evocative, made Tanaka shiver.

"You can surely think of *something* you'd like, some way for me to repay you for your kindness."

Whispering, Tanaka replied, "You don't have to do anything. You owe me nothing."

She felt his fingers curl around her wrist. When he pulled her hands apart, she let them drop to her sides without protest, uncovering herself. The deep, rumbling sigh she heard told Tanaka that Tabor was not unaffected by what he saw. Her cheeks and ears felt warm, and she knew that if she'd had a looking glass to peer into, she'd see the face of a young priestess flushed with embarrassment . . . and passion.

"You're being kind," Tabor said after a long pause. He brushed his knuckles over the crest of Tanaka's breast, then turned his hand around to cup the firm flesh. "There's *nothing* I can do to repay you for all you've done?"

The sensual drawl of Tabor's words incited her passion, but not without drawing an equal amount of ire. Giving her anger free rein, Tanaka turned her gaze upon Tabor.

"You don't *owe* me anything," she said sharply, biting the words out as coldly as Tabor had spoken his warmly. "And I don't like the implication that . . . that *that* is a bartering tool, something that can be traded for."

"I didn't mean to offend you," Tabor replied, taking his hand from her breast. "If you don't want me touching you, then I won't." Even in the starlit darkness, Tabor could see her iciness melt. He issued a half-smile, the one that so many women had said was sensually disarming. "But, of course, if you don't want me to touch you, then it only stands to reason that you should touch me."

Once again Tanaka's fire flashed, but this time Tabor was not put off by it. The sexual repartee had been a ploy, buying him time until the last trace of sleep's fogginess had left him so that all his senses could appreciate Tanaka. He took her by the wrist once again, but this time she resisted.

"It's one or the other," Tabor said, intentionally ambiguous.

Tanaka did not want to be honest with herself. She did not want to admit that she was curious about Tabor and what it would be like to touch him, explore him boldly with her hands just as he had freely caressed her. When he guided her hand beneath the blanket, she resisted, not out of a sense of indignation, but because she thought she was *supposed* to resist. But she didn't put forth much of a struggle, and she curled her fingers around the thick, solid staff of flesh without having to be told. She squeezed firmly, drawing yet another rumbling groan of pleasure from the big Viking she'd coaxed away from the gates of Valhalla.

Every nerve ending in her body was charged. Tanaka could feel Tabor's strong, rapid pulse through his manhood, and it fascinated her. She squeezed a little more tightly, testing him, experimenting, watching the expression on his gaunt, handsome face change as she stimulated him.

133

"It this what you wanted?" she asked, moving her small hand up and down. She watched Tabor's throat pulse as he swallowed drily. If he tried to speak, he failed, though his lips moved as though he wanted to say something to her. She watched him respond to the sensations she caused, and Tanaka reveled in her newly discovered power. It thrilled her.

He's huge! thought Tanaka as she ran her hand along the length of him, marveling at his size and the suppressed might that burned its way through her palm and into her blood. It was immediately apparent to Tanaka that Tabor was a man of considerable dimensions, and this made her shudder slightly. Surely, he was too large to give her pleasure.

Tabor sat up, slipping his left elbow beneath him as a prop. Instantly, fire-like pain blazed in his arm, shooting through his shoulder to explode in his brain. He gritted his teeth and fell back upon the bed of blankets. Tanaka leaned over him, her hands flat upon his chest, holding him down.

"Don't try to move," Tanaka said, whispering. She did not want Sven or Carl or any of the other Vikings bursting in on her small bow bedroom to see what the trouble was. "Lie back. You'll only reopen your wounds if you try to move."

The passion had been destroyed by the bolt of pain that had laid Tabor prone. For long seconds, Tabor lay motionless, his eyes squeezed tightly shut, his breath coming in ragged gasps. Only when the pain finally subsided and his breathing returned to normal did Tabor open his eyes and attempt a smile. His forehead, Tanaka noted, was dotted with drops of perspiration.

"Is it better?" she asked, leaning over Tabor, her face just inches from his. When he nodded, she dabbed his forehead with a corner of the blanket. "Don't try to do too much too soon. You're not going to recover all your strength right away."

If Tanaka thought that Tabor would be dissuaded from his seductive goals, then she had little understanding of exactly what kind of man he was and of the unswerving allure of her own charms. Pain had slowed Tabor, but it had not stopped him, and when his gaze went from Tanaka's face down to her temptingly close breasts, she knew that he had strong desires that had yet to be addressed. As before, she sat back on her heels and crossed her arms modestly over her bosom.

"You've only yourself to blame," Tabor accused.

"You were shivering. I was trying to keep you warm," Tanaka replied. "I meant nothing by it."

Tabor just chuckled. He didn't believe her, and once her explanation had been questioned, she began to doubt it herself. Was it really such an innocent act to strip off her clothes so that her body warmth could go directly to him? Had she really hoped that her life force could be shared by him? Wasn't there just the chance that she had secretly hoped that he would awaken from the black sleep and gaze at her with the look in his eyes that was there now?

The laughter died in Tabor's throat, and when he

135

spoke, his tone carried a mixture of authoritarian command and seductive charm. "Touch me, Tanaka."

She looked at him and felt the embers of passion that had been ignited within herself much earlier burst again to white flame. While looking straight into his eyes, she placed her hand lightly on his stomach, which was almost completely void of hair.

"I'll touch you," Tanaka whispered, her heart racing, her hand trembling as she at last came to a vague understanding of what she was going to do and why. "But you must lie there quietly. Promise me you won't hurt yourself."

Tabor grinned crookedly, wickedly. "I don't make promises to women," he said, which wasn't entirely accurate, since he'd made a promise to Tanaka earlier. "And I *always* try to keep from getting hurt."

Tanaka looked at the scars of varying ages covering his mighty arms, shoulders, and chest. "If that's the case, you'd better try harder. Your body looks like a map."

"A map of all the wars I've been in. Now touch me, Tanaka. Your beauty has me in a spell . . . a spell from which only you can rescue me."

If there had been any doubts in Tanaka's mind of her desire, Tabor's words removed them as seductively as if he'd removed her clothes. She slipped her hand once again beneath the blanket, her fingers sliding over the crisp hair that sprouted above his manhood before curling around his staff once more. He had lost some of his rigidity; but when she grasped him, he recovered instantly, burgeoning to full, awesome size.

"Some—sometimes when I look at you, your strength frightens me," Tanaka whispered, working her hand slowly over him. Tabor's right arm was circled loosely around her hips, and she almost asked him to touch her. She remembered the quiet pleasure she'd taken when she had washed Tabor while he was in the black sleep. "You're the strongest man I've ever seen." *And the most handsome and virile,* she thought, but did not say. "Close your eyes now. Lie back."

If she believed Tabor could remain idle and calm while she remained naked and near, she understood nothing at all of his passionate nature. He ran his fingertips up her spine. Then, slowly, his hand slipped around her body to brush softly against her breast, then he hooked his hand around the back of her neck.

"Kiss me," Tabor whispered hoarsely, pulling Tanaka down to his waiting mouth, hungry for the taste of her lips.

The sigh that Tanaka heard this time was her own. She allowed Tabor to pull her down, and when her mouth covered his, her lips were parted to invite the exploration of his tongue. She melted into him, adoring every inch of him that was in contact with her, trembling as their tongues danced erotically, darting from mouth to mouth. Throughout the kiss, she continued to use her hand on him, squeezing and fondling him with a boldness and confidence she'd never before known.

When Tabor took his hand from behind her neck

to reach around her waist again, Tanaka sighed disconsolately through a kiss. She did so love the way his fingers caressed her hair. But then, even as she was considering asking Tabor not to stop, his large hand cupped her buttocks, the tips of his fingers slipping inward to press temptingly close to the core of her heated sensations.

Remaining on his back, Tabor pulled Tanaka higher, breaking the kiss that had fused them together. At first she protested, wanting to continue feasting on his mouth, but he forced her higher and her breasts slid across the surface of his chest. He grinned up at her, continuing to force her higher until awareness at last dawned upon her.

"You must remain still," Tanaka whispered.

"Then you must feed me," Tabor replied, his tone husky with suppressed passion, his fingers caressing the taut half moon of Tanaka's behind, dangerously near the moist petals that ached for attention.

"I will," Tanaka replied. "I will give you all the sustenance you need."

The bold words were matched by even bolder actions. Tanaka turned slightly so that the taut, passion-darkened crest of her left breast was above Tabor's mouth. She never lost hold of his manhood, continuing to manipulate him in ways she could tell he found pleasurable.

When Tabor captured her nipple between his lips and put his tongue in motion, Tanaka tossed her head back, sending her hair flying around her shoulders to stream down her back in long, curly waves of ebony black. She uttered a low, throaty moan of delight when Tabor's teeth nipped at the sensitive breast. The sensation of his sharp teeth was quickly followed by the raspy moist warmth of his tongue.

Moving her shoulders slightly, Tanaka positioned herself so her other nipple was now directly over the Viking's mouth. As the heat of passion seared her veins, Tanaka had the fleeting realization that what she was doing was wrong. She had no choice but to capitulate to Tabor's carnal commands, she rationalized. . . . but she didn't have to enjoy them as much as she did. And she certainly didn't need to volunteer to do anything!

But how could something so wrong feel so exquisite?

Don't think, Tanaka admonished herself. Though she had little experience in such matters, she already realized that thinking too much inhibited the pleasure of the moment. She trembled as she rocked to and fro, feeding the tips of her breasts to Tabor's tempting mouth.

For Tabor, to feel her small hand working him as he tasted the sweetness of her flesh was the most erotic experience of his life. Not even the throbbing pain from his injured biceps could dampen the excitement that charged through him. He ran his hand up and down over the back of her thigh, touching her from knee to buttocks, letting his fingers play along her velvety flesh.

The sensory delight he experienced while touching Tanaka was a powerful elixir that made him feel as though he had drunk much strong wine. He squeezed her firm buttocks, and, when he reached deeper into the cleft to touch her even more intimately, she issued a cry of surprise.

So wrong! So terribly wrong! an annoying little voice in her mind whispered when Tabor's hand reached the juncture of her thighs.

Tanaka dismissed the voice. She cast the troubling questions and doubts aside because they prevented her from enjoying all the wonderful sensations that Tabor was so capable of making her feel. Deep within herself, in the buried core of her soul, she was hungry for the delights of the flesh that Tabor had taught her were possible. Down low, the rosy petals of her femininity felt wet, tingly, neglected. When Tabor touched her there, then probed cautiously, his finger slipped in easily.

"Ah-h-h!" Tanaka gasped, her head hanging down as she leaned over Tabor. She quivered from head to toe as he suckled upon her breasts and tantalized her with his fingers.

Tanaka was unaware that she had released Tabor's staff. She was unable to concentrate on anything but her own body and the extraordinary joy that she was feeling. Tabor's fingers probed and prodded, arousing the sensitive nub while his lips, teeth, and tongue drew pleasure from her nipples. It was only in a vague corner of her mind that Tanaka was able to realize that she was leaning over Tabor, her hands over the left side of him, her trembling behind on the other.

I was supposed to give him pleasure, she thought guiltily as the tension within her built upon itself,

140

fire feeding upon fire.

She felt it beginning, and this time she knew what was happening and she was not scared. It was that strange release of tension, of passion, that had gripped her body before, when Tabor had taken her into his arms and bed back at Hedeby. Sensations swirled in a vortex, like a hurricane that circles tighter and tighter, engulfing everything in its path.

And then, as she felt the culmination of all sensation fast approaching, Tabor pushed her away. She blinked her eyes, at first having a difficult time comprehending exactly what he had done. She blinked, her body fevered with a passionate insanity that required Tabor if she was ever to be free of it.

"I must have you," Tabor said hoarsely, the strain of desire showing clearly on his handsome face. "Now!"

Tanaka's hunger for Tabor was as great as his for her. She straddled his lean hips, raising up so that she could guide him into her. The heights of her passion were such that she did not even care if he was so large that she could not accommodate him comfortably. She needed to feel him inside her, the joining of their bodies. The communion of their souls.

She lowered herself upon him, opening to him, surprised that all she felt was pleasure—a sweet, blissful satisfaction of extraordinary scope.

Oblivious of other crew members aboard the boat, Tanaka called out her lover's name again and again as she rode him from one culmination to another. He lanced upward, filling her with his power, his strength, and his essence. And when at last she heard his leonine roar as he drove into her higher and deeper than ever before, an overpowering sense of oneness engulfed Tanaka. She slumped down upon him, her breasts pressing against his heaving, perspiring chest. She kissed his cheek and shoulder, but not his mouth as together they gasped to recover their strength.

"Tabor . . . Tabor . . . Tabor," Tanaka whispered, her body tingling.

She kept him inside herself for as long as she could before rolling beside him onto her back. When she was empty of him, she felt hollow inside, and she snuggled close to Tabor, pleased when his strong right arm curled around her shoulders.

"I never . . . dreamed . . . it could be like that," Tanaka whispered.

She was hungry for the sound of her own name on Tabor's lips. Had she pleased him? the nagging voice inside her head suddenly asked. When she looked at Tabor, she saw that he had fallen asleep, his reserves of strength sapped from their shared passion.

Chapter Eleven

Somewhere in the night, Tanaka found the sweet solace of sleep. But before she was finally able to rest, a hundred questions rattled endlessly in her skull.

Why had she made love to Tabor? He was her captor; she, his captive. She could not — *should* not — feel anything for him but scorn and revulsion. No high priestess would ever feel anything but unmitigated hatred for a barbarian who had forced her into his bed.

Only Tabor hadn't forced Tanaka. He hadn't forced her to do anything. Nothing had prevented Tanaka from resisting Tabor except her own desire.

As he slept beside her, Tanaka studied his face, amazed. He had taught her the outer limits of passion and the glorious turmoil beyond.

She fell asleep at last, curled beneath the blankets at Tabor's side, for once not caring to know how far away the pursuing ships were. With Tabor's powerful arm as a pillow for her head, Tanaka drifted into sleep, a faint smile at her lips.

Just past dawn, Tabor groaned, blinked, and

awoke. Tanaka was instantly awake, hearing and feeling her patient and lover reviving.

"Are you all right?" she asked, pulling her knees beneath her, remaining in the makeshift bed.

Tabor's libidinous grin told her he was better than all right, and when his gaze went from her face down to her bare breasts, she saw that his strength had returned.

"I'll bet you're hungry. Let me put my clothes on and I'll get you something." Tanaka reached for her dress.

"Nay," he said, his whisper graveled with emotion. "I am hungry . . . but not for food."

Tanaka gave him a look. "You've been wounded, and you feel strong now. But it would be best if you lay quietly where you are."

"Nay, I don't think that at all. A Viking knows what makes him strong." Tabor placed his palm against Tanaka's cheek. He stared at her lips, remembering the pleasure they'd known. "You make me strong. And right now, what I need is you."

Tanaka had valid reasons to refuse Tabor. She saw their lovemaking as an aberration, a mistake in judgment, an error caused by fear and confusion — anything other than the most breathtaking experience of her life. But looking deep into the fathomless depths of Tabor's blue eyes as he pulled her nearer, could think of nothing but how delicious it would be to taste his lips against her own just one more time.

She moaned softly when their lips met. And it was Tanaka who first explored the outline of Tabor's mouth with the tip of her pink tongue, then probed deeper, emboldened by Tabor's throaty sigh of acceptance and approval.

She kissed him long and hard, sliding down to press the full length of her body against Tabor's, never letting her mouth leave his as she repositioned herself. When at last she felt the comforting heat of his body seeping into her own, Tanaka raised her head to look into his eyes.

"Can you?" she asked in a whisper, too embarrassed to be more specific. "So soon after? . . ."

Tabor took a lock of her ebony hair and twirled it around his thick forefinger. With someone else he would have boasted and disarmed. But with Tanaka, he felt no need for braggadocio.

"Aye," he said at last. "I have been bruised, battered, bloodied, and beaten, but I can still give you pleasure and still receive pleasure from you." He brushed the silky lock of hair he'd twirled around his finger against his lips. "I have been made a weakling by Ingmar's arrow, I fear, but my strength will soon return. Then I will give you the loving you deserve."

Though he spoke from his heart, Tanaka did not entirely believe the Viking. He had been injured, it was true, but he was no weakling. And though she knew now that it was possible to feel pleasure from a man's touch, she could not imagine how Tabor could pleasure her more than he already had.

"Yes . . . yes," she crooned, not wanting Tabor to make promises he could not keep, kissing him to quell his words.

145

She moved with greater surety this time, pressing her weight upon Tabor. This time instead of the blinding, all encompassing sensations of before, she was able to separate the feelings, savoring them.

Could there be anything sweeter in all the world, Tanaka wondered, than the feel of bare breasts against a strong Viking chest? The aroma of their recent passion permeated the blankets, a silent—and erotic—reminder of what they had shared.

She feasted on his mouth, catching his lower lip between her even white teeth. Her fingers played lightly with his nipples, and she was surprised to find that his, like her own, had become erect.

His right arm was around her waist, his injured arm motionless at his side. He did not caress her, but she did not mind. Without the sensory overload it was easier to think.

Tanaka kissed his cheek, then his ear, then his throat, wriggling to press her breasts against him. Raising her knee, sliding her thigh against his, she moved her leg until she felt his hardness burning against the flesh of her inner thigh. That he was already aroused appealed to Tanaka's vanity, though she never would have admitted it. "You're so much bigger," she whispered as she kissed Tabor's shoulder, marveling at the breadth of his chest and how her body responded to him when she could caress him at her leisure. But the moment the words were out of her mouth, Tabor stiffened, and Tanaka knew that what she'd said could have many different meanings.

In a burst of jealous anger, Tabor clenched his

teeth, then forced himself to relax and enjoy the pleasure that this high priestess—if her allegation were true—was willingly providing.

Tabor told himself that it was none of his concern that she had been Ingmar the Savage's captive before he'd received her as a gift. But the thought of her magnificent, golden body being defiled by the loathsome Ingmar the Savage—

"Have I displeased you?" Tanaka asked, cutting into Tabor's troubling thoughts, sensing his sudden change of temperament. "Tell me what I have done, and I will never do it again."

Tabor looked into her eyes, so close to his own, feeling the softness of the heavy hair that spread across his naked chest. She waited for his response, and Tabor—seeing the insecurity of the future—knew he would be a fool to question whatever passion Tanaka was willing to share with him.

"Don't talk," Tabor whispered, passion resumed, his eyes smoldering like heated chips of blue diamonds. "Just kiss me."

Her passion mingled with concern for Tabor's health. Twice he tried to take her into his arms; and both times, she was able to see his pain. To keep him down, Tanaka tossed a leg over him, straddling his hulk as she had during their frantic lovemaking under the stars.

"There," she said, sitting lightly upon him. His arousal heat burned against the small of her back, branding her as his. "Now you've got to stop moving or your arm will start bleeding again, and if that happens, then we'll have to stop all—" she smiled devilishly "—activity. I'll have no choice but to get Sven to help me put a fresh bandage on your arm."

As she spoke, she moved her hips subtly, almost imperceptibly, but the contact of her delicately rounded buttocks against his lower abdomen, of velvet-smooth skin gliding against passion-enflamed manhood, was not lost on either of them.

"Of course, as soon as your men find out how well you've recovered," she continued, "they'll all want to see you, speak with you. . . . and, well, that would mean that you and I would simply have no time for privacy . . . or the things that men and women do when they have privacy."

As she spoke, teasing Tabor with every word, he marvelled at the feminine perfection of this woman, aware that she had changed for him the meaning of "attractive." Her smile was devastating, to begin with. But instead of the small nose of a Scandinavian woman, hers was long and narrow; and though Tabor had previously thought of such noses as unattractively big, he saw Tanaka's as aristocratic, regal, befitting a high priestess. Instead of golden blonde hair that grew in perfectly straight strands ideally suited to braiding, her hair was so dark it appeared blue-black, shimmering in the early morning sunlight. It fell down the front of her body in thick, satiny waves that nearly reached her navel.

"Thor himself would defy the gods to be with you," Tabor said in a low voice, brushing aside Tanaka's hair to view her round breasts. The areolas were small and dark brown rather than large

148

and pink, and this, too, made her different from the women he had known. Visually stimulated, he felt himself growing.

Tanaka, unschooled in Viking tradition, could not know the full importance of what Tabor had said, but she sensed that he had praised her and that such flattering words did not pass glibly from his lips.

"You can touch me," she said, taking Tabor's right hand and placing it over her breast. His eyes, she noted, glinted with passion like the turquoise stone that her people prized.

She guided him into herself again, as hungry for the sensation of being filled by him as he was to possess her. He set the rhythm, raising and lowering Tanaka until she understood what he wanted. At first she felt strong in her desire and her ability to arouse Tabor, but as passion increased, logic failed her. And when Tabor's hand clamped over her mouth while she writhed in white-hot passion it took a while for her to realize that he was only trying to quiet the screams of her ecstasy.

When Tanaka pulled the curtain aside, moving away from her bow bedroom, intent on getting food for herself and Tabor, she realized that on a boat there could be no secrets. The men, knowing she had made love to Tabor, turned away from her to hide their salacious smirks.

Curt was at the rudder. Sven's blanket bedroll was nearby; he was sleeping after spending the night at the rudder himself. They were Tabor's second- and third-in-command.

The men who were awake moved aside, allowing Tanaka to step toward the stern. It galled her that the men did not look at her, and a blush darkened her cheeks and ears.

Men! she thought angrily. *They complicate my life and cause me trouble!* But there was one man who had indeed caused her trouble but had also taught her the heights of pleasure. *But it's just my body that he pleases,* Tanaka thought in frantic, self-delusion. *I'm not responsible if my body responds to that vicious Viking!*

She knew it was a lie, but she clung to it desperately, afraid to ponder for even a second what it would mean if it *weren't* a lie.

"I need food for myself and Tabor," she said to Carl, with more forcefulness than necessary. She wanted to stop the jokes and snickering. "Will you get it for me?"

Though she phrased it as a question, it was a command, and the instant the words were out of Tanaka's mouth, she knew she had made a grave mistake. A woman slave did not give orders to a Viking man, and the tight-lipped look Carl gave her said her insult would not be forgotten.

"Nay, I will not get your food," Carl said slowly, measuring his words as though it were difficult to control his temper. "I will have another man fill plates for Tabor—" he stared straight into her eyes before adding "—and perhaps there will be enough there for you, as well."

If there had been a general humor when Tanaka

had first stepped out from behind the curtain, it had vanished, beneath the tension. As plates were prepared for Tabor and Tanaka, she could almost feel the questions of the men around her. Moments earlier, the men had all wondered whether she was as uninhibited in bed as she sounded. Now they wondered how much influence she had over their leader, whether she was foolish to slight Carl as she had, and whether she knew that sharing a bed with Tabor would protect her from the other crewmen.

When the plates were ready, Tanaka took them to Tabor without a backward glance, hoping that he had not heard the harsh words she'd exchanged with Carl.

"Who's at the rudder?" Tabor asked when Tanaka returned.

He was sitting with his long legs folded comfortably beneath him, a blanket thrown modestly over his lap. He accepted the proffered plate with his right hand but was able to hold it with his left as he ate. Tanaka accepted this as a good sign since it meant he was finally able to use his hand at least a little bit without feeling pain. Of course, with Tabor, such an assumption was only guesswork. He could well be in pain and stubbornly refuse to show it.

"Carl is. He's been sharing the job with Sven."

Tabor nodded approval. "They are both good men. Are we still being followed?"

"I think so, but I can't be certain. I didn't see any boats, but then I didn't really look."

Laughing, Tabor said, "Aye! And that just like a

151

woman! We've had our ranks cut from more than seventy to less than fifteen; we've been chased not only out of our homeland, but out of our home waters as well; we've sailed days and nights without pause—and you forget to check if we're still being followed!" Tabor laughed again, the booming sound full of life.

Sitting upon folded blankets, Tanaka tore into her food, not because she was hungry, but because she was angry with Tabor for laughing at her. She ate in stony silence, knowing that Tabor was anxious to see his comrades, angry that he had not wanted to spend more time talking quietly with her after their lovemaking.

"You can eat at leisure," Tabor said with an attempt at humor that rankled Tanaka. "It's not the last meal you'll get."

"How dare you insult me?" Tanaka snapped, keeping the volume of her voice down but allowing her fury to resonate each word. "How dare you treat me like I'm nothing to you? If it weren't for me, you'd be dead!"

"Don't use that tone of voice with me when—"

"So sure of yourself!" Tanaka hissed, cutting Tabor off, heedless of the danger she was putting herself in, knowing only that she had been slighted by Carl and now by Tabor. She was too proud to accept second-rate status from anyone. "Maybe I am *just a woman* to you, but if I were just *any* woman, you'd be dead. Do you hear me? Dead! I changed your bandages so the sickness wouldn't get in your blood! I bathed you in cool water when the fever was upon you and made you burn! And when you shook with the cold, I held you close—as I would a child—to keep you warm!"

The words angered Tabor, not because he did not believe them, but because they were the truth. But what Viking warrior could accept that he had been sickened and needed to be held like "a child"?

"You tell me you are a high priestess, but you have a most unholy tongue and a temper to match!" Tabor whispered, his eyes hard and unblinking. He had been in jubilant spirits moments earlier, but he was worried that his men would hear her cross words. If they did, then he would have to punish her in a way that would show Tanaka—and prove to his men—that he was in charge of this boat and every person upon it. "If you are indeed a high priestess, then I assume you have the wit to understand that people who cross me suffer . . . unpleasantly."

Tanaka knew that Tabor held all the power in his large hands. Denying that would only get her humbled, hurt, or worse. But as long as she was alone with him, she was reasonably confident she could speak her mind without being beaten.

"And as a leader of men, I assume you have the intelligence to know that there is a difference between having the *power* to punish and having the *right* to punish." Tanaka rose slowly, sensing that once she finished she would do well to put distance between herself and Tabor. "And at the risk of pointing out the obvious, Ingmar crossed you, but

153

he seems to have suffered only the loss of very many arrows and very few men."

Tanaka relished her victory. Then, sure that she had gone too far, she dropped her plate, tossed the curtain aside, and practically leaped into the center section of the boat.

Ingmar sipped the beer and smiled. It was good to be back home in Kaupang, Norway, where he had been born and spent his early years. Beer tasted the way he wanted it to here; the food was mostly the heavy dumpling-laden stews that he loved, and he was surrounded by people who saw him as a conquering hero instead of a pillaging rapist.

To his left, the young maiden who had been sharing his bed since his return to Norway mended his clothes, adding embroidery to his vest and jackets. He'd stolen the embroidered trim from a boat his crew had overrun on their return from Hedeby. At the far end of the longhouse was another maiden — a young woman who had thus far been able to avoid Ingmar's bed, though it was uncertain how long her luck would continue. Ingmar looked at her. Tonight he would coerce her, resorting to force, if necessary, although experience had taught him to be patient if he wanted more than forced affection. This was especially true with virgins.

While Ingmar pondered whether this virgin was worth his patience, the door opened and his brother Hugh entered the longhouse along with a frosty blast of air. Hugh's face said Tabor was still alive.

154

"You coward!" Ingmar spat, tossing his drinking horn aside, spraying beer over his mistress, the floor, and the walls. "He's still alive, and you dare return?"

Hugh, shorter, lighter, and not nearly as strong as his older brother, pasted on an angry expression, but the blood drained from his face and his complexion took on a waxy cast. He advanced a single step deeper into the longhouse, remaining close enough to the only door to ensure escape should Ingmar physically vent his anger.

"We chased him for days," Hugh explained, his voice cracking slightly. He hated that he literally quivered in his boots under his brother's rage. "He's out of our waters for good. Isn't that what you wanted?"

"I wanted him *dead*." Ingmar's words indicated that if he did not get what he wanted, there would be more dead than just Tabor. He allowed his gaze to roll slowly from Hugh to his mistress and finally to the virgin maiden, knowing that the effect was chilling. "I do not like it when I am denied the things that please me. You understand that, don't you, Hugh?"

"Of course I understand. I'm your brother." Hugh's cheeks finally took on a bit of color.

"Then why can't you follow the orders that I give you?"

The menace in Ingmar's words shot ice through the veins of everyone in the longhouse. Ingmar, was known to lash out at whoever happened to be closest. No one wanted to suffer for Hugh's failure.

"Well?" Ingmar taunted, wanting to humiliate his brother before the women.

"I. . . . I don't know."

"There isn't much that you do know." Ingmar replied. "But I'll tell you this, and you'd better listen carefully because your life depends upon your remembering it." Hugh tried to swallow.

"Someday, Tabor is going to return; and when he does, you're going to kill him. You'll kill him before I even know Tabor is here. You'll do this for me because you know that from this point forward, I hold you responsible for any inconvenience that Dane causes me. Do you understand?"

"Aye," Hugh replied.

"Now get out of my longhouse, and don't set foot in here again while Tabor still lives."

Hugh thought better of protest. He had, till then, stayed in the longhouse with Ingmar. He had always lived with his brother. Now he would have to find a new place, and everyone in Kaupang would know that he had been tossed out by his brother.

Inwardly fuming but outwardly contrite, Hugh vowed that the day would come when he wouldn't have to bow to his brother's wishes.

Chapter Twelve

Tabor could feel his stamina increase with each passing hour, and he welcomed the sensation with open arms because he'd need every ounce of strength he could possess very soon. After the early morning lovemaking with Tanaka and the argument that immediately followed, Tabor at last greeted his men. Their confidence in him, showing clearly on their faces, added to his own inner peace. At one point Tabor took the rudder to guide the boat on its southbound course; but his left arm still was not fully healed, and, rather than draining his tenuous supply of energy and possibly reinjuring his arm, he turned the rudder back to Carl.

An unseasonable cooling breeze from the north had enabled Tabor's men to stay ahead of the two ships that had followed them out of Scandinavian waters, past the shores of England, and into the warmer southern seas. On the day that Tabor resumed the leadership of his men, when the sun shone high in the sky at midday, the breeze that had kept them ahead of the deadly stone-tipped spears of Hugh's Northmen suddenly stopped.

Tabor looked up at the huge square green and white sail of the ship, now hanging limp upon the mast, and hissed a curse to all the gods in all the heavens. With a steady breeze and excellent helmsmanship, his boat had created a gap of nearly three miles from the pursuers. Without the wind, the oars would be needed, and seventy strong men could propel a boat much faster than could thirteen men — and one woman.

"What'll we do?" Carl asked, keeping his voice down as he stood beside Tabor to stare at the lifeless sail.

Tabor said nothing. Though Carl was third in command, the difference between his skills and those of Sven's was enormous. At a time like this, Sven was sage enough to stay at the rudder to make the most use of any breeze that might fill the sails and leave Tabor alone so he could ponder their situation.

When it was clear that no answer was immediately forthcoming, Carl grabbed the hogshead and gulped the inferior wine that had first been stolen by Hugh but was taken in turn by Tabor's men.

Tabor turned northward. In the distance were two specks where once there had been three. The specks were sails coursed by strong and savage men who could kill Tabor and his Viking force. To the east was Spain, unless it was France. They could put in to land, but once there, all travel would be laborious. The sailors would be tired, and there would be no food or water except for what they could steal. The huge armada following them would have a distinct advantage on land. Besides, Tabor admitted, he felt

158

more comfortable and more confident with water—not land—beneath him.

At last Tabor turned his gaze toward Tanaka, who sat near the bow, her legs beneath her, appearing serene Tabor knew better; and when she looked up at the empty sail and then at him, he understood that she had read their situation perfectly. For a few seconds, they studied each other warily over the heads of the men that separated them. She at the bow, he at the stern; there was something suitable about the distance that kept them apart and the circumstances that tied them together.

I cannot think of her now, Tabor admonished himself, dragging his gaze away from the beautiful Egyptian priestess and her exquisite passion. She could become his obsession if he weren't careful.

He tried to not think of her, but that was impossible. Her presence was with him constantly. The questions she had asked forced Tabor to look within himself for answers. She seemed to know him better than he knew himself and yet she did not understand the Viking ways. Burning with passion, he dreamed of the countless hours he would spend with her in his arms. He would give her pleasure, accepting the pleasure she could provide, and they would take each other to those breathless heights that were as close to Valhalla as a Viking could get without dying.

When Tabor looked again toward the specks in the distance, they had disappeared. They had dropped their sails and were now rowing. Meanwhile, Tabor's own boat was nearly dead in the water, hardly rising and falling with the small ocean waves.

"Ready your weapons, men," Tabor said, almost conversationally.

Tanaka had not been afraid until she watched Tabor's men prepare themselves for a battle they could not win. With grim determination, the men strapped on their helmets and cawls, the leather fighting jackets reinforced with metal plates. They placed their shields nearby and readied their arrows in neat accessible lines. Beside the arrows rested the swords and spears for the worst fighting, after the boat had been forcibly boarded and the battle had progressed to hand-to-hand combat.

She stepped toward one of the younger Vikings. Less hardened, occasionally he had glanced in Tanaka's direction with something akin to affection. Tanaka hoped that he would tell her what the older warriors would not.

"Why aren't we rowing toward land?" she asked in a whisper as the young man strapped a stiff leather gauntlet to his left forearm.

"Tabor would rather fight on the water than on the land."

"What would you rather do?"

It was inconceivable to the boy even to consider going against Tabor's decision. He had, on occasion, doubted the wisdom of Tabor's decisions, but in the long run, Tabor had always been right. Because of this, the boy was more inclined to doubt his own wisdom than Tabor's.

Seeing that she would get nothing of value from the young man, Tanaka ventured toward the stern. Tabor stood with his feet apart in a broad, commanding stance, holding the rudder in his right hand

and a long, deadly spear in his left. The bandage around his injured biceps was white, and Tanaka was amazed at his recuperative powers. Unlike all the others on the boat, Tabor had not put on a helmet, leaving his long blond hair to flow down over his broad shoulders.

"When the fighting starts, I want you to take cover beneath the sacks of dried meat," Tabor said when Tanaka approached him. "Their arrows will not go through the sacks, so you will be safe there."

There was only a hint of affection in his tone, but it was enough for Tanaka to know that his outward commanding demeanor did not necessarily mean an inner hardness of heart toward her.

"No, I will stay here with you." Tanaka could feel the eyes of other men upon her and knew that many ears were listening. The two trailing boats were less than a hundred yards away, and the Vikings could also hear the Northmen's chanting as relentlessly, their oars cut into the water, propelling them closer.

"Do as I tell you, woman."

"No."

For a moment Tabor was baffled. He had no experience with opposition, especially not under battle conditions.

"You defy me?"

"Yes, I want to help."

"You're a woman!"

"Yes, and I still want to help in this fight." She looked from Tabor to Sven and the other men who were close enough to hear. "I have my life to lose, just as you do. But before I lose my life, I could suffer much more than you." Tanaka raised an inquisitive eyebrow, knowing her logic was sound and Tabor could not refuse her. "You are outnumbered, so what difference can it make if the hands that help you belong to a man or a woman?"

As though to underscore the importance of action, the faintest of breezes ruffled the sails and carried with it the rhythmic chant of cold-blooded killers straining hard at their oars, rowing with synchronized strokes for maximum efficiency.

Through clenched teeth Tabor hissed, "You infuriate me, woman!" But behind his anger, showing clear and blue in the depths of his eyes, there was pride in Tanaka. She was showing her courage; and, for a man like Tabor, courage had appeal.

There really wasn't much that anyone could do except pray for wind, which Tanaka, the priestess, did. The Vikings readied their weapons, paying chief attention to their bows and arrows for the first line of fire. Tanaka knew that if the fighting reached the sword and dagger stage, Ingmar's numerical advantage would make short work of Tabor's well-trained warriors.

The chanting continued, becoming louder with each passing second. With each stroke of the oars, the two ships drew closer. Tanaka, kneeling near barrels of drinking water at the middle of the ship, ran a dagger over a sharpening stone. She glanced at the approaching vessels, then up at the sail, which still hung limply on its mast. The ships were close enough now for her to see the men working hard at the oars, pulling in long strokes. Another two minutes and the ships would be upon them.

"Prepare for battle," Tabor cried.

Upon his command, the best archers moved to the bow of the boat, taking with them quivers bulging with arrows. As the best of the best, they had taken arrows from the other men, extending their supply. In the law of battle, skill and competence reigned supreme; ego died quickly.

Tabor stood at the rudder, his left thumb hooked into the wide leather belt that encircled his waist, his blond mantle streaming over his shoulders. Sven knelt at his side, an arrow already notched on his powerful bow. His attention danced between the approaching Northmen and Tabor, waiting for the command to let the first arrow fly. Tanaka was not surprised to find that Sven was one of the elite Viking archers, and she was sure that if Tabor's arm had not been injured, he would be the best.

"At your direction," Tabor said then, his eyes narrowed to slits.

Tanaka's heart skipped a beat as she watched Sven slowly draw the string back, bending the strong, fibrous bow, raising it up high, estimating the angle necessary for maximum distance.

The *twang!* of the arrow's release made Tanaka gasp. All eyes followed the arrow as it arched through the air, becoming little more than a sliver in the distance. The arrow descended fast, and when it struck an oar of the approaching ship, Sven cursed. But though he had missed hitting a man, the other archers had noted what trajectory was necessary.

"Let fly!" Tabor commanded.

For only a second, Tabor and Tanaka looked at each other. He gave her a fleeting smile, one that he did not truly feel, and she smiled back, knowing that he was only trying to still her fears.

He can be a sensitive and caring man, she thought then. *He doesn't like that part of himself because he doesn't think it is the way a Viking warrior should be, but it's there nevertheless.*

Within seconds, arrows began flying in both directions. Tanaka stayed near the water barrel, and though she could not say for certain, it seemed to her that far more of the Northmen arrows missed their mark than those of Tabor's men. She realized this perception could be prejudice, but as the ships drew nearer, she watched many enemy sailors twisting in agony as arrows struck them. Tabor lost few men.

Tabor, as though defying the gods as well as his enemies, remained standing tall and proud at the rudder. An arrow landed with a *thunk!* near his foot, missing him by inches. Contemptuously, he pulled the arrow from the wood and handed it to Sven.

"Send this back to them," he said.

The arrows no longer had to arch through the air to soar from boat to boat. The warriors were close enough to see their enemy's eyes, filled with the fear and hatred that go through men moments before they are to fight hand-to-hand.

This war is madness, Tanaka thought, and as though to underscore a truth, an arrow struck a Viking who knelt beside her. Without a sound, he fell backward, the arrow protruding from his chest.

Tears welled in Tanaka's eyes, spilling out and rolling down her cheeks as visions of the Viking's future came to mind . . . visions of a future that would never be.

A scant sixty feet now separated the boats. Tabor

recognized the commander of the closer of the two chase ships. Though he did not know his name, he remembered the man to be a smarmy fellow who had ingratiated himself to Hugh. The notion that he, Tabor, Son of Thor, should fall under the onslaught of such scum was beyond belief. Tabor knew, as if in revelation, that he was not destined for Valhalla. Not yet. He would not be sent to the great Viking heaven by men such as these.

He looked from the approaching ship to Tanaka, then up to the huge green-and-white stripped sail, which, at that moment, billowed outward, catching a sudden impossible wind.

Fifteen feet separated the ships. Sven grabbed Tabor's ankle and pulled hard, forcing his commander to his knees to take cover behind a large shield fixed to the rear of the boat. Tabor continued to hold the rudder in his right hand.

Men screamed in rage, in blood-lust, and sometimes in pain. The distance between the lead ship and Tabor's was crossed by arrows in the blink of an eye. The Northmen strained at their oars, propelling the ships forward, but they were easy targets for Sven, who made every arrow count.

The breeze was having its effect on Tabor's ship now, moving it forward. The Northmen ships had their sails down; and, though men were preparing to board Tabor's vessel, their ranks were being decimated by Tabor's archers. But the chase ships continued to narrow the gap.

Tanaka closed her eyes. She prayed to all the Egyptian gods who had guided her since her youth, prayed for wind to take her and Tabor and all his proud Viking warriors to safety.

For more than thirty minutes, Tabor worked speed from the wind while his Northmen counterparts screamed for their oarsmen to work harder. The distance that separated the ships was often hardly more than twenty feet, sometimes as much as fifty. When the closest ship abandoned the oars and worked to raise its sail, Tabor's men made them pay dearly for it, sending arrows into the unprotected Northmen. With neither sail nor oars, the ship soon drifted back until a hundred yards separated it from Tabor's boat.

The second ship kept even with Tabor. But its men were bent at the oars, using all the strength they possessed. The grim, determined, confidence in Tabor's eyes said he would nurse the wind long enough to drain the Northmen of that strength.

Time, he knew, was on his side, but only if the southbound wind continued.

Tanaka closed her eyes and continued praying to the gods. Only vaguely did she consider that perhaps it was wrong for an Egyptian high priestess to pray for a Viking warrior who was her captor.

In the east, the golden glow of dawn greeted Tabor. He leaned against the rudder of his ship, where he had remained through the night, coaxing with his prodigious skill and instinct.

Tabor looked to the north. He saw nothing but endless sea. During the night, the Northmen had, in their inexperience, rammed ships as they tried to align with Tabor. In the night air, he had heard the Northmen shouting from ship to ship, cursing each other, and Tabor had smiled to himself in the dark.

They had begun fighting him, and now they were fighting each other. It was typical of their lack of discipline, and his scorn for the Northmen increased.

To the east, he saw the shore line a little more than two miles away. Though he had not been able to see the coast during the night, Tabor had followed his instinct and not been wrong.

Tanaka lay on the deck of the ship at his feet, a warm woolen blanket covering her so that only her head, with its glorious ebony hair, was revealed. She had refused to go to the bow, where their makeshift bedroom was, preferring instead to stay near should he need her.

So brave, Tabor thought, looking down at her. *She has a Viking heart.*

Sven was sleeping, as the rest of the crew. Tabor himself felt fatigue pull at his eyelids, but the dull throb in his biceps prevented him from giving in.

Reaching down, he caressed a lock of Tanaka's hair before smoothing it behind her ear so that he could see her face without obstruction.

Sighing sleepily, Tanaka blinked her eyes, rubbed them with the backs of her hands, and looked up at Tabor. When he smiled down at her, she knew immediately that they were out of danger and that his superior skill at the helm of the ship had been the deciding factor.

"How are you?" she asked, getting up on her knees. The bandage at Tabor's arm was dotted with blood that had seeped through, but it was clear that the bleeding had begun and ended long ago.

"Strong. Healthy. How else would a Viking be?"

At that, even Tanaka had to smile. Tabor's Viking

167

pride infuriated her, but there was an indomitable quality to it — and to the man — that was infectious. It drew her in despite her reservations.

She glanced at the rest of the crew. A quick count told her two men had died. She had nursed three others who'd been struck less severely by arrows. The men who had died had unceremoniously been dumped overboard, a Viking tradition during war.

"Where do we go now?" Tanaka asked. She sat next to Tabor, looking into his ruggedly handsome face to search for the truth to his injuries and fatigue. The strain of command pulled at his harshly chiseled features, and she could see that he desperately needed sleep.

"We go south. South until we can become strong once again."

"We could go home," Tanaka suggested.

"Home?"

"My home," Tanaka said. She felt a tightness in her heart. She had not planned to say such a thing, but now that she had put words to her thoughts, she could not turn back. "If we follow the land and keep the shore to this side —" she showed Tabor her right hand "— when sailing past the narrow straits, we will find my home. All of Opar will welcome you."

"Only Viking women welcome Viking men. Strangers all fear us," Tabor replied with what he considered was proof that she was either misguided or openly lying.

"You said once that I was not your slave. If that is true, then should you return me to Opar, you will be a hero. You will be the man who has returned the high priestess to her throne. Here, on your ship,

I am just a woman, a woman of little power—"

"But a woman of great courage," Tabor cut in, remembering how she had braved the rain of arrows to assist his wounded crewmen.

Tanaka blushed briefly, looking away in her embarrassment. It was not easy for her to accept compliments, and she did not really want to remember anything of the night before.

She turned her dark eyes back to Tabor. "In Opar, I am a woman of influence. I can give you anything you want. You and your men can find shelter there. With food and time, you will become handy again. Then, when you fight your enemies, you will fight them with strength, not just with heart."

"And we must only go south?" Tabor asked.

"Until we reach the narrow straits. Then we sail into the morning sun."

"It is as far as Alexandria?" Tabor asked, remembering tales he had heard of a fantastic city.

"Not that far toward the sun in the morning."

Tabor turned partially away from Tanaka, thinking about what she said. He had sailed around the southern tip of Spain before, but when he had, he'd followed land to the north. He had heard of others who followed the land to the south, but he had not done so himself. Tanaka had told him of Opar, but Alexandria was said to be an ancient city of breathtaking wealth and beauty.

Much of what she told him made sense. Tabor knew that he and his men needed rest and food. They had fought all they could. To continue fighting meant death, no matter how strong their Viking will. But if he sailed to Opar, he would be far from any

169

land and peoples he had known. . . . and he would eventually have to leave the Egyptian city to return to his own land—without Tanaka.

"You miss your home?" Tabor asked.

"Greatly."

Tabor looked at her, reaching over to cup her face in his palm. He wished that his arm didn't throb, because that alone kept him from pulling her close. He wanted to feel her body against his own, running his one good hand over her ripe curves. Fatigue and pain. . . . these alone kept him from letting his Viking desires soar.

"Then I will return you to your home. We will pass the cold season together. And when the spring comes and the wind again blows strong and warm from the south, my men and I will return to our own seas. Ingmar and Hugh will then pay dearly for their treachery."

With tears of joy filling her eyes, Tanaka took Tabor's hand in hers and kissed it.

"Thank you! Thank you!" Tanaka sobbed.

Chapter Thirteen

By the end of the second day, when the trailing ships still had not been seen, Tabor announced that the spigots for the wine casks were to be set loose. Tanaka watched with amusement as the Vikings drank with wild abandon. Even Tabor, not yet close to full strength, quaffed the strong, vile wine that he proclaimed was hideous and far below standards for any Danish Viking. Since it was all they had, it would have to do.

"Skoal!" Tabor shouted, raising his drinking horn above his head.

The Vikings repeated the toast in unison, their voices ringing loud and proud. Standing near the bow, his back to the blanket that had been stretched across to give him privacy with Tanaka, Tabor tossed his arm around Tanaka's shoulders. His wine sloshed.

"Our Egyptian high priestess claims that we can find safety and strength in her land," Tabor called out, addressing the men. "She says that in her land, we will know peace, and with that peace, we will recover our strength."

Sven replied, "We are Vikings! We are always strong!"

Tabor smiled in response. He knew that Sven was as aware of their precarious condition as he was. Their numbers were few, and their supply of food could not last forever. Besides, autumn was upon them, and with it, the northern breeze. The Vikings lacked the manpower to row against that wind. In truth, they had little choice but to sail south.

"Even Vikings need time to rest and become whole again." Tabor, a bit drunk, pulled Tanaka in a little more, dwarfing her with his great size. Never before had he shown great affection for a woman in front of his men, and it surprised even him that he could do so. "We sail to Opar. When the spring comes and the wind blows warm from the south, we will be strong again. Then we will hunt down Ingmar the Savage and make him Ingmar the Deceased!"

Another shout roared up from the Vikings. Tanaka saw that many of them were quite drunk, but not Sven, who had taken over for Tabor at the rudder. He alone had refused wine until his turn was over. She noticed, too, that the Vikings all looked at her with new respect now that Tabor had his arm around her shoulders. Although the men were aware that she and Tabor had made love, this easy familiarity — Tabor with his arm around her shoulders — was an intimacy that seemed even more important to the Vikings.

Outside, the wind howled furiously, buffeting the longhouse. Ingmar the Savage smiled. This winter, he would not have to worry about whether Tabor, his lifelong enemy, would attack. At long last, after so many years and countless battles, it appeared that Tabor had finally been defeated.

Though the ships that had been sent to kill Tabor had failed to capture the tall Dane, they had chased him far to the south. Tabor's crew was small, Ingmar had been told—much too small to sail the longboat very far. And since there had been no new word of Tabor and his Vikings, then surely they had suffered a dire fate. That was what Ingmar hoped, though he would have preferred to see Tabor's decapitated head in a sack.

There was, however, one good thing about not knowing whether Tabor was dead or alive. Without any solid confirmation, Ingmar did not have to let his younger brother return. Where exactly Hugh was now, Ingmar could not say for certain, and he wasn't curious enough to find out. In the spring, when the sailing and the raiding and the pillaging would begin again, then he would want Hugh at his side. For now, Ingmar intended to spend the long, cold winter enjoying the three women he had taken into his house, the good wine that was stored up, and the plentiful food that he had stolen.

Tanaka closed the curtain so that she had privacy. She groaned, running her hands up her hair-stubbled legs. She hadn't shaved or waxed since Ingmar had captured her months earlier, and though her body hair did not bother Tabor, it bothered her. She felt unclean, and twice she had asked Tabor to let her use his sharp shaving dagger. But he had refused her permission, saying that she had no need to kill herself.

Leaning back in the blankets that she shared with Tabor, Tanaka closed her eyes and thought about her life on the boat. Things could not remain the same much longer, she knew. The food was plentiful, but water was not. Also, the Viking warriors had been away from women for a long, long time. Neither the respect nor fear they felt for Tabor could keep their eyes from straying toward her when she went about the ship. Even Tabor realized that soon it would be necessary to take the men to land.

It was for that reason that Tanaka stayed in their private bedroom area most of the time. She and Tabor continued to enjoy the pleasures their bodies could give one another, but now Tanaka was careful to never make any noise. She did not want to twist the dagger of desire even more cruelly into Sven and the rest of the Viking crew.

Pulling her knees beneath her, she pushed her hair away from her eyes and looked over the edge of the ship. The arid land, so familiar from her youth, was still to her right, as it had been for days now. The north African coastline had to be followed if she was ever to return to Opar. But how far away was she from home? She had no experience in such matters.

But she did know the spires of Alexandria; and far off, looking like needles pointing upward toward the heavens, she saw the familiar twin spires of her homeland.

"Tabor! Tabor!" she screamed joyously, leaning over the edge of the boat, unconsciously reaching out for her home as though she could grasp it in her hand.

The great Viking jerked the curtain aside with such haste that he ripped it from its moorings. He grabbed Tanaka by the shoulders, turning her to face him, his expression showing the concern he felt.

"Home!" Tanaka shouted. "Tabor, we're home!"

She pulled out of his grasp and pointed at the twin spires. Tabor squinted, then a smile creased his handsome features.

"You are sure?" he asked warily. He knew that the mind could play tricks on people, especially if they've been aboard ship too long.

"I know my home," Tanaka replied without hesitation. She wheeled around to face him; and, even though the crew were all looking at them now that the curtain had been ripped down, she threw her arms around his neck and kissed him fiercely. "Thank you," she said, tears moistening her eyes as she whispered into his ear. "Thank you for taking me home. I promise. . . . I promise you with my heart and soul as high priestess to Pharaoh Moamin Abbakka that I will repay you a thousand fold for what you have done for me."

Tabor chuckled, resisting the urge to let his hands slide downward to cup Tanaka's buttocks. He dared not tempt the discipline of his Vikings unnecessarily.

"I have only done that which is honorable, that which I have promised I would do," Tabor replied, pushing Tanaka away. He felt it wasn't right for a Viking leader to show emotion, particularly not the more gentle emotions, in front of his men.

He turned to Sven. "Prepare the men. I want to be ready for whatever happens."

Instantly, the Vikings began readying their weapons, testing their bows and checking their swords and daggers.

"That won't be necessary," Tanaka said, defensive, fearing the bloodshed of her own people. "You are returning me to my land. My people will not harm you. Oparians are peaceful people."

175

"So you say," Tabor replied, moving toward the stern, determined to be at the rudder when they approached land. "But a Viking cannot trust anyone but himself."

So damn stubborn! Tanaka thought, but she was happy and did not voice her thoughts.

She watched as Tabor took the rudder, his blond hair streaming over his shoulders, blowing in the slight breeze. He had lost some weight since his injury, but his left arm was much better now, though it was still considerably weaker than his right. He no longer was in any danger of getting the sickness in the blood, and for that Tanaka was thankful.

Tanaka had seen violence, and she had no doubts about the Vikings' fighting abilities. She went to Tabor's side. Her hand was light against his arm as she looked up into his brilliant blue eyes, but her face showed deep concern.

"These are my people," Tanaka said, her voice barely above a whisper. "Please. . . . I don't want any fighting. There's been too much of that already."

Tabor placed his hand on her shoulder. "A Viking never wants to fight. Sometimes, he simply has no choice. For you, I will make sure we do all we can to prevent bloodshed."

Tanaka turned away from Tabor. She could now see, far away along the hazy blue shore line, the familiar Egyptian fishing ships. Though she couldn't be sure, it looked like one of those boats, perhaps loaded with soldiers, was being sent out. Her heart constricted as she thought of how good it would be to once again be with people who looked like her and spoke her language, people who shared the same gods. Comparing the size of her kinsmen to the extraordinary size—the height and strength—of the Vikings she had spent too much time with in the past months, Tanaka knew that if the soldiers of Opar ever fought the Vikings, her native people had no chance of surviving.

"Tabor . . . promise me there will be no fighting," Tanaka prodded, determined that nothing would spoil her return.

"I am not good at promising," Tabor replied sharply, distracted. He was counting the arrows in his quiver and making a final check on the notched string of his bow.

"I know you're not good at it, but I want you to promise me anyway."

His eyes narrowed, and Tanaka knew that she had made him angry, but she would not be easily deterred. Tabor and his men would fight and kill if provoked, but they were also barely a handful of men compared to all the strong-willed Egyptian soldiers that Pharaoh Moamin Abbakka could send out. In the end, the death of Tabor was assured, and the thought horrified Tanaka.

After much prodding, Tabor finally turned to Tanaka and said, "We will not fight unless we are forced to fight, woman!"

Tanaka smiled, rose up on her tiptoes to kiss his chin, and moved to the high bow of the boat, where she could hear Sven, Carl, and the other Vikings laughing at the domesticity of the argument and at how she had calmed and cajoled Tabor into saying what she wanted him to.

No boat could approach the harbor without Pharaoh Moamin Abbakka sending defensive ships out to meet it. When the first Egyptian boats met with Tabor's longboat, Tanaka stood at midships and called out to the Egyptian commander.

"I am Tanaka, High Priestess to Pharaoh Moamin Abbakka, High Priestess of Opar," Tanaka called out in Egyptian, standing proud, her ebony waves flowing beautiful and black in striking contrast to the coarse woolen dress of Scandinavian design that Tabor had given her what now seemed long ago. "These men you see me with are heroes! They have saved me from my captors and have returned me to my home!"

The boats were very near, and archers on all sides had arrows notched and ready to fire. Tanaka raised her hands above her head, as though delivering a proclamation from her temple. Her native tongue tasted good on her lips; and, though all the faces she saw were tight-lipped and grim, she was certain that she could avoid bloodshed.

"Speak to me! Tell me of your understanding, and that you will escort your high priestess to Pharaoh Moamin Abbakka."

Standing beside Tanaka, Tabor waited to see how the return of a high priestess would be accepted. Though he had learned many Egyptian words during his time with Tanaka, she spoke the language now so quickly that he understood little of what she said and that disturbed him.

"Will your commander show his face to High Priestess Tanaka? Will he come forth to offer me his protection and loyalty?" Tanaka continued, her dark eyes blazing with the inner fire of conviction.

At last a man moved to midships, to the very edge of the Oparian war vessel. His hair and skin were dark, and he wore the headdress of a leader of men.

"The High Priestess Tanaka was taken long ago,"

he said, but there was clearly doubt in his voice.

"I am that woman," Tanaka replied.

"You say you are that woman. How do I know this is not trickery, magic?"

Tanaka studied the man's features. Sixty feet separated them, and she wished that she could stand face to face with him. Though few subjects of Opar had been close to her, virtually every resident of the city had, at one time or another, attended a celebration in which she had given a proclamation. Even in the enormous city of Alexandria she was known. Had she seen him before?

Looking away from the man, Tanaka gazed at the high twin spires of the temple she loved, at the outline of the city that had been her birthplace. She had been through so much since her initial capture by Ingmar the Savage that she was confident the gods would not destroy her now that she had at last returned home.

"If I am not who I say I am," she said, speaking Egyptian and hoping that Tabor could not understand her words, "then explain how I am able to command these massive, pale-skinned warriors from afar to bring me to my home?"

The Oparian captain pondered the statement. Try as he might, he could find no error in the logic. The foreigners, with their light skin, pale eyes, and yellow hair, were large and fierce-looking. If the woman were not Tanaka, High Priestess for Pharaoh Abbakka, then how could she wield power over such men?

"High Priestess, you have me to command," the soldier said, symbolically tossing his spear to the deck of his boat.

The Egyptians lowered their arrows. Tanaka looked at Tabor and nodded, but he did not signal for his men to lower their drawn bows until she scowled at him.

The moment the Vikings lowered their arrows, a cheer went up among the Egyptians.

"What is it?" Tabor asked, standing at Tanaka's side, his hand protectively placed at the small of her back.

"They are pleased that their spiritual leader has been returned to them," Tanaka explained, her eyes sparkling. "Thank you, Tabor, for bringing me home."

She looked up at Tabor, feeling happier than she could remember being in a long time. However his attention was not on her, but on the city of Opar that they approached. She saw the determined set of his strong jaw, the hawkish line of his nose, the resolution gleaming in his eyes. And she could not help but wonder what changes would occur in their lives when they reached the city.

He would be the outsider, not she. How would Tabor handle that difference? Also, in Opar and Alexandria, she held enormous power. Tabor was an unknown to everyone but his own Vikings. She was home now, in the land she loved, in the city that loved her. What would happen to the man she had shared her body with these many nights? Had her heart, despite its shield, become involved with the rugged Viking with the tender caresses? Had she — and Tanaka really didn't want to think about this — actually fallen in love with Tabor? He had never said a word about the future to her; he had never indicated that she would have a place in his life in the future. But the future was now. The future was the city of Opar, her temple, Pharaoh Moamin Abbakka. But was Tabor, Son of Thor, in her future?

Tabor looked down at Tanaka and saw the concern in her eyes. He put his arm around her shoulders, pulling her against his side.

"Do not be afraid," he said, completely misreading her hesitation. "I will be at your side. No one can harm you as long as I am at your side."

"Then you must stay at my side for all time," Tanaka replied.

She would have felt much more confident if Tabor had said he would. He didn't. He just looked at the approaching city, his palm warm and possessive against her shoulder.

Tabor didn't like it at all. Not one bit. The early warning the city had received from the advance ships that High Priestess Tanaka had been returned to her homeland had prompted a city-wide celebration.

Though he understood Egyptian when Tanaka spoke it to him slowly and carefully, he did not understand a tenth of the words that these people spoke to her. The words jumbled together. And, even more difficult for Tabor, the people of Opar were openly effusive in expressing their appreciation for the return of Tanaka.

Men *hugged* him. But it wasn't until he had bodily lifted one man over his head and threatened to toss him to the ground (Tanaka's timely intrusion into the clash of cultures saved the man from broken bones) that the Egyptians finally realized that no matter how thankful they were that Tabor had sailed from far away to bring High Priestess Tanaka back to them, they must *never* touch his person.

"When we get to the temple, the pharaoh will want to see you immediately," Tanaka said, sitting at Tabor's side in a carriage carried by eight strong men. They made their way through the crowded streets, surrounded by cheering mobs. "He will shower you with riches, I promise."

The wary look in Tabor's eyes disturbed Tanaka's sense of peace. A solitary man who understood his Viking warriors and the privacy of women who desired him, he was emotionally adrift when surrounded by this woman.

"But perhaps you would like to bathe, rest, eat? Would that please you more than to meet Pharaoh Moamin Abbakka?"

Tabor, never overly expressive, gave just the slightest nod of his head. But Tanaka knew what was important to him. "I am concerned for my men. They must be cared for before I can accept comforts for myself."

"They will have the finest foods this land has to offer," Tanaka promised. "Food and drink will be plentiful."

"And they will be safe?"

"Guards will be posted."

Tabor grinned. "My men can guard themselves," he said. "Best you put guards around your most attractive women. Sven and the others . . . they have been away from women for a long time."

Tanaka, as high priestess to the temple, had never any fear that anyone from Opar might force themselves upon her. In her position, she had access to and was indulged by men and women of power and status. She was privy to secrets and even knew of Princess Natankin's clandestine affair with a young guard twenty years her junior. Tanaka believed that as long as neither violence nor the threat of reprisal was involved, the gods did not care who shared pleasure with whom.

"Your men will be taken care of," Tanaka said, deliberately ambiguous.

"Then I will accept your hospitality," Tabor said finally.

Tanaka controlled the urge to take his hand. It would be inappropriate for a high priestess to hold hands in public. Her concern for Tabor's well being surprised her. Since he had recovered from his nearly fatal wounds, everything about him seemed invincible. Now, in a strange, foreign land, he had only a few of his Viking warriors at hand. And although he towered over a sea of dark-haired dark-skinned people, he seemed lost. No amount of iron-hard resolve could hide the faintly haunted look in the depths of his sea-blue eyes.

When they reached the quarters in the temple where Tabor would stay while in Opar, he was rendered speechless. Though a wealthy man by Viking standards, nothing that he had in Denmark could compare to the extraordinary wealth of Pharaoh Moamin Abbakka.

"It is . . . amazing," he whispered, looking at the high-ceilinged room with its ornately woven rugs, plush fabric bed, and personal bathtub.

Tabor was particularly perplexed by the tub, which was sunken into the rock floor of the room.

"How does it become empty? It would take many servants many trips with a bucket."

Tanaka smiled, walking down the steps that led into the deep enclosure. She felt a flush of pride in her culture and in the palace she called home.

"See?" she said, pulling out the leather-wrapped stopper at the lowest point on the stone floor. "The wa-

183

ter drains out there."

"And where does it go?" Tabor asked, genuinely amazed at such an invention.

"Beneath the stone floor there are small channels for water. The water runs beneath the floor. I suppose it goes outside the palace walls, though I'm not certain exactly where."

Tabor smiled. "There is much that I can learn while I am here."

Tanaka returned his smile. She was enormously pleased at how readily Tabor accepted new ways. If he let his Viking pride flare, it could cause problems for everyone in the palace. No matter how strong and powerful Tabor, Son of Thor, was, he wasn't in his Scandinavian waters now. He was on land, in the palace of the pharaoh; and if he thought the pharaoh wasn't a powerful man, he was absurdly, even suicidally, mistaken.

Tanaka reached up for Tabor's hand, letting him help her as she ascended out of the tub. When she was on the floor again, she tried to slip her hand away, but his fingers tightened around hers. When her questioning eyes met his, she recognized instantly the romantic gleam.

"Not now," Tanaka said quietly, aware that servants had been dashing about the palace, making sure the Viking guests were treated like heroes.

"Why not now?" Tabor teased, pulling her to him, locking his hands together at the small of her back. "I have brought you home. Isn't that cause enough for celebration?"

He tried to kiss her, but she twisted in his grasp, avoiding his lips. "Yes," she said nervously. "It is a time for celebration, and I would love to share that celebration with you, but right now I must see Pharaoh Abbakka. There are many questions he has for me." With some effort, Tanaka slipped from Tabor's grasp. She saw that he was disappointed, but not defeated. "Be patient."

"Patience is not a Viking tradition."

At that moment, four of the most beautiful servants among the dozens at the palace stepped into the room. Their dark hair was unbound, falling in glistening waves almost to their slender waists. They stood shoulder-to-shoulder, all wearing identical, sheer bustwraps and leggings that left little of their figures to the imagination. It shocked Tanaka when she realized that her first emotion upon seeing the attractive young servants was jealousy. She instantly chastised herself, but the feeling persisted, particularly when she glanced at Tabor and saw that he had noticed their beauty as quickly as she had.

"Tabor," Tanaka said, whispering now so that the young women would not hear, "if you are patient and wait for me to return to you, I promise you, you'll be happily rewarded."

Tabor, aware of Tanaka's unease, felt not in the least inclined to lessen her fears. He let his gaze slide quickly back to the servants who awaited orders.

"I am not a patient man," Tabor said.

Anger now mingled with jealousy inside Tanaka. The servants were all freshly bathed, shaven, beautifully clothed, their hair brushed to a glossy sheen. In comparison, she felt unwashed, her legs and underarms scratchy with a stubbly growth of hair. She was certain the servants had been given the order to provide Tabor with whatever entertainments he might request; and, for the first time in her life, Tanaka

185

questioned the usefulness of having so many servants at the palace.

"*Be* patient," Tanaka said again, a sharp edge to her tone, her dark eyes holding a flame that could burn with passion or resentment.

"Only if you promise me that you will hurry back," Tabor said at last, giving Tanaka a smile that said he was only teasing.

Tanaka felt a warm, melting sensation, an anticipatory feeling that she had come to know well during her days and nights aboard the Viking longboat.

Though the servants walked about the room, preparing the bath for Tabor, Tanaka rose up on her tiptoes and quickly kissed him on the mouth.

"I will hurry," she said, then whisked out of the room without a backward glance. She would see the people she needed to, bath and shave and go through a proper Egyptian toilet, and then return to the much too powerful, far too alluring, and much, much, much too exciting Viking warrior.

Chapter Fourteen

Tabor was too well aware of women not to understand the covetous glances he received from the four thinly clad servants. Although the diaphanous cloth hid the body, it did nothing to hide the tempting shapes beneath. And they were all beautiful and young, although none could compare with the high priestess, Tanaka.

He smiled, watching the women as they scurried about the room, accompanied by short, powerfully-built men who carried huge buckets of steaming water for the bath.

How long had it been since he'd enjoyed a hot bath? In his Viking homeland, baths were a ritual, but only during the worst weather did anyone ever heat the bath water. That would be unmanly. But to not bathe was equally inappropriate, so the Vikings frequently cleansed themselves in water that left their flesh pinkish white and numb and their jaws clamped shut so their teeth would not chatter.

But, when it was possible, there were few pleasures more appreciated than a hot bath with a good bar of soap . . . and, should the high priestess Tanaka return (Tabor had begun to think of her in terms of her formal title, now that he had witnessed the power she wielded in Egypt), he'd have a good and passionate woman to make the water even hotter.

So dark and petite, Tabor thought, looking at a small-featured servant who twice now had brushed against his arm as she hurried past him while readying his room. *Eyes like midnight on the open sea.*

The servant, perhaps younger than Tanaka, met Tabor's stare. Her smile was fleeting, and as she lowered her eyes, she gazed on his chest.

The other women noticed the flirtation and began to make comments. Tabor could not understand their Egyptian, but he was not sure if it was because they spoke so quickly or if they were speaking another dialect.

As soon as the bath was prepared, the men left the room, and with the daintiest of shrugs of small shoulders, the four women slipped out of their blousings. Naked from the waist up, their small breasts pert, lush, and inviting, they stood at the four corners of the sunken tub, now steaming with scented and soapy water, and indicated Tabor was to enter. They would bathe him, it was clear . . . and probably do anything else to and for him that he wanted, the language barrier not being much of an impediment.

"First, I must see to it that my men are well cared for," Tabor said in his gravelly tone, by no means immune to the charms of the young servants who, evidently, were his for the taking. "I shouldn't be gone too long."

He left the room, feeling strange. He knew he had taken the proper course of action by leaving them when he had, but the notion of Tabor, Son of Thor, walking out of a room containing four beautiful, bare-breasted young women did a disservice to his name, his reputation . . . and also played havoc with his senses!

The room closest to his was now occupied by Sven and Carl. Though he had not noticed it before, Tabor realized that there were very few doors in the palace. The doorways were covered by woven rugs of brilliant color, and though this did provide visual privacy, it did little to keep sound out or in.

He eased aside the doorway curtain. Sven sat in a tub of some sort—it looked to Tabor like a huge stew bucket that was used for gatherings, where enough stew could be made at one time to serve three hundred people. A young woman was trying to wash Sven's back, a task made difficult both by his amorous movements and because she was sitting in the tub facing him. Her giggles and his soft laughter told Tabor that the two were understanding each other quite well.

Carl was on a mound of pillows, his head in the lap of a young woman who fed him grapes slowly, sensually, one at a time.

Tabor turned away from the curtain, a smile curling his mouth. His officers were well cared for, he knew. Now he had to find out about the rest of his Vikings, then he could return to the hot bath and the four women that awaited him.

Sometimes, a Viking likes to test his willpower, and the four servants—combined with his own imagination and the possibilities for pleasure that he imagined—provided a test that Thor himself might be unable to resist.

Tanaka felt a jarring rush of fear as she approached

Pharaoh Moamin Abbakka's private quarters in the palace. A ridiculous fear, because the pharaoh had made it clear that she was second only to Neenah, his wife. But Tanaka had not seen Abbakka in many months, and she could not help worrying that she might somehow have fallen out of favor.

Total and complete power rested solely in Abbakka's hands, and Tanaka felt a twinge of apprehension. If they ever had a disagreement, there would be no one whom Tanaka could turn to, for in Opar, there was no higher power than Abbakka.

She lingered in the hallway, smelling the familiar scent of her palace home with its marble walls and stone floors, its bowls of dates displayed where hungry wanderers through the corridors could stop to nibble or sip a goblet of the hearty wine that the good Pharaoh Abbakka was so proud of. Dignitaries visited the palace just for a taste of the wine produced by Abbakka's people.

The presence of so many servants and guards surrounding the entranceway to the west wing of the palace signified to Tanaka that Abbakka and his wife, Neenah, were awaiting her.

The guards saw Tanaka approach, and they snapped to their best military posture, but as she drew nearer, she saw concern in their eyes. And sympathy.

Tanaka stopped at the doorway to Abbakka's spacious quarters. She looked up at one of the guards and asked quietly, "There is sadness in your eyes. Why is that, soldier? Are you not pleased that your high priestess has returned?"

The young man's knuckles were white as he squeezed the handle of his battle-axe even tighter. "It is not displeasure at seeing you again, high priestess,

190

that makes me sad. If I could, I would gladly have traded places with you so that you would never have known a moment's discomfort."

Tanaka felt a tightness in her chest again, and she had to blink away the crystal tears that filled her eyes. She was home with her people—home at last!—and they were happy to have her back. The guard's declaration, she knew, was not mere boasting. She was the spiritual leader for Pharaoh Moamin Abbakka and all who resided in his palace and lived under his rule in Opar, and as their spiritual leader her return meant much more than just the return of a kidnapped woman to her home.

"You are a good and loyal man," Tanaka said quietly. She raised her hand, pressing her palm flat against his chest, over his heart. "Your heart beats with loyal blood. Such loyalty will be rewarded, either on earth or in heaven, or, more likely, in both places."

The guard's smile was such a beam of pure pleasure that Tanaka had to resist patting him on the cheek as she would a young boy.

But Tanaka's happiness vanished the moment she stepped into Pharaoh Abbakka's quarters and saw Priest Kahlid standing near the pharaoh's chair.

For years, Kahlid had been able to hide his scorn for Tanaka, though many people were aware of his resentment. Pharaoh Abbakka had slighted the spiritual guide Kahlid in choosing Tanaka to be his high priestess. Though Kahlid always showed Pharaoh Abbakka a smile and claimed he did not mind being a mere priest to Tanaka's exalted position of high priestess, Tanaka had never believed it.

"She is back!" Kahlid said when she entered the room.

Pharaoh Abbakka burst from his huge, ornately carved chair, his purple robes fluttering. He rushed to her, taking her by the shoulders to examine her at arm's distance.

"You are well?" he asked, honest emotion tightening his throat and filling his voice.

Tanaka nodded. It was always awe-inspiring whenever the pharaoh deigned to show his feelings, and by looking into his face she could tell that he had missed her greatly and that she was being welcomed back into his palace with open arms.

"Neenah and I . . . there has been a hole in our lives, an emptiness in our hearts, since you've been away. We prayed for your safe return . . . but it was difficult . . . so difficult to pray without the one who understands such matters the most."

In formal fashion, Tanaka and Abbakka greeted each other as protocol dictated, with Tanaka kneeling and kissing the back of Pharaoh Moamin Abbakka's hands, signifying her loyalty to him as pharaoh. Then Abbakka bowed and kissed Tanaka's open palms, signifying his respect for her as high priestess.

When they stood again facing each other, Neenah and Kahlid stood on either side of Abbakka.

"I thought of you constantly while you were away," Neenah said softly, her eyes glistening with tears.

It took all of Tanaka's strength to keep her tears in check. In many ways, Neenah had been a surrogate mother or aunt for Tanaka, and though their positions in life were vastly different, it had never seemed to make any difference to them.

"I thought of you, too," Tanaka replied, then kissed the backs of Neenah's hands.

The warmth of the greeting ended abruptly when

Tanaka was forced to acknowledge Kahlid's presence. She had always loathed the man. He used spirituality as a tool to worm his way into the hierarchy of the palace, and Tanaka hoped that Abbakka had seen through Kahlid's mendacity. Perhaps that was why he had chosen her over the older and more experienced man to be the chief spiritual guide for the palace, though it was disconcerting to her to see that Kahlid still held great power in the palace of Opar.

Neenah, however, believed deeply in Kahlid's spirituality, which she called a gift from the heavens. Neenah, unlike her pharaoh husband, was extraordinarily gentle-hearted. She could not believe that anyone would smile at her and then lie. Her sheltered existence as Abbakka's beloved wife insulated her from most of the dangers in the world . . . except from men like Priest Kahlid.

"It is good to see you again," Kahlid said, smiling.

The proof of his danger, Tanaka thought, *is that he sounds sincere.* Only his eyes, that window to his dark and deadly soul, revealed that he was not truly happy with her return. Tanaka looked at him, but said nothing.

"Kahlid has been the spiritual leader for this palace in your absence," Abbakka said. "But now that you have returned, after you have rested and fully recovered your strength and spirit, then you will resume your position as high priestess."

"I need only recover my strength," Tanaka replied quickly. "My spirit is undiminished."

The rage flamed only for an instant in Kahlid's eyes, and it was invisible to everyone but Tanaka. But she had seen it, and there was no mistaking that Kahlid was not pleased about relinquishing the position of High Priest which he had coveted for so long.

"Yes, that sounds wonderful," Kahlid said, his smile broadening to amazing proportions. "It is good that this . . . *unfortunate* business is in the past."

Tanaka looked straight into Kahlid's eyes, but she could not see into his soul now. He was protecting himself, hiding his innermost feelings. She had not thought it was truly possible for her to hate any man who had not actually committed an act of violence upon her, but as she looked at Kahlid, she realized she had that capacity.

"You won't mind giving up your position?" Tanaka asked innocently, again staring intently into his eyes, testing his skill as a liar.

With a casual shrug, Kahlid replied, "Of course not! The sooner you resume your rightful place, the happier all of us will be. It is not right when the world and its people are not in balance."

Neenah piped in, "There! Now that that is settled, I think a feast is in order! A huge festival so that all the people can celebrate Tanaka's joyous return with us!"

Abbakka smiled warmly, first at his wife, then at Tanaka. "She's right. You're as important and loved by the people as you are loved by us. They'll all want to see you." Abbakka's gaze went up and down Tanaka briefly, sadness had etched lines in his gaunt, wise face. "We will swathe you in the finest clothes in all the lands," he continued, his tone soft and sincere, his voice almost prayerful. "You shall be treated with the respect befitting the high priestess that you are."

"Thank you," Tanaka replied.

Kahlid said, "Yes, I'm sure you will be happy to be suitably attired after your . . . *ordeal*." He drew the word out slowly, making it slightly obscene, as though he could not only imagine the horrors that Tanaka had

194

endured aboard Ingmar the Savage's boat but also wished that he could have seen those horrors with his own eyes.

He's happy that horrible things happened to me, Tanaka thought in a flash of intuition. It had never occurred to her before that someone from her own palace would be pleased that she had been kidnapped and treated hideously. *He wants to know all the gory details.*

The realization sickened Tanaka.

"I have summoned extra servants for you," Neenah said. She took a half-step closer and whispered. "If there's anything more you need, just tell them. They know you're to be given anything you want."

It was a superfluous order, since as high priestess there weren't many things that were beyond Tanaka's authority to demand, but she appreciated the intent nevertheless.

"Thank you," Tanaka said, then excused herself, happy to leave the disquieting aura of Kahlid and anxious to return to Tabor. She would show herself to him as a high priestess in her own palace, and then she would joyously give herself to the powerful Viking warrior who had saved her life.

"The wench! The swine! I wish she'd been dragged through the rivers of hell and raped by jackals!" Kahlid hissed, his hands balled into fists of impotent fury.

"We'll think of something to be rid of her," Lysetta said, reclining on Kahlid's bed.

She watched her lover pacing his room, and she wondered whether he would want her soon. Often, his rage triggered a sexual impulse in him, and he always took it out on her. She didn't mind all that much, though she wasn't in any real mood to feel him sweating upon her as he thrust into her with the anger of a madman wielding a dagger instead of a phallus.

"Abbakka made it clear that she's the high priestess once again. He made that *very* clear!"

"Abbakka can change his mind."

Kahlid wheeled to face Lysetta, his eyes ablaze with a murderous fire. "Not Abbakka! Once he makes up his mind, nothing changes it!"

Lysetta realized that arguing with Kahlid when he was in such a state would accomplish nothing worthwhile and it might just get her slapped. He did that sometimes when he was really mad and he couldn't see any other way out of an argument. She raised a hand, crooking a finger for him to come closer.

"I know just what you need to clear your head," she whispered in a husky purr. "Just what will set your mind at ease."

She had not realized how distraught Kahlid was until he turned down her invitation with a distracted wave of his hand. The thought of Kahlid not wanting sexual release, especially when he was this agitated, frightened Lysetta. She sat up straighter on the bed, moving a pillow behind her back so that she could lean comfortably against the wall.

"She must be stopped," Lysetta said, her dark eyes taking on a distant quality as she began plotting Tanaka's ruin. "We've worked too hard to get this close to Pharaoh Abbakka to let that girl cast us aside now."

"But how . . . when every time Abbakka looks at her, he sees a high priestess who speaks to the gods and gets answers from them?"

Lysetta smiled suddenly, and there was a sensual glint in her eyes when she looked at Kahlid. "Do you think she's got feelings for that man who brought her back — that barbarian?"

Kahlid's eyes narrowed with uncertainty and suspicion. "The Viking? I can't imagine her finding anything appealing about him. A massive creature, from what I've been told. His eyes are the color of the sea. Strange . . . how very strange that must be."

"What if I should become . . . acquainted with the Viking?" Lysetta postulated, thinking aloud, formulating the plan as she spoke. "And what if Tanaka really does have feelings for the Viking. Then surely that could prove to Pharaoh Abbakka that Tanaka isn't everything he thinks she is. If she suffered from the mortal failings of jealousy, lust, greed, hatred . . ."

Kahlid scowled. "Abbakka knows that you and I share a bed! He knows everything! What difference does it make to him if she sleeps with the barbarian?"

"It is acceptable for you to have me as a lover," Lysetta continued, her tone growing increasingly confident. "You're a man, after all, and having a lover, or even several lovers, is acceptable for a man, especially a man of your power. But what about a woman, Kahlid? Do you think that Abbakka would turn a blind eye to Tanaka's indiscretions as easily as he would to yours?" Lysetta laughed throatily. Her mind, was deeply sensual and faintly cruel. "And if the people knew their high priestess was spreading her legs for a barbarian! . . . what kind of slovenly harlot would do that? Surely not a high priestess worth respect. And what would the wagging tongues say if Tanaka argued with me about my relationship with the barbarian? What then, Kahlid, would Pharaoh Abbakka say?"

Kahlid looked at Lysetta, eyebrows raised quizzically. "You would go to bed with the barbarian for me?"

Lysetta grinned wickedly, shaking her head. "No, darling, I would go to bed with the blond barbarian for *us*. I don't intend to be a harlot my whole life. When you are High Priest to Pharaoh Abbakka, then I am someone special within the walls of this palace. When you are only a priest, then I am only a whore."

Kahlid nodded in understanding, not even feeling a twinge of jealousy at the thought of Lysetta having sex with the Viking. He resumed his pacing, turning her plot to discredit Tanaka over in his mind.

From every angle, it looked like a solid plan. But what he did not realize was that Lysetta was equally as interested in discovering what it would feel like to have the strong Viking making love to her as she was in seeing to it that Tanaka did not ascend to her former place of stature within the palace.

"You were destined to be with me," Kahlid said quietly, his thoughts far away as he planned the outrage he would display when he "discovered" that Tanaka, the Viking, and his own mistress, Lysetta, were all involved in an utterly immoral triangle of deception and debauchery.

He hardly heard Lysetta leave the room.

Chapter Fifteen

Tanaka's living quarters had not been altered since her kidnap by Ingmar a season earlier.

Had it actually been just that summer? Only a few desperate months that she had been gone from this room, she thought, standing in the doorway to her chambers?

The familiar sights of her quarters almost made her cry. Almost, but not quite. She had been riding such an emotional boat tossed about on stormy seas since her return home that it seemed she was always on the verge of tears, and that simply wouldn't do. She saw herself as a woman with vast reserves of inner strength.

"You remember?" the servant, Habibah, asked.

Tanaka glanced at the girl. Habibah was several years younger than Tanaka and had lived in the palace all her life. Tanaka had always liked her, and the look of concern on Habibah's face told the high priestess that she had at least one servant who was loyal and honestly pleased to have the high priestess return to the palace.

"Of course I remember," Tanaka answered softly, stepping into the huge, open room that had been her living quarters since childhood. The room itself was massive, measuring sixty square feet. The bathing area was the second largest in the palace — second only to the pharaoh's. Various sections of the room were separated by ornately woven rugs and fine silks brought in from Persia, gifts from Neenah.

"We haven't quite finished preparing it for you yet," Habibah said, dutifully following her mistress one step behind and just to the right.

Women of all ages scurried about the room, straightening a pillow here, adding fresh water to a pitcher there. Since men weren't allowed in the chambers of a high priestess, filling the tub with water required two women to carry each bucket instead of one man.

"That's no matter," Tanaka replied, walking to the area holding plush, interwoven blankets. She had slept almost every night of her life upon that mattress of blankets. "I'm just happy to be home."

All her life she had been attended to by a dozen servants, so Tanaka was not overly modest about removing her clothes in front of the women. She sighed softly, pleased to be among her own things, and pulled the coarse woolen dress that Tabor had given her over her head. She dropped the Scandinavian garment to the floor with a dismissive groan. She never wanted to see the garment again. Next came the underdress, which she cast aside with equal disdain. Naked, she crossed to the bath, which was nearly filled.

"How have you been in my absence?" Tanaka asked, descending the steps into the tub. Habibah, she recalled, had been casting glances at a certain young military officer in the pharaoh's army when last they'd spoken.

The water was steaming and scented, almost waist deep, and absolutely heavenly. Tanaka turned to look at Habibah, who hadn't yet entered the bath, and she saw that tears trickled down the servant's cheeks.

"Have I said something wrong?" Tanaka asked, approaching her young friend. "Has the officer been hurt?"

"No, high priestess, the officer has not been hurt," Habibah answered, wiping the tears quickly away. A small gathering of servants had surrounded the bath, and all of them looked upon Tanaka with sympathy. "It is you that I cry for. You have experienced so much, and yet you worry about my heart."

Habibah stripped out of her clothes and entered the bath so that she could wash Tanaka's back and hair.

It wasn't until Tanaka had seen her loyal servant without the usual diaphanous servant's clothes that she realized why all the women were looking at her so carefully, and with such concern. Habibah, like all the others, was carefully shaven and waxed, hair removed, as fashion and the Egyptian sense of cleanliness dictated. Tanaka's body hair, to the women who were her servants, spoke silently and eloquently of hardships they could only imagine.

"Do not cry for me," Tanaka said, looking straight into Habibah's eyes as she spoke, though the words were intended for all of the women in the room. "I have been returned to my home, to the people I love, to the people who love me. I stand before you now as your high priestess, taking my rightful place among my people. There will be no sadness for me. I so decree it."

A decree from a high priestess had to be taken with the utmost sincerity. The servants continued readying Tanaka's living quarters while Habibah, immersed in the five-foot-square bath with Tanaka, washed the Oparian spiritual leader's hair as other servants continued to bring in fresh buckets of steaming water.

The warm, soapy water scented with a jubaleen herb made her skin and hair feel fresh and so soft. Habibah washed Tanaka's long, thick hair, then slowly and carefully brushed it free of tangles. Everything was exactly as she remembered. She had dreamed of these pleasures while she'd been Ingmar's captive. And when Tanaka was given a razor while she sat in the bath, the high priestess sighed with happiness, nearly finished with all that she had to do, knowing that soon she would return to Tabor and at last be able to show herself to him as a confident high priestess, not as a slave or captive.

"Is the wax being readied?" Tanaka asked, inspecting the edge on the razor and finding it satisfactory.

"Yes, priestess," Habibah replied, running a brush through Tanaka's curls. She was pleased with the delicate work she had made of cleansing and brushing Tanaka's hair, very rarely allowing the strands to tug even lightly against her scalp.

"Fine. Now why don't you tell me about that soldier? The officer who had caught your fancy, as I recall," Tanaka said, raising her leg above the steaming surface of the water and working up a thick layer of scented lather with the bar of soap.

Elsewhere in the palace, the occupant of another steaming bath was smiling and finding it particularly pleasant that the Egyptians took as much pride and pleasure in the production of beer as the Scandinavians did. He drank heartily from a gold goblet; and each time he brought the goblet away from his mouth, a young, bare-breasted servant quickly refilled it from a large urn.

"You are sure there is nothing . . . more . . . we can do for you?" a servant asked, kneeling at the side of the tub near Tabor's shoulder. She could not imagine the high priestess succumbing to desire, and consequently never dreamed she might be intruding with a subtle, sexual invitation to the big foreigner with the most beautiful blue eyes she had ever seen.

He looked up at her, understanding most of the words she'd spoken. But when he looked into her eyes, whatever words he did not quite understand were easily translated when she glanced into the steaming water and smiled.

"No, nothing more," Tabor replied, wishing now that he'd paid as much attention to learning Tanaka's language as she had to learning his.

He leaned his head back against the edge of the bath, closing his eyes. A moment later gentle hands carefully lifted his head, then lowered it back down again upon a pillow.

"That should be more comfortable," a rich, feminine voice said.

Tabor opened his eyes, looking straight up at a woman he had not seen before. His first reaction was one of anger, though no one would be aware of this, since his expression did not change at all. It infuriated him that someone had entered the room without his hearing her.

She smiled down at him. The servants who had

been assigned by the pharaoh to stay with Tabor were moving quickly from the room.

"I don't think you'll need those young girls any longer . . . now that I'm here." She knelt near Tabor's elbow, taking the goblet from his hand. There was amusement in her eyes as she sipped the brew, eying him over the golden rim. "A woman is not supposed to drink spirits. But then, a woman is not to be taught anything other than how to care for a man. I am not a usual woman. I have been taught many things." She smiled wickedly. "Some more interesting than others."

Tabor could not keep the smile from his lips. He understood every word she'd spoken, and now realized that he had the most trouble with the native language when it was spoken by someone who had not been given a formal education as Tanaka and this woman obviously had.

This siren who'd entered his quarters was past thirty, he guessed, was exceptionally attractive, and carried herself with a confident poise that was both shocking and stimulating. There was an openness to her sensuality that far exceeded that of the servants who'd been all but throwing themselves at Tabor since he'd been left alone with them, but the openness was tempered and heightened by her lack of haste. It was as though this strange, enigmatic woman had made a decision that affected Tabor greatly and had confidence that her plans wouldn't fail.

"You are — ?" Tabor asked, quite suddenly wondering what she would think of him as he struggled to pronounce the words as Tanaka had taught him.

"Lysetta." With the back of her hand, she wiped water from Tabor's shoulder. "I live in the palace."

"Are you a high priestess, like Tanaka?"

Lysetta's eyes hardened for a second at the sound of the name, but they softened just as quickly. "No. A pharaoh has but one high priest or priestess. I live in the palace, that is all."

"Then you do nothing?"

She understood that Tabor did not intend insult with his choice of words in the foreign tongue. "I do *everything*," she corrected, a sultry purr to her tone as she began connecting drops of water on Tabor's thickly muscled shoulder. "I always have."

Watching her hand moving along Tabor's right biceps, Lysetta could not help but think that he must surely be the strongest man in the world. There was a devilish, evil quality to Kahlid that Lysetta had always found fascinating and exciting; Tabor had a raw, animal magnetism. It drew her to him. Even if she had no ulterior motives for seducing Tabor, she would have wanted him in her bed. On a purely physical level, she had never seen such a man, and her active and erotic imagination was already conjuring up scenarios of the pleasure that would be hers to revel in while he labored above her, giving himself to her for her pleasure.

"If you would like to come out of the water, I can show you what . . . *everything* involves," Lysetta said softly, her gaze locking his with challenge and promise. "Or, if you prefer, I will enter the water with you."

Her gaze shifted from Tabor to the soapy water. She wished that the soap hadn't been lathered so thickly, making it impossible for her to see deeper into the water. An explicit mental image of Tabor flashed in her brain, and she shivered with imaginary satisfaction.

Several seconds passed and neither one said a word. Tabor looked at Lysetta. He wanted her. Though she was a decade older than the nubile, naked servants who had crowded his chambers earlier, she represented a much greater threat to his willpower and to the promise he had given Tanaka.

"I'll take no answer at all to mean yes," Lysetta said with the simple, self-serving logic which had served her well all her life.

Tabor slipped away from the edge of the bath, moving to the center, knowing he should tell this seductress that she must leave, knowing, too, that he was curious to see how far she would go and that he wanted her to stay . . . at least until he had a look at what she was offering. Looking isn't the same as touching, he told himself, and thinking isn't the same as acting.

She stood slowly, her dark eyes pleased. The garment she wore, a shimmering silk robe dyed the color of rubies and emerald, signified her wealth and station. Her education and bearing told Tabor that Lysetta was a force within the palace, even if she did "nothing" and "everything" at the same time.

Lysetta loosened the small knot at her left shoulder. Her robe fell to the sash at the curve of her hips. Her breasts were rich, lush mounds that gripped Tabor with invisible tentacles, though his connoisseur's eyes told him that her breasts were neither as high, nor as round and firm, as Tanaka's.

"You needn't go any further than that!" Tanaka snapped, striding angrily into the room in a flurry of white silk robes that fluttered about her legs like the wings of some angry dove. "No answer does not necessarily mean yes with every man in this palace."

Tanaka stood at the edge of the bath, more furious than she could ever remember being, wishing more than anything else in the world that she could be as calm and aloof as she had been when she noticed Tabor's eyes straying toward the servants.

"Hello, Tanaka," Lysetta said quietly. She intentionally avoided using Tanaka's title. She made no effort to hide her breasts. "I didn't expect to see you here."

"Obviously," Tanaka shot back. She glanced down at Tabor, who was now leaning back against the opposite side of the bath, the gold, beer-filled goblet still in his hand. He looked like he was anticipating a sporting event, and Tanaka's anger flared even hotter.

Turning away from the high priestess, Lysetta gave Tabor one final look at her breasts before readjusting her robe. "Perhaps we can speak more later," she said to Tabor. "Sooner or later, Tanaka won't be around to disturb us, and then we can get to know each other much better."

"Get out of here." Tanaka pointed a trembling finger at the doorway.

Lysetta walked from the room, her head held high. She had flustered Tanaka, which was a significant accomplishment; and she had learned that, no matter what Tanaka said to the contrary, she harbored powerful emotions for the tall barbarian from across the seas. It would be doubly sweet, Lysetta thought, to seduce Tabor, injure Tanaka in the process, and watch the high priestess fall from grace.

As she made her way down the hall, ignoring the frightened faces of the palace servants she passed, Lysetta smiled confidently, feeling superior because she knew that unlike Tanaka, she had no emotions, no love, and no remorse, to get in the way of her plans for the future.

The depths of the hurt that Tanaka felt could not be

207

exaggerated. She had hoped so much that her return to Tabor's quarters would be joyous. She had wanted to please him, but instead had found him ogling Lysetta, a serpent of a woman.

And — worst of all — Tabor had enjoyed the argument she'd had with Lysetta. A smugness in his expression told her he would enjoy seeing who was the victor in this fight for his attention.

"You are mistaken," Tabor said, still leaning against the wall of the bath.

"I know what I saw. My eyes do not deceive me."

"It is not what you saw that deceives you. It is what you think."

Tanaka didn't want to ask another question. Tabor was too smooth with his words, even in a foreign tongue, too quick with explanations that made sense at the time they were given, for her to want to ask. But, as so often was the case when she was near Tabor, she did what she promised herself she would not do.

"How does my thinking deceive me?"

"You think that I would have taken her into my arms, into my bed. That is how you are deceived. She showed herself to me. I did not turn my eyes away, just as I did not turn my eyes away from the young servants who were in my quarters." Tabor paused to sip his beer, but he did not take his gaze away from Tanaka's, holding her in place through the sheer, immutable force of his will. "If I told you that I do not enjoy looking at pretty women, I would lie, and you would know it to be a lie, since you are a pretty woman . . . the most beautiful of all." He smiled then, showing even white teeth and an easy, facile charm, the charm of a man who had soothed the battered egos of many women who were angry with him for showing attention to others. "And since you are the prettiest of all, I enjoy looking at you most of all."

"Do not trick me," Tanaka said, her voice a tangled whisper of confusion and conflict.

A moment earlier she had been furious with Tabor for having destroyed the entrance into his chambers that she had wanted to make. She had imagined the look of pleasure that would be in his eyes when he saw her in the sartorial finery of high priestess. Now, despite his enormously inappropriate conduct with a woman Tanaka loathed, she was unable to maintain the grasp she'd had on her fury.

"After all we have been through, Tanaka, and still you accuse me of trickery. What have I done to make you so distrustful?"

"You were looking at her."

"And that surprises you?"

"No."

"Then why this anger?"

Tanaka huffed with indignation. Why had she ever thought that this man—this maurading Viking barbarian—was capable of feeling? It infuriated her that he wasn't apologetic. In fact was behaving as though *she* were the one acting inappropriately.

"I expected you to look at a serpent like Lysetta," Tanaka said at length. "I had hoped, however, that you wouldn't." She cast Tabor a withering, condescending look. "Obviously, I was hoping for more than you are capable of."

It was not a taunt that Tabor could let pass. He set the gold goblet upon the edge of the bath and began to rise, and Tanaka immediately took a step away from him.

209

"What are you doing?"

"You question what I am capable of," he explained calmly, moving toward Tanaka's side of the tub, his lower body still hidden beneath the soap bubbles. "I intend to show you."

"No, you won't."

"Yes, I will."

"I don't want you to."

Tanaka turned her back to Tabor when he placed his hands on the edge of the bath, about to lift himself out. She had seen him before, of course — many times. But she did not want to look at him now because she was angry with him and she wanted to continue being angry with him. If she gave him half a chance, or loosened the feverish hold she had on her anger even the slightest, or let her body do her thinking for her, then she would forget about the anger that justifiably bloomed in her breast.

She heard the splash of water as he lifted himself from the bath, then the splatter of drops upon the smooth stone floor.

"This isn't what I wanted," Tanaka whispered.

There was something in the tone of her voice that stopped Tabor. Rather than placing his wet hands upon her shoulders to push aside the silk gown she wore, he picked up a large, square cloth that had been laid out by the servants for him to dry himself with. He wiped his hands dry, then carefully pushed her ebony hair away from the base of her neck before kissing her there.

"What did you want? Tell me, and I will make it so," he said, momentarily forgetting that he was in Egypt and that *she* was the one who had the power to change the surroundings, not he.

"I wanted . . ." Tanaka began, then her words died away.

It was futile, she told herself, to try to explain anything to Tabor. He understood fighting and warfare, it was true, and he understood how to give a woman pleasure when he touched her. He knew how to make a woman feel as though she alone held the secrets to truth and beauty within her honorable soul. But what Tabor was utterly and completely incapable of understanding was that there were times when a woman was not confident in herself. A lack of confidence was as foreign to Tabor as the land he now stood upon.

"What did you want?" Tabor asked, his tone deep, husky, his breath warm against the back of Tanaka's neck.

"I wanted to make this special for you," Tanaka continued, disappointed that she had to put to words her wishes. She'd much rather Tabor simply, magically, understand. "Special for both of us. I feel. . . . I feel pretty. I finally feel—after *so* long—like I *want* to feel, Tabor."

"For the first time since you were captured," Tabor said, wondering if it would even be right for him to remind Tanaka of that episode in her life.

"Yes."

"I have told you many times that you are beautiful."

Tanaka turned slowly, but she made a point of keeping her eyes upward so that she wouldn't be too greatly affected by Tabor's nudity. She looked into his eyes, once again aware of how enormously different they were.

"Your telling me that I am beautiful is not the same as my believing that I am beautiful, feeling that I am beautiful . . . feeling it in my heart."

"Now I understand," Tabor said.

But Tanaka was not so sure. Tabor was a man of rough edges and lethally-honed fighting skills. Could he truly understand the tender feelings within a woman's heart? Was he capable of even *feeling* tender emotions . . . emotions like love?

She pushed his hands from her arms, turning her back to him once again, taking several steps away. Why did it always have to be so difficult whenever she was with Tabor? Why was she always riddled with questions whenever she looked into his eyes?

"You worry that you are not beautiful, and that is not surprising," Tabor said.

Tanaka made a bitter, derisive sound. "Thanks. That makes me feel much better." The Viking was incapable of sensitivity!

"You suffer the same as beautiful women in many lands," Tabor continued, moving closer, looking at Tanaka in the exquisite silk robe, wondering what the look in her eyes would be like when he removed the robe from her and proved to her how greatly her beauty and spirit affected him. "You worry about your beauty. You don't believe that you are beautiful. It is only beautiful women who do not know they are beautiful. The women who believe beyond question that men cannot resist them. . . . *they* are the women who are unattractive, both to the eye — and to the soul — of a Viking warrior."

Sensation fluttered to life within Tanaka. What Tabor said touched her deeply, at the core of her being where secret fears lived. All her life she had been praised for her sense of spirituality and for her appearance, but Tabor's words — even with his thick accent that sometimes made his Egyptian difficult to understand — were the most precious ones ever spoken to her.

"Turn. . . . turn and face me," Tabor said, his voice a passion-husky whisper. "Let me look once again at a goddess."

"I am a priestess, not a goddess," Tanaka corrected.

"You are my goddess."

Tanaka turned slowly, already reaching for the knotted sash at her hip.

Chapter Sixteen

Tanaka forced herself to keep her gaze high, so that she would only look into Tabor's eyes. Still, her eyes would not follow the direction of her better judgment, and she could not help noticing once again the breadth of his massive chest or the way his pectorals were so perfectly formed. He was like a sculpture made by a woman artist who had let her sense of perfection be her guide, not that of her mortal, flawed model.

She noticed the white scar on his left biceps where Ingmar's arrow had struck. The arm was strong once again, but Tanaka asked, "How is your arm? Is it giving you any pain?"

"My arm is not the issue," Tabor replied, understanding Tanaka's sudden and perhaps unintentional subject change. "Your beauty is the subject. Considering its importance, I think we should give it our complete attention."

Tanaka promised herself that soon — sometime soon — she would confront Tabor and make him decide exactly what plans he had for her in his future. But for now, there was only the night, themselves, and whatever feelings and pleasures they were able to share.

His body was still wet from the bath." Tanaka watched small streams run from his long, blond hair onto his shoulders, continuing downward over his chest. When her gaze pulled upward again to his eyes, he was smiling sensually. He was a man accustomed to women finding his body beautiful.

His confidence annoyed Tanaka.

"Are you always so sure of everything?" she asked when he placed his hands upon her shoulders.

"I know what I know," he replied with pure Viking logic. "I believe what I believe. There are many things I do not know and do not believe, and those things do not concern me."

She felt him easing his fingers beneath the neckline of her silk robe. If she did not stop him soon, she would not be able to stop him at all; and though she had dreamed many times of sharing this moment with Tabor, this was not the way she had imagined it.

"You say that I am beautiful," Tanaka continued, never letting her eyes stray far from Tabor's. She trembled, still aware of Tabor's naked body. "Is Lysetta beautiful?"

Tabor's eyebrows raised slightly as he gazed down at Tanaka. He pushed the silk aside enough to show her collarbone, which suddenly seemed the most sensual part of her body, making him realize how much he had hungered for Tanaka's return while he'd allowed his eyes to take in the nubile servants.

"Well?" Tanaka repeated, wanting an answer. If a look at Lysetta's breasts had caused Tabor's excitement, then Tanaka didn't want him to touch her. She would not be a substitute for another woman.

"Is she beautiful? Yes, of course she is. I would be lying if I told you she wasn't," Tabor answered.

215

Tanaka wished that just once he would lie to her. She hadn't really wanted the truth. She wanted a sweet lie that would bolster her confidence.

"Is she beautiful in the same way you are?" Tabor continued. "No. Is her beauty comparable to yours? Not in the least." With the pad of his right thumb, he brushed Tanaka's lips, making her feel as if she'd just been kissed. "Hers is a harsh, angry, manipulative beauty. You can see that behind her eyes, where her lies and deceit fester like wounds. Her body and her beauty are weapons, and she uses them skillfully in her war."

Through her silk robe, Tabor cupped the underside of Tanaka's breast, running his thumb across the nipple to make it erect. The contact was shocking in its intensity, and Tanaka's knees trembled, her lashes fluttering briefly against her cheeks. She made no move to push Tabor's hand from her, and she did not allow her gaze to stray. She struggled to pretend to be unaffected by his touch.

"She is beautiful, but she does not have breasts like these," Tabor continued, his thumb brushing back and forth across the tip of Tanaka's breast, the touch of silk heightening her pleasure. "These are the most beautiful breasts in the world. . . . but then, you've known that all along. You don't need me to tell you that."

Yes, I want you to tell me! Tanaka thought frantically, afraid that Tabor would stop. He was shamelessly appealing to her vanity, and she was accepting the praise. Perhaps later she would regret it . . . much, much later.

"I have watched you tremble when we are together," Tabor continued, his voice deep, sensual. He moved closer to Tanaka so that she was forced to tilt her head

216

far back on her shoulders to look up into his eyes. "To see you respond to me, to my touch, is what gives me my greatest pleasure."

Tanaka asked herself how any woman could deny such a man as this. The tone of his voice, the words he spoke, the friction of his thumb touching her nipple through the silk robe — all of it was done with practiced skill. She didn't want to think about whom Tabor had practiced with before he met her. That didn't matter. All that mattered was that he was with her now, and he would please her and show her ecstasy.

"Tabor. . . . I should be angry with you —"

"But you're not," he said, cutting her off, a touch of levity in his tone. "We've done enough fighting with one another and with all the others. . . . now is the time for peace."

The word *peace* sounded odd coming from a Viking warrior. She realized then that there were a thousand things about Tabor that she did not know. She had thought him incapable of understanding her insecurities, and then he destroyed her myth by showing her how sensitive he was to her needs. She had thought him a man who loved violence and lived for war, yet he talked now of putting an end to the fighting and accepting peace.

"You mystify me," she whispered, her bones melting as Tabor's thumb continued its tantalizing strokes.

"Me? I am a simple man. You. . . . you're the mystifying one. You're a high priestess. You are so different from any other woman I have ever known."

When he spoke those words, Tanaka became afraid that Tabor would not like the changes she'd made in herself. The Scandinavian women did not shave themselves. Would it bother him that she had? Would she now be ugly to him? She wished that it were darker in the room so that he could not see her well.

"What is wrong?" Tabor asked.

"Sometimes, I wish you would not be able to see inside me as easily as you do."

"The more I see of you, the more I desire you."

Tanaka at last let her gaze dip down, and when she did, she saw the extent of Tabor's passion for her. She trembled, thrilled with the effect she had on this warrior and a little frightened of the power that she unleashed in him.

When Tabor reached for her, Tanaka melted into his arms. He held her tight and she parted her lips, waiting that eternity of a single second before his mouth closed down over hers. She felt him pressing hard against her stomach, searing her flesh through the silk of her robe.

"Tabor. . . . I can never stay angry with you," Tanaka whispered when the kiss finally ended. Her arms were locked around his neck to pull him down so that they could kiss, but as she looked into his fierce blue gaze, her hands strayed to his shoulders to feel the steely muscles that rippled beneath the surface of the smooth, pale skin.

"Do not even try, priestess," Tabor said, amusement and passion twinkling in his eyes.

He started to pick Tanaka up, taking her into his arms, but she stopped him, twisting out of his grasp. Though it never failed to arouse her when Tabor lifted her into his arms, she wanted to be more in control this night, to act rather than be acted upon.

In a conversational tone, as though her body were not on fire with hunger for the Viking, Tanaka took

Tabor's hand and said, "Tell me, do you like my home?" She led him across the room to the mattress. Tabor did not answer her. "I suspect you will find that many things are different here than in your homeland. Our customs, our way of doing things, our dress and manner . . ."

She pushed against his chest, forcing Tabor to sit. He slipped further onto the mattress, his body gloriously naked, his mind enviously at ease. He stretched out, resting on an elbow to look at Tanaka, and she wondered if she would ever be as comfortable completely naked with him as he was with her.

"Thank you," Tanaka said. With just his eyes, Tabor asked a silent question. "For making me believe that I'm beautiful," she answered. "Sometimes, I'm afraid that my skin is too dark for you, or . . ."

She let the words die away as she loosened the sash around her waist. Her robe was simple but elegant. Made of fine silk, it had billowing sleeves and wrapped loosely around her body. With a shrug of her shoulders, she let the robe fall to the floor. The immediate intake of breath she heard worried Tanaka, and she kept her gaze down, somewhat afraid of what she would see if she looked into Tabor's eyes.

"You don't approve." Tanaka crossed her hands over herself.

Tabor moved quickly, pulling his knees beneath himself, crawling across the mattress until he knelt before Tanaka. He was aware that the cultural differences between what he knew and what Tanaka expected of herself were enormous. He reached out and ran his palm lightly along the outside of Tanaka's thigh. The flesh was firm and smooth, freshly shaven and waxed. Tabor's blood began to burn in his veins.

219

"You don't approve," Tanaka said again, self-conscious.

She tried to kneel, to get down on the mattress with Tabor, but this time he was the one who stopped her.

"No," he said in that commanding tone that brooked no rebuttal. "Stand."

Tanaka remained standing, her hands folded one over the other, as if she could hide behind them. When Tabor took her wrists in his hands, she resisted, afraid their differences in what constituted cleanliness and beauty would be a chasm Tabor could not bridge.

"You mustn't hide from me," Tabor whispered, gently but insistently pulling at Tanaka's wrists, forcing her hands away from her body.

Tanaka blushed crimson. Tabor's response was proof of his acceptance.

"Why?" Tabor asked, lightly bringing his fingertips to Tanaka's smooth *mons,* touching her light as a feather.

"It is our way," she answered. "It displeases you?"

In answer, she felt Tabor's large, powerful hands cup her buttocks, then his lips, warm and moist, kissing her down low. His tongue injected wet, heated ecstasy straight into her veins.

She gasped loudly, tossing her hips backward, away from the contact. But Tabor was strong—much stronger than Tanaka, and infinitely more determined. He held her fast, his long, powerful fingers burying into the tender flesh of her buttocks, his serpentine tongue flashing across her sensitive orifice. She pushed her fingers into his hair, forcing his head away from her.

Tabor was looking up at her when Tanaka's vision at last cleared. There was that twinkle in his bright eyes that she had seen so many times before that whispered of unimaginable ecstasies, unspeakable pleasures that would be shared if only Tanaka would trust him and follow his lead.

"For now, please don't," Tanaka whispered, still keeping Tabor's hair entwined in her fingers, forcing his head away from her. She knew she could not hope to stop Tabor, but perhaps it would be possible to delay him slightly.

"Why?" he asked, his hands still warm and strong against Tanaka's buttocks, forcing her to strain to keep some distance between them. "You enjoy it; I enjoy it. Why deny that which we enjoy?"

"Because. . . . because I want to make you happy," Tanaka said. She was once again irked with Tabor that his commanding nature made it practically impossible for him to allow anyone, even her in this most intimate circumstance, to be in control for even brief moments.

But Tabor released his hold on Tanaka, and she took her hands from his hair. He reclined on the bed, his head on one of the numerous pillows. Tanaka knelt at his hip, ignoring the most obvious sign of Tabor's desire for her.

She placed her hand lightly upon his chest and smiled down at him. "I brought you back to life when we were on the boat," she said softly, her hand roaming over his chest. Would she ever tire of feeling these powerful muscles? "Now let me take care of you once again. This palace is my home. I love being here, and I owe you my life for bringing me here."

"You owe me nothing," Tabor whispered. He laced his fingers behind his head, appearing calm and unconcerned, with one aroused exception which thrust upward impatiently, thickly engorged. "You saved my life, and now you say I've saved your life. We owe each other nothing."

"We owe each other everything," Tanaka contradicted.

Tabor's eyes narrowed as he contemplated what she had said. Every time he was sure he understood all there was to know about her, she threw something at him that forced him to reevaluate.

Even now, it was still difficult for Tanaka to look straight into Tabor's eyes for very long. They were so unflinching, as though they saw everything and were surprised by nothing. Tiny fears, little more than pinpricks of sensation in the deepest part of Tanaka's soul, flared and were extinguished within her.

Let this night be one of magic. Tanaka thought as she watched her hand moving over Tabor's chest. *Now that I am home, let me show Tabor the beauty and splendor of my homeland.*

But hardly had this thought entered Tanaka's head when she realized that if *she* were home, then *Tabor* was far from home. No matter how much desire they shared, they could never both be home simultaneously.

Tanaka banished the thoughts. There would be time enough to worry later. This would be the only time that she would be able to share with Tabor his first night in her palace. From behind the mattress, on the floor, Tanaka produced a small, exquisitely painted container. She removed the stopper and poured a small amount of the thick, clear liquid into her palm.

"What is that?" Tabor asked.

"A balm," Tanaka replied.

She rubbed her hands together, heating the liquid. Glancing down Tabor's body, she was pleased to see that he had relaxed. She knew how hot his passion could burn, and she wanted this evening to be a long, slow exploration of the senses, not a meteoric inferno.

"What is it for?"

"It is for you," she said in a sultry purr.

The balm's actual purpose was for women after shaving, though its secondary purposes were well known in the amorous aristocracy. She took him into her hand, and he came to life, quickly regaining stature.

"Does it feel good?" she asked.

"Whenever you touch me, it feels good."

Tanaka chuckled throatily. As her small hand worked along the length of him, testing and exploring, touching sometimes very lightly and at other times with firm confidence, she could see the strain beginning to show on Tabor's features. She saw it first in the corners of his eyes; and if she had not known him as well as she did, she would not have been entirely certain that she pleased him at all. The pinched look showed more plainly in his eyes, and finally the strain of controlling himself showed in his lips, which were pressed into a thin line of self-control.

"Exactly how long do you think you can continue like this without turning me into a madman?" Tabor asked finally.

"Quite some time, actually," Tanaka replied with conversational composure. "So many times since we've been together you've sent me spiraling into the heavens, it seems to me only fair that I torture you with similar means . . . if I can."

For a moment, Tabor watched as Tanaka's breasts swayed tautly from side to side as she pleasured him. A low, rumbling sound of passion erupted from deep within his broad chest, and he closed his eyes, forcing himself to think of anything but the small hand that touched him with consummate, erotic skill.

It was easier, Tabor noted, to control himself when he was not looking at Tanaka. She was too beautiful, her visual charms too undeniable, for him to remain idle and calm while she touched him, kneeling naked at his hip.

"Don't look away," Tanaka whispered, forcing Tabor back to the present. "I want you to watch me," she whispered. She wanted him thinking of her, the memory of Lysetta still too fresh in her mind. "I want you thinking of me . . . only of me and no one else . . . ever."

"How could I ever think of another?" Tabor asked.

He felt himself losing control, but it did not bother him. He watched as Tanaka took him in both hands, touching him, heightening his excitement so that he felt all-powerful, as though his passion could go on endlessly. He let his gaze follow the curve of Tanaka's back, the delicate line of her buttocks, the tight, straight line of thigh, and the curve of her exquisite breasts. When at last he looked straight into her eyes again, he saw a new confidence behind those ebony eyes that was as exciting as it was shocking.

"Remember how you've teased me?" she asked.

Tabor nodded. He tried to swallow, but his mouth was dry. This Egyptian high priestess was turning the tables on him, and he felt powerless against his desire for her. No woman had ever captivated him so thoroughly, so completely. Despite his best intentions, he was unable to keep his eyes open.

Just let him try to forget me! Tanaka thought defiantly, challenging whatever differences there were that would ever separate them. *Just let him try to think of another woman when he's with me!*

She picked up the balm again and poured a single, thick drop of liquid onto her forefinger, then she slowly smoothed the balm around her lips, making her mouth glisten and shine.

"Watch," she said then, and there was a commanding tone to her voice that had not been there before.

Tanaka waited until Tabor opened his eyes, then she bent forward and kissed him lightly, tasting him briefly before taking him in deeply. Tabor made a growling sound, the predatory animal noise that used to frighten Tanaka but now excited her because she knew that she had affected him. She had stripped away whatever levels of civility he maintained and touched him in the core of his warrior's soul.

His body tightened from head to foot. When his eyes closed, Tanaka released him. "No," she said sternly. "You must watch. You will think of no woman but me."

Uncharacteristically exasperated, Tabor replied, "In the name of Thor and all that is holy, Tanaka, I cannot possibly think of any woman but you! Not now! Not ever!"

"And that," she said, her dark, sultry eyes boring into his as she moved down slowly to capture him once again, "is exactly the way I want it."

Chapter Seventeen

Tanaka tossed a grape into her mouth. "You look almost as weak as you did when you were on the boat," she said. Now that Tabor was so strong, it seemed acceptable to make light of those horrifying days and nights on the longboat when she did not know if he would live another day or whether Sven would kill her if Tabor died.

"Weak?" Tabor gave her the best stern look he could manage while lying sprawled out on his bed, naked, basking in the afterglow of an orgasm that had left him drained of energy. "Come here and I'll show you how strong I am!"

Tanaka laughed again, a tinkling laugh of pleasure. These were the times that she enjoyed most with Tabor, when he did not feel it was necessary to be either a predator or a protector, when all he had to be was her lover, a role he handled spectacularly.

When Tabor reached for Tanaka's ankle, intent on pulling her across the blankets to him, she slipped out of reach. She knew that she had pleased him, but his passion was far from sated. Before she would joyously tumble into his arms, she wanted him to chase her; and until he did, she would remain out of reach.

"Not yet," she said. "You'd better get *all* your strength back first. I'm . . . hungry tonight."

"So I see."

"You'll have to be especially energetic."

"I will do my best," Tabor said, running his palm up Tanaka's calf. "Will my best be good enough for you?"

"It always has been."

Tabor liked this new Tanaka. He knew it was because she was in her own home that her confidence had risen to such daring levels, and he was only too happy to be the benefactor of that confidence.

"We'll have to get you suitable clothes," Tanaka said, her cheek puffed as she nibbled on freshly cut fruit.

"What's amiss with the clothes I have?"

"They're too warm for here. The sun will cook you."

A cat walked through the curtained doorway. Tanaka stretched a hand out to stroke it, then turned her attention back to Tabor. Cats were a part of her divinity ceremony, and several roamed the palace, accorded the status of divine creatures. Tanaka did not recognize the cat and wondered if it belonged to Kahlid. She would have to ask about other changes that had occurred in her absence.

"Besides, I think you would look absolutely delicious in a nice silk robe," she continued. "And maybe a headdress—one made of gold. That would suit you."

Tabor frowned. Tanaka was making decisions for him; and though he enjoyed her newfound confidence while they were touching and caressing each other, he did not appreciate her taking control of his life.

"I need no robes," he growled. "I have the clothes of a Viking warrior. That is what I have always been; that is what I will always be. Why try to look like someone I'm not?"

"Because, my magnificent barbarian, I will think that you look even more handsome than you already do, and there's absolutely no telling what will happen then," she said, deciding she liked *barbarian* as Tabor's sobriquet. "I can't control my . . . *appetites* now," she continued, lingering erotically over the word so that the sensual, timorous quality touched Tabor. "I shudder to think what I'll be like with you wearing . . . hmmm? . . . let's see, what color would be best with those blue barbarian eyes of yours?"

She sat cross-legged, a light blanket thrown over her thighs to modestly cover her, her breasts exposed to Tabor's hungry gaze. Tabor was leaning back against the wall, the opposite end of the blanket thrown across his loins. As Tanaka studied him, she marvelled once again at the man's extraordinary size and strength . . . and at the incredible way that Tabor could miraculously make her feel tall and strong and powerful with a look, a touch, or a word.

"What are you thinking?" he asked, studying Tanaka as he sipped from the gold goblet, quenching his thirst with the hearty beer that had surprised him with its splendid taste.

It took a moment for Tanaka to regain her composure. It was an unsettling possibility that Tabor might be able to read her thoughts.

228

"About you . . . you and all the different things about you that I don't know yet but would like to."

"I'm not a difficult man to know," Tabor said. He shifted on the blanket, clearly uncomfortable. He did not like speaking of himself.

"You're not a difficult man to love, perhaps," Tanaka replied.

She bit her tongue instantly, afraid that she had gone too far by implying a permanence with Tabor that he could not accept. For a second or two, their gazes held, one sea blue and the other midnight black, each asking silent questions of the other, neither having answers.

Tanaka was the first to look away. She promised herself that she would never again speak the word love while she was in Tabor's company.

When she spoke again, it was clear that she and Tabor would both simply pretend that she hadn't mentioned the word at all.

"You'll have to see Pharaoh Abbakka soon. He's anxious to meet you." When she turned back toward Tabor, her eyes held a mischievous twinkle. "I've told him some stories of you. He's quite impressed. Neenah wants to hold a huge celebration on your behalf," she said, knowing how Tabor would dislike such a public display of emotion, particularly if it were for him.

"And what stories did you tell him?" Tabor asked, eyes narrowed suspiciously.

"Just . . . stories."

Tanaka laughed and picked another delicious piece of fruit from the large bowl. This was better, she thought. Laughter and teasing with Tabor worked best. It was only when she mentioned words like "love," or in any way implied there might be some future between them that the happy moments vanished like a puff of smoke, leaving behind only the residual sensations of suspicion and doubt.

"Moamin is very interested in talking to you about sailing and shipbuilding. His men have already looked at our boat—"

"*Our* boat?" He raised an eyebrow.

Tanaka scowled, refusing to accept the singular Viking anomaly to an egalitarian society that said no woman could own a ship. In all other aspects of Viking life that Tanaka had gleaned while with Tabor, women had far more rights than they did in her own land. But whenever it came to ships, the Vikings were as prejudiced as Egyptians.

She huffed, bringing a smile to Tabor's lips, and said, "The boat that I was on for how long? *That* boat!".

Tabor nodded, remembering how astonished Tanaka had been when he first explained to her that Viking women were allowed to divorce their husbands if they were not treated properly and were given half of all the property that had been accrued during their marriage. To Tanaka, that had been unthinkable.

"Pharaoh Abbakka wants to know how you built your boats. Your people seem to sail farther than ours."

Tabor shrugged his broad shoulders. If Pharaoh Abbakka wanted to learn a Viking's way of shipbuilding, he had no objections. Perhaps it would even be possible for him to learn something from the

230

Egyptians. Either way, Tabor was already planning for the time when the winds would blow hot and strong from the south, and when he would want a good ship beneath him and many strong warriors around him for his return to Hedeby. He had a score to settle with Ingmar the Savage, and he would not rest until it had been settled and he'd regained the battle-axe that had been in his family for three generations.

From all Tabor had been able to see in his brief time at the palace, the pharaoh was a man of extraordinary wealth and power. He would be an ally worth having, and an enemy worth avoiding.

"You can tell your pharaoh that I will gladly extend myself on his behalf."

It was Tanaka's eyes that narrowed suspiciously this time. That didn't sound like the Tabor she knew, but she was too happy that he was being cooperative to question his motives.

"And you will find," he continued, a devilish brightness now glittering in his eyes, "that I will extend myself on *your* behalf as well." He looked down at the blanket, which was slightly tented. "As you can see, I am already somewhat . . . extended."

The sexual banter both delighted and shocked Tanaka. Was she, High Priestess Tanaka, really joking about such things? Sometimes when she was with Tabor, she felt like she was another person or at least a new person that had not lived until he'd entered her life.

"On my behalf?" Tanaka asked.

"*Only* on your behalf. *Always* on your behalf."

Tabor tossed the blanket aside and stopped breathing for just a moment when he looked at Tanaka in her naked splendor. She moved toward him, but he placed a hand on her shoulder to stop her. She looked at him questioningly.

"Does it hurt when you do that?" he asked, running the tips of his fingers along Tanaka's smooth thigh, then lightly brushing them higher.

"No. First we shave, then we wax. We do this from the moment that hair begins to grow. Eventually, the hair becomes soft and thin, and we hardly need to shave at all." It was difficult for Tanaka to talk of such things, but the unsettling need for Tabor's approval forced her to ask one more question. "Does it displease you?"

"I like everything about you," Tabor replied, the huskiness in his tone suggesting truth.

Tanaka leaned forward to plant a light kiss on Tabor's lips. "You are a good man," she whispered. "My barbarian . . . my beautiful barbarian." She took the container of balm and poured a drop onto her finger, then carefully smoothed the thick liquid against the entrance of her womanhood. "We use the balm after waxing," she explained as Tabor's eyes widened with approval. "It has, you will find, many purposes."

When she kissed him, then thrust her tongue into his mouth to explore further, his powerful arms wound round her slim voluptuous body. Soon Tanaka lay in a magnificent sprawl upon Tabor's bed, receiving his attention like a goddess receiving homage, taking glory in his extraordinary skill. Tabor added the balm liberally both to himself and to Tanaka, and when at last he was ready to become one with her, Tanaka was sobbing with the need for release.

"Please!" she begged, her legs entwined with Tabor's, her tiny hands pulling at his shoulders. "Now, Tabor! I need you—"

Her words were silenced as he gave himself to her, sharing with her his strength, his energy, the soulforce that drove him. And when at last culmination came, it struck with thunderous force.

Far down the hall, Habibah heard the sound of the high priestess's cry of passion. Discreetly, she continued to clean Tanaka's living quarters, pretending she had heard nothing, praying that the high priestess was not under a demonic spell cast by the blond barbarian from afar.

Chapter Eighteen

Tabor's reaction to Pharaoh Moamin Abbakka was a single thought: *This* is a leader of men.

The pharaoh's bearing was commanding; his visage, stern without anger; his gaze, appraising without condescension or judgment. Even though Tabor was considerably taller than Moamin, younger by more than two decades, and many times stronger, there wasn't a hint of trepidation in Moamin, and this impressed Tabor enormously. He had intimidated countless people in his life, most often unintentionally, and it pleased him that the pharaoh was not easily cowed.

Tabor sensed that in a war, Moamin would be a cool head of reason, a skilled tactician, a formidable foe or an invaluable friend.

"So this is the man who has brought our spiritual leader back to us, eh?" Moamin remarked.

Standing beside Tabor, Tanaka turned toward him and whispered under her breath, in Danish, "You're supposed to kneel to the pharaoh."

Tabor just glanced at her and replied, "A Viking kneels to no man."

Several seconds passed as Moamin waited for Tabor to bow before him as custom and propriety dictated. Then he accepted that Tabor did not understand the custom. But a moment after that, not even the language barrier could hide the fact that Tabor *did* understand that he was supposed to kneel to the pharaoh, he simply *chose not to.*

A murmur went through the crowd gathered in the room. Tanaka felt fear, warm but steadily growing hotter, flame in her stomach, spreading through her limbs. When she looked at Kahlid, she saw a glint in his eye. He was pleased. Tabor had jeopardized himself, insulting Moamin with his refusal to genuflect.

"Pharaoh Abbakka," Tanaka said, her voice soft though more than a whisper. She was not interested in having Kahlid listen to what she had to say. "You must understand that he comes from another land. A land that is far from here and has ways that are different from our own. He means no disrespect."

Tanaka spoke quickly, adding just the slightest change and inflection to her words, but it was enough to prevent Tabor from understanding all that she said. He was fully aware that he had insulted the pharaoh, but he could not—not if he was to continue to think of himself as a warrior and call himself a Viking—kneel to anyone, much less a man he did not know.

Turning to Tabor again, her dark eyes filled with a mixture of anger and fear, Tanaka hissed in Danish, "You're supposed to kneel! Why won't you kneel? He has the power to have you killed!"

"No, his guards have the power to kill me, but before that would happen, he would die by these hands."

Tabor held his hands out, the fingers spread, to emphasize his point. Tanaka—as well as everyone else in the room, though she was the only one who spoke Tabor's language—looked at his huge, powerful hands.

Pharaoh Moamin and Tabor locked gazes again, and this time there could be no disguising the Viking's insubordination.

"You are either very foolish," Moamin said, speaking slowly and distinctly, so that Tabor could understand him, "or very brave. No man has ever dared refuse me so."

"And no man has ever dared make such a demand of me."

The room was stone-silent. Then, finally, a smile creased Moamin's face. Not a full smile, but enough for the crowd to realize that Tabor would not be dragged away and hoisted high in the public square, impaled by spears.

The secondary dignitaries were soon dismissed, leaving Tabor with Moamin, Kahlid, and Tanaka. Though Tabor had learned Tanaka's language, she was still needed to translate many of the words the pharaoh spoke. He understood her better than he did any of the others.

"I owe you a great deal," Moamin said, walking slowly, his hands clasped behind his back, Tabor at his side. "For bringing High Priestess Tanaka back to us—back to me." He shook his head, recalling his emotions when he'd first learned that Tanaka had been kidnapped by seafaring barbarians. He had felt like a rudderless ship, adrift and helpless. For a week, Moamin had refused to see anyone, not even Kahlid.

Tabor listened to Moamin's praise and thanks, but his concentration drifted. He knew he had done the proper thing by taking her back to her home; but now that he was here, it was difficult for him to comprehend the differences between this land and his own. The pharaoh's fortune, Tabor guessed, had to be greater than the combined riches of Hedeby and Kaupang combined. Not only did he see gold statues, numerous guards, and an abundance of food and wine, but the sheer wealth necessary to build the palace was staggering. Among his people, Tabor had been considered an affluent man, but his wealth — even during the best of times after successful raids — was nowhere near that of Pharaoh Moamin Abbakka's.

"I understand you would like me to look at your ships and see how yours differ from those of the Vikings?" Tabor said as he rounded a corner and headed down yet another long hallway.

"If you would," Moamin replied.

Tabor nodded. "In some ways, my people seem far in advance of yours." Out of the corner of his eye he saw Moamin's immediate negative reaction to the comment. He heard Tanaka gasp behind him. "But in other ways, you and your people have advanced far beyond mine."

Tabor smiled then at Moamin, and both men realized they were playing a game — a game of politics. They were experimenting with their own power and with the power of the other, testing courage, honor, and dignity. They were leaders of men — one of many more men than the other — sharing the same goal of honorable leaders everywhere: To do what is best for their people.

"We have much to discuss," Moamin said. "And I don't really think we need anyone to help us with the language, do you?" Tabor shook his head. "Then, High Priestess Tanaka, Priest Kahlid, you may attend to your other duties."

Neither Kahlid nor Tanaka wanted to leave, but the pharaoh's dismissal had been clear.

"Don't start any arguments," Tanaka said quickly, in Danish. The smile she received from Tabor did not calm her.

"There now," Moamin said when he was alone with his Viking guest. "Perhaps I could offer you some of our beer? I believe you will find it most agreeable."

Tabor felt at last like the guest of a powerful man rather than an impoverished barbarian who needed the pharaoh's blessings for every breath he took.

"I was dismissed," Kahlid fumed, pacing back and forth. His hands were again balled into angry fists. The cords in his neck stood out with the strain of controlling his volatile emotions, and his face was crimson. "Dismissed! Like I was nothing more than a servant!"

Lysetta decided it was best not to mention that as palace priest, he was just a servant. She sipped her wine. Never had she seen Kahlid so angry, although Kahlid's anger had been erupting quite regularly since the return of High Priestess Tanaka.

At first Lysetta had fretted over Kahlid when he got this way; then she would become frightened of him, thinking he would again strike out at her; now, she just waited until he'd finished his tirade and received his sexual release by thrusting himself inside her. Then he would calm down and they would be able to talk rationally about the problem that Tanaka represented.

"Dismissed!" Kahlid continued, his robes fluttering against his thighs as he strode back and forth across the length of his chambers. "Never in my life has anyone dared to dismiss me!"

Someone has now! Lysetta thought with a certain amount of glee, even though she liked Kahlid as much as she was capable of liking anyone but herself.

She turned her face away so that Kahlid would not see the smile that pulled at her mouth and brought a brightness to her dark eyes. She realized then that, to at least some extent, she hated her lover.

It was only through Kahlid that she would be able to have the real wealth and power that she hungered for, so she was willing to sleep with him and give him pleasure and release. Sometimes, she even enjoyed the encounters. But she had noticed recently that being with Kahlid and letting him touch her wasn't as much fun as it once had been.

"It's that pale-skinned Viking!" Kahlid continued, oblivious to Lysetta's smile, too concerned with his own emotions to worry about hers. "He's the one who has caused all this. If not for him, Moamin would never have dared dismiss me. They're becoming friends, I tell you, and that will never do!"

"And why is that?" Lysetta asked, her tone cool and modulated, neither disrespectful nor obtuse.

"Because the only person Moamin should trust is me! All my plans hinge upon Moamin trusting me, and he can't trust me if he trusts someone else!"

"Someone like Tanaka?"

"Tanaka's not much of a problem, really. She's a woman."

Lysetta bristled. Though Lysetta had always intended to ride with Kahlid to the top, perhaps she could take the power in her own hands.

"What's the Viking's name?" he asked, at last actually stopping his pacing long enough to look directly at Lysetta.

"Tabor." She had heard that the full name was *Tabor, Son of Thor* and that it had something to do with his sexual prowess, but Lysetta kept that information to herself. She did not want to antagonize a man who did not yet realize she saw him as an enemy, an obstacle to her dreams.

"Tabor? Strange name, that. Just proves how backward he really is."

Lysetta thought of commenting on how far Tabor and his men sailed — drastically undermanned — to reach Egypt. Such an accomplishment could never be achieved by someone "backward," but she kept that opinion to herself, too.

"The first thing we'll have to do is rid ourselves of Tabor," Kahlid continued, his gaze distant and unfocused once again as he planned aloud his ascension to power. "He's not a man I want to have to deal with later."

Lysetta thought, *Meaning you don't want to look over your shoulder to find he's after you.* But even before she could agree with Kahlid's decision, a libidinous voice whispered inside her head, promising passion in the arms of the golden-haired Viking.

"I think it would be a mistake to kill Tabor too soon," she said, unable to stop the desire-driven words. She pretended not to see the angry look that Kahlid shot at her. "We might be able to blame many bad things upon him later. A lot of people are going

240

to die, Kahlid, and it is going to be easier with the palace workers and villagers if we have someone to blame the deaths on."

She saw Kahlid's features softening and knew that she had struck a responsive chord.

"If we can blame Tanaka's murder upon Tabor, and maybe even Moamin's, then surely there could be no uprising against you, the only spiritual leader remaining. The soldiers here in the palace and at the outposts will follow your strong leadership, but only if they do not believe that you are responsible for the death of Tanaka. She is loved by all!"

Lysetta bit her tongue after the last sentence. It was true that the people all loved Tanaka, and many of them were openly suspicious of Kahlid. That had long infuriated him.

"What could be better than blaming all the killing upon Tabor and his men?" Lysetta continued, not wanting to give Kahlid time to think about her *faux pas*. "The soldiers will do all the killing on their own . . . with direction from you at the appropriate time, of course."

"Of course," Kahlid said. He nodded approval. He liked Lysetta's plan. "I had just planned on disgracing Tanaka and through that taking her place . . . but murder . . . murder . . . and if I could prove that I had nothing to do with Moamin's death . . . even Neenah's death . . ."

"Now all we have to do is determine how to blame Tabor and his men for the murders," Lysetta said, but her mind stayed with Tabor and what he had looked like when she saw him in the bath. Before she saw him executed, she wanted to find out if he was really as exciting a lover as his body promised.

241

* * *

Tanaka reclined on the mound of pillows, and one of her servants placed a pillow beneath her knees. Tanaka had missed these luxuries when she had been aboard the longboat with Tabor and his men. She enjoyed the personal servants who gave her backrubs and massaged the muscles in her arms and legs, and she especially enjoyed having delicious, familiar food to eat again. Though her appetite was nothing compared to Tabor's, Tanaka had especially missed the goat cheese and the breads.

"You asked me to remind you of the meeting with the pharaoh," a young servant said, keeping her voice low so that she would not intrude on Tanaka's concentration. "It was to take place when the sun crossed the sky."

Responsibility . . . that was the price of luxury. The high priestess for Pharaoh Moamin Abbakka must always be available for those in need of spiritual guidance or supervision.

"Have we displeased you?" another servant asked, her expression showing that she would rather walk through the gates of darkness than displease the high priestess.

"No, you have been perfect," Tanaka replied warmly. "I sighed because the time that I have spent in this room has come and gone so quickly." Tanaka looked around her own bedroom, now crowded with servants, and wondered what Tabor would think of her living quarters. That thought brought a smile to her lips, and she heard a collective sigh as the servants all relaxed.

"Please leave me for a moment," Tanaka said,

needing just a few minutes to herself so that she could daydream without worrying that one of her servants was reading her mind. "Only for a little while, then please return to help me prepare for my meeting with the pharaoh."

The servants left quickly, clearly pleased that Tanaka had requested their return. If any of them should displease Tanaka in any way and if the pharaoh should hear about it, the punishment would be severe. The pharaoh had decreed that the high priestess's life be devoid of unpleasantness.

When she was alone at last, Tanaka closed her eyes, and in her mind's eye, she was able to see Tabor as clearly as if he were standing in front of her. She could see his eyes, dark blue and intense with passion, looking at her, seeing straight into her soul. She could see, too, his love for her shining in those eyes.

Tanaka sighed. This was neither the time nor the place for such wistful dreaming. She would soon be required to use all her powers of concentration and spirituality to assist Pharaoh Abbakka on whatever decisions he had to make; and after that, she was expected to meet with several groups of young people who wished to be married and had yet to go through the soul-cleansing process, a prerequisite for the ceremony. When she was finished, even if she wanted to and had the energy left for it, she could not invite Tabor to her bedchambers. To have a man in the quarters of the high priestess was a breach of propriety that Tanaka dared not contemplate, no matter how dearly she wished to feel Tabor's strong, gentle arms surrounding her.

With her eyes still closed, Tanaka shifted positions

on the pillows, moving slightly. She felt a twinge of pain down low. A pain that brought a smile to her lips—a smile that would have shocked the servants if they'd still been in the room. She was sore from the vigorous lovemaking with Tabor. She had told him he'd need all his strength to satisfy her, and Tabor had taken her challenge to heart. He gave her all the strength he had, throwing his heart and soul and every ounce of passionate energy he possessed into their lovemaking until his body was bathed in sweat.

How many times had he brought her to that mysterious land where her body burned white-hot and the explosions of desire scorched her every sense? Four times? Hadn't he tried to bring her to a fifth when Tanaka at last cried out that she could take no more?

Another soft sigh escaped Tanaka's lips as she thought about the blissful lovemaking. It had truly been special, and she felt more confident now that she had proven to herself and to Tabor that his desire for her burned no hotter than hers for him.

Lysetta now seemed much less a threat to Tanaka's happiness with Tabor.

When she realized that Lysetta, in a way, was responsible for helping her to shed the last of her inhibitions, Tanaka chuckled softly. She heard a murmur of voices, then realized that her servants were peeking into the quarters. They had heard her private laughter, and no doubt they wondered what had brought such levity to her soul. Dare she tell them? Sadly, Tanaka realized that, at least for the present, she had to keep her love for Tabor a secret. Perhaps there would come a day when she would not have to hide her feelings for him. But for now—at least until she became thoroughly resettled back in the palace of Pharaoh Moamin Abbakka, it was best she keep her feelings — for everyone — to herself.

"Please return!" Tanaka then called out, pushing herself up from the mound of pillows. "It is time for me to prepare to counsel the pharaoh!"

The servants rushed into the huge room, all of them talking at once, each wanting to be the one to receive the high priestess's complete, undivided attention.

Chapter Nineteen

Tabor leaned back against the wooden railing that surrounded the dock, and though his eyes took in the ship the carpenters were building, his mind was on other matters.

It had been well over a week since his arrival on the Egyptian shores; and aside from the first days, when he had shared his passion and joy with Tanaka, he had hardly seen her. To make matters worse, Tabor was discovering that his grasp of the Egyptian language wasn't as solid as he had thought. Though he understood Tanaka well enough, whenever anyone else talked to him, there was much he did not understand. Sometimes, when he had talked with Kahlid, he got the feeling that the priest was belittling him, even patronizing him.

Tabor didn't like feeling cast aside. It made him feel small. Here, he was an oddity. In his homeland, he was a leader of men. But here, his men seemed far more interested in the available Egyptian women than in learning the Egyptian method of shipbuilding.

So Tabor spent most of his time alone or struggling with shipbuilders. Sometimes, he sensed that men were watching him. Tabor had long ago learned to trust gut feelings. He hadn't lived this long with enemies like Ingmar the Savage by not heeding instinct, especially forebodings of danger.

As Tabor pushed to his feet, intent on returning to his living quarters, he decided to tell Tanaka of his worries and suspicions. This time, he would be forceful and make her listen. The last time he'd broached the subject, she'd laughed, dismissing his fears as the product of a man unaccustomed to life in Egypt.

As he made his way toward land, Tabor heard a sailor call out to him, asking him where he was going. Tabor did not reply or react to the question. He was tired of being looked upon as an idiosyncracy among these short, swarthy people, and he wanted his own clothes back. These silk robes might well be the height of fashion here, but they looked more like women's wear than anything a Viking would choose.

As he made his way through the village streets, Tabor was once again aware of how much taller he was than the Egyptians. His long blond hair, flowing over his shoulders in glowing waves, defined him as a foreigner as much as his broad shoulders and his piercing blue eyes.

He thought then that without having Tanaka at his side he felt even more the outsider. He recalled how, when Tanaka had spent time with him, he had delighted in learning about her culture and ways of doing things. Without her, Egypt was just a land filled with people he did not understand or care to.

Could it be that he, Tabor, Son of Thor, had fallen

in love with the Egyptian high priestess? And could it be that she did not love him?

He growled then, a low, deep growl that rumbled out of his massive chest. It was a sound born of frustration and disillusionment, and the animal-threat sound of it caused villagers to part wide to facilitate Tabor's passing.

Tabor was not the type of man who spent hours pondering whether he loved a woman or not. He was a nomadic Viking, a man who found pleasure and companionship wherever it was to be found; and when he sailed on again, he left behind memories, but he kept none for himself. That was his image of himself.

But Tabor refused to delude himself. He could not accept the lie. Tanaka *wasn't* just someone he had slept with. She wasn't a sexual conquest who had been entertaining but was no longer relevant.

"Stop thinking about her," Tabor said aloud in his native tongue. He enjoyed the taste of his own language, which he only spoke when he was with his men or with Tanaka.

He decided then, as he hurried through the village, taking long steps that would have forced a smaller man to run to keep up with him, to spend more time with his men. Granted, Sven, Carl, and the others were a poor substitute for Tanaka, but they understood Tabor and accepted him as their leader. At least in their company, Tabor knew he was surrounded by friends.

The length of his stride, the faraway look in his eyes, and the hard set of his jaw frightened the villagers as Tabor made his way back to the palace from the seaside. He hardly noticed how the people moved aside well in advance of him, and he did not pay any attention to the hushed sigh of relief when he passed without venting his anger upon them.

Tabor was so intent on his thoughts that he did not notice that he was being followed by a small man with intelligent eyes, a devious mind, and a very sharp dagger.

Tabor found Tanaka in a room filled with stacked piles of papyrus and small desks with backless three-legged chairs. Two men were with her, and Tabor was pleased that they were old men. When he entered the room, the scribes squinted to focus on him.

"Tabor?"

It was a simple question, and Tanaka's furrowed brows told him that she wasn't overly displeased to see him, but she wasn't altogether pleased, either.

"I must speak with you."

Tanaka looked at him, then down at her desk, which was scattered with papyrus. The thumb and first two fingers of her right hand were stained with pigmentation. Tanaka set her brush down carefully upon its holder, then opened and closed her hand several times in quick succession. She had been writing for some time, and the muscles in her forearm were cramping up.

"This really isn't the best time," she said.

Her eyes danced right and left to the men flanking her, silently indicating to Tabor that he must not say anything too intimate in front of them. Tabor wondered how boorish she thought he was, but he tamped his anger. It was not the Viking way to show powerful emotions, especially not in front of strangers.

"It is important," he continued, spreading his feet just a little wider apart, putting his hand on his hips. "I wish to speak to you privately."

Tanaka sighed wearily, then rubbed her eyes. She rose from her chair and spoke to her companions. The two scribes toddled out of the room on shuffling feet, their backs hunched from hours of work, their eyes red-rimmed with strain.

"How are you?" Tanaka asked when she was alone in the library with Tabor.

"Concerned. I believe there are people in this palace who mean you harm."

Tanaka moved closer to Tabor. She wanted him to kiss her. It didn't have to be the soul-searing kisses he was capable of, just a light one on the mouth or even on the cheek. She wanted a show of affection from him—something she hadn't gotten much of in the past week. It was thoughts of his kisses that prevented his words from registering immediately in her mind.

"What do you mean?" she asked finally, leaning back against the desk.

"I think you have enemies among your people."

"And how do you know this."

"I can feel it here," Tabor explained, touching his stomach. "People mean to do you harm."

It did not entirely surprise Tanaka. She had lived in the palace most of her life, and she would have needed to be completely blind to not know that all people in positions of power and influence had ene-

250

mies. But she also knew that she was Pharaoh Moamin Abbakka's spiritual leader and personal friend. Anyone plotting against her would soon find himself at the public execution block. The pharaoh was protective of her, and it was Tanaka's awareness of this that kept her from worrying too much about the politics—and dangers—of her position as high priestess.

"There are enemies within the palace walls, I grant you," Tanaka said, smiling, touched by Tabor's concern. "Your intuition is correct, but I think you will find the anger and animosity is not directed toward me."

Looking down at Tanaka, Tabor felt a rush of emotion for her. He saw at last the strain of fatigue pulling at her soft features. She was unconsciously flexing her right hand and rubbing one forearm with the opposite hand.

"Perhaps . . . perhaps my feelings are not accurate," Tabor equivocated.

He normally saw his world as black and white, right and wrong, in absolutes that either were or were not. This change in him, this gray area of doubt, had never existed until Tanaka entered his life.

Tanaka took his hands in her own. "It is the Viking in you. You see treachery everywhere. You needn't worry. I am very powerful here, and Ingmar is far away."

"No one is too powerful for treachery. And though I have fled from Ingmar, in the spring I will return to my waters, and Ingmar will pay with his life for what he has done."

251

"Would it be so bad to stay here . . . here with me?" Her hands went up to his chest. "Forget about Ingmar. I have."

It was not true. Sometimes, at night, Ingmar the Savage's face still flashed in her mind, jarring her awake, her body bathed in sweat, her heart pounding in her chest. She had not forgotten anything about Ingmar or her hideous ordeal. But the nightmares were becoming less frequent, their severity diminishing.

Tabor shook his head. "It is a matter of honor."

"Forget about honor. Stop thinking like a Viking."

With a wave of his hand, Tabor knocked Tanaka's hands from his chest, glaring at her. "Forget about honor? Stop thinking like a Viking? What makes you so superior, high priestess? You would do well to think of honor!"

Tanaka gasped. "Are you saying I am without honor?"

It was the worst thing anyone had ever said to her, and Tabor was the last person from whom she expected such angry words. Not even Ingmar the Savage had accused her of being without honor.

"I can be nothing other than the man I am, and the man I am is a *Viking* man."

In his eyes Tanaka read disrespect, and she was hurt, then angered. She was High Priestess Tanaka, she had lived through the hideous days and nights as Ingmar's captive; and now that she was home in her palace, no one was going to be condescending and disrespectful to her ever again.

"Be a Viking if you want to, but don't assume that my people are *like* Vikings! In this palace, we don't talk of peace, then kill by ambush! That's more than you can say about your precious, honorable Viking traditions."

Tabor did not respond. He turned on his heel and left the library, pushing the elderly scribes aside and nearly knocking them over when they inadvertently blocked his path.

Whether Tanaka believed him or not, Tabor sensed that there was mortal danger in the palace; and he would protect her, whether she wanted him to or not. Her naïveté was something he could not fight, just as his intuition was something he had to heed. She had to look so weary in the library. He had wanted to comfort her, to rub her shoulders gently to ease the knotted muscles, and later, when she relaxed, to show her the ecstasy that even an exhausted body could feel.

But instead, she had let him know beyond all doubt that she saw him as an inferior form of humanity. Treachery, Tanaka believed, was something only Vikings were capable of. Ha!

When Tabor was at last outside the palace and able once again to breathe fresh air, he smelled the ocean on the breeze and headed toward the water. He followed his instincts, pulled by invisible forces of nature that gave him comfort and solace.

Yasir rolled away, breathing deeply, and placed a forearm on his forehead. His body glistened with the sweat of sexual exertion. He felt drained, exhausted, simultaneously powerful and weak because of the woman beside him.

She was Lysetta, and she was the most beautiful

woman he'd ever slept with. She was also the mistress of Kahlid, and if the priest ever found out about this tryst, he'd surely have Yasir killed.

Perhaps that was part of what Yasir found so exciting about Lysetta. She was dangerous, and that aura of spontaneous pleasure and sudden death made the blood flow hot in his veins.

He had been in the village square, idling away his time, when a small man approached him, asking if he was Yasir, the mercenary. Instinctively, Yasir drew his dagger, but the little man merely smiled and said that there was someone very rich and very powerful who wished to speak with him. Yasir at first refused to follow the little man through the winding, crowded streets of the village, fearing attack. But curiosity and the need for money forced him to put aside his caution.

She was waiting for him behind the wine merchant's shop, wearing a veil that concealed her identity. Yasir refused to speak unless she removed the veil. She did him one move better. She opened her robes to show her body, keeping on only the veil. Lush and inviting, her body promised extraordinary pleasure, and the look in her dark eyes just above the black veil that covered her face said she was the kind of woman who enjoyed such things.

Yasir ordered the little man to turn his back, and then he took the woman right there behind the wine merchant's shop, pressing her down into the dirty alley to have his way, not really caring that he couldn't see her face.

He reached his summit quickly, and he'd hardly gotten to his feet when she was up as well, readjusting her fine linen robes as though nothing had happened between them at all.

And then she began talking about murder, political assassination, and how Yasir had come well recommended. When she removed the veil, her smile was wicked and exciting and spoke of death.

The alley was not well traveled, but Yasir wanted to get Lysetta away from prying eyes. He was surprised when she quickly agreed to go with him to his abode.

Yasir had wanted her again when they reached his small stone hut, but Lysetta had refused him. She wanted to talk more, and since Yasir knew that she was refusing his sexual advances so that he had to listen to her, he didn't mind.

She mentioned no names and gave no specifics. Would Yasir be willing to assassinate several people in the near future? How great was his need for money? Had he killed anyone for money other than the three that Lysetta had learned about? Did he have loyalties to anyone? Had he ever killed a woman before?

Satisfied with Yasir's answers, Lysetta satisfied his body once again.

"You were good," she said, pulling her knees beneath her and crossing them. He hadn't been satisfying at all, but satisfaction wasn't what she'd sought in Yasir's bed. She pushed her fingers through her luxurious hair, smoothing the satiny tresses back, unmindful of her own nudity. "That impresses me," she purred.

Yasir moved his arm to look up at her. He smiled, gratified.

"There's something that I want you to do," Lysetta began.

"You want me to kill someone," Yasir cut in. "That's what people pay me to do." It was a flat statement of fact, as though his profession were no different from that of the village carpenter or the wine merchant or the fishmonger.

"Someone special."

"It'll cost you more." Some people were harder to kill than others. Difficulties cost money. It never occurred to Yasir that there might be anyone who could not be assassinated or someone who should be left alone.

"You will be superbly rewarded," Lysetta said with another sultry purr. "In many, many ways." She leaned over, kissed Yasir's naked, sweaty chest, then sat up again. "I want you to kill the high priestess. After that, there are more people who must die."

The high priestess? Yasir had killed a woman before—a wife who had become troublesome to a husband who had tired of her—but never a spiritual leader. Only briefly he wondered if his soul would have to pay a price for killing a high priestess.

"I don't care how you kill her, and I don't want you to do the deed immediately," Lysetta continued when she saw no negative reaction from Yasir.

"Good. I like to have a plan."

Never before had he killed anyone of such power and influence, and the truth was he had never before needed more than a few minutes to plan a killing and his subsequent escape. When he had killed the moneylender's wife, he simply covered his face with a

256

hood, slashed her throat with a dagger, and darted away, disappearing into the crowd. All his assassinations had been handled in similar fashion, but there were too many bodyguards surrounding the high priestess for such a simple method to be successful. The assassination would be even more difficult because Pharaoh Moamin Abbakka was worried that Tanaka would once again be kidnapped by barbarians, so the guards were on constant vigil.

"Have you heard of the foreigner who returned Tanaka to Egypt?"

Yasir nodded. He'd heard the man was a giant with golden hair and that all women found him extremely attractive. This surprised Yasir, since he'd never believed that any woman thought any man was attractive.

"I'll want him killed, too. His name is Tabor. He's a dangerous man."

And you're a dangerous woman, Yasir thought.

"But you mustn't kill either of them until I tell you," she said, thinking that it would be a crime to kill Tabor before she'd sampled the sensuality that he exuded.

"Or before you pay me," Yasir added. His senses were dulled slightly by sexual satiation, but not so completely that he was willing to murder without due reward.

Lysetta smiled at Yasir and nodded slowly. He was a repulsive, ugly man with thick lips unsuitable for kisses. It was uncomfortable to spread her legs for him, but nothing worse than that. Once his usefulness to her was over, he'd never touch her again; and she would hire another assassin to assassinate him.

But as long as she had found a killer to do her bidding, she was going to make the most of it.

"There could be others . . ." she said, letting the sentence trail off.

"If you have the money, then you have the services of my dagger." Yasir placed his hand on Lysetta's naked thigh. He might want her again, and he sensed that as the number of people she wanted murdered continued to climb, the more she would need him. He liked being needed by someone like Lysetta.

"If, perhaps, I could arrange it so that you have a private meeting with the pharaoh, would your dagger cut his throat as easily as that of a common man's?" She saw his eyes widen at mention of the pharaoh's name. She bent over to kiss his chest again. Her tongue quickly circled his nipple, and she was thankful that he couldn't see her grimace at the unwashed taste of his flesh. "And what about Kahlid? Can you kill a priest as well as a high priestess?"

Again, she felt Yasir flinch, but Lysetta was not concerned. She had the ugly little assassin under her spell, and she was certain that he would do anything she wanted.

Yasir felt her lips and tongue working on his flesh, and he closed his eyes. Killing a pharaoh was bad, he knew. Very bad for the afterlife. And what about killing Kahlid? He knew that she was Kahlid's mistress. She was dangerous—even more dangerous and deadly than he was—and even Yasir knew it. . . . but somehow that didn't really disturb him, especially not when she kissed him so intimately, purring words of praise, telling him how handsome he was, how virile, how lucky she was that he would allow her to touch him, kiss him. . . .

"Just tell me who you want killed," he heard himself whisper.

"I will. I will," she replied.

Chapter Twenty

Tabor looked at the young man standing guard outside the library door. He thought he knew all the guards who had been assigned to protect Tanaka, but this was a new face . . . new, and different. He didn't have the fresh, energetic, dedicated look in his eyes common to the others. He did not look like a man whom Tabor would want to be aboard ship with and call a fellow Viking. Rather, he had the sallow look of the early stages of dissipation.

"What is your name?" Tabor asked, stepping close to the man. Was that wine on the guard's breath?

The man looked straight into Tabor's eyes, but he did not respond. His mouth twisted into a sneer. He glanced at the guard positioned at the opposite side of the door and smiled, an insulting smirk that leaped over cultural barriers to deliver a direct slap to Tabor's face.

"Little man," Tabor hissed, struggling to speak the language as distinctly as possible and to keep his anger in check, "if you do not answer me, I will take your throat in my hands and see if I can squeeze the answer *from* you." He leaned down so that his nose nearly touched the guard's. "Speak!"

"My name is Abdul," he said at last, scowling. "And what is your name?"

Tabor straightened and moved just a little closer to the guard, making it clear that he stood half a head taller than the Egyptian.

"My name is Tabor. Your pharaoh has made it clear that I am allowed to come and go as I choose, wherever in the palace I wish to go. You should know that you cannot ask questions of me. . . . or perhaps you were too drunk to remember what you were told?"

"I'm never that drunk, though sometimes the smell of foreigners affects my stomach."

Tabor had promised Tanaka that he would not be violent with any of her people, but this man was pushing his promise as far as it could be taken. For a second, Tabor stepped back and wondered how angry Tanaka would be if he gave this impudent cretin the beating he clearly deserved. Abdul was strong, and he had the look of a man who had been in many fights. Still, never for a second did Tabor fear that his own powers and prowess would be insufficient to the task.

"Speak your mind, if you have one," Tabor whispered, staring at Abdul.

"I have nothing to say to you," he drawled.

Tabor looked at the other fresh-faced guard, who wanted no part of the argument.

"What is your name?" Tabor asked of the quiet guard.

"Menna."

"Menna, I want you to keep watch on Abdul as

261

well as on High Priestess Tanaka. If Abdul does anything wrong, I will hold you responsible."

Menna blanched, but he squared his shoulders and nodded in agreement, averting his eyes from Abdul, who muttered vague threats under his breath.

When Tabor entered the library, he found Tanaka once again hunched over the small desk, brush in hand, writing on the papyrus. At his entrance, she put her brush down and smiled broadly, a smile which warmed Tabor's heart.

"I was hoping you would come to see me," she said.

With the faintest flick of her wrist, she dismissed the two old scribes who had been her almost constant companions since her return. When she was alone in the library with Tabor, she went around the desk and rose up on her tiptoes to kiss his mouth.

"What's wrong?" she asked, looking up into his eyes.

"What makes you say that?"

"I can feel the tension in you." She placed her palm on his chest, feeling his strength through the fine linen robes the Egyptians were famous for. "Tell me."

"I don't like your guards."

"Them?" Tanaka laughed softly. "You needn't be concerned. They're loyal."

"You've got a new one. I haven't seen him before."

"They're soldiers. They change frequently."

"He's got the bearing of a murderer."

Tanaka moved away from Tabor. "I don't want to argue with you," she said. There was exhaustion and exasperation in her tone. "I'm weary of all the responsibilities I've had thrust upon me since my return," she continued. "No one maintained decent records of what supplies the palace had or where those supplies were kept, where the grain was being stored, or how much we have."

"What does that have to do with the guards?"

Tanaka turned on her heel, her dark eyes suddenly flashing. "It doesn't have anything to do with the guards, Tabor! It has everything to do with me! I'm tired, exhausted! I've been working hard to try to restore some semblance of order to the palace, and I simply do not have the energy or the inclination to worry about who is standing outside that door! It just doesn't matter, don't you see? I've got more vital matters to concern myself with!"

Tabor looked at Tanaka and shook his head. Every time he walked through the palace, his sixth sense warned him that treachery was afoot, brewing thick and pungent. He could smell deceit in the air. And though he did not know Moamin well, he respected the pharaoh's judgment, and assigning a man like Abdul to protect the third highest ranking member of the palace did not seem characteristic.

"I am concerned for your protection, and you respond to that concern with scorn and insults." He threw his hands up in frustration. "You must be a brilliant woman to know everything there is to know!"

"I know that you're thinking like a Viking, and that's why you see trouble where there is none!" Tanaka shot back, not at all abashed by Tabor's anger. "Now unless you've got something else to say, I'll thank you to allow me to return to my work. I have many responsibilities in this palace, and I take them seriously."

Tabor stormed out of the library, his teeth clenched

in rage. He half hoped that Abdul would get in his way so that he could knock the vile Egyptian to the ground, but Abdul moved aside. If he had so much as said a word, Tabor would have put a fist in his mouth. But—fortunately for him—he said nothing at all.

The Viking headed for the sea to think. Tanaka was in danger. He knew this because he sensed it and he trusted his senses. He also knew that she had let the power of her responsibilities blind her to the world around her; and because she was so overloaded with work, so exhausted with the duties that had been neglected since her abduction, she was not thinking as logically as she ought.

Her words had cut him to the marrow, but he would not allow his anger toward her affect his judgment, which said that at all costs he would protect her from danger within the palace . . . even if she didn't think there was any.

"Pardon," the young man said, standing obediently just outside Lysetta's doorway. When she met his gaze, the young man entered the room.

"What is it?" Lysetta asked, slipping into a robe. Kahlid had left her bed only a few minutes earlier, and she had been lying naked, plotting what needed to be done if she was to hold in her own hands the wealth and power she craved but which had thus far eluded her.

"You said that I was to inform you immediately if the tall man with yellow hair and High Priestess Tanaka ever spoke in anger to one another again."

Lysetta's dark eyes glittered with excitement as a

series of new plans and plots snaked through her mind.

"How long ago?" she asked.

"I came here immediately."

Lysetta smiled at the eager youth and patted his cheek. "You'll be rewarded for this," she said, her voice sultry, promising much more than monetary remuneration. "Leave now, and tell my servants to attend me. All of them! Do you know where Tabor has gone?"

"Toward the docks, I believe."

Lysetta waved the young man away, no longer needing him.

Tabor was going to the water again. Lysetta had noticed that whenever he was troubled, he sought the ocean.

She wondered briefly what Tabor and Tanaka had been arguing about, then cast the thought aside. It mattered little. They were arguing, and that was all that Lysetta needed if her plans were to work as she hoped.

She tossed off her robe as half a dozen female servants entered her chambers. Nobitia was among them, and Lysetta was pleased because the girl was particularly artful in applying eye makeup.

"Lay out my finest robes," Lysetta demanded. "And get my perfume flask. The green one."

"But you said you'd use the perfume in the green flask only if—" Nobitia began.

"Silence! This is an *emergency!* I want to be at my absolute best, so bring the green perfume flask to me *now!*"

Nobitia scurried away, her shoulders hunched as though she carried a great weight. It was the last time she would ever question Lysetta about anything.

Soon Lysetta left her chambers, trailing a rich, delicate perfume in the air, a gown of exquisite violet linen draped loosely about her body yet defining its curves and valleys. Dark makeup highlighted her eyes, and red dye had turned her cheeks pink and her lips crimson. On her feet were the finest sandals of goatskin. Dangling from her ears were precious gems secured with slender gold wire.

When she stepped out of the palace and into the street, Lysetta could feel eyes upon her, though she pretended to be unaware of the attention she was attracting. Men turned their heads to watch her as she passed.

It would be impossible for Tabor to deny her this time. She was more certain of it than she had been of anything in her life.

The closer she got to the pier, the more Lysetta was aware of the differences between herself and Tabor. She could smell the Mediterranean saltwater in the air, and even the faint scent of fish. She wrinkled her nose at the smells. She had done all she could to avoid areas like this, to insulate herself from people like those who now surrounded her. They were laborers, thick-muscled and perspiring in the heat of dusk. They wore harsh durable linens, always left in the natural beige color that Lysetta found repugnantly common.

Yet this was the place where Tabor felt most comfortable, where he put his mind and soul at ease. Did she really want to be in the arms of a man like that?

Yes!

Her body shouted the immediate answer. She

wanted him *because* he was so different from the social milieu that sanctioned backstabbing delivered with perfect manners. He was raw and primitive, and everything about him suggested that sex would be powerful, uninhibited, and endlessly satisfying.

She was aware of her body as she walked. She could feel the empty hunger and the swishing of the fabric against her thighs as she walked.

By the time Lysetta at last found Tabor, her mind had worked her body into a feverish state of anticipation.

"Hello," she said, walking down the narrow plank to the boat.

When Tabor turned his head toward her, his expression was grim. She hoped he would smile upon seeing her, but he did not. He acknowledged her presence with the faintest nod of his head, then resumed inspecting the new fishing longboat that carpenters had just completed that afternoon.

As Lysetta stepped off the plank onto the boat, she looked around quickly. There was no one around, and though the boat was hardly the most romantic location Lysetta could imagine for a tryst with Tabor, she was pragmatic enough to realize that this was where *he* felt most comfortable. The empty boat offered enough privacy for her, but she'd heard the Viking was less comfortable about having his body seen by others than Egyptians typically were.

"Do you like it?" Lysetta asked. She sat down beside Tabor, who continued to study the Egyptian method of tying down the sails. When Tabor shrugged his shoulders, Lysetta slipped closer so that her knee touched his. "You look good in your new clothes."

"They're slippery," Tabor replied. "Smooth and slippery."

"We have the finest looms and weavers in all the world," Lysetta explained.

"Perhaps, but I still prefer the feel of my own clothes."

"But they're so rough and scratchy."

"They feel like clothes are supposed to feel."

"Viking clothes, perhaps."

Tabor turned, his eyes bright and piercing. "And I am a Viking. Shouldn't I be wearing Viking clothes?"

Lysetta looked away. This wasn't the conversation she'd planned to have with Tabor. She hoped that his anger toward Tanaka was what was making him behave so brusquely with her.

"Yes, you are a Viking," she said, and almost casually dropped her hand to his knee. "Everyone can see that. You tower above every man in the palace."

Tabor looked at the small hand upon his knee, then his gaze moved slowly up her arm until it met Lysetta's. His expression was unreadable, acknowledging that she touched him but not giving approval or disapproval.

"You seem sad," Lysetta said, her voice low now. "Sad and lonely. Is there anything I can do to make you feel . . . less lonely?" Her hand moved along his thigh. She squeezed his leg, and though he was relaxed, his muscle seemed solidly flexed. Tremors of excitement raced along Lysetta's spine. Why wasn't he doing anything?

"Sadness and loneliness are not Viking emotions," Tabor said sternly. "You are the one who seems lonely."

Lysetta leaned away from Tabor. Curiosity compelled her to ask, "What makes you think I am lonely? I have people around me whenever I want them."

"Yes, whenever you want them. They answer when you command them. My men do the same thing. But my men spend time with me without being ordered to. Your servants do not."

"And what does that tell you? *I* don't want them near me anyway!"

Lysetta stood quickly and almost walked away from Tabor. What did he know? He hardly spoke the language. How could he truly know what her life was like, what her innermost feelings really were?

"Why did you come here?" Tabor asked, appraising her. He noticed the added touches of makeup, the gems at her ears, and the exceptional color and quality of her gown. He knew she had made an effort to look especially attractive for him and that she'd sought him out. The pier was not a place Lysetta frequented.

"I was . . ." Words faltered as Lysetta contemplated lying. Why did he have to be so handsome? It would be so much easier if he were just an ugly barbarian! "I was looking for you. I heard that you had an argument with the high priestess. I thought you might like companionship."

Tabor stood then, and Lysetta sighed. So tall and handsome, and his blue eyes were not ugly, like Kahlid had insisted, but beautiful, brilliant, and beguiling.

"You have spies?"

"I have friends in the palace. They tell me things. I know what happens."

"You have servants," Tabor corrected. "Do those

servants tell others what you do just as they tell you what others do?"

"You don't have to worry. I wasn't followed here. I am alone, and anything we do will remain a secret."

Tabor shook his head, looking out to sea. Why did she have to be here now? He hungered for Tanaka's touch, and she was in no mood to listen to what he had to say, much less enjoy a few passionate hours of loveplay. Now he had Lysetta throwing herself at him. If Tanaka had been anyone other than who she was, Tabor would have easily taken the pleasure that Lysetta offered. But Tanaka had touched him deeply, and her influence over his actions extended beyond those moments when she was with him.

"I must leave," Tabor said suddenly, feeling the hungers of his passion building as his strength of will slipped.

"No, you don't," Lysetta replied with equal resolve. She grabbed his wrist with both hands, preventing his departure. She hugged his hand to her bosom. "You don't have to go anywhere. There's nothing she can do for you that I can't. And believe me, I will do it much . . . much . . . better!"

Tabor weakened. Lysetta leaned into him, pressing her breasts against him as she tilted her head back to invite a kiss. When Tabor did not immediately accommodate her needs, she hooked a hand around his neck and pulled him down.

"I will be so much better," Lysetta purred, her breath warm against his lips. She felt his resistance, but she was unshakable. "Forget all about that child, and taste the pleasures of a woman!"

She kissed him and sighed loudly, wanting Tabor to know that she was passionate and uninhibited, experienced and not afraid of a man's touch. When the kiss did not become more fevered on Tabor's part, Lysetta parted her lips invitingly. Still the kiss did not deepen.

"What is wrong?" she asked, a hint of self-doubt in her tone. She grabbed Tabor's hand by the wrist and forcibly placed his palm over her breast. "Does this not please you?"

Tabor looked at Lysetta, feeling her breast against his palm and feeling shame, anger and frustration, too. He did not want her, and the only reason that he didn't was because he was under the influence of a high priestess who made other women seem bland and unappealing.

"It does not," Tabor said quietly. "But the blame is not with you, it is with me." He took a step away from Lysetta, and her expression changed from passionate hunger to cold-blooded fury. "I have been vexed," he said honestly, not knowing why he felt it was necessary to speak the truth to this woman who despised him. "I am under the spell of the high priestess. She has me in her control."

Lysetta spewed invectives so quickly at Tabor that he was unable to understand a single word. Then she left the boat, her purple gown glittering and flashing against her legs in the evening breeze.

Tabor watched her stomp toward the village, and when she was out of sight, he went to the end of the pier and sat, hugging a knee to his chest, staring out to sea. Never before had he turned down the advances of one woman out of loyalty to another.

What would Sven think if he discovered what Tabor had done? He would laugh, that's what he would do. He'd toss his head back and laugh aloud because

Tabor had long bragged how no woman would ever capture his heart exclusively, and now there could be no denying that Tanaka had done exactly that.

So engrossed in his thoughts was he that Tabor did not notice the small, furtive man slinking away, keeping to the shadows, heading back toward the palace from which he'd come.

His eyelids fluttered briefly, and Kahlid emitted a low, ominous monotone. Then, suddenly, his eyes opened wide and he looked directly into Neenah's frightened eyes as she sat at the opposite side of the table from him.

"I fear we will all discover that the foreigner and his men bring with them grave danger for all in the palace," Kahlid said softly, his voice carrying with it all the sadness and concern that he could manufacture.

Neenah was literally aquiver with fear as she listened carefully to Kahlid's every word. She could hardly breathe she was so scared for the lives of her husband and the people she loved who lived in the palace and the village.

"And High Priestess Tanaka has changed, too," Kahlid continued, sensing that Neenah was receptive to anything he had to say. "Since her return, the influence of the foreigner has been apparent to all, has it not? She has usurped power that was never hers, and she has complained and criticized all who labored to do her work in her absence."

Everyone in the palace knew that Tanaka was furious with the way the records had been kept by Kahlid and his minions, and she'd made no effort whatsoever to spare anyone's feelings when discrepancies were discovered. Gold, wine, perfume, and other precious goods such as grain and dried fish in the palace warehouses were missing. Though some suspected Kahlid had fattened his own purse with the goods, no one—not even Tanaka—dared point an accusing finger without irrefutable, undeniable proof.

Kahlid had immediately initiated his own rumors, complaining that the errors were in Tanaka's accounts, and perhaps it would not be out of line to inspect her personal accounts.

So when Kahlid mentioned Tanaka's attitude shift since her kidnap and return, Neenah was sadly forced to agree that she had, in fact, changed greatly from the happy, young high priestess who had been ripped from their loving embrace so many months earlier.

"Do you think the foreigner is responsible for this change?" Neenah asked, needing to hear the words from a priest, someone she could believe without question.

"Very likely. . . . his power over others is great. . . . it is almost unworldly the power he has—"

"Power from the underworld?" Neenah gasped.

Kahlid had carefully led Neenah to the conclusion he wanted without having to push her. And now that she was there, it took almost no skill at all to push her over the edge.

"Perhaps. . . . I cannot see where his power comes from. . . . I am a spiritual man .•. . powers that come from the underworld . . . their source is murky to my inner eye. Evil from that source blinds me."

Neenah was openly shivering now. The thought of a huge Viking like Tabor wielding powers from the underworld shook the foundations of love and tolerance that Neenah had long prided herself in.

"Tanaka . . . the high priestess. . . . she has changed, but she is not completely to blame for all that has changed. . . . she is under a power . . . a great, evil power . . ."

And then, with a heavy sigh, Kahlid slumped forward, dropping his head onto his forearms as though greatly fatigued by the visions he had seen.

He said nothing for several minutes, letting Neenah ponder the suspicions he'd sown on the fertile soil of her mind. Though Kahlid had initially intended to have Neenah killed when Moamin and Tanaka were executed, he thought now of letting her live. It might be easier for the soldiers to believe that he was governing by divine right if someone from the pharaoh's family was at his side. Neenah believed in him completely, never questioning anything he said. If he could convince her that Tabor was responsible for all the murders, Neenah could serve as a figurehead. Otherwise, the villagers and soldiers might come to believe that Kahlid was behind the deaths.

Of course, to follow this plan meant that Lysetta must be murdered with the others, but this caused Kahlid only a moment's displeasure. Though Lysetta was a stimulating bed partner, he'd been growing tired of her. Assassination was as good a way as any to rid himself of a mistress that had outlived her usefulness and excitement. Besides, his spy had said that Lysetta had gone to the pier and was seen kissing the Viking barbarian. Kahlid did not believe that he should be true to just one woman, but he insisted on fidelity from his mistress.

Chapter Twenty-one

Tabor looked at Kahlid, who met his gaze unflinchingly. The two men did not like each other, though harsh words had never been exchanged between them. As they sat now in the anteroom waiting for Tanaka to finish her tarot reading for Moamin, there was no reason for either of them to be more than civil.

"What is it about me that bothers you so?" Tabor asked suddenly. He always preferred confronting problems and people directly, and the bluntness of his question had the effect on Kahlid that he'd wanted—it threw him off balance.

"Nothing," Kahlid answered. Then, quickly, he regained his composure, leaning forward on the granite bench to place his elbows on his knees. He scratched his chin, pulling at the small beard there. "Actually, there is much about you that I do not like, if we are being honest, but since what I do not like has no bearing on the pharaoh, or this palace, I see no reason to put my feelings to words." He smiled then, the devilish smile of someone very much pleased with himself. "What is it about *me* that bothers you, Tabor? I've seen in your eyes the hatred you feel. It'll do you no good to deny it."

Tabor had to control his temper to keep from grabbing the priest by the front of his fine robes and shaking him the way a cat does a mouse. But he'd promised Tanaka he would never use violence against any of her people.

There was another reason why Tabor did not let his baser instincts dictate. He believed that Kahlid was an enemy far more dangerous, perhaps, than any enemy that sailed the seas near Hedeby. Kahlid's power and wealth were enormous, and if he was indeed foe, then Tabor did not want to let his true feelings be known.

"I deny nothing," Tabor said in his quiet, rumbling way, speaking the Egyptian language slowly. "All in this palace know I have feelings for the high priestess, and that she has spent her days and many of her nights working with you and not with me."

Kahlid grinned then, nodding. "As the palace high priestess, she has many duties that must be fulfilled. I am the next highest ranking spiritual advisor, and there is much that we have needed to consult on together. You needn't be jealous of me. I have no designs upon Tanaka."

Tabor nodded and looked away, as though contemplating what Kahlid had just said, a jealous man trying to come to grips with his own irrational fears. Actually, he was wondering exactly how badly Kahlid wanted to be the palace high priest, a position he had filled—badly so, according to Tanaka—when Tanaka had been kidnapped and away at sea.

"Sometimes, when a woman fills your heart with unease, the best way to make your heart feel good again is to be in the arms of another woman." Kahlid grinned lustfully, as though he was a good friend of Tabor's and they were sharing a licentious joke. "But surely, you know what I mean."

Tabor nodded, but he was thinking, *You and Lysetta deserve each other. I don't know which one of you is more treacherous than the other.*

"Perhaps, when you have the time, you might like me to read the cards for you," Kahlid continued. "You will find the tarot can tell you things about yourself and your future that no one else can."

Tabor shook his head. "I do not believe the tarot can tell me anything," he said, intending offense. "If ever I have so much time with nothing to do, perhaps I'll find a beautiful Egyptian woman to spend it with."

An icy hardness slid over Kahlid before he forced the false smile of camaraderie back to his lips. "Of course."

Silence surrounded the two men as they sat outside the huge room that Tanaka used as her private temple, the room she felt had the greatest spiritual energy. Then the huge door, made of cedar and reinforced with bronze and copper, opened smoothly upon its well-oiled hinges, and Pharaoh Moamin Abbakka stepped out, flanked by Tanaka.

"Most enlightening, Tanaka. Most wonderfully enlightening," Moamin beamed.

"I try to be of help when I look at the cards," she replied modestly, clearly happy that she had pleased her pharaoh but uncomfortable with his effusive compliments. "It is a gift. I really can't accept credit for the visions myself."

"A gift from the gods," Moamin said, his voice

hushed as though he feared that speaking such words might cause the gods to take away Tanaka's powers— powers which the pharaoh counted on when he made decisions of state.

With barely a nod of recognition to Kahlid and Tabor, Moamin turned and entered a circle of his most trusted bodyguards and advisors.

"It's good to see you here," she said, her tone conversational, as though she could trick Kahlid into thinking that her relationship with Tabor was just that of a spiritual advisor to a man needing counsel. "Won't you please come in?"

Kahlid began to follow them, but Tanaka stopped him. "You won't be needed," she said.

Kahlid had come to the temple hoping to be of service to Moamin, only to be snubbed when the pharaoh asked that Tanaka read the tarot cards for him. And now, after waiting nearly two hours, he was being cast aside once again.

"You may leave. But I do thank you for your consideration," Tanaka continued, hardly glancing in Kahlid's direction, able only to look at Tabor.

When Tabor and Tanaka were alone in the temple room, the door closed and the bolt thrown, Tanaka threw herself into his arms, kissing him full on the mouth.

"Thank you for coming to me," she said, her hand resting lightly against his cheek. "I have so wanted to read the cards for you, and it seems like my duties consume all my time . . ."

She let the words trail away. Would it be some hideous offense to the gods if she should make love to Tabor here, in the temple room? she wondered. She thought it wouldn't be. She had searched the cards,

278

her heart, her soul. She had looked deep inside herself for an answer, and nothing that she could see indicated that sharing her heart and soul and love with Tabor was wrong—even if that sharing took place in the temple room.

Taking his hand in hers, she led him across the great room illuminated with countless candles and oil lamps made of gold. There were sections of the temple room for the reading of tarot, for prayer, for the writing of holy dictates and royal decrees. Only the elite of the palace were granted entry to this room, but this was not known to Tabor.

"Sit there," she said, indicating the pillows on the floor in front of a short-legged wooden table. She sat opposite him shuffling rectangular pieces of papyrus stiffened with beeswax and intricately painted.

Tabor watched Tanaka's hands and the tarot cards. He did not believe, but in an effort to find common ground with Tanaka, whom he had not seen nearly enough of lately, he had agreed to let her read his tarot.

"Lay your hand upon the cards," Tanaka instructed, placing the papyrus down on the table before Tabor. "Think of the questions you would most like to have answered."

Tabor placed his hand upon the tarot cards, but he was looking at Tanaka as he did so. "What I most want to know is when Kahlid plans to betray you."

The words spilled from Tabor's mouth before he could stop them, and as soon as they were spoken, he was filled with regret. Tanaka stiffened, her face turning first angry, then hurt. Tears pooled in her large, dark eyes as she stared, unblinking, at Tabor. Tension thickened in the room.

"And. . . . and I was foolish enough to think that you'd actually come here for me . . . to be happy . . . with me!"

Tabor wanted to take her into his arms and say the gentle, loving words he knew she wanted to hear. But what she *wanted* to hear was not what she *needed* to hear. Tabor had no proof but his gut told him Tanaka was in danger. Grave, mortal danger. He believed the forces came from within the temple — forces quite likely controlled by Kahlid, a man who stood to gain a great deal if once again Tanakah were unable to serve as high priestess to Pharaoh Moamin Abbakka.

"I do want to be with you," Tabor said at last. "I want to make you happy and keep you happy. I don't ever again want bad things to happen to you. That's why I must stay on my guard, Tanaka. Treachery and deceit are everywhere."

Tanaka sprang to her feet, a flurry of purple and white, ebony hair flying. She had planned an exciting, romantic tryst for herself and Tabor, something she felt they both desperately needed. Now he had turned that new tryst into an old argument.

"Treachery, treachery! Treachery and deceit are all you can see!" she shouted, backing away from Tabor as though he might leap at her any moment. "This is not your homeland! Can't you understand that we do not behave that way here?"

"Can't you understand that you are not as loved as you think you are?"

"Certainly not by you!" Tanaka shot back. And then the tears began to flow because there could be no denying now that Tabor did not love her. If he did, she reasoned, he would not try so hard to destroy every gentle moment the two of them might share.

"That is not what I said."

"You didn't have to say it! You say it all the time in everything you do!" Tears streamed down her cheeks. Tabor moved around the table toward her, but Tanaka held her hands up to ward him off. "Leave! Leave me now! Get out of my temple, you barbarian!"

It was the first time that Tanaka had ever called him by the name with damning intent. It was an insult not only to Tabor, but to everything he was and everything he stood for.

She watched a muscle flex in his jaw. His huge hands, capable of violence and tenderness, were balled into enormous, threatening fists.

Without another word, Tabor turned and left the room. Once alone, Tanaka slumped onto a mound of pillows, giving in to the sobs and tears that shook her body, feeling further away from Tabor than she ever had.

Tabor stormed through the village, pleased that the people moved aside when he approached them. The anger he felt more than altered his expression; it seemed to ooze out of his pores so that even if a person weren't looking at him, the anger could be felt.

It's always crowded in this land, Tabor thought, heading once again toward the water. Perhaps he could find a small fishing boat and spend time alone on the water. That would restore his good spirits. To restore the strength of his soul, he needed to be alone. His mind worked most clearly when there was no one near to disturb his concentration.

Barbarian. The word had been spoken by Tanaka many times, but only once had she ever meant to wound him with it. And she had succeeded.

High Priestess Tanaka could not be bothered with the opinions of a lowly foreigner like Tabor. That's what she meant. She believed that her people, her ways, her beliefs, were vastly superior to his, and that was why she could not believe that an Egyptian, especially one living within the palace, would ever do anything to hurt her.

It was dusk. In a few minutes the sun would be down and the villagers would be safely nestled in their sun-bleached homes with their families. Tabor knew that he should return to the palace and began walking in that direction. But then he felt that feeling—that indefinable feeling that he had ignored only once before, once, when Ingmar the Savage had nearly killed him.

His stride lessened and the villagers stopped studying him with quite so much trepidation. He even smiled when an elderly woman carrying a basket laden with bread and onions—the staple diet for these people—paused in her work to look at him.

He was being followed.

Tabor knew it without having seen the man or men who followed him.

Who followed him? And why?

The pharaoh had assigned bodyguards to Tabor. When Tabor explained that this would not be necessary, that if he ever felt he needed bodyguards he would have his own men perform that task, Moamin then assigned a battery of bodyguards to follow Tabor discreetly. Tabor had spotted the men almost immediately, and, when he spoke with Moamin again, asked once more that the bodyguards be removed. So Moamin had promised that he would allow Tabor to handle his own security. But had he been true to his word?

Tabor didn't want to think about the political ramifications of killing an Egyptian who was only trying to ensure his safety.

It was still nothing more than a feeling, but Tabor behaved as though the danger tingling in the pit of his stomach were irrefutable. Rather than heading straight for the pier, he paused at several of the stands where villagers were selling their wares and casually inspected some linens and jewelry, neither of which he had any interest in purchasing.

He turned holding a square of linen, acting as though he wanted to inspect it in the waning sunlight. But he was not looking at the cloth, and when he turned, he saw a small man suddenly stop walking to inspect a live duck.

Tabor summed the man up with a glance. What he saw did not surprise him. The man was short, had fleshy lips and small, cruel eyes. An ugly man, Tabor realized, ugly in ways that transcended cultural differences and prejudices. He had the furtive look of a man who felt life had been unfair to him and, because he was the victim of this unfairness, any atrocity he committed was therefore acceptable.

Tabor neatly refolded the linen and handed it back to the merchant, then continued on his way, with apparent aimlessness. Though he walked slowly, his eyes darted right and left, and his mind examined dozens of possible courses of action to take.

He made his way in the direction of the pier, but eased far to the west of it where there would be fewer people. If he were to discover who was directing the ugly little man's actions, he would need to appear to unwittingly fall into the man's trap, then turn the tables on him.

Thirty minutes later, Tabor was convinced that there was only one man following him. At the outskirts of the village, few people milled about, and the sun was just minutes away from disappearing beneath the horizon.

He followed a narrow path that sheepherders used, exchanged pleasantries with a cheesemaker who was closing up his stand, then slipped behind a building, pressing his body against the wall, enshrouded in shadow. Tabor removed the slender-bladed dagger strapped to his stomach. The dagger had saved his life many times in the past, and the feel of its smooth, polished handle reassured him now.

He waited, hardly breathing, holding the dagger at his side, hoping to use it only as a threat and nothing deadlier.

The little man's footsteps were quick and light, but Tabor heard them. When he rounded the corner of the cheesemaker's building, Tabor made his move, his powerful body uncoiling from the shadows with fluid grace and awesome, frightening swiftness. Swiftly he fell upon the little man, leading with a huge left fist that connected solidly with the Egyptian's jaw and sent him staggering. A heartbeat later Tabor smashed the butt end of the dagger against the back of the little man's head.

Tabor straddled the body. He'd hit the man harder than he'd intended, anger steeling his muscles. The little man groaned, and Tabor breathed a sigh of relief, knowing that he had not killed him.

"Quiet," Tabor said in Egyptian. He placed a big foot on the man's chest. Had he been back in Denmark, Tabor would have tossed his head back on his shoulders and given a victory scream over his vanquished enemy. "Speak only the truth. Give me only answers. Do you understand?"

The little man nodded.

"What is your name?"

"Yasir."

"Why are you following me?"

"I have been paid."

"Who pays you?"

Yasir's thick, fleshy lips glistened with saliva. They moved, but he did not speak.

"If you do not speak, you will have no need of a tongue," Tabor said, twisting the dagger in his hand, indicating that if he wanted to cut Yasir's tongue out, he would do so.

"Lysetta paid me."

"What does she want? Your time is running out, and when it does, so will your life!"

Yasir managed a babbling sound, and more spittle glistened on his lips. Finally, his eyes wild with fear, he said, "She will kill me if I tell you! Promise me you won't tell her."

"I promise I'll kill you if you don't tell me everything you know."

"She paid me to see if you are with any women. I . . . I think she wants you for herself."

Yasir continued talking until Tabor threatened to cut his tongue out if he said another word. Tabor did not completely believe the story. He knew that Lysetta wanted him, that she had been furious with him when he'd refused to share his body with her. But he believed he'd met women like Lysetta before, and those types of women went on to other men when they felt spurned. They didn't kill the man who had spurned them. Dangerous and compulsive, true, but their danger was short-lived and lacked the essential lasting hatred of an Ingmar the Savage.

"Get away from me," Tabor said, taking his foot off Yasir's chest. "If I ever see you again, I'm going to break both your legs. Then I'll never again have to wonder whether you are following me."

Yasir was gone in seconds, disappearing into the shadows.

Alone, Tabor wondered whether Yasir's story was true or false. His words appeared true, but his fear hadn't seemed entirely real. It was as though he were exaggerating his fear so that Tabor would believe his story.

Was Yasir cunning enough to invent a ruse like that? Was he telling a half-truth? Sometimes half-truths were the worst kind of lie, the deadliest and most destructive kind.

Tabor headed back toward the palace, to rejoin his men. He trusted them and he was certain they would protect Tanaka. He believed Yasir was both telling the truth and lying. . . . and knowing where truth ended and the lie began was impossible.

Tabor felt certain that both his life and Tanaka's were in peril. Even if she didn't believe her own people would hurt her, he did; and as long as he did, he would do everything he could to protect her from the fatal foibles of her own gentle heart.

Sven refilled Tabor's goblet with beer, then sat beside his leader. They were in the chambers which Sven shared with Carl. The two Egyptian women that had been seeing to their needs were in the room as well, though they were tending to Carl, who lay on a cot, his head and body heavily bandaged. Only a few hours earlier he'd been found in the village, lying in a pool of his own blood. Egyptian men—four of them, Carl had explained through puffy, bleeding lips—had attacked him from behind. They used their fists on him until he was beaten to the ground, then they used their feet to kick him into unconsciousness. Even then they did not stop until the villagers began to scream.

"You're sure that Carl didn't do anything to provoke the attack?" Tabor asked, speaking fluidly in his native tongue with the one man in the world whom he trusted completely. He did not have to worry about the Egyptian women overhearing them because they did not speak the language.

"Positive. You said not to cause any trouble, and we haven't. He was just out looking, that's all."

Tabor scratched his cheek, Staring at the amber liquid that he swirled in his goblet. Fury brewed in his stomach. Egyptians had attacked one of his men and beaten him badly . . . nearly to death. That kind of offense demanded a response from Tabor. He lived by an old, honored code: When someone hits you, you return the blow twice, striking flesh twice as hard, and they'll never hit you again. But whom could he hit? And if he *did* let his violent frustrations and sense of duty prevail, if he did let his fists do what they ached to do, then what chance would he ever have of once again knowing peace and contentment with Tanaka?

"Listen to me," Tabor said, choosing his words with care. "I believe that soon there will be great violence within the walls of this palace. I believe our lives are in danger."

"From the pharaoh?"

"No, I believe he is a good man, but the men near him are evil. That evil will seek to destroy us . . . and Tanaka as well." He looked Sven in the eyes. "You are the only man I have ever trusted completely. I love Tanaka, and I fear for her life. She does not believe that she is in danger."

"I will protect her with my life."

Tabor nodded. Theirs was a friendship that required few words.

Chapter Twenty-two

"I didn't come here to argue with you," Tabor said, his hands on his hips. It was a defiant stance, one that suggested he was more inclined to speak than to listen.

"I'm glad you didn't come to argue because there's something very important that I must tell you." Tanaka saw the cross look that flickered over Tabor's face, but she was determined to be the first to speak. "Last night, some of your men raped a woman in the village and—"

"What?" Tabor bellowed. "That's a lie! My men would never do such a thing! They know my penalty for that, and it's a penalty no man wants to pay!"

Tanaka refused to be intimidated by Tabor. She had spoken with Kahlid, who had spoken personally with the family of the girl who'd been attacked. Kahlid had said the barbarians reeked of beer, laughing when the girl begged for mercy. The hideous memories of her own abduction were still too raw in Tanaka's memory for her to feel any mercy for men guilty of such an atrocity. It had only been serious discussion with the pharaoh that restrained Tanaka from having the guards drag all the Vikings out of the palace and put the spears to them.

"It was your men, Tabor! They were seen! Who else has yellow hair except your men?"

"My men would not do such a thing," Tabor repeated with conviction. "They sail with me. I trust them, and they know what I will not tolerate."

"Well, maybe you'd better tell them again."

"That is not why I came here to speak to you," Tabor continued, as determined as Tanaka to voice his thoughts. "I came here to warn you."

"Warn me about what this time? It seems to me I'm in much greater danger from your people than from my own, though you seem determined to accuse my people of all crimes, real and imagined."

"I tell you once again that you are in danger."

Tanaka looked straight into Tabor's eyes, detesting the fact that once again they were fighting. "You're right. . . . but the only danger I can see has blue eyes and blond hair. It's your men who endanger me, not my own people."

"One of *my* men was attacked by four Egyptian soldiers! Would you explain that?"

"Probably attacked by a father and three irate brothers," Tanaka shot back without a moment's hesitation.

"Four against one? And you try to tell me how superior your people are to mine! Ha! In a fight man to man, Carl would have thrashed them all, but instead they attacked him like a pack of wolves!"

Even Tabor was aware of how ridiculous the argument had become. He had promised himself that he would not raise his voice while he was with her, nor would he criticize anything about her way of doing things. He had intended merely to state that one of his men had been hurt and, for the safety of everyone in the village and in the palace, the attackers should be found immediately and punished so their reign of terror would end. Never had he dreamed that she would lambast him with such a preposterous notion that his men were running riot through the village raping innocent girls.

"What do you intend to do about the accusations?" Tanaka demanded.

For long, tense seconds Tabor looked at her. It would do no good now to tell her that her life was in jeopardy from someone within the palace. It would also do no good to say that he knew in his heart that his men were not responsible for the rape if, in fact, a rape had occurred. Finally, with a resigned sigh that piqued Tanaka's ire even more, he said, "I will talk with my men. Perhaps they have heard something. That is the best that I can do. And please, for your own safety, be careful. Be wary of everyone. I fear terrible things will happen — soon."

They did not kiss when they parted, though they were unattended in the library. When Tanaka was alone, she sat in her chair and wept. The chasm between them grew wider and wider, and though she loved him — loved him as she had never dreamt she could love any man — she began to feel that she would never again know happiness with him. He was distant. They were separated by more than miles, separated by social position and stature, by beliefs, by their notions of truth, by their fears. She was beginning to fear that Tabor, despite his protestations to the contrary, was unable to love a strong women. He *said* he adored her strength, but Tanaka could see that Tabor's words and actions were not the same.

"This is the perfect time," Lysetta said, her eyes wild with excitement as she peered at Kahlid. "Tanaka and the barbarian have been fighting constantly, and the villagers are beginning to believe that the barbarians have been making raids on them in the night."

"I don't want to hasten into this," Kahlid replied, pushing himself a little further away from Lysetta on his bed. "I'm not sure the soldiers are willing to follow my command."

Lysetta huffed softly through her nose, then rose and walked naked across the room. She poured herself a goblet of wine. She made no effort to hide her disappointment in Kahlid for not immediately ordering the assassination of the pharaoh, the high priestess, and Tabor.

"The soldiers are sheep," Lysetta said quietly, shaking her head in open contempt. "Kill their leader and you become their leader. It is as simple as that."

"There's much about power that you do not understand," Kahlid replied, aware that Lysetta was anxious for his ascent to power so that she could share it. However, he had no intention of rushing his plans, particularly since, once they began, Lysetta would be one of the people to be assassinated.

Lysetta pouted at his insult, but then smiled. When she walked back to Kahlid's bed, there was a seductive sway to her hips. She curled beside Kahlid and offered him the goblet.

"Yes, there is a lot that I do not know," she agreed. "And I am impatient. But I only want what is best for you. I want you to have what you deserve. And you can't tell me that Tanaka deserves to be the high priestess."

"The pharaoh is a fool," Kahlid said. "But his foolishness will end soon. I have . . . given money to a man." He looked into a candle, watching the flame, his gaze distant and unfocused. "A dangerous man. As much in the way as the high priestess is to my plans, she's still just an annoyance and nothing more. The pharaoh is the real problem. Once he's out of the way, then nothing can stop me."

He turned his head slowly toward Lysetta and gave her a sleepy, dreamy smile. Everything was proceeding exactly as he wanted it to, from the rumors spreading about the abominable behavior of the Vikings against fair Egyptian maidens to the worsening relationship between Tabor and Tanaka.

"We've got to be patient," Kahlid continued. "If we rush this, something could go wrong. If we take our time and act only when the omens are right, then all our dreams will be realized."

Lysetta did not frighten easily, but as she listened to Kahlid and watched his eyes glaze over, she felt a marrow-deep fear shiver through her. Kahlid talked about *we*, but she sensed he really meant *me*, that she was no longer involved in his plans for the future.

"There are still few key soldiers I need to have aligned with me, but once I gain their allegiance, there'll be nothing to hold me back. If you control the soldiers and you are the spiritual leader, then you shackle the people with chains no one can break." He raised a finger heavenward, nodding his head, speaking slowly and distinctly, but to himself. "I have to be patient, that's all. Soon . . . everyone who has ever

293

prevented me from receiving what is rightfully mine will receive just punishment."

Lysetta felt panic rising like molten lava inside her. She did not want to be patient — she *could* not be patient. Not with Yasir lurking in the village, possibly crowing about his affair with her; not will Tabor living like a prince and rejecting her when she let him know that she was his for the taking.

A few days earlier, Tabor had caught Yasir and threatened his life. Yasir rushed immediately to Lysetta and said he could not go through with the assassination: Tabor was too skilled a warrior for Yasir to assassinate him single-handedly. But Lysetta knew of no other assassins, and she was rightly afraid that the more men she confided in, the greater the chance of Kahlid learning of her plans. Seeing that Yasir was on the verge of walking away forever, Lysetta had seduced him. Previously, when she'd let him touch or kiss her, it had been repulsive but something she was willing to endure to achieve her goals. But this last time with Yasir was more than even her calloused sensibilities could take. His rubbery lips seemed to be everywhere on her in his frantic search for fulfillment — pressed against her mouth, her eyes and ears, her neck and breasts — and everywhere they touched, they left saliva behind.

The longer Lysetta had to keep Yasir in line, the more often she had to sleep with him. . . . and she simply couldn't do that ever again.

No wealth in Egypt was worth that.

"Kahlid, aren't you being a little over-cautious?" Lysetta asked softly.

Was that really fear she heard in her own voice? What if Kahlid had found someone else to satisfy him? Lysetta knew she was beautiful, but she was no longer young, and sometimes a man like Kahlid could only feel young and virile in the arms of a young girl. She pushed the thought from her head. This was not the time for such notions.

"I'm being as cautious as the situation warrants," Kahlid replied. When he looked at Lysetta again, she could tell that he had returned to the present. "What makes you think I'm making a mistake?"

"I never said I t-thought you were making a mistake." Lysetta tried to smile, as though to dismiss her own words, but her lips quivered instead, giving her the appearance of a woman on the verge of tears.

"Yes, you did," Kahlid replied, suddenly getting to his feet. With his passion so recently sated, Lysetta's flaws were glaringly apparent to him. "You just didn't say it quite that way, but you did mean that I am making a mistake."

"No, I didn't."

"Have I made a mistake with you? Have I misjudged you, Lysetta? You're a brilliant woman. We both know that. What we don't both know, though, is what thoughts go through that brilliant head of yours."

"Nothing! Nothing at all, really!"

Kahlid laughed then. He hadn't seen Lysetta squirm in a long, long time. In a day or two, he'd give Abdul a thick, gold coin, and tell him to let the killing begin. And once he'd given that order, the time that Lysetta would spend alive would be drastically limited.

"I'm glad that nothing is going through your head," Kahlid said with a smile. "I truly am. I know that you're lying, of course, but that doesn't really matter.

You wouldn't tell me an important lie, would you?"

"No, never an important lie!"

"You'd only lie to me about the unimportant things, isn't that so?"

There was no answer that Lysetta could give that would absolve her. He had intentionally maneuvered her into this defenseless position, so she said nothing. For a second she wondered if seduction would free her from his tightening web, but she dismissed the idea. Kahlid did not have a licentious gleam shining in his eyes; and if she weren't so confident in her own beauty, she might even have believed that he was looking at her naked body with a certain amount of scorn.

"No need to answer me," Kahlid said finally, breaking the silence. "You'd only be telling yet another lie, and I've grown quite weary of your lies."

"May I enter?" Tanaka asked, leaning against the heavy marble doorway.

Tabor sat on a thick pillow before the hearth. When he looked up and saw Tanaka, his blue eyes were wary. He set aside the gold plate of honey-glazed baked duck, a delicacy in Egypt, and Tabor's favorite meal.

"Please," he said at last.

Tanaka stepped in, smiling to herself. The remains of the duck had been picked almost perfectly clean. Her great Viking warrior had a hearty appetite, and that was just one of the many things that she so adored about him.

"Did you like the duck?" He nodded, his eyes still wary. "Good. I ordered it especially for you."

"Thank you."

She hated it whenever Tabor was stiffly formal with her. She enjoyed her barbarian the most when he was exactly that—her loving, gentle, uncivilized barbarian.

"I know it is your favorite," Tanaka continued, walking slowly into the room, her mind spinning as she tried the impossible—to read what was going through Tabor's mind. When he wanted to hide his thoughts and feelings, Tanaka's powerful intuition was useless. "I wanted to do something to please you."

"My belly is full of good food," Tabor said, his voice devoid of emotion. "I need only to clap my hands and a beautiful servant will rush into this room and fill my goblet with beer. What more could I wish for?"

Tanaka would have been happier if he hadn't been quite so aware of how beautiful his servant was. And it would have put her mind more at ease if he didn't seem quite so contented. But she had planned for this evening with diligence and care, and she wasn't going to let residual anger get in the way.

"I know you well enough to know that there is *much*"—the word came out as a breathy purr of sensuality—"more that you could want. I've spent too many days and too many nights with you to believe that you've got everything you want."

"*Too* many?"

"Not nearly enough."

Tanaka took another step closer, then stopped. Tabor had not risen to greet her, nor had he genuflected as everyone else in the palace, with the exception of the pharaoh and his wife, would have done. There were times when that annoyed Tanaka, but not tonight. Tabor treated her as a woman, just a woman, nothing more, nothing less. She was not a high priestess when she was with him — at least not in his eyes. And tonight, being just a woman was as much as Tanaka wanted.

She had prepared for the evening with much forethought. Her gown was made of the finest woven linen in the land, dyed a shimmering midnight black, trimmed with polished seashells. The gown draped over her left shoulder, where the material was gathered and held together with a red ribbon two inches thick. From there the material spread out across her chest and back, covering her bosom. The slanting material was gathered again at her hip, the twin halves sweeping gracefully, forming a diagonal line high across her thighs. She wore sandals of goatskin that had just been made by craftsman that day. Around her left ankle was a slender gold chain, ornamented with bright gems held by gold wire.

"You look . . ." Tabor began, then stopped himself. There had been too many cross words between himself and Tanaka lately for him to forget them so quickly.

Tanaka knelt on a pillow near Tabor's hip, and her gown split, revealing the curve of her right thigh all the way to the hip. She noticed that Tabor's gaze went down to her legs and noticed, too, with some disappointment, that he did not let his gaze linger upon her very long.

She folded her hands in her lap, wishing and waiting for Tabor to finish his sentence. She took a shallow, calming breath and turned the full force of her ebony eyes upon Tabor, determined — with a rational, confrontational logic that under other circumstances would have pleased Tabor enormously, since she'd learned it from him—to get to the heart of their problem.

"How do I look, Tabor?" she asked.

"Beautiful."

"Then why didn't you tell me?"

His eyes narrowed briefly, and there was just a hint of a smile curling his lips. "You'd made it clear that my opinion should remain unvoiced."

"Not with everything," Tanaka said.

She felt her confidence growing with each second. She was beautiful. She'd never really known it until Tabor had convinced her, and, now that he had, she wasn't going to let anyone—not him or the Fates or the gods—convince her otherwise.

"What do you want, Tanaka?"

Tanaka realized that it was a last bitter shard of pent-up anger that forced Tabor to question so bluntly, so rudely. She was determined to see beyond it, not to let minor problems prevent her from enjoying—sharing—major pleasures.

"You, of course. I've wanted you since you taught me to want you. But lately, rather than making each other feel . . . glorious, we make each other angry and despairing. And rather than reaching out across the differences that separate us so that we can hold hands, we point again to the differences, then turn our backs on one another."

Tabor smiled at the clarity and forcefulness of Tanaka's words. He pushed a hand through his shimmering blond hair, the muscles in his arm flexed. Seeing those muscles and that lustrous blond hair touched Tanaka in deliciously exciting ways.

"You've been feeling as though I only have time for

299

you after I do everything else," Tanaka continued. She shifted her shoulders just slightly, so that the bodice of her gown separated enough to display the inner swell of her breasts. "I'll admit that I've let my position and power in the palace rule me. It's felt good to be back where I belong, doing what I've been trained to do. But *you* must admit that you've been less than accepting of our way of life here. You've told me and everyone else who would listen how superior your boats are to ours."

"But they are superior," Tabor replied.

Tanaka silenced him with a comically stern look. "Such a stubborn man," she murmured, shaking her head.

"Will you do me a favor?"

Tanaka hesitated. "What?"

"Let your hair down," Tabor said quietly, in that sensually raspy tone that said he was not nearly as calm as he pretended to be. "For me," he added, as though whispering a prayer.

I will do anything for you, Tanaka thought. She did not say the words because this was not the time to voice such a truth. Later, when her erotic little plot had come to fruition, then she would tell Tabor everything she thought, everything she felt.

Slowly, feeling his heated gaze upon her, Tanaka reached up and removed the four shell combs that held her hair in place. Then she shook her head gently, sending the midnight tresses falling down her back and over her naked shoulders in waves of ebony splendor.

"Better?" she asked.

"Much," Tabor said, then reached for her.

Tanaka slipped away quickly, getting to her feet.

She saw the flash of annoyance in Tabor's eyes, the tightness that hardened his lips, and she responded with a smile, secure that she was playing this out exactly as it should be, having been taught by Tabor—the master teacher—that anticipation heightens satisfaction.

"I'm leaving you now," Tanaka whispered, her body tingling from head to toe as she looked down at Tabor. "But we'll be together again very soon. You've thought that I placed my position as high priestess above you. Tonight, with the help of Thoth, I'm going to prove to you that you're wrong."

"Thoth?"

"Thoth is the Egyptian god of wisdom and sorcery. We look to Thoth for wisdom . . . and magic."

"How with Thoth help us?" Tabor asked. He reached for Tanaka's ankle, by nature an impatient man, but she skipped out of reach with a laugh.

"Tonight, you're going to be where no man has ever been," Tanaka whispered, the words too important to say louder. "Tonight, you are going to go to my quarters. The guards will be gone. I'll dismiss the servants. No one will ever know that you are there. And tonight, my darling barbarian, I will show you how much I have missed our happiness together."

"But you have said it is forbidden for a man to enter the high priestess's quarters."

"It is. But you taught me how pleasurable the forbidden can be."

Tanaka yearned to kiss Tabor. She wanted to kiss him before she left him, but she also knew that if she did, if she allowed herself to touch him, she would not be able to let him go . . . not until the burning, wet hunger that gnawed at her was satisfied.

The look in Tabor's eyes told her that whatever their differences and whatever their arguments, they were forgotten now, at least for this one night.

"Meet me tonight," she said as she backed toward the doorway. "When that candle has burned down, come to me, my darling." She pointed to a stubby candle that would be extinguished in two hours. "Come to me, and I will prove that I think only of you."

Tanaka turned then and ran from the room, gems tinkling at her ankle. If she had not run from Tabor at that moment, no power in heaven or on earth could have made her leave.

Chapter Twenty-three

"I want to see him when he dies," Lysetta said, and the tremble in her voice was from excitement and anger, not fear.

Yasir looked at Lysetta, and at that moment, he realized he was employed by someone who was much deadlier than himself.

"If you want to see him die, it'll cost you more," Yasir said, but only because he could think of nothing else to say.

"I've given you enough already," Lysetta replied. Without a word, she reminded Yasir of their sexual encounters and that not all of them were completely without coercion. "In fact, I've given you more than you deserve."

He turned away from her then because he did not want her to see the fear in his eyes. She was lethal, like a cobra, and he sensed that she was ready to strike. He could only hope that she wouldn't strike at him, because he was certain that whomever she turned her venom on would never survive.

"It's got to begin now," Lysetta continued, her

senses ready for violence. "Give me what I paid for . . . now!"

Yasir's inclination was to stall Lysetta, but the look in her eyes he had seen before in the eyes of savage young men. Men who had become soldiers because they wanted to kill for the joy of killing and because being a soldier was the only way to murder without suffering the wrath of the pharaoh.

They left then, Yasir following Lysetta through the palace to Tabor's quarters. He kept his eyes down, not wanting to meet anyone's gaze. He was following a woman, accepting a subservient role without complaint, and he realized then that he had at last met someone more evil than himself. When this night was over and the killing came to an end, he would run from the palace and never return.

Yasir was taken aback when they approached Tabor's quarters. Never before had there been a guard at the door, but there was one now. Did it mean that Tabor had been forewarned of the assassination?

"We cannot do this now," Yasir hissed beneath his breath.

Lysetta turned on him with a smile of pure bloodlust. "We cannot *stop* now. Kill the guard first, then we will go on to Tabor."

She turned then toward the tall blond man standing near the entrance to Tabor's room, and the smile that pulled at her mouth was genuine, since she was happy that she would get more death for her money. He watched her approach with wariness in his eyes. He did not remove the short, thick, deadly sword from the sheath at his hip, but he did grab the handle tightly, preparing himself for danger. He did not watch Lysetta as much as he watched Yasir, who followed her several steps behind.

"Is Tabor within?" Lysetta asked.

The foreigner looked at her uncomprehendingly. He did not speak her language, and she did not speak his. Lysetta then noticed the redness near the man's left eye and the puffiness of his jaw and realized that he was the man Kahlid's men had beaten. His powers of recuperation astonished her, and Lysetta's sultry smile slipped a fraction. She moved so that the muscular guard could not see both her and Yasir at the same time. She asked another question of the guard, studying his face carefully to see if he could understand her better than it appeared. His expression did not alter at all.

When Lysetta tried to slide over to peer into Tabor's quarters, the guard moved to block her path. She looked at him, smiling, and remembered then that someone had called him Carl. That he was one of the closest associates to Tabor pleased Lysetta. She remembered hearing how Tabor had insisted that this man and another enjoy nothing less than the finest accommodations in the palace.

"You can't understand me, can you?" Lysetta asked, inching closer to Carl. She ran the tip of her finger up his forearm, which was thick with muscle. In a face-to-face fight, she knew that Yasir wouldn't stand a chance against him—but that wasn't the way Yasir killed his victims.

"You're Tabor's friend," she said, the tip of her tongue playing lightly around her lips.

"Tabor?" Carl said, understanding that one word, his eyes darting back and forth from Lysetta to Yasir.

"His good friend. That's important. You see, he was given the opportunity to be with me, and instead he . . . chose not to. That was a mistake. I don't offer myself to just anyone, so when I do make the offer, I become offended when I am refused. And since he hurt me by his refusal, I'm going to hurt him." As she spoke, she was moving subtly, her eyes boring into Carl's, her voice a universal caress that bridged the gulf between their languages. "I'm going to hurt him in a special way. I'm going to hurt him by killing you."

It was at exactly that moment, when Lysetta had manipulated Carl so that his back was to Yasir, that the sharp dagger was thrust between his ribs. Even Carl's great Viking heart could not continue, and he had departed his body and was lifted toward Valhalla before his corpse hit the granite floor.

A shudder went through Lysetta as she stood over the corpse. This wasn't exactly as she had imagined, but it was good enough to have been worth the effort. It had also proven to Lysetta that Yasir could do the job.

"Tabor is next," Lysetta said, unable to look away from the corpse.

She had fantasized what it would be like to look into a man's eyes as he died, and her expectations had been fulfilled. But then, as she looked down at the corpse, a crimson pool formed beneath the body, bright red against the white marble. The smell of fresh blood filled Lysetta's nostrils, but the gory reality of murder was not what she had hoped.

"I . . . I think you can handle it from here," she said, her voice barely above a whisper. "When you're

306

finished with Tabor, come see me. I'll be in my quarters."

There was a ringing in her ears, and her stomach churned. Lysetta forced herself to walk, not run, away from Yasir and the dead foreigner. Not even her great hatred for Tabor could make her stay to watch him die.

It was at that moment, in a section of the palace far from Carl's lifeless body, that Kahlid grit his teeth in impotent rage. He stood outside the pharaoh's quarters, summarily dismissed. He had offered to do a tarot reading for the pharaoh, who had said that that important service would be handled by Tanaka alone. From the way Moamin spoke, Kahlid knew that even if Tanaka died, the pharaoh would not appoint him high priest. Moamin did not trust him, and that meant that Moamin, too, had to be disposed of.

With long, angry strides, Kahlid returned to his quarters, where Abdul awaited him.

"It's time," Kahlid said. "I want you to go immediately to the high priestess and kill her. When you're done, kill the pharaoh. He won't be heavily guarded."

"The high priestess first?" Abdul asked quietly.

"Then the pharaoh."

"Where is she now?" He was clearly more interested in Tanaka than in Moamin.

"In her quarters. Hurry now," Kahlid said, picking up a jeweled goblet. "There'll never be a better moment." He grabbed the front of Abdul's robe, balling the cloth in his fist. "Don't fail me," he said with chilling menace. "I'll lure Moamin away from his guards, and then it is up to you to kill him. Just don't fail. When the new day dawns, either we will both be successful or we will both be dead. Our destiny is tied together."

Abdul did not look away even though he was surprised at the vehemence of Kahlid's words. Surprised, but not afraid. When he had finished the killing, he would be the friend of a powerful man. Such a friendship had its benefits. All he had to do was kill and stay alive until Kahlid could consolidate his power. Life would be easy from then on for the foot soldier whose life and military career had thus far been undistinguished.

He left Kahlid's quarters imagining the advantages of being the personal assassin of a high priest.

Abdul could tell that something was different as he approached the high priestess's quarters, but he could not say what had changed. He reached inside his robe, curling his fingers around the haft of his slim dagger. It was a reassuring feel, one that let him know he was in control and that all who opposed him would die. But he did not draw the dagger, not wanting to alert any guards to his evil intentions. . . . and that's when he realized what was different.

There were no guards. And there were no servants. No retinue of women surround the high priestess and her living quarters.

Abdul stopped walking and withdrew the gleaming dagger from his robes. He held his breath and listened. There wasn't a sound to be heard, although there were over a hundred people in the palace.

The archway that led into Tanaka's wing was the

last place for a man to stand guard. Again, no one. Abdul passed through the archway, stepping into an area where no men were allowed. Being a man in an entirely female world appealed to him. Inhaling deeply, he thought even the air itself smelled differ-ent—fresher, as though the women who breathed it were distinctly superior to the soldiers that were his usual companions.

Which doorway led to the high priestess? There were a half-dozen doors. Abdul had not been told which room was Tanaka's, and he had not thought to ask.

He glanced through the nearest doorway. The room was empty. He moved inside, driven by curios-ity and the perverse pleasure he took in being in a woman's room while she wasn't there. The room be-longed to Tanaka's servants, and there were clothes of fine linen present. Abdul took a garment and held it to his face, sniffing. The fabric was soft—much softer than anything he had ever owned—and it had the aroma of a woman's body in its soft folds.

Abdul dropped the garment. To smell the scent of woman on the cloth reminded him that he had a job to do. He felt the tingling rush of adrenaline through him. In a nearby room, one of the most beautiful women he had ever seen was waiting with no guards to protect her.

His heart was pounding, his palm sweaty as he gripped his dagger. Abdul realized that if he were truly alone with the high priestess, there would be no one to tell Kahlid what he did with Tanaka before he killed her.

The third room that Abdul looked into was more

luxurious than the others, and there could be no doubt that it was the high priestess's room. Abdul stepped in cautiously, respect making him question whether the gods would intervene and prevent him from doing the foul deeds he planned.

The room itself was dark, without so much as a lamp or torch for light. But from a side room Abdul saw a pale yellow glow. He froze, unable even to breathe. Very, very faintly he heard the lilting sound of a woman humming. He waited several seconds, forcing himself to relax, to remember that if he were discovered in the high priestess's quarters, Pharaoh Moamin Abbakka would have him summarily executed, his corpse dragged through the streets.

Abdul pressed his back to the wall, waited for his nerves to calm, then peered around the ornately carved doorway into the area enclosing High Priestess Tanaka's bed. The breath caught in his throat.

She was reclining against a mound of pillows, wearing a sheer gown of royal purple only loosely knotted at the waist. Her long, ebony hair was neatly brushed over her shoulders to follow the parted lapels of the robe. From his vantage point, Abdul was able to see the full, smooth inner swells of her breasts and the large gold *ankh* suspended from a gold chain resting in the valley of her breasts. Reclining on the bed, one knee raised, her thigh exposed, her body relaxed and voluptuous, she was fiercely arousing. He stepped slowly into the room, a cruel smile twitching on his lips and a sharp dagger in his hand.

What's taking him so long? Tanaka thought with the petulance of a child forced to wait for a gift.

310

Almost immediately, she chastised herself for her impatience. After all, hadn't she been the one to insist that Tabor wait until the candle burned down before he come to her?

She felt totally different, powerfully alive, and terribly naughty. Tonight would bring an end to all the arguing. She was certain of it. Tonight, she would prove to him, to herself, and to whatever and whichever gods were watching that the love they shared was too powerful to be denied.

She opened her eyes briefly and looked at the ceiling overhead, where the finest artists in the village had depicted the scene of her ascension into the heavens. Her smile broadened. *Yes*, she thought, *tonight I will indeed ascend to the heavens . . . and I'll make the voyage in Tabor's arms!*

It was terribly wicked of her to arrange this tryst with Tabor in her own quarters, in a place where no man — not even the pharaoh himself — was allowed to enter. But she wanted Tabor to know exactly what he meant to her, what his presence in her life truly meant. By inviting him in to her sanctuary, Tanaka was refuting her past. She was not ignoring or pretending those hideous days she'd been Ingmar the Savage's captive had never happened, but she *was* putting those days and those experiences behind her. She could not control that which had already happened — she could not rewrite her own personal history — but she could influence her future. . . . and more than anything or anyone else, she wanted Tabor in her future.

Tanaka hoped that Thoth would understand and accept her actions.

She heard the heavy sound of a footstep. It surprised her. Despite Tabor's great size and strength, he was extraordinarily lightfooted. She felt disquieting fear pool in her stomach, fear that demanded action. Her first impulse was to heed it, to run from some approaching danger. But even as her muscles tensed in preparation, she smiled, willing herself to relax into the comfort of the pillows, firmly dismissing her fear. She was as paranoid as Tabor, who saw peril lurking everywhere. She could not remember a time when she'd heard his step, but she dismissed this as simply the result of his impatience to see her.

"I wondered how long it would take that candle to burn out," she said, keeping her eyes closed, wondering what was going through Tabor's mind as she lay in a sensual sprawl upon her bed, her robe opened just enough to give him a glimpse of what waited for him beneath. "Have the guards all gone? Did anyone see you? Oh, Tabor, I'm such a wanton woman where you're concerned."

"No one saw me."

The fear exploded in her soul. That was not Tabor's voice!

She sprang off the bed, pulling her robe more tightly around her, tugging at the sash to secure it. Only vaguely did she recognize the man who had entered her private quarters, and it was only her own impropriety and the desire to keep it a secret that kept her from screaming for guards to take the intruder away in chains. Only moments earlier she'd dismissed everyone, sending them to the far sections of the palace, thereby insuring that her passion with Tabor could be vocal, if desire so dictated, and yet still remain secret and private. There was no one to hear her screams, whether passionate or fearful.

"The pharaoh will have you killed for this!"

Abdul smiled, twisting the dagger in his hand. "The pharaoh would have me killed for being here? What makes you think the pharaoh is going to be alive tomorrow? Besides, what do you think the pharaoh would think about the Viking being invited here? A wanton woman *and* the high priestess? I don't think the pharaoh would like you being both."

Tanaka crawled backward on the bed until she was against the cool granite wall. She had seen the look that was now in Abdul's eyes in a man's eyes before — in Ingmar's when he knew he had her captive and that she was helpless against him. It was her helplessness that had most excited Ingmar, and Tanaka sensed instantly that Abdul shared the same depravities. It was no mistake that he had come to her bedchambers, just as it was no mistake that he held a dagger in his hand. His eyes were darkly feral.

"Get out of here," Tanaka said, trying hard to sound authoritative. "I'm warning you . . ."

Abdul chortled. "You like the yellow-haired foreigners? That's not right. If you're going to give your body to a man, you should give it to an Egyptian!"

The sight of him sickened Tanaka. Looking at him reminded her that she had argued with Tabor about the inherent treachery of his people compared to her own. The foolishness and naïveté of that position now seemed ludicrous.

"Who sent you here?" she asked, walking backward off her bed, keeping a distance from Abdul as he advanced. "Why are you here?"

313

Abdul was a powerfully-built, stupid man whose closest association to people of power and influence was to guard their doorways. Gazing at Tanaka, he knew that he would never again get so close to such a woman; and, deep in his soul, he sensed that he would never live through this night of planned carnage. Since he valued his life so little, nothing prevented him from behaving however he wanted. Right now, what he wanted more than anything else was to feel Tanaka writhing beneath him!

"Can't you talk? What's wrong with you?" Tanaka demanded, backing along the wall, moving deeper into the room as Abdul advanced at exactly the same speed.

"Kahlid sent me." It took a moment for Abdul to realize that he had actually spoken the words. But when he saw the shock in Tanaka's eyes, he was happy that he had told her. "He's tired of having you around, so he hired me to see that you have another accident."

"Another accident?"

"Do you really think it was just coincidence that you were kidnapped from that boat when everyone else upon it was killed? Don't you remember how Kahlid encouraged you to get on it, how he said it would be good for you to breathe in the fresh sea air?"

Tanaka froze. It all came back to her. Kahlid had said that she looked pale and needed to breathe the sea air. He had said he never felt so spiritually pure as when he was in a boat far out in the Mediterranean. He had said that going out to sea with the vil-

314

lage fishermen would be an experience she would never forget. . . .

"But . . . but how?" she stammered, momentarily forgetting the threat that Abdul represented, her gentle heart finding it difficult to believe that even a man like Kahlid was capable of such mendacity and deception.

"He met up with the foreigner in Alexandria. They were trading, and Kahlid told him that a fortune was to be made if you were taken from the fishing boat and killed." Abdul chuckled softly, almost within arm's reach of the high priestess now. "But he didn't kill you, did he?"

"He tried to kill my spirit, but he failed . . . just as you will fail!" Tanaka hissed, angry and defiant.

She thought then that it should not surprise her that evil such as Kahlid and Ingmar should be in league. It didn't matter that they did not speak the same language or sail the same seas. What mattered was that they were evil—hideous and vile—and that they preyed on helpless victims. It was only natural that such men should seek each other out. . . . and it was only natural that such men should be blotted out of existence, banished from the face of the earth into exile in the underworld.

"If you leave now, I promise that nothing will happen to you," Tanaka whispered, her voice trembling as she resumed her slow retreat from the intruder's advance.

He laughed again. "If I *don't* leave, I promise that something *will* happen to you."

It could not happen to her all over again. Not when Tanaka had at last thought she had put the

315

past behind her and that the scars seared into her soul by Ingmar the Savage had healed sufficiently so that she was able to open again to life and to love.

"I'll kill myself before I let you touch me," Tanaka whispered.

Abdul laughed openly then. He knew there was no way for the high priestess to kill herself before he had forced himself upon her. And once he had satisfied the savage fire in his soul, then he would be the one who would kill.

He held the dagger but kept it safely out of the way when he lunged for Tanaka. He did not want to cut her, to mar her extraordinary beauty in any way. Not until he had finished with her, and then he would make it a quick, painless kill.

She screamed a high-pitched cry of fear as she leapt away from the outstretched hand that grabbed for her robe. Her scream was ecstasy to his ears, and Abdul's laughter became a steady huffing sound, like a winded man forcing himself to continue running when his lungs ache for a rest.

"Don't fight me," Abdul said, moving closer. He reached again for the high priestess's sleeve, but she skipped out of reach to the side. "I won't make it painful for you if you don't fight me."

He watched the way her breasts moved beneath the sheer robe she wore, the way her ebony hair fluttered against her cheeks, the way her slender thighs scissored as she rushed from him, moving deeper into the room and farther away from the one door that offered her only chance for escape. Everything about her, from the glittering of fear in her eyes to the way her moist lips trembled softly, excited Abdul. Whether he lived to see another day no longer mattered to him, not if he was able to know the power, the thrill of mastery, over this woman.

"You are mine," Abdul said softly, like the hiss of a cobra before it strikes. "There's nothing you can do to stop me."

A deep voice, thickly-accented, deadly serious, replied, "She may not be able to stop you, but I can."

Abdul wheeled to see Tabor bearing down on him. His hands were empty, and Abdul felt only momentary relief, since he was certain that in a fair fight with daggers or swords he would have no chance against the big Viking.

"Stay out of this or die, foreigner!" Abdul hissed with far greater courage than he felt. "Do not die for something that does not concern you!"

Tabor continued his approach, but now he moved slowly, his eyes icy blue, dancing back and forth between Abdul and Tanaka, assessing the situation, determining the best course of action.

For Tanaka, Tabor's presence had never brought greater relief, but his intrusion once again into her world was a two-edged sword: she was glad he had come to save her, but she was frightened for his safety. Even if she failed to defend herself against Abdul, if he did not kill her when he was finished, then she could once again try to put the hideous event behind her and get on with her life with Tabor. But if Tabor should die defending her, then there would be nothing left for her. She would have her life, but she would have lost her life's greatest joy.

"Tabor, no!" she whispered, taking the opportunity

to move away from the corner in which Abdul had trapped her. "He has a dagger!"

"Yes. And I've got my hands," Tabor replied, holding his large, powerful hands out for Abdul to see. His forearms bulged with thick muscles, blue veins scoring the pale surface of his skin.

It was the certainty in his tone more than anything else that unnerved Abdul. Even though Tabor did not have a weapon, Abdul would lose this battle. It was one thing to die from the blade of a dagger, quite another to feel the strength in a man's hands as his fingers squeezed the life from you.

Abdul blanched at the thought. He held the dagger out in front of him, close to his hip so that Tabor could not easily pull it from his grasp.

"You'll die," Abdul said.

"Someday . . . but not this day," Tabor replied, moving forward in a crouch, hands out in front — a stance he had used as a boy when he wrestled with other boys. He advanced stealthily, his body tensed and poised, ready to spring like a mighty lion upon his prey.

"You frightened my love," he whispered in guttural Egyptian through teeth clenched in rage. "You frightened her, and for that you will pay."

Abdul's nerve failed him. But he was a skilled fighter. He was confident of this. He had also felt his nerve slip before, and he knew that the surest way to recover faltering courage was to draw first blood. Whenever he'd done this, each time he had seen his enemy's blood flow, his courage and confidence had returned with renewed vigor.

He feinted to the left, and then stabbed straight

forward with the dagger. For such a large man, Tabor moved with startling swiftness.

Abdul's hideous laughing-breath rattled again as he advanced. His dark eyes glittered menacingly.

"Yellow-haired swine," he hissed. It was the worst thing he could imagine calling anyone, and it was mildly disconcerting that the foreigner didn't seem to fully understand the meaning of the insult.

Abdul watched as the crisscrossed muscles just above Tabor's right knee swelled, the thigh bulging powerfully, and he knew the foreigner was going to make his attack. Rather than waiting to make his defense, Abdul made a half-hearted, straight-ahead stab at Tabor's face with the dagger, forcing his foe to lean backward. In the next instant, Abdul slashed sideways with the dagger, drawing the blade over the Viking's left forearm.

Blood spurted from the four-inch wound, and Abdul's cry of victory mingled in the huge, echoing room with Tanaka's scream of fear.

Abdul had drawn first blood. He knew he would be victorious. He could not lose to an infidel! He lunged forward, stabbing with the dagger, certain that the Viking would realize that his only chance for survival was to retreat, to run from the greater might of Abdul!

His confidence vanished the instant Tabor's huge hand clamped tightly around Abdul's wrist. In a moment in time lasting no longer than a fraction of a second, he felt the barbarian's fingers tighten around his wrist with such strength—inhuman strength, his frightened mind concluded—that he dropped the dagger. He looked into the barbarian's eyes, blue as a

319

summer sky and cold as death itself, and tried to pull away, but he could not free himself from the fingers that clutched his wrist. Abdul felt himself being turned, twisted so that his back was toward Tabor. An eye-blink of time later, Tabor's other hand cupped Abdul's chin. The assassin felt his head being forcibly turned, and he thought that no man on earth was powerful enough to force his chin over his shoulder. No man, that is, but Tabor, and as Abdul's chin was wrenched over his shoulder, he felt a stab of pain, heard the high, sharp crack of bones breaking . . . then heard nothing at all ever again.

Chapter Twenty-four

The sobs finally ended, leaving behind only hiccuping gulps. Tanaka pressed her cheek against Tabor's chest and trembled in his arms as he whispered reassuring words, stroking her hair, promising that all would be well.

"I was so terrified," she cried. She rubbed her face into Tabor's robe to wipe away the residual tears. "I was so afraid for you."

"You shouldn't have been. You've seen me fight before. You've even seen me bleed before."

"Yes, but I didn't love you then."

It was a simple declaration, and one that Tanaka had not intended to voice. But now that she had said it, once and for all time, she was happy that it was out. She pushed against Tabor's chest just enough to be able to look up into his eyes.

"Is that so terribly bad of me?" she asked quietly, honestly. "I just want to love you, to be with you, to live in peace with you. I wanted you here with me tonight because I wanted you to see that you're more important to me than anything or anyone else. I would even challenge the wrath of the gods to be with you."

"That's why you invited me here, to your chambers where no man is allowed to be."

It was a statement, not a question, and the full magnitude of it caught Tabor by surprise. This beautiful, brilliant, courageous woman—who was as much a mystery to him as she ever was—loved him. . . . and it seemed to Tabor at that endless moment that he had found Valhalla on earth.

"And I love you, Tanaka," he said quietly, smoothing wavy hair of black satin from her eyes. "I will love you for all time. I want to live with you and have children with you and never be parted from you." He stroked the pad of his thumb over her full, trembling lips. "Without you, I have nothing; with you, I have more than I ever dreamed I'd have." He put his hands on Tanaka's shoulders and pushed her backward, holding her at arm's distance. He leaned down and looked straight into her eyes. "That's why you must be my wife. I cannot live without you, so you must be my wife."

Tanaka looked away, fighting pangs of disappointment. "Your declaration has great force, but not much romance. I am not one of the Vikings you can command."

For an instant Tabor closed his eyes and silently cursed himself. It was his Viking ways that made him think he could demand the world and all the people in it to change their lives to suit his desires. But this mysterious woman before him was not to be commanded. Not now, not ever. Tabor knew that if he was to seize his chance for eternal happiness, then he

322

must convince Tanaka that he had the power to make her happy.

He took her hands in his and knelt on one knee before her. Though speaking from the heart was not something that he enjoyed doing, when he spoke to Tanaka again, his tone was clear and strong and lacked its usual authoritarian air. Instead, his words were sweet and gentle, wrapped in the perfumed folds of a rose.

"High Priestess Tanaka, will you marry me?" He looked from her eyes down to the small hands held in his own. Her fingers looked frail, and he had to consciously remind himself to loosen his grasp for fear that he was hurting her. "Please, Tanaka. . . . I never dreamed I had the power to love like this. I know the gods will never smile down upon me like this again, so you must — you simply *must* — become my wife."

Tanaka smiled then, unable to resist the joy surging through her bosom. Tabor, her loving Viking, was still demanding and forceful, still telling her what she must do rather than asking her what she would do, but he loved her. He was a Viking and always would be. She couldn't make him anything other than what he was. But at least he was *her* Viking, and his declaration of love was a promise that she believed.

"Yes," she said, and when his head snapped up and his face broke into that brilliant, rakish smile that she so loved, she added, "but in an Egyptian ceremony, not a Viking one."

"As long as the ceremony is immediate, I don't care if it is a Northman ceremony," Tabor replied, rising to his feet to scoop Tanaka once again into his arms, relaxing his grasp only when she squealed with glee and discomfort that he was holding her too tight.

Yasir was frightened. Saliva dribbled from his thick lower lip to drip from his chin onto his chest, completely unheeded. He sat in a dark corner of the long hall that led to Lysetta's chambers.

What to do?

He had crept through the palace to the high priestess's chambers and reached there just in time to watch the enormous barbarian break Abdul's neck. It was the most frightening display of deadly strength Yasir had ever seen, and shivers of fear still twitched up his spine.

After witnessing Abdul's death, Yasir rushed back through the palace in time to watch the barbarians being rounded up and taken to the dungeon. Kahlid, as palace priest, had accused the Vikings of raping and stealing, and he intended to personally torture each and every pale-skinned Viking until he discovered which ones were responsible for the hideous crimes. Kahlid let all who listened know that it was his opinion that all the foreigners were equally guilty, but since he was a fair and just man, he would torture them first to determine the truth.

"There are enemies in the palace!" Kahlid continued. The soldiers' blood already ran hot. They had arrested the Vikings, foreigners who had received special treatment. "These strong, powerful enemies have faces we know and recognize. We believe they are our friends, but they are *not* our friends, good soldiers! These enemies will destroy all that we love unless we act now to protect our pharaoh, our village, and ourselves!"

"Who are these enemies?" a voice called out from the crowd. "Do they have a leader?"

"Yes, and it is Lysetta, my friends! Lysetta has supped with the pharaoh and pretended to be my friend and yours, but she is loyal to no one! She works in legion with the nether world for the destruction of all that we love!"

"What should we do, Priest Kahlid?" another soldier asked. By raising his sword above his head, he made it clear what choice of action he felt was in order.

"We should take the traitor Lysetta and lock her away with the barbarians!" Kahlid replied, his face flushed with excitement. "Do it now, good men! Do it now!"

Yasir had been able to hide in the crowd of rushing soldiers, then disappeared down a hallway. He'd watched as Lysetta was taken from her chambers and dragged away screaming, professing her innocence and claiming that she was not to blame, others were, and if the men would just give her a moment she would tell them.

Yasir had no doubt that Lysetta would accuse him of whatever she was blamed for. He had enjoyed the flattering things she had said to him and about him when they were in each other's arms, but he'd never believed them. He'd known that she said those things to please him, just as she had touched his body because she needed him to kill for her. Now all that had changed. Lysetta would be his worst enemy.

He closed his eyes and tried to think. What would

325

Lysetta confess first? Would she tell how he had stabbed the foreigner in the back? Probably, Yasir concluded, but that wouldn't be such a bad thing since Kahlid had now turned the soldiers against the Vikings.

But there was still Tabor, the leader of the Vikings, to consider. Tabor was with the high priestess Tanaka, and he was protected by her just as she was protected by him. The soldiers, under Kahlid's orders, had the power of numbers and the authority of a priest to arrest the foreigners. However, this power and authority did not extend to Tabor, loved by the high priestess and respected by Pharaoh Moamin Abbakka himself. Sooner or later Tabor would find out that Yasir had stabbed one of his men in the back. . . . and then, Yasir had little doubt, his own neck would break with the same hideous snapping sound as Abdul's.

So he had to go, to escape . . . but to where? And with what money?

In the shadows, he saw a figure move. Without hesitation, Yasir thrust straight ahead with his dagger, driving it into the body of a young servant girl returning to her quarters.

Yasir stood above the corpse, glad he had killed a woman. Women always let him know how ugly he was; women caused problems. If only he could kill Lysetta as quickly as he had killed the servant girl, then his life would be exactly as he wanted it. He felt better now that he had killed again.

"Don't get angry," Tanaka said as she finished applying one more bandage to Tabor's wounded forearm. "But it was Kahlid who ordered that man to come here."

Tabor's expression hardly changed. Only a slight narrowing of the eyes and a tightness to the lips indicated the murderous rage within.

"I knew he was evil," Tabor replied, deceptively conversational. "He wants to be high priest; and, as long as you live, the pharaoh will never allow it."

"Such a foolish reason to kill," Tanaka shook her head. She was pleased that Tabor held his temper in check.

"Where is Kahlid now?" Tabor asked.

Tanaka took his hands in hers and said sternly, "You promised me that if I told you, you wouldn't seek revenge!"

"Your murder would not have made Kahlid the high priest. Pharaoh Abbakka does not trust Kahlid, and Kahlid knows that. The only way for him to achieve his goal is to murder *two* people—you and Moamin. Only then does he have a chance at what he covets."

Tanaka considered Tabor's words. A chill washed through her, starting in her stomach and spreading swiftly until she could feel its chilling truth even in the tips of her fingers.

"Neenah trusts Kahlid," Tanaka whispered, as though afraid someone else would hear her, though she was alone with Tabor in her chambers. "With the pharaoh dead, Neenah would take his place. She is kind-hearted, but she is not a leader. She would look to Kahlid for strength. . . . and then he would have more power than if he were high priest!"

327

Tabor swore in his native tongue, and Tanaka did not understand because he had never before used that kind of language in front of a woman and certainly not in front of the woman he loved.

"We've got to do something," Tanaka cried, clutching Tabor's muscled arm. "We can't let Kahlid win!"

Tabor growled his low, lion's rumble of frustration. This was not his fight, yet he was inextricably linked to Tanaka's troubles and he could not turn his back on the problems that now plagued the palace. As much as he loved Tanaka, it was his sense of justice that committed him to the fight. Strong men, he felt, must protect the weak from powerful evil, or that evil will grow stronger and stronger until it cannot be defeated.

"By Thoth and the thunder of Thor, I will destroy the evil in this infernal palace!" Tabor vowed. "Stand by me, woman, and I will slay the fools who dare defy me!"

Never before Tabor included her in his battle plans. Yet he clearly wanted her with him, and he would not rest until the enemies of the palace—by extension, her enemies—were slain.

"Thank you," Tanaka said softly, angry that she herself did not have the power to fight against the assassins and soldiers of her enemies. "Thank you for being everything that you are."

"Thank me when I am victorious." Tabor checked the bandage on his arm and stood. "Stay here," he commanded, opening and closing his fist to test the severity of the wound. He was pleased to learn that he had not lost any of his strength.

"No, I'm coming with you."

Tabor conceded. Arguing would only delay them further.

"When the killing begins, turn your head away," Tabor suggested. "I know you do not want bloodshed; but there has already been so much blood spilled, the only way the killing will end is to kill the killers."

Tanaka's gentle heart insisted that she protest. Yes, too much blood had already been shed, but violence never truly answered violence. On the other hand, these were savage matters wrought by savage people, and Tabor had a better understanding of what was needed. Crystal tears glistening on her cheek, she gave in.

Tabor headed out of the chambers, and Tanaka followed him. He was formulating a plan. He wanted Sven at his side; he always felt more confident when his lifelong friend was at hand. However, as they entered the long hallway, three Egyptian soldiers saw Tabor and leaped for him. With a scream of rage, Tabor freed himself, but three *more* Egyptians wrestled him to the floor.

"Run, Tanaka! Run for your life!" Tabor shouted even as a powerful forearm was placed cruelly across his throat, cutting off his breath.

He could hear Tanaka screaming. The sound of her voice and the knowledge that if he failed now this woman that he loved would die urged strength into his limbs. With a lionlike roar, Tabor thrashed on the hard granite of the palace floor, dislodging four of the six men who held him down. He grabbed a soldier by the throat, his fingers digging into soft flesh, but the haft of a broadsword smashed hard against the base of Tabor's skull. Brilliant lights flashed in his head, and his fingers went numb. He could still hear Tanaka's scream, but from very far away. And then the blackness that he fought against overcame him with a velvet embrace.

Chapter Twenty-five

It seemed only moments later to Tabor when he opened his eyes. Tanaka was sitting on the floor, cradling his head in her lap. She stroked his hair and searched his face with grave concern. And the assassins — the Egyptian soldiers who had jumped and clubbed him — stood above him, their concern nearly matching Tanaka's in intensity.

"Why?" Tabor asked in Danish so that the soldiers would not understand him.

Tanaka smiled, relieved that Tabor had not drifted irrevocably into the black sleep and that he was thinking clearly.

"Kahlid told the men it was the foreigners who caused our problems in the palace. He had your men arrested and thrown into the dungeon."

"I'll kill him!" Tabor pushed Tanaka away, determined to free his men immediately.

"Be still," Tanaka cooed, grabbing Tabor's wrist. "Your men are being freed as we speak." She stroked the side of Tabor's face lovingly. "You're lucky I was with you. I alone had the power to convince these men that you are innocent and that Priest Kahlid is the real enemy."

"You saved my life."

"Yes," Tanaka replied simply, her smile broadening. "I'm getting rather good at it by now, don't you think?"

Her smile rankled Tabor's Viking pride, but there was truth to her statement—and impish charm in her eyes. When he let her help him to his feet, he became aware of a throbbing in his head and a lump behind his ear, but the dizziness had passed.

"We must go to the pharaoh," Tabor said in Tanaka's tongue and with sufficient volume for the soldiers to hear. "Kahlid will not rest until all his enemies are slain."

Tanaka followed the men; and for the first time, the palace seemed strange and unfamiliar. The long hallways were empty. No servants milled about. No children laughed or played. Everyone, it seemed, was hiding. . . . and though she tried to deny it, Tanaka could smell death in the air.

As they approached the pharaoh's private chambers, they passed the two guards who always stood on either side of the entrance. The guards lay on the floor, arms and legs strewn in a death sprawl.

With hardly more than a glance, Tabor deduced that the men had not died simultaneously. First one guard had been killed, then the second one struck down as he gazed at the corpse of the other.

With Tabor leading the way, the men burst into the pharaoh's quarters, only to stop instantly at the scene unfolding before them.

Kahlid stood behind Neenah, one hand against her

332

throat, the other holding a dagger behind her ear. And Pharaoh Moamin Abbakka tried desperately to buy her freedom with his own life. Yasir knelt on the floor, scooping Neenah's jewelry into a leather pouch.

"Drop the dagger," Tabor said, his Egyptian bad, but sufficiently good for Kahlid to understand. "It's over for you. You've failed."

"Get out!" Kahlid retorted, adding an ounce of pressure behind the dagger. Neenah let out a scream of primal fear.

"Stop!" Moamin shouted. "It's me you want, not her!"

"Tell them to leave!" Kahlid shouted back.

"All of you, drop your weapons and be gone!"

The soldiers could not disobey a direct order from their pharaoh, and they were out of the chambers in a breathless second. Tabor, sword in hand, stood his ground, surrounded by the abandoned weapons of the fighting men. Tanaka stood at his side, surveying the scene.

"You, too," the pharaoh said to Tabor. "You must leave."

Tabor shook his head, his glittering blue eyes sharp and deadly as the sword he held. "I am Tabor, Son of Thor, and I take orders from no man."

"Leave or I'll kill her!" Kahlid hissed.

Tabor shook his head. "If I leave, you will kill her, then you will kill the pharaoh. But if I stay . . ."

With valuables overflowing the leather bag, Yasir got to his feet. Clutching his looted wealth, he wiped saliva from his thick lips with the back of his arm.

"I killed your friend," he said triumphantly, believ-

333

ing there was nothing Tabor could do to exact revenge. "I put my dagger in his back and watched him bleed like a slaughtered goat!"

Yasir laughed until the heavy broadsword that had been in Tabor's hand an instant earlier flew toward him. In all his years of fighting, Yasir had never known anyone to throw a heavy broadsword, nor had he thought any man would have the strength to throw such a weapon. He had no time to react before the blade sliced cleanly through his clothing, but he did have an instant to looked at the handle of the sword and the growing red stain on his shirt before he fell face down. He did not move again.

In the silence that followed, Tabor retrieved a bow and arrow from the floor and notched the arrow.

"Never underestimate me," Tabor said quietly.

Kahlid ducked behind his captive, using Neenah as a shield. "Drop the bow!" he shouted, peering at Tabor from behind the pharaoh's wife. "Drop the bow or I'll kill her!"

"Drop the dagger, or I'll kill you," Tabor replied.

Moamin Abbakka inched further away from Tabor, whose skill, he hoped, would free his beloved wife. As he moved, he kept up a steady discussion with Kahlid, trying to convince the would-be assassin that nothing would happen to him if he would put down his dagger and release Neenah.

"I'm warning you!" Kahlid cried out, his body twisted sideways so that he could remain behind Neenah, but she was much shorter than he. "Put the bow down now or I'll kill her!"

Tabor had the bow fully drawn, the taut line barely touching the tip of his nose. Thick blue veins bulged in his forearms as he bent the bow, needing only to relax the fingers of his right hand to release the string and send the arrow on its deadly journey.

"Walk away from this," Tabor whispered. His eyes were unblinking, his voice as cold as death. "You can't win by hurting any more people."

Kahlid laughed hollowly, hysterically. He pressed the dagger's tip to Neenah's neck and drew a single drop of blood.

"*You* walk away, barbarian! Foreigner! I'm where I belong!" Kahlid's spittle sprayed from his lips as he spoke.

Then, almost incoherent, he cursed Tabor. Babbling, he bobbled, shifting position behind the pharaoh's wife. Tabor's arrow remained pointed straight at him.

"You can have whatever you want," Moamin offered, his tone steady, but not strong. "Don't listen to Tabor. He doesn't speak for me. It's not Neenah you want, it's me. I can get you what you want. Money, women—tell me and you shall have it."

Kahlid swore again, and the eyes that he turned to the pharaoh were filled with loathing and contempt.

"What you'll *give* me?" Kahlid asked, a peal of hateful laughter erupting from his throat. "Whatever I want, I'll *take!*"

"But I can help you!" the pharaoh said, nearly shouting now. Experience told him that it was nearly impossible to negotiate with desperate, irrational men. And they were completely impossible to predict.

Tabor stood solidly, his feet at shoulder's width, moving only his upper body to correct his aim, always readjusting to Kahlid's movements. The only way for Kahlid to leave the room was to pass by him. The tall blond man with the taut bow had every intention of making that escape quite impossible.

"I don't want your help," Kahlid said. "I want your blood, you dog!"

Tabor had to strain to fully understand the priest's guttural language, but there was no mistaking the rage. Kahlid had been living under a great tension he'd kept buried for a long, long time—tension that was finally erupting. Soon—perhaps in no more than a few seconds—Kahlid's mind would snap, breaking like dock moorings overtaxed by the weight of a great ship buffeted by stormy seas.

Tabor, more than anyone else in the room, knew the great price often paid in negotiating. Tabor had believed that Ingmar the Savage might want peace, although a trap was more likely. Tabor's instincts had told him—warned him—that he should not listen to Ingmar, that anything the cruel Northman had to say would be a lie. But instead of listening to his inner voice of reason, Tabor had allowed his desire for peace to substitute for judgment, and that illusion had cost the lives of many of his men and nearly his own as well.

Negotiating with villainy was a mistake that Tabor would not make twice.

Twenty feet separated Neenah and Kahlid from Tabor. Kahlid peered over the woman's shoulder, only his eyes and forehead visible to Tabor.

"Tanaka, close your eyes," Tabor said quietly.

"If you miss, you'll kill the pharaoh's wife!" Kahlid spat, never for a moment believing that Tabor had the skill or the courage to attempt such a dangerous shot.

But Tanaka knew Tabor better. She closed her eyes and turned her back. She heard the *twang!* of the bowstring being released and the sound of an arrowhead piercing flesh and bone.

Neenah's frightened scream echoed through the quarters. Tanaka kept her eyes closed until she felt Tabor's large hands at her shoulders. Then his strong arms encircled her, and her head lay against his chest.

"It's all over," he said softly, stroking her hair and back. "We can be at peace now."

Chapter Twenty-six

It had been months since the carnage, but there were still times when the violence rippled across Tabor's sense of ease.

The winds were blowing steadily from the south now, strong, warm spring breezes that would carry him back to Scandinavian waters and the unfinished business of Ingmar the Savage. Soon he would be sailing to a land of violence and away from a woman—his wife Tanaka—whom he loved and adored.

"Much is weighing upon your mind," Sven said, moving beside Tabor on the dock, in front of the twin boats that the pharaoh had had specially made as a gift to Tabor for his valor and service.

"The boats. I think they will serve us well."

Sven smiled, shrugging his broad shoulders. He knew Tabor and knew that it wasn't the construction of the ships that had silenced his tongue more than usual. It was leaving his wife behind. He also knew Tabor well enough to avoid suggesting once again—he'd already done so three times, and the last time precipitated a shouting match with Tabor—that

Tanaka accompany them on their journey back to Hedeby.

"We will still leave at dawn?" Sven asked.

"Aye."

Sven glanced sideways at Tabor, wanting to say more, to find the words that would convince his good friend that Tanaka would be safe in their absence and that she would be a faithful, loving wife no matter how long their separation. But Sven was no better with words of tender emotion than Tabor, so the two Vikings stood shoulder to shoulder in silent accord, each knowing the other's thoughts almost as clearly as if they'd been put into words.

"Will you be moving back into the high priestess's quarters?" Tabor asked. He pushed himself away from the table, which was piled high with the delicacies of Egyptian food that the pharaoh had ordered brought to him on the night before his departure.

"I don't know," Tanaka replied. "I haven't thought about it very much. Not at all, actually."

She had moved in with Tabor when they were married, and they lived in the quarters the pharaoh had provided. He had not moved into hers because it was still an issue that the high priestess had taken a husband. It would have compounded the scandal if he had committed the great blasphemy of living in her quarters.

"You understand that I must leave, that I really have no choice?" Tabor pressed.

"Yes, I understand. We've talked about this a dozen times, and I'm resigned to the fact that as a Viking you must return to your homeland to do what you can to get rid of Ingmar the Savage. He is a vile man and he must be dealt with. I understand all of this."

"You're being very reasonable," Tabor said.

She was being reasonable. . . . and it bothered him. Initially, there had been tears. She didn't see why her husband had to leave. Then, when he spoke of honor and leadership, Tanaka demanded that she go along. Tabor's laugh—surely any woman who wanted to go along on a war ship had been made senseless by too much sun—infuriated Tanaka and made her all the more determined to go with him. She demanded that as his wife she be allowed to go with her husband wherever he went, but Tabor refused. Tanaka even begged the pharaoh to use his influence on the stubborn Viking. The pharaoh said no. Perhaps it would be best, he suggested, if Tanaka did not make too much of an issue of being Tabor's wife. The ceremony itself had been unorthodox, since it was the pharaoh who officiated it for the high priestess and not the other way around, and no one—not even Tanaka herself—was altogether sure of the propriety of such a ceremony. No high priestess had ever married before, and many people did not think the pharaoh should have allowed Tanaka to marry at all—and certainly not to a blue-eyed barbarian.

And then, as the boats' construction neared completion and the sailors were selected so that Tabor and Sven would have a full complement of men, Tanaka had abruptly quit arguing.

"I know you, Tabor," Tanaka said, finishing the last of the honey-glazed roast duck breast. "When you make a decision, you never back down. I can argue with you until I haven't a breath left in my body, and I'll still never accomplish anything. . . . so why waste breath better used on other words?"

Every word that Tanaka spoke was irrefutably true, but that still didn't make Tabor feel any better about the way she was accepting this. He would have actually preferred her tears and protestations to this quiet, Viking-like acceptance of the inevitable.

"There is only one thing that I will ask of you," Tanaka said.

"Tell me, and I will make it so."

"That you don't expect me to watch you sail away. When you leave, I don't want to stand there as you disappear into the distance."

It was not the request Tabor had expected, though he hadn't been certain what she might ask of him, but he nodded his acceptance.

"I will return to you as quickly as possible," Tabor said.

Tanaka smiled pleasantly. "I'm sure you will." Her nonchalance ripped holes in Tabor's peace of mind and made him question how much his wife loved him after all.

They set sail at first light, Tabor at the helm of

one ship, Sven piloting the other. The crew was mostly Egyptian, the finest sailors and soldiers that the pharaoh had in his command. From the time the pharaoh had commissioned the boats for Tabor's voyage to his homeland, the Egyptian men had been schooled in the Danish language so they could speak and understand Tabor, Sven, and the other Vikings.

The wind blew from the south, strong and warm, and Tabor took this as a good omen. If the wind continued strong, he would be back in his home waters in only a few weeks' time—perhaps less.

He looked back at the pier, where the pharaoh and his wife still stood, though he could no longer distinguish them from the rest of the crowd of well-wishers.

Tabor's heart felt heavy, his chest tight. Hundreds of people stood on the pier and along the shoreline, assuring Tabor and his crew that they would be missed in their absence and welcomed upon their return. But Tabor did not want many hundreds of strangers to wish him a safe voyage, he wanted only the wishes of one special woman as he left upon his perilous mission of revenge and retribution.

But that one woman was nowhere to be seen.

True to her word, Tanaka had remained away. She had said she wouldn't be there, but Tabor hadn't believed her. He'd expected that her icy resolve would melt and he would see her at the last moment, teary-eyed, running along the pier to throw her arms around him, to kiss him, and if the Fates and the gods were smiling, to tell him she loved him and would wait—no matter how long it took—for him to return to her.

Tanaka didn't come.

Tabor turned his back to the shore once again, concentrating on the rudder to nurse every bit of power from the wind. He used his strength of will to hide his disappointment. At least the ship that Pharaoh Moamin Abbakka had had made for him was truly a spectacular vessel. It incorporated the finest features both of the Egyptian and the Viking longboats, and his crew was absolutely first-rate. When he returned to his home waters and hunted down Ingmar the Savage, there was the possibility that Tabor would still be outnumbered, but the skill of Tabor's men, both as sailors and as soldiers, could not be overestimated.

To his right and slightly north of Tabor's position, Sven sailed with his crew. Tabor allowed himself a smile as he remembered the stoic Viking's almost childlike giddiness when he learned that he would be the leader of the second crew, the captain of a finely-crafted sailing vessel.

These would be the good days, Tabor knew. The days when all the men had to worry about was getting the most of the wind and keeping land in sight. Later, when they were in the treacherous Scandinavian waters with submerged rocks that ripped the hulls from even the strongest ships, then sleep would be difficult and fear would be a constant companion. Those would be the days when, even while sleeping, Ingmar the Savage's face would never stray far from their thoughts.

343

Soon, even the palace that had become Tabor's home was no longer visible. Tabor concentrated on the task of guiding his ship, his thoughts occasionally drifting to the battles that would be fought when he returned to his home. And whenever the thought of Tanaka entered his mind, he pushed it away forcibly. Until he returned to her, she was in his past; and to dwell upon her memory for long was neither healthy nor befitting. Besides, she had not thought him worthy of a personal farewell, so in all likelihood she had forgotten him — or was trying to — and was getting on with her life and the responsibilities that were hers to bear as palace high priestess for the Pharaoh Moamin Abbakka.

Dusk was approaching when Jafar made his way back to where Tabor stood at the rudder. Tabor smiled at the young Egyptian sailor, pleased to have him aboard. He had seen Jafar's skill with bow and arrow, sword, and spear, and the young sailor's attitude and disposition were excellent.

"Tabor, Son of Thor, I have bad news for you," Jafar said, standing with his shoulders square, looking straight into Tabor's eyes, as he knew he must if he were to be considered a man in his leader's eyes.

"Yes?" Tabor was not worried. The first day of the voyage had gone without incident, and his instincts told him that a favorable wind would continue for many days.

"We have a stowaway," Jafar said. "In your chambers."

Tabor cursed furiously. Knowing that Jafar did not understand the words pleased him. When the

344

crew had been assembled, every young man in the village had wanted to travel to foreign lands and fight the enemy that had caused the high priestess Tanaka so much pain. Tabor and the pharaoh had evaluated all the candidates for the two ships, and though they had selected exactly one hundred, there were still five times as many who had been rejected. Every Egyptian man knew that if he sailed with Tabor and lived to return, he would be a hero in the eyes of Pharaoh Moamin Abbakka and in the eyes of the young women of the village and palace. Life would be considerably easier, and there were many advantages in a life of ease.

"Take the rudder," Tabor said, not at all sure what he would do with the stowaway.

He stormed to his quarters, which had been uniquely designed, different from anything that Tabor had ever seen on a ship. A room, fifteen feet square, had been built at midships, just ahead of the ship's large single mast. There Tabor would sleep, protected from the elements, though the rest of the crew would not know that luxury. Tabor had insisted that it was not necessary to coddle him, but the pharaoh—urged on by Tanaka—insisted that Tabor, as a leader of men, deserved such comforts.

He opened the door to his chambers, ready to roar like a lion to scare the young whelp with the temerity to sneak aboard a fighting ship. He opened his mouth to bellow, but his jaw dropped open in silent surprise. Tanaka lay upon his mattress, dressed in a diaphanous gown of pale white that made the darkness of her skin and her ebony hair that much more pronounced. The gold *ankh* between her breasts reflected the light, making Tabor remember that it was the Egyptian symbol of life . . . and that life without Tanaka was hardly worth living.

"I should be furious with you," he said, stepping into the room, closing the door behind him.

"Yes, you should be, but you're not." Tanaka pushed herself up just a little higher, leaning against the pillows and the wall behind her. The shimmering bodice of her gown opened more, almost to the navel, to display the dark, smooth, inner swells of her breasts. She felt an instant warming of her blood when she saw Tabor's gaze go to her bosom and linger there.

"How did you get on board without my seeing you?" Tabor asked. He knelt at the edge of the mattress, finding it difficult to keep from taking Tanaka into his embrace when she looked so magnificently inviting. "I watched everything that was brought aboard."

"Yes, you did. . . . but you are forgetting that I am a high priestess and, though the Egyptians aboard are loyal to you, they are even more loyal to me. And, frankly, in their eyes, I have greater rank."

A twinge of anger went through Tabor. He did not like being out-ranked by a woman, especially not when aboard his own fighting ship. It also bothered him that he had men beneath him who clearly were participants in this subterfuge.

346

"Which men helped you aboard? Who helped deceive me?"

"If I told you that, you'd only be angry with them. There's no need for that." Tanaka reached up to draw the tip of her finger along the line of Tabor's jaw. "You looked so disappointed when I said I didn't want to see you off. Oh, Tabor, as much as you hate to admit it, there is a tenderness to you."

Tabor pushed her hand from his cheek. "No," he said. "I am a Viking." His mood swung to and fro, from pleasure to fury. Tanaka would be in great jeopardy when he returned to do battle with Ingmar the Savage.

"You are a Viking, Tabor, but you are also a man. A tender and thoughtful man. It is one of the reasons why I love you as much as I do."

Tanaka pushed herself farther away from Tabor, giving him room to lie on the mattress beside her. When she moved, the bodice of her gown opened a fraction more, and the garment split to reveal her thigh—exactly as she had known it would. She had been planning this evening for several weeks. "Sit beside me, and I will show you how much I love you, and you will show me how tender a strong Viking can be," she said.

"No."

It was a single, angry, defiant declaration, put forward on principle. Tabor had insisted that Tanaka stay in Egypt and she had promised she would, then had done exactly the opposite. Tabor had sworn his Egyptian sailors to an oath of loyalty, some of them—perhaps all—had conspired with

347

Tanaka to steal her aboard the ship without the leader's knowledge and against his expressed wishes.

This was not the kind of control over his life and his men that Tabor enjoyed.

"Don't be stubborn, my darling," Tanaka said, her tone as velvet-warm and smooth as the gown she wore, sultry with the implicit promise of ecstasy and mutual fulfillment. "It won't accomplish anything, and it will prevent us from enjoying ourselves."

Tabor shook his head, but the blue light in his eyes suggested that his anger was yielding to humor and passion. He thoroughly lacked the ability to keep a firm grasp on his anger when Tanaka was dressed as beautifully as she was, looking incredibly alluring in the sheer gown that concealed only the crests of her breasts, highlighting the hardness of her nipples beckoning beneath.

"So this is why you wouldn't bid me farewell; and this is why you stopped arguing when I said you couldn't make the voyage with me."

Tanaka nodded. She caught her lower lip between even, white teeth, her expression beguiling, subtly sexual.

"And this is why you insisted that this be built," Tabor said, extending a hand in a circle to indicate his chambers. *Their* chambers.

"I did want a little more privacy than we had on our voyage *to* Egypt. And, to be truthful, I never did enjoy being rained on and sleeping with the wind blowing straight through me."

Tabor smiled, the last of his anger fading rapidly.

"High priestess, you are not a Viking. A Viking would never complain about sleeping aboard an open ship."

"You're right, I'm not a Viking. . . . but I *love* a Viking . . . very much . . . much more than that Viking may ever really know. . . . but if he doesn't know it, it isn't because I haven't tried to show him."

Tanaka patted the mattress near her hip, wanting Tabor beside her. She felt an exuberance in having kept her plan a secret from Tabor all these weeks. Her intent to be with him always was working out better than she had dared hope.

"Why continue battling the inevitable?" she asked with impish charm. "You love me. I love you. I'm here on this boat with you, in this tiny little room that I had built especially for us so that we would know some privacy. Doesn't it seem to you that your stubbornness is getting in the way of our happiness?"

Tabor pulled loose the knotted cord at his throat to remove the light cape. "I do not like being played the fool," he said, tossing aside the cape. He removed his boots; and as he did, he felt Tanaka's hand upon his shoulder.

"It is the last time I will do anything like that," Tanaka said, watching as the powerful muscles moved beneath her husband's shirt. She tried to remain docile, but the desire charging through her was too intense, and she quickly got her knees beneath her and cuddled close behind Tabor.

"You intentionally lied to me."

"Yes. Must we keep bringing up that little, unfortunate point?"

Tabor was distinctly aware of Tanaka's breasts, warm and enticing, pressing against him. He felt her lips whisper against the side of his neck, and a moment later the tip of her warm, moist tongue followed the sensitive curve of his ear. It was all that Tabor could do to appear unaffected by her, pretending anger and ignoring the lengthening and thickening of his manhood, which had never been immune to Tanaka, no matter how great his fury.

"You disobeyed me."

"If you wanted a wife who would tremble at the sound of your voice, I'm afraid you've fallen in love with the wrong woman."

Tanaka leaned more firmly into Tabor. Her breasts felt tight, irrationally compressed, the nipples distended and tingling, hungry for the pleasure they would know when Tabor at last put his silly, intrusive pride away and paid attention to them the way she wanted him to.

She moved her shoulders from side to side, rubbing her breasts against his biceps, blatantly forcing him to be aware of all he would have left behind if he'd been allowed to embark on this voyage of revenge without his wife.

"I'm not the docile, obeying type," she said, stating what had long been obvious.

Tabor began unfastening the stays on his shirt, his blood coursing furiously through him. He seemed perfectly calm, though perhaps slightly annoyed, as though he were being forced to endure

350

some minor hardship that he felt he should not have to bear.

It was only in the depths of his clear blue eyes — and only then if a woman knew him well — that this deceit was revealed. In his eyes glinted lust. And an almost adolescent humor, the mischief of a man feeling like a teenager again. He was giddy with love in all its panoramic newness, oblivious to everything but that one special someone that made life not merely worthwhile, but exquisite. Sleeping was an abominable waste of time; it prevented him from being conscious of her.

"I've been a bad wife," Tanaka continued, almost laughing. She sensed the falseness of Tabor's anger, and it lightened her heart and heightened her playfulness. Her eyes took on a pathetic, doleful expression as she clutched theatrically at Tabor's arm. "Please forgive me, husband Tabor!" she wailed as he pulled his shirt completely loose, exposing the pale, hard-muscled expanse of his chest.

Slowly and deliberately, each move a study in sexuality, Tanaka stretched herself over Tabor's thighs, rubbing her breasts against his legs and against the prominent bulge in his trousers as she moved over him, lying sideways across his lap.

"I've been very bad," Tanaka whispered, her voice a husky, sensual purr that said she could be very, *very* bad with a little coaxing, and that if she were, Tabor would be very happy about it. "In some families, if a child has been bad, the father takes that child over his knee and brings his palm down upon the child's backside."

As she spoke, Tanaka raised her gown to reveal the taut buttocks that she had been wiggling ever so slightly as she writhed on Tabor's lap. The moment she revealed herself to him, she felt the warmth of his hand against her, and the strength of his fingers as he squeezed her. She spread her thighs further apart.

"I've been very bad," she purred, no longer making any attempt to keep the smile from her lips, though she was able to continue the seductive, submissive game she'd started. "So very, very bad." She wiggled, offering her backside to Tabor, knowing he would never strike her. She could feel his heat and hardness through his trousers and her gown, pressing firmly against her, a portent of things to come.

Tabor closed his eyes for just a moment, forcing his raging emotions back under control. He tried rather foolishly to convince himself that he was a man of considerable experience. This was not the first, second, or even third time that a woman played a coy, seductive game with him in order to receive his attention and perhaps gain a measure of forgiveness for some transgression. And if Tanaka had been anyone else, Tabor *would* have been able to maintain his composure—but if she had been anyone else, he also would have been able to maintain his bachelorhood. Instead, he'd given it up without a glance backward or a single moment's regret.

When he opened his eyes, he found that his hand rested on Tanaka's backside. He squeezed one buttock, then the other, watching his fingers compress the taut, satiny flesh, astonished as he always was that anyone could be this arousing, particularly when there wasn't anything *physically* about Tanaka that he had not fully touched, caressed, and tasted. But time could not diminish the fire that burned in his soul, and never had that fire burned hotter than it did at this moment, when — by all rights — he should be absolutely furious with his wife.

As though the hand belonged to someone else, he watched as the fingers dipped into the cleft of her backside to graze along her smooth, shaven petals. He felt instantly the heat and wetness of her readiness.

A deep, rumbling groan escaped Tabor, and his manhood became even harder with the understanding of how ready Tanaka was for him.

"You've been very bad," Tabor said, though the tightness in his throat made the words sound as though they had been spoken by someone else.

"Yes, so very bad," Tanaka replied, her eyes closed, total concentration on the hand touching her backside, the fingertips brushing temptingly against the entrance to her womanhood. Her thoughts danced between savoring the satisfaction she had known from her husband's caresses and the pleasure she would know on this particular evening. By this time, her fear that Tabor would be so angry that he'd turn the ship around and row against the wind to return her home had been abandoned, forgotten.

"Very bad," Tabor repeated.

He pushed the tip of his finger into Tanaka. She uttered a tiny cry of pleasure, her body twisting against his thighs. She tossed her head to throw her hair away from her face, then looked over her shoulder at Tabor, aware of how she must appear to him. She was still astonished that this man who had known so many women intimately was so enamored with her. After all the times that they had made love, his hands still trembled, his breathing grew ragged and uneven. She looked into Tabor's eyes, their gaze holding in silent understanding. And when she felt Tabor withdraw his fingertip, she sighed again, intentionally, so that he would know how much she appreciated everything he did.

"I've been naughty," Tanaka whispered, her dark gaze held magically by Tabor's.

"Very," Tabor said.

And then, his eyes never breaking contact with Tanaka's, he brought his fingertip to his lips and sucked it. Tanaka sighed, closing her eyes momentarily, and when she opened her eyes again, she realized that Tabor had waited so that she would be looking at him before he continued.

"Very, very naughty," Tabor said, then returned his hand to her, smoothly reinserting the finger he had just moistened.

She let out a harsh little cry of ecstasy, and that brought an end to the game. Tabor, who had already shown greater restraint with Tanaka than ever had before, stood abruptly, unintentionally and rather unceremoniously allowing her to roll off his thighs onto the floor of the boat. He pulled at his shirt, struggling with the garment to remove it from his long arms. Even before he had the chance to pull loose his trousers, Tanaka had accomplished that task for him. Seconds later, he had removed his final garment and had stripped Tanaka of her gown with equal haste.

"Wife, you will be the death of me," Tabor whispered, pulling Tanaka against him as he stretched out on the foot-thick mattress made of the finest duck down in all of Egypt.

"No, my darling barbarian, I will be the life of you," Tanaka replied, curling into her husband, her arms encircling his familiar chest.

She leaned into him as they faced one another, lying on their sides. She pressed her breasts into his hard chest, trembling softly as the warmth of his body heightened the sensitivity of her nipples. She pushed her fingers into his long blond hair, astonished once again at its silkiness and how her body reacted so spontaneously to the feel of it against her fingertips. She felt his strength, his love, his desire, the very essence of him. . . . she felt it all, in everything that Tabor said and did—and even in the things he was unable to say because of some unfortunate Viking custom of stoic silence that Tanaka could not comprehend.

"Wife . . . wife," Tabor whispered, his lips nuzzling Tanaka's as he spoke the single, precious word.

"Husband . . ."

Tanaka had never thought that she would call any man "husband," especially not after she had been kidnapped and captured by Ingmar. But then Tabor had come into her life, and now the thought of spending a night, much less a week or a month, without him beside her in bed was intolerable. So she had looked him straight in the eyes and lied to him. She was Tanaka, high priestess to the Pharaoh Moamin Abbakka, and she would lie, coerce, use every ounce of power and influence she had, and even defy the gods themselves if they threatened to come between her and the husband she loved.

Tabor pulled Tanaka in closer, his manhood trapped between them, furiously rigid in its yearning. He stroked the satiny, ebony hair from her eyes, then kissed her mouth quickly, more in love with her at that moment than he ever before, even more than on that blessed day when he had stood with her before the pharaoh, confessing his lifelong love, and took her as his wife.

"I should be angry with you," he whispered, looking into her eyes, his hand sliding down to the rounded curve of her buttocks. "But I cannot be angry with you for long, just as I cannot help but love you for all time."

His words were too profound for Tanaka to accept calmly. She rolled onto her back, pulling Tabor with her, desire and passion strengthening her in ways nothing else could.

"Love me now, you barbarian!" she hissed, almost angry with herself and with Tabor because she needed him so much.

He entered her in a long, breathtaking plunge, filling her, driving into her so that when at last he stopped, Tanaka felt she had been at once invaded by her husband and surrounded by him. His ardent desire for her made her feel feminine and strong. She was desired by a man who desired no other. And she was free to be uninhibited in her personal quest for the ultimate fulfillment, for the pinnacle of passion that no woman before had even imagined, much less attained.

Chapter Twenty-seven

The gods smiled upon them. The winds continued, warm and strong from the south, propelling the two-boat armada westward through the narrow straits, then northward, as they followed the western coastline of Portugal.

Somewhat grudgingly, Tabor had to admit that the Egyptian sailors now under his command were at least as good as his own Vikings—in many cases, superior—both as soldiers and as seamen. There had, however, never been so much talking on any boat Tabor commanded. He mentioned this to Tanaka, and she laughed. Tabor's views toward the Egyptians, she promised, would evolve slowly, until, at last, he would agree that her culture was, in fact, quite superior to his. Tabor, answered with a teasing laugh that the sun would turn black as night for all time before such a preposterous lie would ever pass his lips.

With the specter of their separation removed, the lovers enjoyed themselves and their lives together. No longer did they have to live with the knowledge that Tabor would sail into battle, leaving Tanaka to wait and worry in his absence.

Tanaka spent much time shuffling and reading her tarot cards. Though she never showed Tabor anything but a brave face, she had heard the men talking. She overheard them say they would be outnumbered when they returned to Hedeby. No amount of confidence in Tabor's fighting skill, or in the skill of the men under his command, could make Tanaka forget what it had been like during those painful hours so long ago, when Ingmar the Savage, with vastly superior numbers, had attacked Tabor. The slaughter, the wanton destruction of property and people. . . . it all played heavily on Tanaka's heart, though she kept it to herself.

Tabor, she knew, had enough on his mind without having to worry that she was unhappy.

The sun was high overhead as Tanaka sat crosslegged on the deck of the longboat, her back against the bedroom wall of their chamber. Tabor was at the rudder, and the boat moved along at a steady pace.

Holding the thick papyrus cards loosely in her palm, Tanaka concentrated, then divided the cards in half. She turned over the top card of one pile. It was the Universe card—for the third consecutive time!

She felt power surging through her. It did not frighten her. An energy directed her, and Tanaka knew that if she followed the path, she would find something beautiful.

Why did she feel this way?

Tanaka dismissed the question almost immediately. She felt the energy, felt the dawning power of it as one feels the strength of nourishing food making the body powerful and invigorated. She could not prove that the energy was present, leading her in a direction that seemed divergent with that of Tabor's intended goal, but it was there.

With tranquility and confidence, Tanaka neatly arranged her cards and put them away. When she emerged from the room, her face was as radiant and sunny as the sky itself. She smiled at the men as she passed them on her way to the stern of the longboat where Tabor stood with his hand on the tiller.

"You're looking pleased about something," Tabor said as his wife approached.

Secretly, he was hoping she was about to tell him that she was with child. They had discussed the possibility of her having a baby, and Tanaka had said that she would hope that the child would wait until they returned to Egypt. She did not want her child to be born in Denmark in the middle of a protracted war with Ingmar the Savage.

Tabor's attitude was different. For most of his adult life, he had worried that he might become a father before he was ready to accept such responsibility. Now that he had at last taken a wife, he wanted all the responsibilities that went with being a husband—and that meant children, *lots* of children. Tabor liked the idea of having a pregnant wife at home, safe and warm while he fought mighty battles. A pregnant Tanaka would add to his confidence, and he believed that the gods would smile favorably upon him during battle if they knew that he would soon be bringing a child into this world with Tanaka.

"How far are we from England?" Tanaka asked, her smile as bright as ever.

Tabor's brows furrowed. "Not far."

"We must go there," Tanaka said, making the statement calmly, as though she were not asking for something unusual.

"Why?"

"Because if we do, we will conceive a son . . . a son who will have great powers and be a leader of men."

For an instant, Tanaka froze, looking into Tabor's blue eyes, listening to her own words. She had not consciously thought the words. They had simply come from her lips, and she heard them and felt the impact of their significance—of their truth—at the same time Tabor did.

For an instant, Tabor's eyes narrowed into thin slits as he peered suspiciously at his wife. But then, only a second or two later, he displayed a wide, beaming smile.

"Thank you," she said, reaching up to grab the lapel of Tabor's leather jerkin. She pulled him down so that she could kiss him quickly, even though she knew that it bothered Tabor immensely to show outward signs of affection toward her in front of his men. "I can't tell you why it is necessary or why I feel this way, I only know that—"

"Shhh!" Tabor placed a long finger against Tanaka's soft lips, silencing her. "You are my wife. You do not need to explain why you want something. You need only want it, and I will make it so."

Intellectually, Tanaka told herself that her husband could not control the earth and heavens to make her life as pleasant and comfortable as she would like. After all, despite Tabor's nickname "Son of Thor," he was not a god—or even a demigod. But at that moment, as she looked up at him, seeing pleasure etched in his features, Tanaka believed that her husband could direct the stars in the sky. She knew this could not be so, but her heart did not, and it was her heart that always spoke loudest.

Taking a more westerly course presented no problem for Tabor. He knew exactly where he was in relation to England and to Denmark. He could redirect his ships to England if it would make his wife happy. . . . and if it would make him the father of a proud Viking son. To achieve that end— to have a son, strong and proud—Tabor would sail off the edge of the earth.

Tabor propelled the rowboat through the water. He had his back toward shore; and over Tanaka's shoulder, he could see his own longboat and Sven's. The boats would wait off the English coast exactly seven days and then sail on, with or without Tabor and Tanaka. It was Tabor's order that should the ships be confronted—which was decidedly possible, since Tabor had made his fair share of enemies in

England—they were to flee northward. But in his heart he doubted that Sven and the rest of his Viking crew would leave him behind in the den of his enemy, and he knew the Egyptian sailors would not desert their high priestess. Even though many of the men did not approve of Tanaka marrying (especially a pale-skinned foreigner), she was their high priestess and they would defend her with their lives to the end.

"You're sure about this?" Tabor asked, putting heft to the oars as he rowed the small boat toward shore.

Tanaka nodded, her mind unclouded by even a hint of doubt. She did not mention the tarot, which had first directed her to England, because she knew that Tabor took no stock in such things.

"I feel it here," she said, placing her hand lightly over her heart.

Tabor grinned wickedly, continuing to pump away at the oars. "That is not where you feel a baby."

"It is to begin with. It is only later when you feel a baby here," she said, moving her hand to her stomach.

Tabor wondered why he was following Tanaka's direction without more complaint. Perhaps it was because she seemed so unwaveringly certain of herself or maybe it was his overwhelming desire to have a child—a son—with this extraordinary woman who could "know" things without having to be told them and "feel" things, which no one else sensed.

When they reached the shore, Tabor began to hide the boat, but Tanaka stopped him.

"There is no need to hide it. No one will steal the boat. No ships will approach Sven. When we return, no one will ever know that we have been here."

"If this boat is stolen, we will have no way of returning to our ship," Tabor said.

He looked out to his boat, which was several hundred yards off the coast, safe in waters deep enough for its impressive keel. He knew he could swim to his ship, if need be, but he doubted Tanaka would have the necessary stamina.

"The small boat will still be here when we return, as will the longboats," Tanaka said complacent with confidence. "Come, we must travel in this direction." She picked up the satchel that held the dried fish and bread they would live on during their time on land.

"What lies this way?" Tabor asked, the first hints of disbelief now coloring his tone as he hefted the waterskin onto his shoulder.

"I do not know. I know only that it is this way, and it is where we must go."

They headed from shore, Tanaka leading the way, following what to Tabor appeared to be no particular path or direction, moving inland and slightly northward. He followed her; and when he began to doubt, he used his Viking will power to chase the thoughts away.

For the first time, Tabor was following another person's lead without question or explanation. He was, fully and completely, trusting Tanaka, even though she could provide for him not one single bit of information to make him believe that there was a reason for her confidence.

He saw it in the eerie, moonlit distance, and it was unlike anything he had ever seen before. Huge stones, each one many tons in weight, stood in a circle in the grassy valley. Some stones, extraordinarily large, had been placed across two of the huge monoliths to bridge them.

It was a temple, and even from a distance Tabor felt its eerie, mystical power. He knew now why he had followed Tanaka.

"What is it?" Tabor asked, placing his hand on his wife's shoulder, pulling her against his side as he looked at the monolithic boulders in the distance.

"It is called by some a temple," Tanaka answered.

"How do you know that?"

"I just do." Tanaka raised her hands, palms outward, toward the stones as though testing the comforting heat of a campfire. "This is what has called me," she said. "This is why we have come all this way."

They picked up their belongings and walked into the valley, Tabor holding the haft of his sword loosely in his hand, his senses alert, his eyes searching the darkness, checking the shadows for unseen danger.

Tanaka's response was different. At first sight of the monolithic, outdoor shrine, a beautific, utterly serene smile creased her mouth. She felt the power of the place, felt it in her bones, in her soul. She had been right to follow her intuition.

"This is where we are supposed to be," she whispered.

Tabor did not answer her. He, too, felt a strange, mystifying power, but to him, feeling anything that was mystifying meant that he must be wary. He held his sword at his side, prepared to strike out at anyone or anything that approached them.

"Yes, this is what has called to me," Tanaka explained quietly, speaking in a reverent whisper, though there was not another soul around. "This is what spoke inside my head."

When they reached the nearest boulders, Tanaka placed her palms flat against the stones. She felt a tingling sensation race through her, and her smile broadened.

"Touch this," Tanaka said. "Feel what I feel."

Tabor's brows pressed together in confusion, but he held his tongue. He placed his palm against the boulder near Tanaka's, but all he felt was the cool, rough texture of the stone. Tanaka realized he did not sense what she did. It was not easy for her to accept that they were different people and that their views on life and perceptions in and of life also differed.

"What is this place?" Tabor asked, at last breaking his silence as they moved inside the circle of stones. He was finally convinced that they were alone and that enemy soldiers would not ambush them from the boulders.

"It is our place," Tanaka replied simply, without the slightest doubt that she might have made some mistake.

She had no name for the temple, though she knew in her heart that it was the place she was meant to be with Tabor. She did not know that other people—ancient people—had named the temple Stonehenge.

Tanaka walked to the center of the circle of stones, took Tabor's cape from him, and spread it out on the moon-silvered grass.

"I know you want to look around," Tanaka said, aware of her husband's inquisitive nature. "Do what you must, then come back to me."

Tabor, pleased that his wife knew him as well as she did, bent to kiss her briefly, then left to investigate the mysteries of the stones.

Tabor felt he was being watched, though his investigation assured him that he was alone with Tanaka in the grassy valley.

From all that Tabor could glean, looking at the huge boulders in the moonlight and studying their location, the temple had been made many years before and was not in continual use. He thought that perhaps the area was used as a gathering place once a month, perhaps only when the moon was full. The temple couldn't be used much more often than that, Tabor reasoned, or the grass would be more trampled down than it was. Whatever the answer, the stones meant something, but what, he could not say.

Confused, Tabor leaned against one of the upright stones and turned his attention toward the center of the circle.

Tanaka was sitting cross-legged, her head tilted slightly back on her shoulders as though to look up at the moon, but Tabor could see that her eyes were closed. He looked at her, wondering what she was thinking, whether she was praying, whether the gods could, in fact, speak directly into her mind. That might explain how she had known about this mysterious place on the island of England, though Tabor, ever doubtful, found the explanation too difficult to accept.

Will this place really give me a son?

The question taunted Tabor. He wanted a son with all his heart, but it was not this strange temple that would give him a son, it was Tanaka.

And it was at precisely that moment, when he was thinking about the joy he would know at being a father to a child that Tanaka would bear him, that she stood, in a single, fluid motion, and raised her arms high above her head, as though reaching to touch the moon. In her diaphanous white robes, she looked ghostly, and for the most fleeting moment, Tabor wondered if perhaps he did feel something, some strange power that emanated from the ground or from the stones or perhaps from the moon glowing overhead. He closed his eyes, trying to concentrate on the power, but whatever he had felt vanished or, more likely, had never actually been there in the first place.

He opened his eyes again, looking to Tanaka, and watched as her hands came down slowly and she unfastened the knotted stays at her throat, then at her hip. With a shrug of her shoulders and a tug at a sleeve, her garment fell down around her ankles and she stood in naked splendor.

Once again, she raised her hands toward the moon, tilting her head far back on her shoulders, her wavy hair shining blue-black in the moonlight, cascading down over her shoulders and breasts.

The sight of her took Tabor's breath away. *I'll never tire looking at her,* he thought, pushing himself away from the stone, approaching his wife slowly, quietly, drawn to her with the same inexorable force that she had been drawn to the temple.

Chapter Twenty-eight

The closer he drew, the more clearly he could see her and the more beautiful she became. Her skin, olive-hued, literally glowed. With her hands raised toward the moon, her breasts were pulled high and, though hidden by her hair, their roundness was undisguised. Her stance exaggerated the line of her ribs and the narrowness of her waist, the delicate, womanly curve of her hips, the graceful tapering of her thighs. From the distance that separated them, Tabor could not distinctly see her womanhood, but what his eyes could not see, his mind could recall with enticing clarity.

Tabor tried to speak, but he could not. The beauty of this woman rendered him speechless. He felt virginal.

And then, breaking the spell, Tanaka turned her face from the moon and smiled at him, her arms still raised high as though reaching for something celestial that she could see but Tabor could not. Everything in Tabor screamed for him to take action, to rush to her and throw her down upon the cape beneath her feet. His Viking blood called out for him to do it, but he listened to the mystical blood of his Egyptian high priestess wife who, for this one magical evening, directed his actions. Hastily, he cast aside his own clothes — along with any doubts he might have had about whether this was a trap set by the gods to separate him from his men, any doubts that Tanaka might be wrong to think that in this strange place they would conceive a son who would be the leader of men.

He stepped up to Tanaka, placing his palms lightly on the curve of her hips, and looked down into her shining eyes. He bent down to kiss her, and she twisted her arms loosely about his neck in greeting.

"Thank you," Tanaka whispered after the tentative kiss. "Thank you for bringing me here . . . and for trusting me."

"You are my wife. What is important to you is important to me," Tabor replied, but he did not understand why or what had directed Tanaka here. He accepted, though, that she could feel things he could not and hear voices that did not speak to him.

She brought her hands down slowly from his shoulders, touching his chest lightly, scraping his small, blunt nipples with her fingernails to draw a low, raspy groan of pleasure from him. Tanaka marvelled at Tabor's body, at its sculptured perfection, at the curving, hard line of his pectorals, and the rippled, granite-hard surface of his stomach. And letting her gaze and her hands roam lower, she marvelled, too, at his manhood, long and rigid. Slowly, almost cautiously, she took him in her hands, squeezing firmly to draw another groan of pleasure from her husband.

"So beautiful," Tanaka whispered.

"That?" Tabor asked with a deprecating grin.

Tanaka looked up into his eyes, smiling. "Yes, this." She squeezed him again, leaning forward just enough so that the sensitive tip pressed against the warm, smooth surface of her abdomen. "This and everything else about you."

"I am a Viking warrior, scarred in many places," Tabor said dismissively, never one to easily accept compliments.

I have many scars, too, only they are not visible, Tanaka thought. *But the scars are healing, thanks to you, my barbarian husband with the tender heart.*

She released him, then tossed her hair over her shoulders, knowing that her husband enjoyed seeing her breasts. At the sight, he inhaled deeply, and Tanaka felt a deep, heated rush of emotion. Her legs began to tremble. She reached out to Tabor, taking his hands.

"Sit," she whispered. "Lie down."

Tabor hesitated. It was not his style to accept orders, especially not under such intimate circumstances, but then nothing about his life now was the same as it had been before — before Tanaka. Still loosely holding Tanaka's hands, he sat down on his cape. He tugged at her, but she resisted, slipping from his grasp.

"Not yet," she whispered, and the glint in her eyes

said that if Tabor were patient, they would both be happier.

Leaning back on his hands, Tabor kicked his long legs out in front of himself, looking up at his wife. His desire for her was so strong that he ached to take her into his arms, to feel her naked body pressing against him, writhing against him as he plunged deeply into her. His manhood throbbed painfully, fully engorged, woefully neglected.

"Can you feel it?" Tanaka asked, moving so that she straddled Tabor's legs.

"Feel what?" Tabor asked, his voice strained with suppressed desire.

"The power. The energy." Tanaka extended her hands in either direction, fingers spread, palms toward the stones. "Perhaps you can't. No matter. I can feel the power, and it is going straight into me . . . into my blood."

Looking up at her, Tabor groaned softly, a sound of pain and pleasure woven together. His restraint, his will power, was being tested beyond endurance. Tanaka stood over him, her smooth, shaven petals glistening invitingly in the moonlight, shining with the honeyed moisture of desire.

"I feel the power," Tanaka repeated.

She looked down at him, her body trembling, her skin tingling. Tabor sat, his hands behind him, his magnificently sculpted, powerful body tensed with self-control. She stepped forward then, audacious and bold, and bent just slightly to push her fingers into Tabor's hair.

"Kiss me!" She pulled Tabor to her.

373

He kissed her between her legs, his tongue flashing with knowing expertise, devastating her. Tanaka cried out sharply, her body jerking at the exquisite contact of Tabor's moist tongue against the fulcrum of her sensations.

She allowed him to kiss until she could no longer remain standing. She sank slowly, pressing herself against Tabor as she bent her knees, taking his face between her palms.

"My lover . . . my husband," she whispered.

Their union, the joining of their bodies in the center of Stonehenge, was directed by unseen powers. As Tanaka slowly lowered herself onto Tabor, his manhood entered her easily, without hesitation, without guidance. She paused briefly, not yet fully engulfing Tabor's manhood, and kissed him deeply, parting her lips to receive his searching tongue.

"He will be a wonderful son," Tanaka whispered, lowering her lean hips a little more, taking more of him. "He will be a man good men respect."

Tabor could not speak. He remained with his hands behind him, holding himself up as his wife slowly descended upon him until he felt the silky backs of her thighs pressing against the fronts of his.

"Complete . . . I feel so complete with you inside me," Tanaka whispered.

She contracted around him, and the pleasure it brought was such that Tabor could not stop a low moan from escaping. He wondered if he would be able to contain his excitement long.

374

"Lie down," Tanaka whispered.

Tabor was almost grateful for the command. He relaxed his arms and lay back immediately, feeling the cool, smooth fabric of the Egyptian cape beneath his shoulders and buttocks and the prickly sensation of the grass against the backs of his long legs. Once on his back, he reached up to fill his hands with Tanaka's breasts.

"Yes-s-s!" Tanaka purred, placing her hands over Tabor's, forcing his fingers to press even more deeply into her.

She began raising and lowering her hips, moving to bring the maximum amount of pleasure to herself. She watched Tabor's face, seeing the ever-changing tapestry of passion painting color and light over his handsome features. Part of her was curiously detached from the blinding pleasure, as though she were watching two other lovers instead of being one of them. But this detachment in no way diminished her pleasure.

"You will be a wonderful father," Tanaka whispered, her hands on Tabor's chest as she impaled herself upon his thrusting manhood. "You will teach him everything you know and I will teach him all I know. . . . and he will be the best of both of our worlds."

Tabor focused his vision. His hands were filled with Tanaka's taut buttocks to guide her movements. His manhood felt searingly hot, and surely it was either burning Tanaka or being burned by her. . . . or, more likely, it was the fire of their shared passion that fueled him further.

Tabor felt the pressure building inside him. He could not withhold his passion much longer. Hooking a hand behind Tanaka's neck, he pulled her down so that their lips met in a heated, breathy kiss.

"He will be the best of both worlds," Tabor said, the strain of passion strident in his tone, "but you are my world!"

His words triggered her response. She bolted upright, tossing her head and flinging her hair against him. Her eyes, glazed with the fiery emotions steaming through her, could barely see the glowing moon high overhead. With a tremulous cry of ecstasy, Tanaka reached her pinnacle of pleasure, and the contractions that shuddered through her stimulated Tabor and he followed her into that mysterious, magnificent land.

Tanaka rolled onto her stomach, propping her chin in her hand. She felt gloriously well-loved, complete, whole. Tabor was everything that she had ever hoped he would be, and though she could not explain why she was certain of it, she knew — simply *knew* — that she and Tabor had conceived a son.

She did not feel cool at all, despite the evening breeze. Tabor's loving had heated her and it felt good now to spend a few moments alone, by herself, so that she could concentrate and be one with her feelings.

Tabor leaned against an upright stone, inspecting it. He was naked, his body glistening with a fine sheen of perspiration from their lovemaking in the moonlight; the nickname "Son of Thor," fit him perfectly as he pushed against the boulder, testing its mammoth weight.

She felt a stirring in her soul, and this surprised her since Tabor had so recently satisfied her passion thoroughly.

If I stopped looking at him, I wouldn't be such a wanton, Tanaka thought with a certain amount of logic. She did not, however, look away from her husband for even a second. *He's my husband. I can look if I want.*

He disappeared behind one of the pillars, and when he reappeared, he stepped back away from the rock, smoothing his long blond hair away from his face and placing his strong, gentle hands on his hips to study the stone.

Curious man. Tanaka thought, pleased that he was so. *A man of action and a man of thought. Such an unusual combination of traits.*

He turned slowly—pirouetting—to look at the entire collection of stones. She tensed her buttocks against the stirring within her, pressing her pelvis harder against the fabric of Tabor's cape. A smile curled her mouth as she watched Tabor inspect another of the numerous boulders at the temple.

She pushed herself to her knees, suddenly cool, the residual heat of their ardent lovemaking at last diminished.

I am a wanton woman. Tanaka thought as she tossed Tabor's cape over her shoulders and tied the drawstring at the neck. On Tabor, the cape came down to his knees. On her, it fell to her ankles. Beneath her bare feet, the cool grass, tickled her arches. She approached her husband slowly, renewing the excitement of their pleasure.

"Any conclusions?" she asked, pulling the robe around her.

He shook his head, his eyes exploring the gigantic boulder. Tanaka could almost hear his mind seeking the purpose of the temple and its ancient design.

"Aren't you cold without anything on?"

That brought a half-smile to Tabor's lips, pulling his mouth to the side so that his dimple showed.

Without taking his gaze from the stone, Tabor asked, "Does my lack of modesty offend you in this place of worship?"

"Quite the contrary," Tanaka said with a purr.

The sensual timbre of her voice drew Tabor's attention away from the boulders and to his wife. She slipped her hand inside his, delightfully devilish. He knew that look and liked what it promised.

"What are you thinking?" Tabor asked, though it was clear his wife had mischief on her mind.

"Nothing." Tanaka moved her shoulders slightly so that one breast peeked out through the opening in the cape.

"Why don't I believe you?" Tabor faced Tanaka directly. He loved it when she revealed this impish spirit.

"Because you're the suspicious kind," Tanaka replied.

Tabor bent low then to kiss her, and he was surprised that she did not kiss him back with matching ardor.

378

"I'm a little sore," she explained. "Your loving was . . . energetic."

She saw his expression change. It disturbed him whenever her body ached from their lovemaking, even though she had told him he should not feel guilty.

"Don't!" she said quickly, placing her fingertips against his mouth to silence the apology before it was spoken. "You were wonderful. You *are* wonderful."

He smiled with mixed emotions. "I don't like to hurt you, that's all."

Tanaka could tell that Tabor's attitude had changed. He had wanted to make love to her again, but now he'd quashed his desire.

"I know you don't," Tanaka said, her fingers tightening around Tabor's hand. "I also know that you want me again." She moved closer to the large boulder, pulling him with her.

"I will survive without enjoying your charms again this evening. Weren't you the one to teach me that patience has its own rewards?"

Tanaka took Tabor by the shoulders and turned his back to the boulder. She ran her hands boldly over his chest and stomach, her eyes locked with his.

"Yes, I taught you to be patient," she said in a husky purr that promised a sensual reward. "And you taught me many things. But tonight, here in this special place, we have created a child." She slipped the cape out of the way. "And tonight, your passion runs hot in your veins." She took his manhood into her hands and sighed when she felt it return to life, awakening from its sated slumber, thickening once again. "Just because I am unable to maintain the pace that you have set for us doesn't mean that you should be . . . deprived."

Tabor reached for Tanaka's breasts, but she took a step away from him, quickly releasing him from her grasp. "No, you mustn't touch me," she whispered, her eyes now aglow with excitement. "Don't even look at me."

Tabor's roguish-smile was incredulous. "Tanaka, I can't keep my eyes off you when you're clothed. How can you expect me to look away when all you're wearing is my cape and even that hides nothing?"

She placed her hands on her shapely hips, elbows akimbo to keep the robe behind her, blatantly exposing herself to Tabor, fully aware of the influence she had over him and relishing it.

"Are you going to trust me or not? I have yet to guide you wrongly."

Even though Tabor could think of some instance where she had been wrong, he did not disagree. After all this time together, Tanaka continued to excite and tantalize him.

"Well?" she prodded, her expression firm, the nakedness of her body seemingly forgotten, though Tabor knew she intentionally flaunted her charms.

"Yes, High Priestess, I will do as you say," Tabor at last replied with solemnity.

"Good. Now look at the moon."

"What?" Tabor exclaimed. It was hardly the request he anticipated, especially when he had seen the fiery passion that simmered within his wife's soul shimmering in her eyes.

"Look at the moon. Perhaps, if you look at the moon, you will understand the majesty of this place." Tanaka moved closer, her steps light and tentative, her heartbeat accelerating.

"You are more beautiful than the moon. Can't I just look at you?"

"No. You must do as I say."

Her authoritative tone brooked no dissent. She was the only person in the world who dared use that tone of voice with Tabor. She took him into her hands again, cradling the length of him lovingly, gently in her palms.

"Look at the moon, Tabor. Experience its power."

Her voice was a purr. She leaned forward to kiss his chest, her tongue tasting his flesh, salty from the exertion of their lovemaking. He tasted like a man recently active, and his scent washed her with memory.

She stroked her hands back and forth along his rigid length, feeling his heart pumping blood into him. The heat of his manhood burned through her palm, heating her own blood.

"Look at the moon, my darling, and feel its power," Tanaka whispered, looking up to see that Tabor had tilted his head back, resting it against the boulder as he stared at the moon. "Feel the power of the stone against your back, of the stones around you."

She kissed his chest, his throat, the hard ridge of

381

his ribs as she bent her knees, moving intently lower. She placed a hand flat against his stomach, feeling the solid muscles beneath the thin layer of smooth flesh, felt the faint flutter beneath her fingertips that signaled the intensity of Tabor's emotions.

Tanaka settled at last, her knees pressing into the cool grass of Stonehenge, her buttocks taut against the backs of her heels. Tabor's magnificence filled her hands, and she stroked him slowly, wondrously, her gaze alternating from that which she held to the face of the man she loved.

I will never tire of pleasing him, she thought resolutely, but for an infinitesimal second she recalled the women that her husband had known before he fell in love with her.

She cast the disquieting thought aside and gave Tabor a smoky, sensual smile. "The moon, you barbarian," she whispered, her breath warm against his inflamed flesh. "You're meant to be looking at the moon."

Tabor's self-control was strained. His powerful body was an interwoven mass of taut muscles flexed and bulging beneath his pale Scandinavian skin. He grasped a lock of Tanaka's hair, twirled the ebony strands around his forefinger, and rubbed them with his thumb, savoring the satiny texture.

"The moon, darling, the moon," Tanaka whispered, wanting Tabor's attention directed elsewhere, self-conscious despite her courage and determination to please her husband.

She waited, but still Tabor continued to gaze at

her, his huge chest swelling and contracting with his deep, uneven breathing, his icy blue eyes barely open as he struggled for control against the raging passion that seared his veins. Tanaka kissed the tip of his shaft, and the resulting groan told her that she pleased him.

She tasted him then, her tongue flicking out experimentally. Tabor groaned again and stared, unseeing, at the moon.

Gratified that he followed her request, Tanaka did not realize that he had done so because if he had continued watching her his control would have slipped away. In a slow, sensual dance, Tanaka gauged her husband's sensitivity. Deliberately, she drove him to the edge of ecstasy and the brink of madness.

Leaning back, she looked at him with as much objectivity as she could manage and decided that her husband was a physical marvel, the most beautiful creature she had ever seen. His thighs were hard and flexed, veins bulging as he fought to hold his passion back. Tanaka ran her hands up and down his legs, touching every inch of him, ignoring his manhood so that he might regain control lost to passion. When she looked up into his face again, frantic wildness burned in his eyes.

"I'm not stopping," Tanaka whispered and, to emphasize the point, dragged her tongue along his length. Sensual, confident, she moaned with satisfaction.

Unwrapping her hair from his finger, Tabor reached for Tanaka. "I must love you," he said through teeth clenched with strain.

But she would not be denied the pleasure of pleasing. Tanaka caught Tabor's hands as he reached for her, then slowly, gently, laced her fingers in his. Then, trapping his hands, she leaned forward and kissed the center of his passion.

"But you *are* loving me," she whispered, her feline eyes glinting in the moonlight, wickedly magical and supremely confident. "And I cannot stop. I mustn't stop. . . . and you don't want me to stop."

"You *must*," Tabor whispered, his control at the breaking point.

She held his hands tightly, not caring that he squeezed her fingers with near-bruising force. Then, her gaze still holding his, she said, "I could stop, but I'm not going to," and took him deep within her mouth.

Tabor closed his eyes, feeling the warmth of her descending over the length of him. He struggled for will power he no longer possessed; and, even as he felt the onrushing tide of his passion sweeping him away, he was distinctly aware that his wife created in him a hunger that only she could satisfy.

Chapter Twenty-nine

The smell of smoke and burning flesh was in the air, but it afforded Ingmar little pleasure. As the village burned and his men attacked the last remaining strongholds of resistance, Ingmar stood twisting a battle-axe slowly in his hands.

Tabor's axe. Throughout the winter, it had been his most prized possession. He knew the value that Tabor, Son of Thor, placed on the axe. By taking it, he had defeated his lifelong enemy.

Except rumor said that Tabor's defeat was not permanent, that he had been seen sailing near Kaupang in a two-ship fleet of boats unlike any ever seen on the Scandinavian seas.

Ingmar heard a familiar shout, and he looked up to see his brother Hugh signaling to him. Ingmar turned his back. Whatever source of entertainment Hugh had found, Ingmar wanted no part of it—or *her*, as was more likely the case. There were more important problems to worry about than the conquest of yet another comely wench.

It had only been the previous summer that Ingmar had tricked his Danish nemesis. When he closed his eyes, Ingmar could still see how he had aimed at Tabor's back—and how his arrow had missed its mark when the Egyptian woman intervened. Throughout the winter, Ingmar had convinced himself that his arrow, which had pierced Tabor's biceps, had eventually killed him. But then there came the rumor that Tabor had returned, as fit as ever, the Egyptian woman still with him, and his ships manned by a dark-skinned crew that spoke a strange and alien language . . .

"He couldn't have gotten her people to sail with him," Ingmar said aloud.

But what other explanation was there?

A short time earlier, Ingmar had raised his deadly axe against a village elder.

"You can kill me with Tabor's axe, but the Son of Thor is back and he will kill you!" the white-haired old man had said.

Those words had taken away the pleasure he had gleaned from the destruction of the village.

What if Tabor were back? Ingmar had seven ships. That would be enough against Tabor's two.

Ingmar the Savage would keep his ships and all his men close to him. No longer would he allow them to sail on their own and return with stolen goods to share with him. He wanted all his men around him because he knew that if Tabor were back, the Viking would want to exact his revenge. Personally.

It felt good to be on land. It felt even better to

feel secure. Tabor had promised Tanaka that she would be safe in the cove and that, for at least two days, she could relax with nothing to make her anxious.

Overhead, the skies were bright with stars; and the smell of beef roasting over an open fire wafted on the light breeze. The boats were not far from shore, and the small village they had discovered was only too happy to receive a returning hero, slaughtering two cows for the evening feast.

Tabor had built a small campfire just for Tanaka so that she could have privacy. That, anyway, was what he had said. She knew, though, that he had done it because he wanted her separated from the men and the villagers. Tabor did not want Tanaka to hear of the atrocities that Ingmar the Savage had committed in their absence. She smiled, pleased that her husband wanted to protect her whenever he could, even though she herself did not feel she had to be coddled like a child.

The blanket on which she sat was thick and supple to the touch. Tanaka removed the Scandinavian-style shoes that she usually wore. She did not like wearing the shoes. They pinched her toes. In her homeland, she only wore sandals, which were always loose and unconstricting. It was at times like these, even though she had not been gone long, that she missed Opar and her beloved Egypt.

The fighting had gone well. On three occasions Tabor's Vikings had engaged Ingmar's men and had emerged victorious. Though she found all warfare repugnant, Tanaka was pleased that the Egyptians who sailed and fought with Tabor had proven themselves courageous to a man. Even Tabor, who had often teased Tanaka about the Egyptian men's diminutive stature, had ceased his teasing, voicing nothing but praise for the swarthy warriors.

As she waited for the beef to finish cooking over the two large fires, Tanaka picked up her tarot cards. Perhaps they would tell her something about the future, she mused.

Holding the cards loosely in her open hand, Tanaka closed her eyes and thought about her husband and his complaints since their return to Scandinavian waters. Fragments of conversations filtered through Tanaka's consciousness. Most of the talk concerned Ingmar and how he had kept his ships and his men around him, denying Tabor a numerically-even war.

A smile creased her lips; she had her question: *How can Tabor defeat Ingmar if he remains surrounded by his men and ships?*

Tanaka moved the cards at random, concentrating on the question before laying several cards out on the blanket. The cards were the High Priestess, the Princess of Swords, Strength, the Lovers, Judgment, and Justice.

She studied the tarot intently, divining its meaning. And as she studied the cards, she felt the quickening of her heart and the slowly but steadily building conviction that if she followed her intuition, Tabor would soon defeat Ingmar the Savage.

Tanaka closed her eyes for a moment, afraid that her desire for a quick end to the fighting and bloodshed had somehow tainted her vision so that she saw only what she wanted to see. When she opened her eyes again, the cards had not changed.

The High Priestess. That represented her, Tanaka, and she believed this meant she should listen to the words that whispered in her heart. Tanaka knew she must look inside herself for the answers to her troubles.

The Princess of Swords. This meant that she must be a warrior, like Tabor, if the fighting were to end. She could no longer simply be a passenger aboard the ship with Tabor, an appendage to him. She must, as his wife and his partner in life, be at his side, equal in every way, yet complementing and balancing him, completing him as night completes the day.

Strength. Even though she was appalled at the violence that she had witnessed, she must have the strength to transcend her own convictions to see a greater good—the end of Ingmar the Savage. To that end, even she would have the strength to be a warrior and take up arms against her enemy.

The Lovers. She must aid Tabor in his quest, just as he must help her. Together, as lovers, they were undefeatable, an unconquerable force that even the heavens would not challenge.

Judgment. For Ingmar the Savage, judgment would soon be delivered. He had violated the laws of humanity, wantonly stealing, killing, and torturing to satisfy his lust for power and wealth. But soon, judgment would be at hand and Ingmar the Savage, along with his murderous younger brother

Hugh, would pay the price for the great and lasting hardships they had caused so many.

And lastly, Justice. When the fighting ended, justice would be served, and the good men — like Tabor and Sven — and women like Tanaka would be the ones to mete out that Justice.

Tanaka read the cards once more; she knew that something was missing. Something, but what? She had spread the cards out before her for the reading exactly as she had been taught long ago.

But her intuition told her that the picture was incomplete.

She watched her hand, as though directed by a power other than herself, go to the stack of remaining cards, cut the cards in half, and turn over the top card of the nearest stack.

The Moon.

Tanaka looked at the card, curious and confused, never having been challenged in quite this way. And then understanding dawned upon her, and she nodded agreement with the gods.

On the day of her birth an extraordinary celestial event had occurred. As her mother wrestled through the labor of childbirth, the moon, on its arc across the sky, moved directly into the path of the sun. The moon ate all the sunlight, even though it was the middle of the afternoon. And as the village was bathed in the strange darkness brought about by the moon's consuming the sun, Tanaka was born. A few moments later, when the moon gave the sun back to the people so they could enjoy its light and warmth, the people in attendance at Tanaka's birth realized that she had been blessed. She was a miracle child, a true-born priestess.

That strange, celestial occurrence of the moon eating the sun at the day's height, casting darkness over the land, was about to happen again! Soon.

Hardly had Tanaka realized she had correctly interpreted the tarot when she found herself face to face with another problem, one which she feared might very well be utterly insurmountable.

How was she to convince Tabor that the sun was going to be eaten by the moon in the afternoon? He took little stock in her powers as a high priestess, though he usually listened to her predictions and proclamations with tolerance or amused indifference. How could she convince Tabor, a man who believed in himself, in his own strength—but not much else—that she had the power to help him, if only he would look at her tarot?

"Woman, do you truly expect me to believe such a story?" Tabor asked, hands on his hips, his voice hushed and low so that it would not carry beyond the walls of the small room on the warship that was their only place of privacy.

"It *is* the truth. I feel it here," Tanaka replied, placing a hand over her heart. "The sun will be eaten at midday by the moon; and at that moment, the events of the earth will be changed!"

She saw disgust flicker across her husband's face. He had listened to her when she said she needed to go to the temple in England, where the stones had been turned upright and the earth's energy was strong. He had believed her then. . . . but now he looked at her without respect.

"You can't keep fighting Ingmar the way you have," she continued. "Ingmar's forces are too strong. He has too many men and too many ships. The only way you can defeat him is to divide his troops into smaller groups or attack him when his guard is down." Tanaka felt a pang of panic chill her heart and heard a whisper of warning. "You told me that yourself! You can't keep fighting Ingmar as you have! Sooner or later he'll be able to surround you and your men. You know I'm speaking truth!"

Tabor glared at his wife in the dim light of the small room. Yes, he knew she was telling the truth; he was the one who had explained it to her. "Keep your voice down," he said. "I do not want the men to hear."

For an instant, Tanaka closed her eyes, letting her head droop. Sometimes Tabor could be so cruel, so insulting. Was he afraid that he would appear foolish in front of his men if they heard her warning? Would they think their leader had taken a madwoman for a wife if they knew she could see the future?

"You must believe me," Tanaka said, whispering now, knowing she could not push Tabor any harder or she would lose him altogether. "If you don't, something horrible will happen. I know it. I can't tell you how or why I know, but it is so!"

"There are things to be done," Tabor said dismissing her contemptuously. He opened the door. "I have responsibilities."

He left Tanaka alone, stepping out onto his boat to be with his men. In the darkness of the cramped room that she shared with her husband, Tanaka lay down on their goose-down mattress and wept.

All she wanted was to live in peace and happiness with her husband—and the child she was certain that she carried. That's all Tanaka wanted. . . . but the way it looked now, by the time her child was born, either her husband would be dead or he would have left her, thinking her a madwoman beyond salvage, unworthy of his love.

Tabor brought the sharpening stone along the edge of his sword one final time, then inspected the edge. It was sharp enough to cause hideous damage—exactly what Tabor needed.

A cool evening breeze fluffed his hair around his shoulders. Distracted, Tabor pushed it back from his eyes. He knew he should cut his mane, but Tanaka liked it because it was long and blond, so it remained untouched.

Thoughts of the argument they'd had that afternoon still plagued Tabor. How could she possibly believe that the moon would—what was it she had said?—eat the sun? It was the most absurd statement he had ever heard her make, although he had heard her voice *many* ridiculous things.

But what if she were right about the sun being eaten? That would give him an enormous tactical advantage. To be at the right place, at precisely the right time . . . then a surprise attack, while Ingmar's savage warriors were confused by the sudden disappearance of the sun. . . .

Contemplating the possibilities brought a smile to Tabor's wide mouth. Even when he was furious with his wife, he couldn't help but think about her and be baffled by her. She could talk such nonsense . . . and such sense. Sense, like how Tabor could not continue fighting Ingmar the Savage with the same tactics he was using.

Ingmar kept himself surrounded by warships and mercenaries, men who sailed and fought with him because they were well paid to do so and because with Ingmar at the helm, they were allowed to commit virtually any atrocity with his cruel encouragement. The Vikings who sailed with Ingmar were the lowest, darkest form of humanity. The kind of men that thoroughly sickened Tabor.

Sooner or later, those hideous men would be able to surround Tabor and Sven. Two ships against six or seven or perhaps even more were no match. If, perhaps, the odds were only two to one, then maybe Tabor would consider a straight-ahead, all-out fight. He had enough faith in his men to believe that such odds, though unfavorable, would still provide a victory for a righteous Viking.

He sheathed his sword, then picked up the quiver of arrows near his feet. Before he inspected the arrowheads, he looked up. The men were quiet, readying the weapons of war.

A murmur of voices drew his attention, and he saw Tanaka walking toward him. With pride, Tabor noticed that the expressions on his men's faces reflected their joy at the sight of a beautiful woman. He noticed, too, that not one of the men aboard his ship looked at Tanaka in lust. If any of the men did have lustful designs on Tanaka, they hid their passion.

"Will we anchor tonight?" Tanaka asked. She sat on the small cushion at Tabor's side. The cushion had been placed there by Jafar, the Egyptian sailor. He had noticed that the high priestess often spent hours sitting beside her husband while he piloted the boat and she was forced to sit on the hard wooden bench.

"No. I have heard that Ingmar's ships are moving. I don't want to get caught in one place."

For an instant, their eyes met, and the silent question was asked: Are you still angry with me? Though not a word was spoken, the tension that still loomed between Tabor and Tanaka could be easily felt. The men who had been sitting nearby discreetly rose and moved closer to the mast to give them privacy.

"Let me tell you a story," Tanaka said, moving closer to Tabor at his post at the rudder. "It's a true story."

Tabor set the quiver of arrows aside. He tried to keep the wariness from showing in his eyes, tried to push the doubts he had of his wife from his heart, but that was not an easy thing to do, not even for a man with his strength of will.

"Continue," he said.

Tanaka felt the undercurrent of tension in her

husband's voice. He was afraid of what she was going to say to him in front of his men. She folded her arms together over his knee, looking up at him with a sincerity that begged him to believe her.

"When my mother was bringing me into this world, a miracle occurred in the sky. As my mother lay straining, trying to push me into the world, the moon ate the sun and the land was swallowed up in total darkness. There was a cry throughout the land. Even the strongest and bravest of men became frightened, trembling over the mysterious thing that had happened. But then, not much later, the moon no longer liked the taste of the sun and returned the fiery ball to the earth. When there was sunlight once again, I lay there on the blanket, pink and healthy. It was determined then that I was special, that I was destined to be a priestess."

"Not high priestess?" Tabor asked, fascinated with the story despite his hesitance to believe such things.

"Only a pharaoh can anoint a high priestess," Tanaka explained. "But my birth was destined. I became what I am because of what the moon did to the sun in the sky. That is what I have tried to explain to you."

"I see," Tabor replied. He took a thick lock of Tanaka's wavy black hair and began twisting it, rubbing the smooth strands with the pad of his thumb. "What *you* must see is that I am responsible for ninety-nine other men. They must trust me to give them commands that will keep them alive in our fight against Ingmar the Savage. No leader of men would ever allow his heart to make decisions that should only be made with the mind."

So that's that. Tanaka thought.

It surprised her that she wasn't bitter. Because of his responsibility—his duty—to his men, he could not allow himself to believe what she felt, because feelings must be secondary to strategy.

Tanaka placed her head on her forearms, which were still crossed on Tabor's thigh. It was a tender act, their touching, and it rather surprised her that Tabor continued to caress her hair even though his men might see him.

I'll convince him . . . somehow. Tanaka promised herself. *I'll make him believe my prophecy, and how it can help him triumph over Ingmar.*

And then another voice spoke within her.

If you do not make him believe you, the voice warned, *Tabor will die.* Tanaka tried not to shiver with fear.

Chapter Thirty

The survivors had buried the dead by the time Tabor arrived in the village. Some women had been spared. Some of the children had managed to flee into the woods and hide until the carnage ended. Not a single building remained undamaged, and most had been burned to smoldering cinders. Ingmar, aware that even the youngest male child would grow up and seek revenge upon him, had had all the men and boys, no matter how old or young, slaughtered.

As she walked silently through the village, wanting to help, Tanaka cried, the tears trickling down her cheeks unheeded. If anything melted Tabor's heart, it was the sight of his wife's tears. Nothing else affected him so powerfully or filled him with such rage. But there was nothing he could do to prevent her tears or to take away the cause of her suffering.

The carnage—the senseless, brutal murders—was the work of Ingmar the Savage. And as Tabor walked from one smoldering home to the next, he focused on a single new awareness: As long as Ingmar lived, more people would die.

Thus far, Tabor had been able to hit Ingmar's outlying ships quickly then disappear into the night or sail away into the fjords at a speed unsafe for Ingmar's ships. Now, once again confronted by the death and destruction that always lay in Ingmar's wake, Tabor realized he had to devise a plan, a brilliant plot to end a heinous reign of terror.

The survivors, mostly women, were given whatever blankets and food could be spared. Tabor's men acted quickly to build two large shelters to keep the women warm and dry. Ingmar's men had not bothered to burn the crops in the fields, but they had lost their geese, cattle, and sheep.

"It is all we can do . . . for now," Tabor said to Tanaka as they left the village. "Until I destroy Ingmar, tragedies like this will continue."

Tanaka made no reply. The whispered warning she had heard before stayed in her thoughts, and though her heart ached for the unfortunate women in the village whose husbands had been murdered by Ingmar the Savage, Tanaka did not want to join their ranks.

The wool blanket rested lightly over them. Tabor lay on his back; Tanaka, on her side, her leg thrown loosely over his, her hand resting on his chest. It was the position they usually assumed before sleep, talking in the dark, hands straying downward.

Since their argument neither had been feeling ardent.

"I can almost hear your thoughts," Tanaka whispered, her head on his shoulder. She could hardly see his profile in the thin light, though she could tell that he was still awake.

"Ingmar must be stopped. Soon."

It was a flat statement. What remained unspoken was the death that the word "stopped" represented. The thought of more violence, more bloody warfare, appalled Tanaka, though she kept this to herself.

Then a thought struck her so forcefully she flinched as though physically hit. The idea came fully formed, instantaneously whole. She suspected its source was godly, for at last she had the final piece of information she had sought.

"What is it?" Tabor asked, feeling the change in his wife, although she had said nothing.

"I . . . I had a thought." Tanaka was leery of telling Tabor what had come into her head. She waited, wondering what she should do, afraid that Tabor — with this new information — would find some convenient, safe place for her to stay. He would get her off the ship, and perhaps — probably — never come back for her.

Tabor, his arm loosely around her shoulders, gave her a little shake. "Well, out with it. You've never been shy with your thoughts before."

As long as he asked, he can't criticize me for what I think, Tanaka decided.

But even as she spoke, she realized that warfare was something she knew too little about. If she were wrong in her prediction, she would be putting her husband and all the men in his command in great peril.

"You've been telling me how inferior Ingmar's men are to your own," she began, speaking slowly and distinctly in the darkened room, her hand resting on Tabor's stomach. She reasoned that if her words made Tabor angry, his breathing would quicken and she would be able to feel it. She could stop herself then, before she stretched his patience and credulity too thin.

"They are filth," Tabor hissed venomously. "Only rats and vermin would sail under Ingmar's command!"

"And you've told me that you must find some way to crush Ingmar completely, to get at him directly."

"He is afraid," Tabor said, flatly. Ingmar *was* afraid, but he was still a deadly foe.

"He nearly destroyed you because he knew that you do not like fighting. He called you to Hedeby to talk, to negotiate a peace. And when you went there, your forces were divided; and through this deception, he was able to gain an advantage."

"There is no need to remind me of failings in myself that I have not forgotten for a moment since that cursed time."

"What if you should use the same tactic against Ingmar?"

She felt Tabor's pulse quicken, and she knew it was not because he thought she was a madwoman. No, it was the possibility of dealing a fatal blow to his enemy that excited Tabor.

"Explain yourself. I do not understand," Tabor said. Only to Tanaka would he ever admit to puzzlement.

"What if you were to take all your men to see Ingmar, using an advance guard to inform him that you wanted to talk, to see if it is possible to have some sort of peace?"

Tabor guffawed. "Ingmar would laugh at such a suggestion. He will not rest until he destroys me, just as I will not rest until I destroy him. I am a Viking, and that is the way of the Vikings."

"Yes . . . but what if you pretended to be acting irrationally because you have fallen in love with an Egyptian high priestess and she has you under a spell? What if she convinced you that you could be peaceful with Ingmar the Savage?"

Tabor chortled. "Wife, you could never, ever convince me that I could believe anything Ingmar has to say."

"I know that and you know that. . . . but Ingmar does not know that."

"Hmmm . . ."

"And what if, when you and *all* your men are in the heart of Ingmar's camp, the sun gets eaten whole by the moon? You and your men would be prepared for it, and it would not confuse you. But Ingmar and his men would not know what it was or that it would not last long. They would be frightened . . . confused and scared; and their fear and confusion would give you the advantage you need."

"As much as I would like to believe there is a way of getting past Ingmar's defenses to destroy him, I cannot allow myself to believe such a plan is possible. If the sun does not turn to night, my men and I will be surrounded. Ingmar will slaughter us just as he has slaughtered everyone who has ever stood in his way."

"But the moon *will* be eaten by the sun," Tanaka continued, knowing well she was entering dangerous waters with her husband. But she was driven by the fear that if Ingmar were not destroyed soon, Tabor would be. "It will happen six days from now, when the sun is high and bright. A voice has told me this is so, and I believe the voice."

"What makes you so sure of this?" Tabor asked.

In the dim light of the small room, Tanaka merely looked into Tabor's eyes; and, with that look, she conveyed to him her conviction.

Tabor rolled his eyes.

"You really believe this . . . this *voice?*" he scoffed.

"Yes, I do." Tanaka looked straight at Tabor. She could not be intimidated by him as so many other people were. "It will happen, just as I say it will; and if you are to stop the beating heart of the monster called Ingmar the Savage, then you must be near the heart of that monster."

Tabor stared at the ceiling. He found logic easier when he wasn't looking at Tanaka, his sense of reason dulled by her beauty, muted by his love and passion for her.

"Do you believe that what I tell you is the truth?" Tanaka asked softly.

Tabor's reply was ambiguous. "I believe that you believe. More than that, I cannot say."

A full day had passed since Tanaka had told Tabor of her vision of the eclipse. During the day, she had questioned herself a thousand times, searching for a flaw in her analysis. But her conviction grew stronger, not weaker, with further scrutiny.

And, with certainty, she understood that if she did not act upon this singular knowledge Tabor would die. Eventually, Ingmar men would trap Tabor in a cove; and, once surrounded, Tabor's hundred good men would stand no chance against barbaric Northmen who killed for sport, destroying everyone and everything they touched.

Time was fleeing faster than a thief pursued by the pharaoh's own soldiers, and nothing Tanaka could say or do would slow its pace. If she did nothing at all—if she simply let Tabor fight his war against Ingmar in his own fashion, at his own pace—she knew her husband's luck and skill would have to run out. But if she *could* convince Tabor that her vision of the future was correct, then he had a chance for victory . . . providing her vision was accurate. If it weren't she would be leading her husband directly into the jaws of a beast that would hungrily devour him.

What was she to do? What could she do?

The questions never left her, not even for a moment, and it wasn't until she found herself searching for Jafar, the Egyptian warrior who had assisted her in stowing away on the warship, that she knew what course of action she would take.

Tabor surveyed the encampment, a tingle of apprehension in the pit of his stomach though all seemed peaceful. Once again he checked the position of the guards—one near the craggy bluff overlooking the water, the other on the highest point of land to the south. From these vantage points they could prevent a surprise attack from either land or sea. Only two campfires remained burning, and almost all of the men were asleep.

So why didn't the tickle in Tabor's stomach fade away? Why, when everything around him seemed at peace?

A movement to his right caught his attention, and Tabor's hand tightened around the haft of his sword. A moment later, out of the midnight darkness, he recognized Jafar and relaxed. He had seen Jafar in two brief skirmishes against Ingmar's men and knew him to be a brave and fierce warrior. Among the Egyptians, he was one of the ablest, and that placed him in an elite league of men.

"Hail, Jafar, my friend," Tabor called out.

He did not dispense titular compliments lightly, and, despite their cultural differences, Jafar recognized the praise.

"Sleep eludes you?" Tabor asked.

He motioned for Jafar to sit on the ground beside him. With their backs against the same Norwegian pine, so they were shoulder to shoulder. The Egyptians had a habit of standing much closer than the Danish when talking, and Tabor had learned to circumvent this by seating the Egyptian sailors before talking to them at length.

Jafar did not speak until he was seated, looking out at the ocean. He cleared his throat and spoke slowly and precisely in his native tongue, using that language because Tabor was more fluent in Egyptian than Jafar was in Danish.

"I am here to deliver a message from Tanaka. She—"

"Why doesn't she deliver this message herself?" Tabor demanded, turning instantly to face Jafar.

"She has gone—"

Tabor's hands lashed out in a heartbeat, taking Jafar by the shirtfront, pulling him so close their noses nearly touched. Suddenly, the source of Tabor's uneasiness become clear; fear for Tanaka's safety made him violent.

"Where has she gone? Why have you let her go?"

Tabor was much larger and more powerful than Jafar; and, though the smaller man tried hard to present a brave facade, the traces of fear showed in the corners of his eyes.

"She has given me a message to give to you. Hurting me will not help you or her."

"Speak! Tell me!" Tabor said sharply, thinly controlled panic rising rapidly within his breast. His wife, he knew from experience, was capable of any behavior.

"She has gone to the enemy—to Ingmar."

Tabor's hands went from Jafar's shirtfront to the man's throat. Anger and fear vied for prominence, and though his large hands surrounded Jafar's throat, he did not squeeze.

"She wanted me to tell you that when the sun is at its highest, two days hence, it will be swallowed by the moon. She is with Ingmar, telling him that you wish a council for peace. If you are there with her and Ingmar when the sun disappears, she says you will be able to defeat Ingmar. His men will be frightened. We will not."

406

Jafar looked, unflinching, into Tabor's eyes. He had tried hard to convince Tanaka, his high priestess, to change her mind. Then, when it was obvious that she was determined to go straight to Ingmar's camp, he had begged to be the one to travel with her as her bodyguard. She refused him that, too. Tanaka knew her husband well; and if there were to be any chance at all of Tabor's believing what she had done, it must come from an Egyptian he held in high esteem.

"You should have stopped her," Tabor said, close to defeat.

"I tried. She said this was something she must do if we are to live in peace." Jafar looked away for only a second. "We will fight with greater strength and courage than any soldiers ever have," he said, indicating himself and the other Egyptians sailing with Tabor. "She is your wife, but she is our high priestess. To us, her life is more important than our own."

Tabor's warrior instincts urged him to take his revenge out on the Egyptian. After all, this instinct whispered, if Jafar were as concerned with Tanaka's welfare as he professed, he would have stopped her instead of acting in complicity with the dangerous, foolhardy plan.

But another voice spoke to Tabor as well, a voice he heard had more and more since Tanaka had entered his life, particularly since they had exchanged marriage vows. This voice—that of reason and compassion—reminded Tabor that no one in the world could love Tanaka more than he did, and even he—Tabor, Son of Thor, leader of men *and Tanaka's hus-*

band—was unable to make her do something she did not want to do or stop her from doing something she was determined to do.

"It is not your fault," Tabor said. "I do not hold you responsible for my wife's foolish behavior. Tell me everything all over again, and this time I will listen with a clear mind. I want to know all that Tanaka said; and, together, we will do what we must do."

Jafar breathed an audible sigh of relief when Tabor relaxed the hands at his throat. Then, from the very beginning, he told Tabor of Tanaka's plan to destroy Ingmar the Savage.

The rocky terrain caused Tanaka to lose her footing several times, a problem exacerbated by clouds that blotted out the moonlight at the most critical moments.

"How far do you think we have gone?" she asked Hanif, the young Egyptian man who had volunteered to travel with her.

"Far enough so that Tabor will not find us," he replied, answering the question that Tanaka had wanted to ask but hadn't.

Tanaka paused for a moment, looking back. The terrain—rocky, hilly, and thickly wooded—differed from that of her own land, and this difference heightened her loneliness. She felt displaced. She had gone far enough from the encampment so that should Tabor discover her absence before Jafar revealed it to him, he would not be able to catch her. But she was still a long way from the port village of

Karak, where Ingmar the Savage was said to be anchored. What would happen if she couldn't find Ingmar? What if he didn't believe her when she told him that Tabor wanted a second try at a negotiated truce?

She pushed such doubts and fears forcibly away. She *would* find Ingmar; he *would* listen and believe her, and the moon's eclipse of the sun *would* happen exactly as her tarot had predicted.

"Let's keep going," Tanaka said quietly. "I want to get there as quickly as possible."

And I want to stop worrying with every breath I inhale.

Quietly, Tanaka leading the way, the two travelers continued in the darkness, walking to meet a man Tanaka loathed with every fiber in her body.

Chapter Thirty-one

As the men ate their morning meal, the low buzz of conversation relayed the news that Tanaka had left in the night. News beyond that was sketchy. There were several stories making the rounds, but the main tale had it that Tanaka couldn't accept the fighting another moment and was determined to walk back to Egypt. This story was accepted by some of the men, but hotly denied by others who said the high priestess would never abandon the men or her husband. Besides, you couldn't *walk* back to Egypt. Tabor understood that the men had to talk this out of their system, had to let their imaginations roam — at least for a little while.

Only when all had finished eating did Tabor move to stand in the midst of the men, surrounded by ninety-nine curious, wary warriors.

"Men, listen carefully," Tabor began, speaking loudly so that all could hear. "Tanaka has gone to Ingmar." There was an immediate murmur of disbelief among the men. Tabor raised his hands for silence. "She has not become a traitor. The opposite is true."

Slowly and carefully so that there would be no misunderstanding, Tabor told the men of Tanaka's "vision" and how she believed that if they were in Ingmar's camp when the moon ate the sun, they would be able to attack and defeat the Northmen despite the difference in their numbers.

"I can't make you go," Tabor said. "If the sun does not turn to night when Tanaka says it will, we will be in the belly of Ingmar the Savage. Have no doubts. . . . if he thinks he can kill us, he will. The man shows no mercy. You've seen what happens when Ingmar and his men raid . . ."

Tabor paused, letting the men contemplate the gravity of his words. Stark images of razed villages and the hollow-eyed numbness of the few survivors preyed on the minds of the men.

"I'll be going to Karak, where Ingmar has made camp. There is no dishonor to any of you who do not wish to come."

Sven was smiling, shaking his head in private humor as he slipped his quiver full of arrows over his shoulder. "Of all the women in the world, *you* had to fall in love with one who has visions!" he said, then laughed aloud.

It had never even occurred to Sven that he might not follow Tabor.

Tabor was surprised, though he later felt that he should not have been, when every single man volunteered to go with him to Karak. Twice more he explained the dangers to the Egyptian men, as well as to his own Vikings, just to make certain they understood the dangers of what they were about to undertake.

Not one soldier wavered in his commitment.

411

* * *

"This is a trick," Ingmar said, scowling.

"She has only one man with her," Hugh said. He had expected his older brother to be more pleased with the news that Tanaka was in Karak — and with him for being the messenger of that news. "I put extra guards at each station, thinking — like you — it was a trap. But it's no trap, no trick."

"Where is she now?"

"In my house."

Ingmar was impatient to see Tanaka again, but he did not feel it would look good if he went to her. "Bring her to me," he growled, throwing himself in the heavy pine wood chair. "Just her. Leave the man under guard elsewhere. And make sure she doesn't carry a hidden dagger, a needle, or a vial of poison. She's a clever woman, and she must have good reason for coming here."

Hugh left the inn. This was his chance to return to his powerful older brother's good graces. It had been a long, cold winter, for Ingmar had blamed Hugh for Tabor's escape. Now, miraculously, it appeared as though his chance for redemption had literally walked into his grasp.

The village of Karak had several hundred permanent residents, though it could swell with large numbers of Vikings temporarily staying in the many hostels and inns for which the village was famous. Heads turned as Hugh ran down the hard-packed main road, moving past ox-drawn wagons, linen-sellers, and the money-lender's shop. Hugh didn't care if it were undignified for him to run. Everyone under Ingmar's command knew of Hugh's humiliation and demotion after Tabor's successful escape; but if he was successful now, everyone would hear how he had regained his status as Ingmar's closest and most trusted advisor.

The guard was still at the front door of the small hut where Hugh lived, though, against Hugh's orders, he had made himself comfortable on the ground.

Soon enough, the men will heed my commands just as carefully as they obey my brother's. Hugh thought angrily, striding past the guard.

She was squatting on her heels on the mattress Hugh used for a bed. The swarthy man with her, Hanif, was sitting on the dirt floor. For an instant, Hugh was taken aback by Tanaka's beauty and the thought of forcing her to comply with his lusty wishes before taking her to see Ingmar filtered through his brain. If Hanif had not been there, he would have.

"Will he see us?" Tanaka asked, breaking into Hugh's violent, lustful reverie.

Her tone was imperious as she rose to her feet, and it annoyed Hugh, but he said nothing. She had made it absolutely clear that she had something very important to say, but she would say it only to Ingmar, implying that she didn't really like having to deal with inferior types like Hugh.

"Just you. Your friend stays here," Hugh replied, wishing passionately that he had the time to force Tanaka to respect him.

"Why?"

"Because I say!" Hugh snapped. He hated having to explain anything to her, his prisoner, and it was especially annoying that her companion held murder in his eyes. "We leave now."

With her shoulders square and a strong, dignified

413

aura surrounding her, Tanaka walked with Hugh through the streets of Karak. All who looked at the beautiful stranger with the dark skin and the waist-length wavy black hair saw a woman perfectly poised, comfortable with herself and her surroundings. But that poise was a facade. Inside, her stomach quivered with fear, her heart beat erratically, and her mouth felt dry as a desert wind.

As Tanaka walked, she looked at the homes and buildings lining the narrow road and was disheartened to see the squalor that the residents of Karak took for granted. The homes were small, one-room structures with thatched roofs, painfully similar to the pockets of poverty and despair that peppered areas near the piers in her homeland. She wondered whether there was any wealth and prosperity in Karak or if it was a land of desolation, a place fit for the likes of Ingmar the Savage.

Then she looked into the eyes of an old-before-her-time woman with stringy brown hair holding a child to her breast. There were two more children, very young, clinging to the girl's dress, their faces dirty, blank, wooden in their sadness. Tanaka saw resentment, disillusion and malice in the eyes of the young mother. Clearly she recognized that Tanaka was in trouble and, since she herself led a miserable existence, she felt all other women—especially attractive ones—had no right to happiness.

As they neared the inn, Tanaka sensed immediately that Ingmar was inside. The inn was, by Karak standards, a lavish establishment, clean and well-kept, but the four men who lounged outside were unwashed, hard men who were out of place in clean, orderly surroundings.

Fresh waves of black, oily fear washed over Tanaka. The surroundings were different, but the atmosphere was identical to what she had experienced with Ingmar. Tanaka could practically smell his presence in the air, and the memories that awareness triggered sent a primal tremor through her spine.

When Tanaka hesitated at the door, Hugh put a hand on her shoulder and shoved hard. As Tanaka stumbled through the doorway, Hugh chuckled gleefully. Tanaka, and all women like her, had always been beyond Hugh's reach; but now that he had her within his grasp, he would make the most of it.

"There's no need for that," Tanaka hissed through clenched teeth, spinning to face her tormentor. "Keep your hands off me!"

Hugh enjoyed Tanaka's anger. When he remembered how Ingmar had been afraid that she was an assassin, his smile broadened.

"Put your hands out," he said, placing his fingers on the haft of the dagger at his hip. The threat was unmistakable. "I must be certain you are unarmed."

As soon as Tanaka extended her hands, Hugh reached for her breasts. If his face hadn't been twisted by such a pathetic leer, perhaps Tanaka would have been more frightened. As it was, she was merely disgusted by his brutish attempt to fondle her. She slapped his hands before he could touch her and took a step back.

"I came here of my own free will to speak with your brother, not to endure your clumsy hands."

Hugh pulled his dagger, his eyes red with hatred. Only the sound of Ingmar's deep voiced checked his violent impulses.

"I don't think we need to worry about her," Ingmar drawled, leaning against the doorjamb behind Hugh. "Let her pass. . . . and don't put your hands on her again. You can have her in due time, little brother, but you must wait until I am finished."

Their attitude turned Tanaka's stomach, but she kept silent behind a blank expression. She followed Ingmar into a large room. A small fire burned, and food bubbled in a heavy kettle, filling the room with its aroma. Ingmar tossed his heavy frame into the thick wooden chair that he favored and leered at Tanaka, making it insultingly clear that she should remain standing.

"I'm surprised to see you again. I'm even more surprised that you've come to me this time," Ingmar said, as his gaze traveled openly up and down Tanaka. He vividly recalled the days of her captivity.

"As opposed to being kidnapped, you mean?" Tanaka arched a disrespectful eyebrow.

Ingmar was shocked at how well she now spoke the language. It surprised him, too, that even after nearly a year, she still did not have that glazed, defeated look that was so common among captives—and so pitiful. He wondered why.

"Kahlid had an accident," Tanaka continued, bluffing, pretending she felt no fear at all. "He went against Tabor. It was a . . . *fatal* mistake."

It wasn't until she saw Ingmar's reaction to her news that Tanaka was absolutely certain that Kahlid and Ingmar had conspired to kidnap her. She had possessed all the facts before, but she hadn't wanted to believe a priest from her own temple could possibly practice such dark deceit.

For several long, silent moments the two looked at

each other. Then, sensing there was nothing left to hide, Ingmar smiled. "Kahlid is dead? Killed by Tabor? That doesn't surprise me. Kahlid was ambitious, but he inspired no loyalty from his men. I knew they would turn on him eventually."

"His men didn't betray him. Tabor figured out that Kahlid was responsible for the bad things that had happened to me, and. . . . he took matters into his own hands."

"And that is why you are here? To warn me that Tabor wants to kill me?" His short, coughing laugh held no humor. "If that is all that you have come to tell me, then we don't need to wait any longer to resume where we left off when I gave you to Tabor."

Tanaka raised her hand. The gesture indicated that she did not want Ingmar to rise from his chair. He would have ignored the silent command from anyone else. But with Tanaka—whether it was the hard, determined look in her eyes or the confident pose she struck, Ingmar could not say—he was frozen in place for a moment. He was distinctly aware that the beautiful Egyptian woman possessed a unique, unnerving power.

"If you listen to what I have to say, maybe you won't end your life with Tabor's arrow piercing your throat, like Kahlid did."

"I have no reason to fear Tabor," Ingmar boasted, but it was such a bald lie that he knew Tanaka did not believe it. He did not believe it himself. "I chased him from these waters once; I will do it again."

"Are you going to talk or listen?" Tanaka asked, her gaze dark and penetrating, boring into Ingmar.

"The last time you were with me you weren't so loose with your tongue," Ingmar replied testily,

417

clearly not pleased with the Egyptian's confrontational attitude.

"That was last season," Tanaka replied flatly, dismissively. "This season, I'm a free woman, and the man who worked with you to see that I got kidnapped is rotting dishonorably in a beggar's grave.' Tanaka forced her lips into a hard, thin, contemptuous smile steeled more by bluff than courage. "Times change. Not even you can alter fate."

Ingmar leaned back in his chair, crossing his legs at the ankle, letting his eyes roam over Tanaka. Her behavior, so cold and confident, shocked him. To be sure, she had never been demure, never cowed or broken by circumstances, but before she at least hadn't been openly abusive or challenging, as she was now. Had it been anyone other than Tanaka, Ingmar would have meted out immediate punishment for such temerity, but something in her bearing and poise whispered a warning in his ear.

She would not be behaving so brashly if she were not protected, Ingmar reasoned. He smiled then, to himself, feeling superior, believing he had seen through the first phase of Tanaka's deception.

"Why not tell me why you're here?" Ingmar said at last.

This time it was Tanaka's turn to be a little surprised. She hadn't thought she could hold Ingmar at bay and make him listen to her proposal so easily.

"May I sit?"

As a chair was brought round, Ingmar allowed himself a single, genuine smile. Tanaka's asking to be seated was an act of civility that surprised and pleased the ruthless Viking leader.

"Tomorrow, Tabor and all his men will be sailing

into Karak," Tanaka began. She watched as Ingmar struggled to control his reaction to the news. Try as he might, he couldn't hide the trepidation that came with knowing Tabor was on his way. "He's not coming here to attack you. He's coming here to speak with you."

Ingmar laughed, hatefully but with relief. "Speak to me? He'd rather use his breath to spit in my eye!"

"Even if that were true, you could hardly blame him."

"Then you admit that he is planning to ambush me?"

"Not at all." Tanaka looked away, taking a moment to gather her thoughts. Such lying and deception did not come easily to her, no matter how great and worthy the cause. "Actually, Tabor is almost happy that you turned against him, because you at last taught him that if he wants to surround himself with certain luxuries, then he must surround himself with certain people. People like you, Ingmar. You are a man of strength as well as vision. Tabor has regained his physical strength, and he now has two ships in his fleet. His men are second to none. Surely, you must know that yourself by now, since Tabor has engaged your men several times in the past weeks."

A muscle ticked in Ingmar's jaw. Yes, he was only too well versed on the fighting skill of the men who sailed with Tabor. Every time the fighting started, Ingmar's men started dying; and, to the best of Ingmar's knowledge, not a single man in Tabor's command had suffered a fatal wound.

"He realizes that if he joins forces with you, together you will be so powerful that no one will dare challenge your strength."

419

"No one dares challenge me now."

"Except for Tabor," Tanaka corrected, with the slightest arching of a slender, mocking eyebrow.

"He pretends. He toys. He does not challenge."

"For now. But how long will it be before another leader with fifty or a hundred Vikings 'pretends to toy' with you? And then another? . . . don't carry resentment for Tabor in your heart."

She gave Ingmar her most guileless look, not nearly as sure of the logic of her argument now as she had been while mentally rehearsing the story during her trek to Karak.

"Tomorrow, Tabor is going to sail here to speak to you. He knows that if he does this, you'll have him and all his men surrounded. But Tabor also knows that you are an intelligent man—intelligent enough to have tricked and almost killed him nearly a year ago. Looking Tabor in the eye and calling him friend is better than looking for him over your shoulder and calling him enemy."

Ingmar nodded his head slowly, looking at the beautiful woman seated across from him but thinking of a man called Tabor, Son of Thor. Soon, if what Tanaka said were true, then he would have Tabor at his mercy. This time, Ingmar would not fail to kill Tabor. His forces were many, and they were gathered around him.

He sipped from a goblet of wine, then scowled. The wine in Karak was very bad, and the beer was even worse. Perhaps it would be possible to find wine and beer in another village in time for the victory celebration over Tabor and his men.

"You can go to Tabor and tell him to come," Ingmar said, almost giddy with happiness now that

420

victory seemed inevitable.

Tanaka stood a bit more quickly than she had intended. "He'll be here. He knew you'd talk to him."

Before Ingmar had the chance to ask anything more, Tanaka slipped out of the room, astonished that Ingmar was letting her go free.

In the outer room, Hugh waited and, when he saw Tanaka, leaped to his feet, thinking she was trying to escape. Then Ingmar bellowed, calling for his brother. Hugh watched as Tanaka left the inn, her expression unreadable.

"You're sure about this?" Sven asked, standing next to Tabor at the bow of one of the warships.

Tabor ran his fingers through his hair, not looking at Sven, who had found—to Tabor's annoyance—great humor in the events of the past days.

In point of fact, Tabor was absolutely certain that what he was about to do was the most foolish thing he had ever done. Even worse, he knew he was leading his men into a battle that—unless absolutely everything Tanaka had predicted turned out to be true—would prove nothing less than suicidal.

The men advanced slowly, using the oars for greater control over the speed at which they approached Karak. Behind the lead ship, Jafar sat at the helm of Sven's vessel. When the fighting began, Tabor wanted Sven at his side.

The Viking inhaled deeply. The scent of the salt air never failed to please him. It was late morning, his favorite time of the day, and all his nerves were battle-ready. But it was not yet time to lead the warships into port.

He turned and gave Sven a grin. "We've been

through many battles, my friend."

"Aye, but never have we gone into battle . . . following your wife's lead."

They laughed then, both of them, at the hilarious absurdity of their situation, drawing the attention of the other men on the boat. Tabor was concerned about each man who sailed with him, just as each was fiercely loyal in return. But the ties weren't as deep, as heart-strengthened, as the bond between Tabor and Sven.

"On the morrow, when the fighting has ended and Ingmar is at last feeding the fish and Tanaka is at my side once more, then we will concentrate our energies on finding *you* a wife. You've been without one too long already."

Together, they laughed once again, and the sound of their merriment encouraged the other Vikings. It let them know that even though they were about to go into battle, their leader was confident, his passion for victory unwavering.

Chapter Thirty-two

They continued to move in slowly. Every man had his weapons ready at his side, though none were allowed to use them until Tabor gave the order. It was clear that news of Tabor's arrival had spread ahead of them. Many people lined the banks, watching the slow, steady progress of the two strangely-designed longboats that rumor had described, but few had actually seen.

Although Tabor's lead boat was still at a distance from the nearest section of the pier, he could already recognize Ingmar, his silhouette distinctive because of his great height and breadth. And beside him, so small and dark, stood Tanaka.

"She's with him," Sven said, his gaze riveted upon the scene.

"She's *beside* him," Tabor corrected testily.

The respect he had for his wife rose slightly, and Tabor smiled proudly. Tanaka had walked through the night into the enemy's camp and she had lured that enemy out onto a pier where he would be most vulnerable, just as she had said she would. Surely, this was the kind of woman that would be a legend, her life and bravery spoken of by storytellers at campfires for generations to come.

"I never thought she could do it," Sven admitted in quiet confession.

"Neither did I," Tabor replied. "Now let's get her out of there."

They were close enough so that Tabor could see Ingmar and Tanaka clearly. He was relieved to see that his wife looked just a little pale and fatigued but, other than that, none the worse for her ordeal. In that single, shining moment, advancing on his wife and the deadliest enemy he had ever known, Tabor realized how desolate his life would be without her. An eternal winter with no sun or warmth. Endless gray, frigid, lifeless days until death claimed him. She was his Valhalla . . . his heaven on earth.

Tabor raised his hands above his head, showing his palms to Ingmar in the gesture of peace, proving that he was unarmed. Ingmar immediately did the same, and both Sven and Tabor snorted at the hypocrisy. Tabor and all his men had a full supply of deadly weapons within arm's reach just as Ingmar and all his men had their lethal weapons near at hand. But for reasons of mendacity and treachery, both sides found it necessary to pretend benevolence.

"Keep your wits about you," Tabor murmured to Sven. When Sven glanced upward toward the sun, Tabor hissed, "Don't look! You don't want to give our plan away!"

Sven grinned ruefully "I know what our plan is, and I still don't understand it."

Scant space and water now separated Tabor from Ingmar and Tanaka. He tried to avoid looking at her, afraid. Afraid that something in his eyes would tell Ingmar of his duplicity; afraid of the whole lunatic notion of Ingmar believing they could find a common ground; afraid that the illogic of the entire battle plan would be written plainly upon his face. Surely, Ingmar could not for a second believe that Tabor was willing to negotiate a peaceful end to their confrontation.

Ingmar called out, "Tabor, you still don't wear a helmet! Must you show off your good looks even now?" He smiled. To the people nearby, who knew no better, he appeared an amiable man at jest with an old friend. But those who did not know better were few; the hatred between these old enemies was legendary.

"I do it just in case you have a mistress worth taking!" Tabor replied, smiling back, his dimple showing as he scanned the crowd on the pier, intentionally making openly seductive eye contact with several women near Ingmar. Avoiding Tanaka's eyes. He did not want Ingmar to know the extent of his emotion and loyalty to Tanaka for fear his enemy would use it against him. Throughout the performance, he smiled with his mouth, but his eyes were hard and cold.

There was the typical commotion as the two battle ships were brought to the docks and tied up. The tension in the air — the thick, explosive distrust — was so apparent that even those few people who knew nothing at all of the Viking leaders inched away. No amount of curiosity could keep them close to the smiling combatants.

Tabor leaped onto the long pier, and Sven immediately followed him, but they were the only ones to get off the boats.

"Have your men come ashore," Ingmar said. "There is good beer and wine to be drunk, good food to be eaten, good women to be kept warm."

"The beer and wine in Karak is foul; the food, worse," Tabor replied without malice. "My men will stay aboard ship for now."

"They are yours to command. But I have no intention of speaking to you at length while standing here. These matters are best discussed in private."

Tabor shook his head. "Nay. In private, a man lies. I have nothing to hide, and if you have nothing to hide, then you, too, will find this a suitable place to discuss a truce."

"Truce? I thought we would discuss a partnership, combining our forces to increase our profits and crush anyone who dares sail against us."

Tabor had thus far managed to keep from looking at Tanaka, but Ingmar's suspicious tone forced him at last to look at his wife. What had she told Ingmar? he asked with his eyes, the question warring with his need to show her his love.

"Which is it, Tabor?" Ingmar asked, a sneer on his lips, his eyes narrowed and hateful. "A truce, a pact. . . . or is this just another of your lies?"

Tabor looked away, as though disgusted with the line of questioning and with Tanaka for having failed to do as he commanded. Out to sea, blocking Tabor's boats, a Viking warship with the characteristic high brow frontpiece moved into position. Escape without confrontation was now impossible.

He turned back toward Ingmar, a playful grin dancing on his lips. "Leave it to a woman to get things wrong, eh, Ingmar? I gave her a simple task to perform, and it appears to be too difficult for her. But then, the dark-eyed one does not speak our language that well."

426

"She speaks it well enough," Ingmar replied skeptically, his gaze darting from Tabor to Tanaka.

Unable to resist the impulse, Tabor looked up at the sky. The moon was strangely located near the sun. . . . but could it, as Tanaka claimed, truly devour all the sunlight? Ingmar looked up, too, but he saw nothing but sky.

"I have prepared a tavern room where we can discuss these matters," Ingmar continued.

His keen, warrior's senses detected Tabor's unease. He knew there was something that Tabor was not telling him, some trick to be revealed later, but he felt no anxiety. Before the plan had any chance of succeeding, Ingmar would make sure that Tabor was dead, killed by his own treasured battle-axe. In the tavern, Hugh waited with the axe. Ingmar had outlined a dramatic, torturous production. He would receive the axe from his brother, and then—when Tabor had been suitably taunted, forced to plead repeatedly for its return—Ingmar would indeed give it to him. Right in the middle of his forehead.

Since she had been silent for so long and since his attention was centered on Tabor, Ingmar was startled when Tanaka spoke, her voice clear and resonant, speaking as a high priestess might address a large assembly.

"Today is an historic day," Tanaka began, looking at Ingmar but raising her hand to include everyone. "Two Viking men—Tabor and Ingmar, their hatred for each other legendary—have now come together to bring peace to this land and to these waters."

A murmur rose up from the citizens of Karak who, though criminal in their own right, had long ago tired of the needless bloodshed and murder that this feud had spawned. Ingmar's men, who greatly profited from the lawlessness they adored, looked from one to the other, each posing the unlikely question: Does Ingmar the Savage really want peace? The Vikings who sailed with Ingmar had been told that every man in Tabor's command was to be slaughtered. When they'd received this command the previous evening, they had cheered long and loud. Now, the dark-skinned beauty from Egypt who had returned to their midst was telling them the carnage they enjoyed was coming to an end.

"There is nothing to be gained by violence," Tanaka continued, her voice rising as the murmur of disapproval from Ingmar's men grew louder.

Outwardly calm, Tanaka's fear constricted within her belly. The moon was in line with the sun, just as the tarot and her visions had foretold, just as they had been on the celebrated day of her birth. But the two celestial bodies were still too far apart. Her palms moist and clammy, she clutched the woven wool sash that circled her waist. She had to keep Ingmar from forcing Tabor into the tavern. Once there, the effect of the eclipse would be lost and victory for Ingmar would be assured.

"Silence yourself, woman," Ingmar said, displeased. "This is no place for you to speak."

But panic gripped Tanaka too tightly for her to be so easily repressed. Ingmar had kept his voice low, not wanting his execution of Tabor or his lack of control over Tanaka to be publicly displayed. There lay his mistake, for the Egyptian high priestess took another step and her voice rang loud with authority.

"I am Tanaka, the high priestess of Opar," she continued. Only those close to her saw the wild fear in her eyes. "I see into the heavens and know what will be! I am powerful! My visions are sought by the wise and the brave!"

"Silence yourself, or I'll cut your tongue out here and now," Ingmar hissed through clenched teeth.

All eyes were upon Tanaka, even those of Ingmar's men. Though they were a barbarian lot, the information that Tanaka was a high priestess was unsettling, especially when she claimed to see visions and have power.

"You have heard that there is to be fighting here on this day," Tanaka continued, now in the grip of primal fear. She was certain that Ingmar meant to slaughter Tabor, his men, and her. She was equally certain that Ingmar's Vikings were not pleased with the thought of not being able to kill on this day. Her hesitation and doubt, her concern that by attacking first she was no better than Ingmar vanished as she looked at the dirty faces and the hate-filled eyes of those who sailed with Ingmar.

"There will be no fighting on this day, no matter what Ingmar has told you! You will not be allowed to kill Tabor, Son of Thor, nor his men . . . because if you do — if you even think of war when we come in peace — I will have the heavens turn black as midnight and death will fall upon you!"

Along the pier, men moved out of the way as Hugh rushed forward. He had been in the tavern, waiting impatiently for his brother and Tabor to arrive. When he heard the Egyptian woman's words, he raced to his brother's side, foregoing the dramatic impact that Ingmar had hoped for.

"That is my axe!" Tabor spat when he saw what Hugh held in his hands.

Tanaka stole a glance toward the sky. The sun and the moon nearly touched.

"Do not damn yourselves to a living, eternal inferno!" Tanaka continued, her voice rising to a defiant shout. "I know you want to spill the blood of your enemy, but my power is great. To prove my power, I will turn day to night!" Her voice rose in crescendo as she pointed toward the moon and sun, now touching and headed for an imminent, shattering collision.

Ingmar roared, his patience at an end. He grabbed Tanaka's arm and threw her roughly to the ground. "Cease your foolish babble, woman!" He sensed the fear growing in his men, fear that her words held truth. "Are you such cowards that you would believe such madness? Madness spoken by a woman?"

But even as he spoke, the sun and moon hastened their soaring travels across the sky, their speed lending credence to the unnerving prophecy of Egypt's high priestess. Not one of the nearly three hundred people gathered at the pier uttered a word. Everyone looked at Tanaka, then into the sky, where the sun and the moon crushed against each other.

Even Tabor stood frozen in place. Could it be that her "vision" of the future was in accord with his vision of the present?

The moon had blotted out half the sun before anyone dared breathed. And then, on land, the villagers of Karak, those who had never believed Ingmar and Tabor could ever be anything but mortal enemies, ran for the protection of their homes. The dark-skinned woman who spoke their language but looked so different from them had said they would suffer greatly if treachery was at hand, and they wanted to be nowhere near when she sought her vengeance. Powers such as those she claimed to have—and now *proved* she had—were not to be trifled with.

"Attack!" Ingmar suddenly shouted, his bellow shattering the silence, drowning out the buzz of growing fear among his own men and the villagers of Karak. He reached for the battle-axe that Hugh held, ripping it from his grasp. "The woman lies! Attack! Attack!"

His words inspired immediate action, but not the kind he wanted. His men were like their leader, savage and ignorant, essentially cowards. Tanaka had promised eternal agony to any man who attacked Tabor's Vikings when they came in peace. Now they believed she had the power to rid the sun from the sky and curse their lives with agony. The men began clamoring from the docked longboat seeking safety, and the freedom to run and hide. Not a dozen men had made the leap from the boat to the pier when the sun at last was completely blotted out by the moon. Midnight darkness fell over the land as black and complete as winter's ice.

"Down!" Tabor shouted, groping in the darkness for Tanaka, grabbing her by the arms. He covered her body with his own to protect her.

"Leave me alone! I want to help!" Tanaka shouted, fighting against Tabor. She could not forget how the tarot had said she must be a Princess of Swords and fight at her husband's side as an equal in spirit if not in skill.

A moment later she heard the sound of bowstrings being released, sending forth their arrows. First it was a single bowstring, then dozens upon dozens of *twangs!* reverberated in the darkness. Tabor had given his men orders that the moment the sun disappeared they were to fire upon Ingmar's men. He had been sure that they

431

be concentrated near the pier in readiness for an attack upon his Viking and Egyptian forces.

Shouts of men struck down by arrows mingled with hideous cries of fear. Men ran blindly. Some fell from the pier into the water; others intentionally threw themselves into the sea, fearful that the inferno Tanaka had promised would claim them.

The total eclipse was brief, but in that time, Ingmar's Vikings were decimated. The Egyptian warriors who sailed under Tabor's command, unlike their leader, never for a moment doubted Tanaka's vision. Unhindered by surprise, they had reached for their bows and arrows as everyone else stood transfixed, watching the sky. Their targets had been picked in advance; and, though they fired blindly in the darkness, they fired accurately. The toll they took upon Ingmar's men was enormous.

When at last Tabor could see again, he rose to his knees, searching first for Sven, then for Ingmar. Sven, too, had lain prone upon the pier so that he would not be accidentally struck by an arrow from his own men. When his gaze met Tabor's, he smiled and drew the long, lethal sword at his hip.

"Where did Ingmar go?" Tabor asked.

Sven nodded down the pier, and Tabor looked just in time to see Ingmar's broad back disappear into the crowd as he knocked people down in his headlong escape.

Tanaka got to her feet with Tabor. All around her she saw the horrible evidence of the effectiveness of her prophecy. Many of Ingmar's men had frozen in place when the eclipse occurred; they had been the first to perish under the barrage of Egyptian arrows.

The moment the sun regained its reign over the sky,

Tabor's men escalated their attack, using both arrows and swords as well as fighting spears. Though shorter than their Scandinavian counterparts, the Egyptians fought mercilessly and skillfully. Each man had heard of the horrors that had befallen their high priestess when she had been kidnapped and held captive by the Vikings. Tanaka herself was a forgiving person; the warriors from her homeland were not.

"See that she is protected," Tabor said to two of his men, taking Tanaka's arm and pushing her toward them.

"No, I want to stay with you," she shot back, fighting against her husband. She was afraid that if they were separated, she would never see him again.

"Where I am going there will be bloodshed and killing," Tabor replied. "You do not need to see your husband do these things. Stay here. The wounded need your help."

He cupped her face in his huge, calloused hands, touching her gently, his eyes asking for a greater understanding than words could communicate. He bent low to kiss her first on the cheek, then on the mouth.

"There are things I must do," he said. "I do not want your gentle heart to have to see such actions. You are a loving woman who would best serve the men who serve her by tending to their wounds. Take their pain away, my darling, and I will do what needs be done."

He kissed her on the lips again, then turned away. Tanaka watched, two crystal tears on her cheeks, as her husband strode down the pier with Sven at his side. It was best, she knew, to let him hunt down Ingmar on his own. The stars had dictated long ago that one day Tabor and Ingmar would settle their feud man to man; and, while

Tanaka hated that truth with every fiber in her being, she had come to accept it.

Steeling her courage, she began shouting orders for the wounded to be brought to her, concentrating on the task she had been assigned, praying that her husband's prodigious strength and cunning would see him through this one last battle against his deadliest enemy.

Chapter Thirty-three

Tabor moved at an easy trot, holding his huge broadsword in his right hand, his dagger in his left. Already, the battle was being decisively won by the Vikings under his command and many of the vermin who sailed with Ingmar were on the run, putting as much distance between themselves and the men who attacked them as possible. The dark-skinned "Vikings" who sailed with Tabor appeared to have the wrath of the gods behind them.

Occasionally, he'd catch a glimpse of Ingmar through the crowd and he'd feel a fresh burst of anger surge through him. He had to pace himself. Though many of Ingmar's men had turned tail and run, there was still the possibility that one of them, singling Tabor out, was drawing a bowstring on him at this very moment.

Tabor had learned his lesson well. He would not forget that foolhardy behavior had nearly cost him his life once before.

Tabor and Sven ran shoulder to shoulder, their eyes darting right and left, scanning the sparse crowd, looking into the eyes of the people they passed. It was their shared belief that the eyes were the window to the soul and if there were to be an attack, intentions would be revealed in the eyes.

"Ingmar is mine," Tabor said as he jogged on.

Sven did not reply. He knew that the hatred between the two was more than just that of two combatants. It was a blood feud that could only be dealt with personally. Tabor himself must kill the man who had betrayed, deceived, and very nearly murdered him.

They ran inland until they came upon Hugh, who waited in ambush with his bow, an arrow already notched. In unison, Tabor and Sven paused a fraction of a second — just long enough for Hugh to raise his bow and take quick aim — then each leaped to the side, away from the other.

Hugh, confronted with two targets instead of one, was confused. An inferior soldier, he inadvertently aimed between Tabor and Sven, hoping to hit one of the two instead of shooting toward a specific target. When Tabor and Sven leaped to the side the arrow passed between them, leaving them unharmed.

Hugh realized his error the moment he released his shot, and he ran immediately. He ran as if he feared the Anubus, the jackal-headed Egyptian deity who Tanaka said escorted the dead on their journey to the afterlife. The Vikings were too close. He could not stop running, notch another arrow, and take aim; and panic overtook him.

The smell of smoke was carried on the wind, and Tabor knew that Ingmar's ships had been set ablaze. It didn't surprise him. The Egyptian soldiers were an unforgiving lot, and they held Ingmar responsible for the misfortunes of their high priestess. They did not want peace with Ingmar the Savage, they wanted revenge and retribution. Not even Tanaka's forgiving nature could stop them from seeing that justice — Egyptian style — was meted out.

Ahead of them, Hugh ran as fast as he could, his arms pumping as he labored to stay ahead of his pursuers. But the years of intemperate living had taken its toll upon his body and soul, and now he would have to pay the ultimate price.

"Don't catch him too soon," Tabor said, maintaining a pace that kept him close enough to Hugh so that he could not rearm his bow yet far enough away so that he felt he still had a chance. "He'll lead us to Ingmar."

Hugh looked over his shoulder and stumbled, his arms flying out as he nearly fell face down in the rutted road that led out of Karak. He dropped his bow in his struggle to break his fall. Then, regaining his footing unarmed, he continued on, running faster than before. He tossed away the quiver of arrows he'd slung over his shoulder to lessen his load, and the laughter he heard from the two men following him told him that although he was winded and nearing the end of his strength, the stronger Danes were far from exhausted.

Men and women, some of them recognizing Tabor, others simply sensing that he was a dangerous man not to be bothered, rushed inside their homes. This was not their fight.

Hugh's legs were growing weak, and he stumbled frequently. Tabor's mouth was set in a grim, determined line as he followed, letting his quarry wear himself out before ending the confrontation.

They wove their way through the heart of Karak, past the tawdry taverns, the sail-repairman's shop, and the hostels for itinerant sailors, and then Hugh's legs failed him. He landed hard on his face in the dirt, his lungs on fire, his legs molten lead.

Hugh tried to wipe mud from his palms. He dug in his tunic for the small, hidden dagger, but Tabor's right fist connected explosively with his jaw. Hugh's head snapped back, but before he could tumble and sprawl, Tabor caught him by his leather vest, hoisted him to his feet, and tossed him into Sven's waiting arms.

"Where's your brother?" Tabor asked.

Sven held Hugh's arms pinned to his sides. Tabor removed Hugh's dagger as he voiced the question.

"I don't know," Hugh replied, when his breathing had calmed and the ringing in his ears had quieted enough to make speech possible.

"Where?" Tabor repeated.

When Hugh did not immediately respond, Sven tightened his arms around the man's ribs in a bone-crunching squeeze. The cowardly assassin's face turned blue. Sven relaxed the muscles in his arms, and Hugh sucked in breath.

"He's going . . . to the . . . women," Hugh said between gasps.

Tabor cursed loudly. He should not have been surprised that Ingmar would surround himself with people. Since he had no regard for any life other than his own and he knew that Tabor would protect the innocent, being surrounded by women lent Ingmar a decided advantage.

"You turn traitor on your own brother so easily," Tabor said, shaking his head. "You and Ingmar are of a feather."

"I owe him nothing!" Hugh replied, struggling to salvage some sense of dignity. "He's never done anything for me."

Tabor could listen to no more. Hugh was everything that Tabor found repulsive in men.

438

"Be merciful," Tabor said to Sven. "He's told us where to find his brother." Then he turned on his heel and jogged away.

Hugh felt Sven release him, and the joy that swept over him was so great that he nearly fell to his knees and wept with happiness. It seemed almost unimaginable to him that he should be captured by Tabor and Sven and live to tell about it.

"Let me know when you have caught your breath," Sven said, unbuckling the clasp that held his sword at his hip. "Then we can begin."

"B-Begin?" Hugh did not like the implacable, lethal expression he saw on Sven's face. "You heard Tabor! He told you to be merciful! He *ordered* you to be merciful!"

"And so I shall be." Sven tossed his sword and axe aside, then loosened his shirt at the throat so that it would not constrict his movements. "Have you caught your breath?"

Hugh, on the verge of hysteria, realized that Sven intended to fight him bare-handed. Man-to-man, Hugh didn't stand a chance.

With quivering pathos, Hugh reminded Sven, "Tabor told you to be merciful."

"I have allowed you to catch your breath and regain your strength. Your death will be quick and clean. That is more mercy than you deserve." His voice dipped low as he added, "And that is more mercy than you showed my friends when you slaughtered them nearly a year ago. You must answer for those murders now, Hugh."

Sven advanced slowly, his eyes cold and blue.

Far away now, Tabor continued on, not slowing his pace until he saw the collection of small, unkempt huts at the outskirts of Karak. These were the homes of the prostitutes who made their living from the sailors that traveled through the port. When Hugh had said that Ingmar had gone to the "women," Tabor knew immediately that he meant these women. Ingmar liked to surround himself with prostitutes. He bragged that he never had to pay for sexual favors, finding it easiest to rape prostitutes, who put up less of a fight. When the deed was done, there were no fathers, brothers, or uncles seeking revenge in defense of the family honor.

Tabor listened carefully. He heard nothing. The only sounds came from the pier, where the Vikings fought Ingmar's men.

Tabor was certain there were women inside the homes. He could sense their presence. And there was at least one man — Ingmar — hiding in their midst, holding Tabor's battle-axe in his hands and waiting to kill the Son of Thor.

"Ingmar, come out and fight me like a man." Tabor demanded but received no response. He was not surprised. Ingmar had no interest in a fair fight. If there was to be an end to the blood feud between them, Tabor would have to seek his enemy out and force the final confrontation.

Tabor grinned. It was fitting that Ingmar hid among the prostitutes.

Two women huddled in a corner of the first house. They turned frightened eyes to Tabor when he kicked their door in. Ingmar was not hiding within.

"Where is he?" Tabor demanded.

"He's a bad man," the older of the two women replied in a quivering voice. "If we tell you, he'll kill us for sure. He's killed for less, I tell you!"

The woman's fear was genuine, marrow-deep. Tabor demanded no more of her. He moved on.

There were three more small homes, and he was certain that Ingmar lay in ambush in one of them.

In the second home, three women cowered in fear. When he asked for Ingmar, they claimed he was not there. But the puffy red eye he saw developing on one of the women told him that Ingmar had been there—recently—and that his presence had been in no way welcome.

When Tabor left that house, instinct told him that in the next house he would find Ingmar . . . and the final battle would begin.

He put his boot to the flimsy door, and it splintered, bursting open, swinging crookedly upon its ancient hinges. Tabor peered inside but did not enter. Behind a mattress, lying flat on the floor, a young woman stared up at him, terror in her eyes. Then another woman appeared, slightly older than the first. Hesitating, she pressed a professional smile upon her face and rose out of hiding.

"Come in," she cooed. "I know exactly what you're looking for, and you won't need that sword and dagger filling your hands to get it."

She smiled, lewdly revealing a missing tooth. She stepped closer to the door, waving to the frightened girl behind her to rise and greet their guest.

"Back," Tabor said, keeping his sword and dagger at the ready.

"But there's no need for—"

"Now."

She stepped backward then, nearly stumbling over the mattress that had hidden her. Tabor paused at the door, his senses alert. The old prostitute babbled, her wiles eluding her. The young one looked at Tabor as though he promised salvation.

441

"Come on in," the older one said. "Let me show you what you need."

Tabor stepped over the threshold, and the girl screamed, "Behind the door!"

In a move that drew as much on instinct as experience, Tabor lunged to his left and blindly threw his dagger at his unseen enemy. He hit the dirt floor of the house, rolling immediately, lifting the huge broadsword for defense, holding the long haft with both hands.

He righted himself, raising up to his knees, his broadsword horizontal to block a strike. And then the battle-axe, the one that Ingmar had stolen from Tabor to use against him, fell harmlessly to the ground at the Viking's feet.

Without a second thought, Tabor dropped his sword and retrieved the battle-axe that he had lost long ago when Ingmar's arrow sliced through his biceps.

Ingmar reeled backward on his heels, shocked by Tabor's unexpected move and the courage of the young prostitute who had betrayed him. Tabor saw the blood dripping from Ingmar's cheek and realized that while his dagger had not dangerously injured his foe, it had jolted him, cutting his face and forcing him to drop the battle-axe.

"Hiding behind skirts again, eh, Ingmar?" Tabor asked, rising quickly to his feet.

Ingmar said nothing. He had no weapons. Only a short knife still buried in the pocket of his jacket. He had believed that the prostitutes of Karak were all too frightened of him to betray him.

"Outside," Tabor said.

"I have no weapons."

Tabor hooked the toe of his boot under the blade of the broadsword and gave it a kick, sending the weapon

442

flipping through the air. Ingmar caught the long handle quickly, a smile of surprise creasing his bearded countenance.

"Outside," Tabor repeated. "You've got a weapon now. It's you against me."

Ingmar chuckled as he stepped outside into the sunlight. He wondered, but did not care how Tanaka had made the sun disappear. He was alone now with Tabor, their only audience a cluster of prostitutes. If he could not defeat Tabor in their duel, Ingmar would run. It did not matter to him if he lost face in front of these women.

"They hate you, you know," Tabor said, squaring up against Ingmar. The familiar feel of the battle-axe's smooth, thick handle in his hands filled Tabor with security and confidence. With this battle-axe, he felt certain that he would not—could not—be defeated by Ingmar the Savage.

"The women? So what? I take the ones I want and leave the rest to do business. They mean nothing to me. Nothing at all."

The two men circled each other slowly, looking for an opening in the other's defenses, knowing that one wrong move meant death.

"They may mean nothing to you," Tabor said, hoping his words would distract, ready to use every tool and trick he'd gleaned over the years to defeat Ingmar. "But one of them warned me about your trap. Without that warning, you would have had me."

A muscle twitched in Ingmar's jaw as he clamped his teeth in anger. He had always hated women, though he needed their bodies for sexual release, and this betrayal infuriated him.

"She'll be sorry," Ingmar vowed. "I had a little fun with

443

her," he said. "Just a little pleasure, and she turned against me!"

"Apparently, she didn't think it — you — so enjoyable."

Ingmar scowled. Tabor tensed the muscles above the knee of his leg. It was a feigned preparation for an attack. Ingmar backed away three steps. He believed he could read Tabor's moves in advance.

The third time Tabor pretended to prepare for his attack, Ingmar took the offensive, slashing hard at waist level in a long, smooth arch. Tabor leaped backward, curling around the sword's point as it barely missed his stomach.

They squared off again, too tense now to waste breath on insults. Always moving, each looked for some sign of weakness in the other. Soon, the women who had been hiding came out from their homes. Some of them, emboldened by the news from the pier and recognizing Tabor, ridiculed Ingmar, taunting him. They cast aspersions on his sexual prowess and anatomy.

"How does it feel to be surrounded by so much love?" Tabor asked sarcastically.

"How does it feel to be dead?" Ingmar replied, lunging forward, leading with his broadsword.

Tabor parried Ingmar's thrust, spinning to his left, and swung hard with his axe, hoping to keep his foe sufficiently off balance to prevent an immediate second attack. But Ingmar was not brushed back by the sharpened blade of the battle-axe. Rather than passing harmlessly past his nose, the blade struck him solidly above the ear as he lunged toward Tabor. Ingmar crumpled to the ground, unmoving.

"You killed him."

Tabor looked at the woman who had spoken. It was the young prostitute who had warned him of the surprise attack. She looked upon Tabor now as though he had killed the Devil himself.

"He'll never bother you again."

More women came from the houses now that Ingmar was on the ground. One walked up to the corpse and kicked it. Another did the same.

Tabor turned away, not having any desire to watch the desecration of his old enemy. He looked at the axe in his hands as he made his way back toward the pier.

From afar, he heard a shout. Looking up, he saw Tanaka. She waved and rushed toward him. Tanaka . . . his future. As he watched her run toward him, he thought about the son she'd said they'd conceived on the mystical ground in England. Tabor smiled, amused that sometimes his wife had the silliest ideas . . .

Epilogue

His name was Thor, Son of Tabor; and though he was only fourteen, he already possessed a physique that caught the eye of Egyptian women in the city of Opar. His smile was the mirror image of his father's, and there wasn't a female heart in all of Egypt that hadn't melted for Tabor, the too-handsome blond Viking who had moved to Egypt and married the high priestess of the palace, Tanaka.

Thor was navigating his boat into port, smiling as he always did whenever he was upon the sea. As usual, he was late returning to port. His mother would be worried, afraid that something unfortunate had happened to him to cause his tardiness; his father, Tabor, would be angry, not because he was late, but because he had caused his mother worry.

There were four other boys in the small boat with him. They looked to Thor for guidance and leadership. Though he was unaware of it himself, Thor had been born for leadership, conceived on hallowed ground and entering the world while his mother and father sailed from Tabor's homeland to Egypt.

"Some day, I'll get us a bigger boat and a larger crew," he promised. "Then we'll really do some adventuring, eh, men?" And his companions heartily agreed as one.